UPSTANDING YOUNG MAN

SHARON DOERING

HYPERION AVENUE
LOS ANGELES   NEW YORK

Copyright © 2025 by Sharon Doering

All rights reserved. Published by Hyperion Avenue, an imprint of Buena Vista Books, Inc. No part of this book may be reproduced or transmitted in any form or by any means, electronic or mechanical, including photocopying, recording, or by any information storage and retrieval system, without written permission from the publisher. For information address Hyperion Avenue, 7 Hudson Square, New York, New York 10013.

First Edition, August 2025
10 9 8 7 6 5 4 3 2 1
FAC-004510-25149
Printed in the United States of America

This book is set in Adobe Caslon Pro, Knockout, Chronicle Display, Arabesque Ornaments, and Verdana
Designed by Amy C. King

Library of Congress Cataloging-in-Publication Data

Names: Doering, Sharon, author.
Title: Upstanding young man / by Sharon Doering.
Description: First edition. • Los Angeles : Hyperion Avenue, 2025. •
    Summary: "A star wrestler with a bright future goes missing weeks before his high school graduation, and his mother falls under suspicion. In this pulse-pounding thriller, secrets threaten to destroy everything—and someone will pay the ultimate price"—Provided by publisher.
Identifiers: LCCN 2024055772 • ISBN 9781368113793 (hardcover) • ISBN 9781368113809 (trade paperback) • ISBN 9781368114820 (ebook)
Subjects: LCGFT: Thrillers (Fiction). • Novels.
Classification: LCC PS3604.O3385 U67 2025 • DDC 813/.6—dc23/eng/20241211
LC record available at https://lccn.loc.gov/2024055772

Hardcover ISBN 978-1-368-11379-3
Paperback ISBN 978-1-368-11380-9

Reinforced binding for hardcover edition

www.HyperionAvenueBooks.com

Logo Applies to Text Stock Only

For Sammy, Jon, and Ed.

*You're the sparkling light in every dark story I write.
I'm so incredibly proud of you three, always.*

(Also, maybe don't read this one. Like, ever.)

CHAPTER 1

MEG

THE DAY THE POLICE GET INVOLVED, 6:50 A.M.

Joe looks dead. Mouth agape like Jaws the moment before someone loses a leg, head hinged back on his pillow, everything about him overextended and extreme. How is his mouth that open?

My cheek on my warm pillow, I scrutinize his chest for signs of life while holding my breath. His bare chest, once muscular and masculine, is now soft at forty-six. His skin is pale beneath dark, wiry hair. The tattoo on his shoulder—a cartoon-style shark—has faded to washed-out denim. It used to make me laugh, how obnoxious it was. Now it makes me sad. His chest inflates. Decidedly not dead.

Joe, my husband. My boyish, clever, and marginally famous husband who, more recently, has turned into something strange and frightening.

Me, I barely slept. I cycled through bursts of sweaty panic so many times, I smell sour. My mind goes to last night like peeling back a hangnail, knowing it's painful and self-defeating, yet I can't resist.

Don't think about that. Think about today.

Today. It's 6:53 a.m., which is good because no one's late yet. I need to be sharp today. I should try for more sleep, but the spring sun is eager, poking at the curtains. No way can I sleep. Even if the sun didn't have a hard-on, I couldn't sleep. I roll away from Joe.

A spider perches high in the vaulted ceiling beside a half-assed, blowsy web. He's out of reach, taunting, accusing. *I saw what you did, nasty woman. I saw.*

To kill that spider and wreck his lousy web, I'd need a roofer's lean-to and someone to spot me. I have neither. Stupid cathedral ceilings. What a waste of real estate. I imagine 1980s moguls wearing colorful Rick Astley jackets, sipping bourbon and stinking up a restaurant with their fat cigars, talking open spaces and vaulted ceilings. One saying, "Hear me out. We build *nothing*. We spin the open space as a luxury, the suckers eat that shit up, and we pocket the cash saved on lumber, see?"

I hate this room. Our bedroom. I used to love it. Truly. But over the past twenty-some years since Joe and I bought this house, it has fallen into a state of neglect: suspicious urine-colored wall stains, scarred furniture, and piles of miscellaneous: negligibly worn clothes, cheap picture frames, cheaper jewelry, and shoeboxes holding shoes so old the faux leather is cracked and coming off in dandruffy flakes.

Joe and I, we're not hoarders, but several areas of the house display disorderly tendencies. It can happen to a bedroom. It's a private room, unseen and unjudged by outsiders. If you're not diligent, it's the first place to come undone.

There is a crack along the wall opposite our bed. Joe has smoothed joint compound over it several times, but the crack keeps breaking through like a stubborn poltergeist. This room needs a good painting. I can't imagine that's going to happen anytime soon.

I turn toward Joe once more. That jaw like he's trying to silently swallow my whole world in a single gulp. He is, in a way. He *has*.

Like the house, twenty years ago I loved him. Truly. Handsome, with a child's energy, fast reflexes, and a mind clear as cold river water. He made me laugh till I peed my pants. His skin smelled of stern soap and testosterone. He was a man of the people, a minor celebrity, in fact. Beloved by poor men who came home with sawdust wedged under their nails. Beloved by men so rich they walked into strip clubs carrying nothing smaller than a fifty.

He used to fight. He won the Golden Gloves tourney at twenty. Riding the prestige of that title, he boxed at iconic venues like Madison Square Garden, MGM, and Staples Center. He had two lucrative years—we bought this house with his fight money—before he shattered his shoulder in a car accident. Joe worked diligently in physical therapy for six months—trying to coax the stiffness out of his shoulder—and boxed three more fights before he realized he wouldn't be making that comeback.

But he had *Golden Gloves winner* behind his name, and males of a certain age lusted over it. When they found out who Joe was, they'd lick their spittle-glistened lips as if he were a juicy plum hanging heavy on a tree. With thirsty eyes and their throats working, they'd hold their handshake seconds too long, silently brainstorming how they could weave his minor celebrity into their business ventures and social standing.

Then, if they remembered I was standing there, witnessing their adoration, they'd clear their throats, smile wide and open at me, their pink tongues wet and thick, and say, "Gotta watch this guy, am I right?"

Why, yes! Because there's nothing more hilarious than domestic abuse.

Joe hasn't hit me. If only it were that straightforward.

Like the room, Joe has accumulated unappealing tendencies. Suspicious behaviors have bled through like water stains. There is a crack in him that seems unpatchable. It's not that I hate him. No, I am devoted. I'll keep his secret, but he scares me. It's hard to relax into love when being near him feels like walking barefoot across a kitchen of broken dishware. Tiny slivers waiting to catch you by painful surprise.

His skin still smells like soap, but there is an undertone I can't put my finger on. A salty, sick smell. Days old semen–slick sheets. Maybe it's age.

I study the coarse shadow of hairs coming in along his cranked jaw and shake off an unpleasant feeling. I would not like to be a man. All that bristly hair sprouting from every pore. Face. Legs. Ears. Ass. Fucking unescapable. I zone in on the hairs peeking out of his nostrils. He could use a nose-hair trimmer. Maybe for Father's Day.

I wander out of our bedroom wearing the long T-shirt I slept in. My feet ache. My whole body feels off. My back is pulling in strange places. Neck in knots. For a split second, I wonder why. Then last night comes rushing back to me. My heart flaps so hard, my hand flies to my chest as if to keep it pinned down. Today is going to be hard.

I pass Whitney's closed door first. I don't have to touch the sweaty brass knob to know it's locked and she's already left for school. Whitney is my most secretive child.

Next, McClane's room. His door is open, and his spindly medusa lamp is on, lighting up everything in jarring LED. Wide-open door, light left on carelessly: all very usual for McClane, but it doesn't feel usual.

The house feels swollen, like a water balloon ready to burst. That flapping in my chest starts again. My hand goes to my breast, sternly this time, without patience. *Clamp that shit down. You can do hard things.*

I pass the bathroom. On the counter is a mess of hair products and a glob of red toothpaste like a small harvested organ. A pile of clothes and towels on the floor. Whitney's mess.

The last two bedrooms on my way to the staircase are empty and dark. Beds, neatly made. They haven't been slept in since Christmas, when my two older children visited.

Downstairs, the kitchen smells like stale lasagna. Last night I tossed what was left in the trash, sauce splattering against the garbage can liner, but forgot to take the bag out to the garage. I reach for the drawstrings and spot a smear of blood on my knee. Panic prickles my skin like an itchy wool sweater. How could I have missed that? Forget taking out the garbage, I scour my knee with a wet kitchen towel until the wrinkled skin is pink and tender.

I microwave a cup of water and drop in a tea bag, Earl Grey—"Old Lady Grey," McClane liked to joke—and pick up my phone.

Big day, today.

I sigh the heaviest sigh ever sighed. I copy and paste the text I wrote late-late last night, so late it was pretty much morning. I attach the video. Do I really want to hit send?

Out the kitchen window, Griswold, the neighbor's tabby, sits on my patio, watching a cardinal nip seed from my feeder. I rap at the window, getting his attention. "Don't eat my birds, Gris," I say. If the kids were around, they'd get a kick out of me.

Late April is a good time for the yard. Rainy nights, cold wet mornings, sunny warm afternoons. Everything in full bloom, busting at the juicy-green, earthy seams. My eyes look for each of the kids' trees. My touchstones.

First, David's tree. An ash, sturdy and straight. Chosen by him from a local tree nursery when he was six. He was the type of boy who could name the make and model of any car. Decent at football. Loved working on his Boy Scout badges. Now he's twenty-four, confident, and always with a plan. He started a job with the FBI nine months ago, and I tell anyone who will listen.

Then Jamie's tree. A weeping willow, loose and sucking up all the water in the yard. Bought when she was eight. Now she's twenty-two and has tattoos on her ankles and wrists, a different hair color every time she visits, and aspirations of being a prize-winning journalist. She is my slightly embarrassing child with dreams too big, full of poor choices made boldly. She is also possibly my happiest child.

Next, McClane's tree. A quaking aspen. Heart-shaped leaves, small and delicate. A seemingly simple tree, until the wind blows. Then its shimmery exotic flair draws your eye, and you can't look away. Bought when he was in middle school because that's when we got around to it, and he was never an asker. He turned eighteen last month. The kid was offered a wrestling scholarship to Indiana University—a full ride. McClane's gorgeous, like a male version of Snow White: light blue eyes, dark wavy hair, and slender. And, like fairy-tale princesses, always with a sleepy side-smile because they suspect the story ends well for them.

Finally, Whitney's tree. A honey locust, bought because Whitney liked the name Honey for a tree. Bought at the last moment on the same day we'd bought McClane's tree, carelessly because she was the last child—*Yes, okay, we can buy you one too, hurry up and pick.* Since it had been last minute, we hadn't checked the tree's sex. We'd accidentally bought the female—the nasty sex, we'd found out. The one with thorns. Promptly loved even more by Whitney because it looked like a magical tree, with its dangerously sharp and elegant thorns wrapping around the trunk, locking you out. Like Whitney. She's sixteen now, dark wavy hair, gray eyes, beautiful and guarded. Clever and smart.

There are more trees in the backyard, but these four ground me. This house, it's important. It is a place of barbed secrets and velvety memories. It captures our stories. Our stories capture it. Keeping this family together is everything.

I look at the text I've written, the video I've inserted. I bite my quivering lip and hit send.

No going back now.

You can do hard things.

I like this saying but find affirmations cheap. They weren't always a thing, after all, so they might sour. Did affirmations start with those imitation Tuscan kitchen decorations that demanded you Live Laugh Love? Sweet, yet bossy. And a helluva lot to ask, really.

Anyway, it's a good affirmation. *You can do hard things.* I used to tell the kids this when they were small. Now I tell myself.

My phone rings in my hand, startling me as if it were a snake that bit me, and I drop it in the sink. Fuck. The sink's clean, but still. A plumber once told me he'd choose toilet work over sink work, and that hasn't stopped troubling me. I pluck my phone from the sink and wipe a wet smear away, which accidentally answers it.

"Hello?" comes a small voice. "Hello?"

Shit. I put the phone to my ear, cringing as wetness touches my cheek. "Yes, I'm here."

"This is Patty with the attendance office at Sugar Glen North. Did you forget to call in McClane?" Such a friendly way to point out a kid's truant. The woman's voice is singsong and has a tired quality. She's probably said this same line dozens of times this morning, inserting a different name, and has grown weary of teenage listlessness and shitty parenting.

McClane. Memories of our argument last night gust inside my head, a sudden tornado of whirling accusations and hot contempt. Warmth creeps up my neck. I gaze out the window again. Griswold and the cardinal are gone.

"Oh, yes," I say. "He had an appointment. Thank you for calling." I hang up before Patty can ask a follow-up. What a job. Telling people their kids are not where they're supposed to be. Delivering news that triggers panic or rage.

McClane's not at school. I lied about where he is. My heart beats like a hummingbird's wings. Should I call the police, or is it too early for that yet?

Too early, I decide, and baby-sip my hot tea.

CHAPTER 2

MCCLANE

28 HOURS UNTIL MISSING

I love being whipped.

What started as a joke months ago, a finger poke in the ribs to piss me off, make my cheeks blaze red, has become cherished. Nothing can scrub my proud smile. Jack and Hudson know this, but they keep up the game for their amusement. One month left of senior year, and we're all burnt-out on school. Bored and a little jumpy for the next inevitable step. Me being "whipped" is the joke that keeps on giving, something to file in our high school memory playlist, and none of us want to let it go. Not even me.

"You're whipped like Jimmy Haby got us in Little League," Jack says. "Remember when he pitched it right into your eye? Dude, I wish I could unsee that."

"Whipped like my bloody eye," I say.

"I wish I saw it." Hud.

"He's going to University of Iowa, you know? Haby," Jack says. "Baseball scholarship."

"Worked his ass off for it," I say.

"Being born with a baseball arm doesn't hurt," Jack says.

Predictably and abruptly, Hudson takes our running joke further. "Whipped like Jack's dad begged his mom last night, knees all trembly and shit." Hud laughs, his voice rising like he's high on something. He might be.

Jack pretends to not be annoyed. He's sitting on the wooden dock, his sweaty socks nestled inside his sneakers next to his tackle box, his huge pale feet in the lake. Pole across his lap as he rethreads. Jack looks like the guy you'd want to back you up in a fight, but he's not that guy. He's tall and meaty, yeah, but he's slow, has an awkward gait, flat-footed or something, and doesn't have a fighting bone in his body.

I'm lying on my back behind Jack, my calves burning on the sunbaked wood of the dock. It's hot for late April, and the golden afternoon sun warms my skin. The fish-and-rock smell of the lake is coated with the burnt stink of asphalt because they repaved the parking lot yesterday and this dock is closest to it.

My phone in one hand, my other raised to cut the sun's glare, I scroll through the crazy stuff kids post on Snap. I'm looking for something that will crack up Jack and Hud. "If this is whipped, I never want out," I say, trying to lighten the tension between my friends. I mean it, though, about being whipped. I love her like crazy.

Natalie is dark wavy hair and brown eyes shot with amber. I'm talking movie-star eyes that gut you. You can't look away. This upper lip that tilts up at the top like the creamy peak of a Cool

Whip dessert. Flawless skin. Great-grandparents from Italy, I think. Actually, I have no idea. Maybe it's Spain or Mexico. I don't care much about her dead ancestors or where people were born.

This feeling, it's like seeing fireworks for the first time when you're a kid: bright brilliant lights exploding through thick dark, the boom rattling your chest a beat later, and the fiery sizzle raining around you as ashy papers, edges curling to a singe, feather to the grass. I am fucking pulsing with good vibes, let me tell you. That's love, I guess. Maybe infatuation. But also love, I think. Yeah.

Hudson splashing in the lake pulls my attention. He's moving around the water's silty edge, sloshing in his sneakers, looking for good skipping rocks or fat spiders to fuck with or maybe for treasure. He found a crumpled twenty once.

He's small and skinny, but scrappy and with an unpredictable streak of crazy. Sophomore year we joked he was going to shoot up like bamboo and pass Jack and me both, but it didn't happen. It might have been because of poor nutrition, which gives the memory of the joke a bad aftertaste. But he's the one you'd want to back you in a fight.

We're at our fishing hole. That's what we call it, for a ring of authenticity, or maybe because one of us called it that when we were in elementary, but there is nothing "hole" about this scene. It's fucking picturesque. I'm talking postcard worthy.

Green Lake is large enough that you can't see it end to end. Five wooden docks along this side of the lake, forest scrub edging the water. Opposite us, the lake meets fifty vertical feet of rocky scrag. Our town, Sugar Glen, is mostly flat like the rest of Illinois, but we have this one sheer cliff at Green Lake and a bit of hill here and there.

Sugar Glen is one of the dozens of Chicago suburbs with a population hovering around forty thousand. An hour's drive to Chicago, most commuters take the Metra to Union Station in Chicago's business district. My parents used to do that.

Out here, grown-ups are a mix of city commuters, working class, some richies tucked away in hidden nooks with horses penned in by pretty white fences, and those who've fallen out of work. We have a lot more of these lately. Someone's holding up a homemade cardboard sign at most of the major intersections these days.

We have our share of corn and soybean farms owned by farmers who have held up their middle finger for a long time to developers, holding on to their ten-hour workdays instead of taking a cash payout. Stupid, if you ask me. I'd have taken the cash the first time they offered, bought a sweet ride, and ridden away with the top down. But, sure, Farmer Guy, you rage against the machine and all that, I guess. Old people have so many weird hang-ups and imagined problems.

Jack, Hud, and I used to fish here. Now most of the time it's just Jack. He's hanging on to what we had before we head to college. It'll be Western Illinois for Jack, law enforcement like his dad. Me, I'm not sure which school yet, but I'm ready for my future. Natalie and college, for sure. Hudson is deciding where he fits.

Some other kid along the lake, out of sight, shouts, "Screw you, Crunkey." The kid's voice echoes, bouncing off the rocks. There's laughing and splashing too. The lake meanders a bit on this side, so you can't see the other people. It's kind of nice, the feeling of privacy, even if it's fake.

We laugh too. Crunkey's one of the gym teachers at our high

school. Jack shouts, "Crunkey's got a sweet ass. Hand me a smaller towel, sir."

Laughter rings out from the other group. Impromptu camaraderie is better when the comrade is a stranger. Even better when you can't see who it is.

Jack says to us, "Whipped like Coach Crunkey does in the locker room after everyone's changed."

"Nice," I say.

"Nice," Hud says.

Jack says, "Ask Natalie if she's got any friends who can't find a date for prom. Maybe Olivia or Lucy? Not Tiana, though. Her voice makes my balls cringe."

"Look at this guy, acting like he has his pick," Hud says, a laugh deep in his throat like he's hacking. "You'd be lucky to go with Durst, son." Durst is our old-lady gym teacher. Hud looks at me, expecting me to join in laughing.

My tongue feels dry. I brought a drink but left it in the car.

"Dude?" Hud says. "Come on, now. You haven't asked her?"

"I think . . . Well, I assumed, right?" I say. "But thanks for reminding."

"So chill this sir don't even ask his girl to prom." Jack.

"Brain so whipped he forgot about prom." Hud.

They laugh. On my back, sun warming my clothes, I smile.

———•———

Natalie is my third girlfriend but my first serious. She's one of those girls who doesn't ping on most guys' radars because she avoids radars.

No makeup, hair in a knot, pajama pants and flip-flops. No boy chasing, no flirty voice, no trying to be seen, but then her friends talk her into going to the homecoming dance senior year. She joins in the pregame effort partly for a joke, and she's so drop-dead gorgeous in her little lime dress with her hair and makeup done, no one can believe they didn't notice her before. Like, bro, did you see Natalie? Like, whaaaa? Bro, bro, like, seriously. Did you SEE?

Yeah. I saw her. I noticed her before the dance. I actually noticed her sophomore year but was too chicken to do anything about it. I didn't talk to her until my senior-year chill finally kicked in. There's this magic to senior year, it's like our shells crack open and we're all loose limbs in warmth and wetness and unselfconscious chirps and trills, flocking and piling together. But, yeah, me and Nat had a vibe going a few weeks before the dance.

It isn't her looks, though. I mean, that's what I noticed first. I mean, c'mon. But when I paid attention, man, when I took in her whole deal, she carried herself differently than the rest of us. She wasn't attention-thirsty and didn't have a nervous fake laugh. Her movements were savvy and calm, and her tone was rich like the smell of a bonfire late at night. She was more grown than the rest of us. We were deciding who we wanted to be, and it seemed she already knew.

Third week of senior year, I was passing out badminton rackets for Mrs. Durst and handed one to Natalie. "Senior year already," I said, my palms sweaty. "I wonder why we've never had a class together."

Her movements were minimal, but her eyes lit with humor, and one side of her mouth slid up. "I'm in the smart classes, McClane."

I smiled big, showing my teeth like a retriever.

"That was a rip, by the way." She winked like I was dumb and she was trying to help me out.

"Yeah, but you know my name." My smile grew.

If this is whipped, I never want out.

Natalie. Her parents call her Tally, or Natalia when they're feeling stern. Hearing her name is like chugging a Bang. I could step into the high school gymnasium during assembly and spot her in an instant. Her heart-shaped face, those dark, shiny waves, that curved upper lip. Like she is the only girl in the world. The beat-up gray Nissan she shares with her siblings is the only car I see in the lot. It, like, glows. Seems like this year, senior year, is the only year I've been alive. These past seven or eight months I've lived enough for a whole life. Drugs. Sex. More. I am a live wire, flailing and shooting sparks.

——— • ———

"Are you going to catch something or keep rethreading?" Hud says.

"Don't disrespect, son," Jack says. "This. This is, like, my zen."

"His yoga." Hud laughs, high and untethered. "It's his downward dog, man."

I laugh because it's funny. I laugh because I love when the old Hud resurfaces. The creative and unselfconscious Hud. Lately, well, Hud can be strange.

I say, "I should bring my pole one of these days."

"Yeah, yeah," Jack says.

"You say that all the time." Hud.

It stings to get called out, but it's comforting that they know me so well.

Jack says, "Whipped like Hud's dad whips a six-pack."

Hud pauses a beat. Turns a flat stone over in his hand, takes a few steps into the still water, and sidearms it. We all count. Seven skips. Not bad. He's done better. I figured he'd snap back at Jack with a fat joke. He doesn't. "Fair," he says. "But it took you a while to think it up."

Hudson's story is like the flu. Everyone felt sorry for his bad luck but stayed away like it was contagious. He grew up in a solid brick house on a good street, his mom a kindergarten teacher, his dad a foreman, whatever the hell that is, cement or lumber or something. Two years ago his mom got diagnosed with ovarian cancer and died months later. It had silently spread everywhere in her gut, she had no chance. In those four months, Hud's dad had slacked at work and got himself fired. They'd let their life insurance policies lapse during the chaos of her being sick, so that was the kicker.

Hud's dad lost their house, and now the two of them live in an apartment on the uglier, industrial side of town, paying rent on fumes. Hud's dad occasionally has a job but more often he's got a beer in his hand before school's out. Hud was habitually truant, and the teachers felt bad for him, so everyone let it slide. They thought they were helping him, not calling him out, but it was more like neglect. Hud's grades tanked, he didn't take the SAT, he didn't apply anywhere. He's got no post-high-school plans. He's got no car. He walks to his shifts at the gas station a half mile from his apartment complex, Shady Grove. Maybe he'll go to Hope Junior College for a two-year degree. He's been hanging with the Shady kids. I don't know them, but they seem lazy and nice and slightly dangerous. Anyway, Hud's been straddling between us and them, deciding.

"Hey, don't sweat it, Hud," I say. "My dad's fucked too."

He nods once and steps back onto the shore, his blown-out sneakers sloshing. They know my dad's been distant, but they don't know the half of it.

"You accept your full ride from Indiana, Mick?" Jack.

My heart sinks, and my good vibes wither. I drop my phone on my chest and cradle the back of my head in both hands. A heron lifts off at the other end of the lake, its wings big as a dinosaur's. "Don't think I'm gonna."

"No shit," Jack says, actually looking over his shoulder at me. "You don't like Indiana?"

"I like it. I just don't think I want to wrestle."

"Better hurry up and decide," Jack says. "You only got a few days." College Decision day is coming fast.

"Won't your parents kill you?" Hud says, jumping up onto the dock, excited for someone else's misfortune. He's not a dick, just looking for connection.

"Probably." My mom loves telling people I was offered a full ride. She loves to brag about us kids, show us off like sparkly jewelry. She's proud of us, I get it, but it's cringe, you know? I used to be jealous when I'd hear her telling everyone about Dave and his job with the FBI and how he's got it all figured out. Now that her attention's on me, I don't want it. Then there's my dad. If I tell him the truth, I don't know how he'll react.

Hud laughs. "McClane Hart, of the beloved Hart family, semipro daddy, turns down his full ride. Come on, now. They're gonna fuck you up, son."

"You don't want to wrestle no more?" Jack says, earnest.

"It's complicated." It is. Private, too. I'm not sure I'm ready to tell them what's going on. And I don't know that I need to. I'm in a good place with Natalie, thinking about my future, overall feeling fine. What good would come from shining a light in the dark, secret corners?

"You ain't gonna turn it down," Hud says. "You'll limp-dick it and tell them you accidentally missed your deadline."

"Maybe." Because ripping off a Band-Aid is hard. Better to let it wilt under the spray of the shower and lose its stickiness slowly. Because I can't imagine telling my parents why I can't wrestle anymore.

My ringtone plays the mellow guitar-strum start to the song "Lover," and I feel a jolt in my chest. My worries evaporate. God, even her ringtone lights me up. She's texting.

"You have to buy a bra and panties with that ringtone, McClane?" Hud laughs. It's a good laugh, the kind of solid unselfconscious laugh he used to have.

"Yep," I say. "G-string. You wanna borrow it?"

"Only if it's red," Hud says.

"Is that Taylor Swift?" Jack says, curious.

I say, "That, my friends, is a man who's confident in his sexuality and taste in music."

"Pay attention, Hud," says Jack. "Girls like that shit."

I can't read her text under this sun. I roll to standing and head for the shade under an oak tree, closer to the parking lot. A second text comes through. I can't make that one out either.

A car pulls into the parking lot fast, tires screeching. Rap blaring, bass thumping, and lighthearted yelling at Hudson. Three guys I don't think I've ever seen. One of them says, "Yo, Huddy. Bro, let's roll."

I don't like that they call him *Huddy*. There's camaraderie, but there's mocking there too. I feel protective of Hud, who he used to be, what he's been through.

I stop and look over my shoulder. Hudson grabs his sun-dyed, frayed backpack, pauses like he wants to tell us something, then says, "Later." He passes me and walks the grass toward the blacktop. Eyes cast down, looking too skinny.

Reading my mind, Jack says, "We need to buy him a few double cheeseburgers."

"Tomorrow," I say, and step under the tree to read her texts. My eyes adjust to the shade.

This text isn't gonna seem real. It's real tho.

I'm pregnant. Not joking. I know.

It's like inhaling gasoline. Thick and noxious. Good thing the tree's there to catch me. My hand falls against the rough bark. The bird chatter around me amplifies. A sudden wind gust rattles the leaves above.

My fingers shaky, like too much caffeine on an empty stomach, I text back.

Wow. Just wow. I'm coming to you. At your house?

My forehead tips against the tree trunk, cool and rough. I close my eyes.

She's keeping it. I don't have to ask, I know. She's my best friend, and I know.

My parents are going to kill me.

CHAPTER 3

MEG

THE DAY THE POLICE GET INVOLVED, 7:55 A.M.

McClane doesn't have an appointment.
    My instinct is to lie. Always. I came from a household of liars, after all. My proclivity for lying was nurtured by my parents. Like Wagyu cows fed beer to marble their beef, I was fed the richest of lies. *Don't worry, you're safe. Trust me. He wouldn't hurt a fly.*

    I put McClane out of my mind. He's eighteen, technically an adult. What mother of an eighteen-year-old calls the police if her kid doesn't show up for first period? It's the last month of his senior year. Kids ditch.

    Calling the police would look henny-penny, suspicious even, and I'm the type who worries how things appear. I'm not afraid to admit that. I've gone out of my way countless times to make sure everything seems normal. Better than normal! I like my home life to have a glossy sheen—the thick VOC smell and satin finish of a new coat of paint—that keeps people from asking questions.

Also, I have work. I can't afford to get fired. Truly. Financially, things have been fragile for us. I grab my first coffee of the day and a breakfast bar that is more candy bar than granola—it's what the kids eat, and I like to stay current. I head to my home office. Basically, a creamy white (garage sale) desk set up in the farmhouse living room near the front window.

I warm my cold hands around my mug, breathe in the steam, and glance at the Dalí-style melting clock ledged on the bookshelf. I bought it four or five years ago to make the room more interesting, to make me more interesting, but lately, honestly, I have become too interesting. Vulgar and villainous. Detrimentally interesting. I frown at the clock. It feels like it's become a metaphor for my slippery, sideways life.

I power up my laptop and log in. My password is *LifeIsGoodAt40!*. I should probably change that. I am forty-four at the moment, and life is lots of things, few of them good.

I used to take the Metra to Union Station. Post-pandemic, when people started being forced back, my company was one of the good guys who said, *No way are we going back. This is working, people! Also, saving us money in office space. Let's keep it remote, and, by the way, see how hip we are? Whatdoyousay you owe us around-the-clock availability, and we'll call it even?*

I have a vanilla candle on my desk and a bird feeder outside the window so I can mingle work life with indulgent, creativity-boosting scents and the mindfulness of birdwatching.

Working remotely is lucky lucky lucky. Truly. Stress-free bathroom breaks, laundry breaks, micro naps, not worrying about the food stuck between your teeth. You can't beat that. Though occasionally I feel like one of those naked bodies in the Matrix, plugged in twenty-four/seven as they suck my life force. I've become less human, somehow. When you're isolated, you lose touch, I think. You lose your common sense. You become a figment of your own imagination. Sure, I talk with my family. But family shares the same domestic dysfunction, so it's not enough to lure you out of your head.

I work for an offshoot of a major tech company everyone's heard of. With a background in art history, I'm the flaky one on a team of mostly software engineers that's training AI to become a creator. Everyone uses AI chatbots, right? My team is creating a NextGen model—an honest-to-God *creator*. When Joe and I used to go to parties, I compared my job to that '80s movie *Weird Science*. I'm like those two geeky boys feeding photos into a computer to create the perfect Kelly LeBrock, but in my case, I feed the software *Far Side* jokes, Karin Slaughter novels, and Andy Warhol art. And then I feed it millions of pieces of analysis of each, so it can reflect.

AI can do this for itself now; my job has already become redundant. As I bide my time until an impending layoff, I've been learning a bit of coding, so I can threaten sabotage when they decide they don't need me. Companies can be douchebags (especially as you slide into your fifties). It's good to have a blackmail strategy in your back pocket. That has become my approach to life: planning for the worst.

Our CEO named the software Eileen. I used to start my day by singing "Come on, Eileen" in the fun, tipsy roar of Dexys Midnight Runners' front man. On tired days, I say it in the tone you'd use with your dog when he's sniffing the fire hydrant and you're freezing cold and want to get back inside. *Come ON, Eileen. Je-sus.*

Yes, I feel sorry for the next generation of creators. They have no chance. Eileen is getting stronger by the day. I feel a little like Doctor Frankenstein, having patched together this brilliant beast. Banksy's street art as the foot, Miyazaki movies as the leg, *Game of Thrones* as the genitals, of course. It's not that I'm malicious and out to destroy the youth. Jamie's a journalist for a second-rate newspaper, after all. I don't want her living in a box beside a dumpster, sharing breakfast with rats.

Still, I like the idea of being Doctor fucking Frankenstein. When you're middle-aged and on the outs, there is nothing quite like the buzz of relevancy.

Today, I type, *Good morning, Eileen. I think you're fucking fabulous.* Eileen could, one day, figure out how to slit my throat, and I'd like her to hesitate at that moment.

My job is a lot like raising kids, actually. Like trying to create a better version of yourself. You give them everything, all your hours of sleep, your vitality, your brainpower, they literally suck golden marrow from your tit, you prop them up, let them beat you at everything, and then they grow and daydream fondly of your death and inheriting your IRA.

After an hour or so of work, I gaze out the front window and sip my coffee. Lukewarm. I imagine a half-dozen squad cars pulling up from both sides of the street and into the grass, their red and blue lights alarming and out of place on this bright sunny day.

The weird thing about life: The sum of what you've done means nothing to your kids, your friends, your neighbors. It's that one bad thing you've done they remember you by.

My heart flutters. McClane.

When would a normal person call the police? Dinnertime? How long can I wait? When is it appropriate to freak the freak out?

Not yet, I think.

I am not someone with conviction. I am not a person who knows the right thing to do quickly. I have friends like that. Nurses and elementary school teachers. They don't even have to think, their reflexes are simply correct.

I have to consider all the angles. Try an idea on like a cami dress and decide if it hugs my curves just right, because I get flustered if it doesn't.

I know McClane didn't ditch. I *know*. I just don't know when to call the police.

And then it happens. A car pulls up fast to the curb, driver's door flying open. There are no blue and red sirens on the roof, but the urgency's the same.

Hairs on my arms rise. I should have planned for this.

She is running to my front door. The doorbell rings twice, one right after the other. Demanding my response. My back stiffens. Then it rings a third time.

I'm out of my chair and rushing to the door. Natalie stands on the porch, her cheeks flushed, a strand of hair across her smooth cheek and caught in her mouth. She sets her eyes on mine. She has a tiger's eyes, flecked with amber, cunning and serious. Pulling the hair loose from her mouth, she steps even closer to the screen.

"Mrs. Hart." She's out of breath, but speaks with conviction. "Something's happened to McClane."

CHAPTER 4

M<small>c</small>C<small>LANE</small>

27 HOURS UNTIL MISSING

I drive fast, repeating what I'm gonna say.
Whatever you want to do, I'll support. I love you.
I say the words over and over. I don't want to forget them when I get to her house and look into her eyes. Sometimes when I look at her, I forget everything I want to say. When I'm with her, it's like warming myself on the beach. I feel sun-drunk and dumb.

Problem is, I'm rehearsing too much, and the words are blending and losing their meaning. *WhateveryouwanttodoI'llsupportIloveyou.*

I don't like the way it feels, those words losing their meaning. It's a hungover, stale feeling. Like a line that might come out of my parents' mouths. When they say *I love you* to each other, it means nothing. It's like neighbors saying *Is it garbage night already?*

If there is one thing I don't want to be, it's my parents.

I mean those words, though: *Whatever you want to do.* Well, mostly, but you've got to be careful when it comes to girls. Natalie, especially. She doesn't miss a single fucking beat. If I say something too casual, too honest, like, "Yeah, I abso-fucking-lutely don't want a kid right now, why the fuck would I? But I support your choices, I love you," she'll latch on to the first part, replay it over and over until she's sweaty sick, tossing and turning all night.

I don't want to do that to her, so I need to think about what I say before I open my big fat mouth.

The streetlight ahead turns yellow, and I gun it. But the minivan opposite me jumps the gun on her left turn so I slam the brakes and stop ten feet past the pedestrian line. The back of my neck is all cold sweat. I roll down my window, stick my elbow out, exhale like I've got a mouthful of smoke.

The streetlight's greenish blue again, and I'm off. I love the drive to Natalie's, even now with my balls sweaty, my neck cold. First, there's the two-lane road with a stretch of forest on both sides. Then it's past the squat industrial buildings. There's an inflatable kids park in one of those flat-roofed buildings. We used to go when we were kids. With all those generators powering air pumps, the place is loud as a runway. I can almost smell the thick plastic and ozone and hear the kids screaming, joyful and urgent. Man, I loved that place.

I pass the Lachlan steel plant with its two flues pumping smoke against a fiery sunset. Then I'm over the steel bridge. A block after the bridge, my car rattles and bumps over a single set of cargo train tracks. There's a great hill just past these tracks. If you take it fast, you can catch air under all four tires and feel like you're Vin Diesel for about half of a second. I take it fast. Habit.

I can get to Natalie's house in sixteen minutes, but it feels far.

Same town, different counties. She's in the old part of Sugar Glen. Small houses, smaller yards.

I like it, though, her neighborhood. I like it better than my street. There's a more authentic vibe to the happenings on Natalie's street. At night, people sit outside on broken lawn chairs, drinking and laughing, their cigarette butts glowing in the dark. Off-leash dogs sniff around their yards. People don't worry about how shitty their cars are or the stained mattress they put out on the curb for garbage night. They are more dickish to each other but easier going somehow. One night last month when Natalie and I sat in my car on the curb, her neighbors were arguing so intensely, I thought it might end up physical. On Sunday afternoon, the same neighbors sat together in the driveway, listening to preseason baseball on the radio.

No one on my street argues, ever, but their conversations are dry and brief. They talk weather, that the mail carrier comes later every year, and did you hear the coyotes last night? Nothing colorful. Nothing daring. Nothing honest.

I turn down her street, and I'm distracted so I forget about the pothole on the corner. My front tire drops down, then bumps up. Damn. I'm usually more careful to avoid that.

I smooth out my steering and drive slowly down her street. My car is a twelve-year-old Corolla, so it fits in here. It used to be Dave's. He named the car Cool Hand Luke after some cowboy in an old movie I never saw. Dave is the type of guy who names cars.

When Dave went to college, the car became Jamie's. She liked that he'd named it and kept that joke going. Now that Jamie's gone, the car's mine. My parents pay insurance, and I pay for gas. I delivered pizza over the summer, like Dave and Jamie did before me. That hot, yeasty beer smell has been baked into the vinyl seats.

My tire seems to have survived the pothole. I say it one more time—*Whatever you want to do, I'll support. I love you*—as I pull up along her curb and realize I've fucked up, big-time.

I'm an idiot.

The whole drive here, I've been worrying about the wrong thing.

Her parents. I should have thought about what to say to her parents, in case they found out. I know it's a possibility. Her mom knows *everything*. It's like her superpower or something.

The yelling is so loud inside her house, I catch full phrases all the way out on the street through my open window.

"...not responsible enough..." Natalie's mom.

"...cannot believe..." Her dad.

"Hypocrite." Natalie.

"...ruin your whole goddamn life..." Her dad.

"...only five dollars..." Her mom. This fragment is a mystery.

"Fucking hypocrites." Natalie.

My heartbeat bangs around inside my throat. If there were ever a time in my life I've wanted to run away, this is it. I could do it. Drive home, grab some money, and head for the coast. I'm considering it, I shit you not. I could crash for a while with Jamie in North Carolina. It's gorgeous there. Or with Dave in Tennessee.

Natalie's parents have joked with me, cooked for me, taught me card games. They like me. They consider me family. But I have no doubt they wouldn't hesitate to grab a knife from their butcher block right now and stick it between my ribs. Between my legs, maybe.

I'd do anything right now to avoid their house.

My palms sweaty, I step onto the curb and walk up their asphalt driveway. Their small, uncovered porch holds two chipped pots, cilantro in one, basil in the other. Her mom showed me how to pick basil last week. *Two hands, Hart, so you don't rip out my roots.*

The front door is open but it's dark in their foyer. The smell of onions sautéed with ground beef drifts through the screen. The late afternoon sun beats on the back of my neck. They're still yelling. The blood rushing in my ears is louder. I never thought ringing a doorbell would be suicide.

I ring the doorbell. Their yelling stops, as if someone flipped a switch. Total silence. I stop breathing. One Mississippi. Two Mississi—

Tyson starts yipping. Natalie's dad mumbles a few words, then someone's walking briskly to the door, the dog's collar jingling alongside. Natalie's mom. She steps to the screen and stares at me with cold eyes, her jaw tense.

This is a woman so strong and wild, she once told her husband to buzz off about asking her to quit smokes because she pushed out five babies for him—she deserves her cigarettes. She plans to die at seventy-five anyway, after she's taught her grandbabies to make empanadas. She wants him to dress her dead body in her skinny black dress and make sure everyone gets drunk at her funeral. She calls me by my last name because she loves the sound of it.

Tyson's a Pomeranian, and he always bites my ankles. Now I'm outside the screen and he's in. What I wouldn't give for that little shit to be biting my ankles, because that would mean everything was okay.

Natalie's mom strains to keep her voice down. "I might have

expected this from Natalia, but not from you, McClane. How could you be so careless?"

"Thanks a lot, Mom," Natalie says from behind her. I can't help but notice Natalie's wearing shorts and flip-flops, because this is the first day she's worn shorts this year. They're frayed and short, and her legs are so smooth, I lose track of time for a second and forget the gravity of the situation. She shoves past her mom, bumping carelessly against her shoulder, and then she's out the door, saying, "I can't stand hypocrites."

I wait a second, thinking I'm supposed to do something for her parents, apologize or something, but that feels wrong. Sorry for fucking your daughter? I look at Natalie's mom's eyes. They're muddy with anger but also desperation. Like maybe she wants to pull me into a big hug, then lop off my head with her favorite kitchen knife. My stomach burns with indigestion. "I worked my ass off to do better for my kids," she says to me, her jaw tight. "Then she makes the same stupid mistake I did. She has no clue how hard it will be." She doesn't mention me, but her words are meant for me.

Nat's mom walks away from the screen and turns to walk up the stairs. I want to remind her she's got dinner cooking on the stove. I don't. I search for signs of Natalie's dad, but there's no movement.

Nat's already in the passenger seat. She slams her door shut before I can close it for her. "I don't want to talk," she says. I drive, not glancing back at her house. She puts on the radio, goes for an oldies station, blasts it. "Hash Pipe." Weezer. Good song, but I can't stand her silence.

"Where to?"

She rolls her window down all the way, slips off her flip-flops, sticks one bare foot out the window, then drops her seat all the way down and says, "Breakneck."

That's what we call Green Lake sometimes. When we were freshmen, a bunch of juniors parked at the lookout after homecoming. They were drinking and smoking weed and messing around. On a dare, one of the guys stripped down to his boxers and jumped.

They found his body just before dawn. It was bumping up against one of the docks. His neck was broken.

Sure, it's barely fifty feet. An easy jump in the day. But the rocks jut out in a few spots, so jumping dark is suicide.

When our hearts are light, we call it Green Lake. When our hearts are wild, we call it Breakneck.

"Park on the cliff," she says.

CHAPTER 5

MEG

THE DAY THE POLICE GET INVOLVED, 9:18 A.M.

I like Natalie, I do. I mean, no girl could ever be good enough for McClane, but I like her. She has good posture and knows her worth. Both are hard to come by in eighteen-year-old girls. Still, all I can think is: Get this girl off my porch.

"McClane's car isn't here," Natalie says. He usually parks low in the driveway, so I can swerve around him. Her eyes probe past me, searching for something inside my house. "Is he home?"

"No."

"Something happened." She inhales like she's going to tell me what but she only presses her lips together. She's a beautiful girl. Smooth skin, a full upper lip that gives her a seductive look whether she likes it or not, and, well, those eyes. Curious cat eyes.

"What's happened?" I step out onto the porch with her. Me

stepping out, it's become a habit. Joe doesn't like when I let people inside.

She steps off the porch to give me room. She's familiar with our habits too, our lack of welcoming hugs or offers of food. She presses her palm against her forehead. "He didn't show at school this morning. He hasn't answered any phone calls. He's just, like, vanished."

"Maybe he went somewhere with friends today? Burger King? Fishing?" I picture him fishing at Green Lake with Jack and Hudson. They started going by themselves on their bikes when they were ten. I used to drive by the parking lot in stealth mode to check on them. Ten's a funny age. Their imaginations are too big for elementary, but they're still so little. Making them think they were freer and more independent than they were was one of my kinder tricks.

Natalie could take that as a put-down, like I'm telling her he's closer to his guy friends, but she doesn't. She's not overly sensitive.

"No," she says, meeting my eyes without hesitation. "I messaged Jack and Hud. They have no idea where he is." I admire her fearlessness with being interpreted as demanding or confrontational. I would like my daughters to demand the same respect. At the same time, I find myself mentally defending McClane and his male streak of unaccountability, his resistance to daily responsibilities and considerations. He doesn't owe you his GPS, young lady. He's not your dog on a leash.

"Wait. Why aren't you in school?"

"I have lunch period. Seniors can go off campus for lunch." She pulls her phone from her pocket, checks it, and slides it back into her pocket.

I'm about to say *It's barely breakfast*, but I remember how high school schedules work. Last year McClane had lunch third period, which was basically nine a.m., and this year Whitney has lunch seventh period, which is nearly two p.m. It's no wonder kids compare high school to prison.

"Maybe he took the morning off to be by himself, think about school, meditate on life." I'm half joking, but it strikes a chord with Natalie. She stiffens and looks away, her eyes settling on my bird feeder.

Her expression shifts. She's keeping a thought to herself, and it makes me briefly think of her as my equal. This girl has her shit together. Probably in a healthier way than I do. My shit is together, but it's duct-taped together like you'd duct-tape someone you kidnapped and tossed in your trunk.

"No." Natalie's attention snaps back to my face. "Something's happened. You need to call the police."

"The police?" I say it as if I haven't considered it yet. "They won't do anything, he's eighteen. He's an adult. He could have driven to Vegas."

"That's not McClane." Her eyes tighten, skeptical of me. "You aren't worried?"

"Natalie, I'm always worried. I worry all the time about my kids, but that doesn't give me the right to fly off the handle and make a mess of things." I say this as a jab, but also because it's true. If there's one thing parenting has taught me, it's the art of mentally numbing myself. Kids do too many things to quadruple your pulse inside a second, from jamming a full hot dog in their mouth to running across the street without looking to not checking their blind spot and narrowly missing getting rear-ended by a ubiquitous Ford pickup. You have to calm yourself to the point of lobotomy. Even when you're not calm, you have to pretend that you're calm so people don't think you're crazy. So that you don't take a regular scene and turn it into a traumatic memory. When you're sitting in the passenger seat and they're driving, you have to inconspicuously tighten your grip on the door, push your shoe against the footwell, and keep your mouth shut.

And teens are dramatic, that's just how they roll out of the factory. Everything is a four-alarm fire, from someone posting an ugly photo of them to you forgetting to run the dryer for them on tumble dry.

My neighbor's lawn mower grinds to life, and Natalie looks across my yard. "Okay," she says calmly. "I can see why you don't want to call the police. But I'm positive something is wrong. I'm calling them."

Well, fuck. I can't afford that, can I? The optics of that would be smeared in shit.

"I'll call." I pull my phone from my sweater pocket and call the police right there on the porch. Phone to my ear as it rings, I tell Natalie, "I don't think they're going to do anything. He's an adult. You saw him last night."

I talk to a tired police department receptionist for a few minutes. Turns out, I'm wrong. They're sending someone over. My knowledge of police procedure is dictated by gory *Dateline* stories and crime shows on Netflix, and apparently, television shows are not reality. Apparently, in a moderately sized suburb in the Midwest, the police will come to your house if your high school senior hasn't been seen since last night.

"They're sending someone," I say. "You can go on back to school. I don't want you to get in trouble. I'll call you if they have any questions for you or they hear anything. I'm sure he's fine, though."

"Do you have my number?"

"Oh, I don't think I do." I add Natalie's number to my contacts list and watch her walk back to her car. I'm proud of McClane for choosing someone as confident and grounded as Natalie.

Still, I can't resist nitpicking. Natalie has no plans for college. Instead, she's planning to take Realtor classes. She's under the impression peddling homes is a stable profession. Hell, maybe it is. It just doesn't seem like it should be the fresh-out-of-high-school dream. Realty strikes me as the hustle you settle for after your dreams go stale in a bowl of bar pretzels and whatever's cheapest on tap. Before you realize you have to wear lipstick, heels, and a pantsuit every time you make a late-night grocery-store run for toilet paper because you never know where you might be able to drum up a sale. I think her parents should encourage her to reach higher. She has the grades. She's responsible. They should tell her *House Hunters* is not an accurate depiction of reality. That selling houses is not all well-timed jokes and beautiful bathtubs. That Realtors occasionally walk into smelly houses to find dogshit on the shag carpet.

I close the door, relieved she's gone. Too many cooks in the kitchen and all that. I pep-talk myself again. *You can do hard things.* I brush my hair and rub cream blush onto my cheeks and lips.

In the room off the kitchen, the television is on. Joe must have turned it on when I was outside with Natalie. He doesn't watch it—just walks in, flips the switch, and wanders away. I don't ask why.

On the morning news, a woman in a bright yellow pantsuit is saying, "—body of missing Missouri woman, Angie Giano, has been found along the bank of the Ohio River in Cairo, Illinois. Police are asking the public for information."

My sour stomach twists. That's the last thing I need, lady. I don't want to hear about some other missing person who turned up dead.

I turn the TV off and brew another cup of coffee. I need to be sharp for the police. I need to make a good impression. Strike them as unsuspicious. Which reminds me.

I delete the message I sent this morning.

CHAPTER 6

M<small>C</small>C<small>LANE</small>

26 HOURS UNTIL MISSING

Back at Green Lake, we're parked at the scenic lot overlooking the water. Which is not green. More like the color of a shadow, a thin black, except on the west side. There the sunset casts flaming amber light along the surface.

The parking lot up here is big enough for two dozen cars. Natalie and I lie in a small patch of grass under a crabapple tree in full bloom. I can't smell the bursting pink flowers. Instead, tail pipe exhaust and hot engine metal.

We both have our eyes on a hawk. It's perched on a NO JUMPING, NO SWIMMING sign a dozen feet away, right in front of the lookout rail. I see hawks all the time around the lake, but not up close like this and not with legs like these. Feathers cover the hawk's meaty legs all the way down to the claws. It's not a red-tailed hawk. I'm not sure what this one's called. It lifts a claw, then puts it back down on the sign, talons clicking against the metal. The hawk doesn't seem to be zoned in on prey. Seems like it's just chilling.

"I wonder what he'd do if you got close," she says.

"I know what he'd do. Rip out my throat."

Her head is heavy on my stomach. It's such a conflicting feeling when someone's lying on you. You absolutely love it. You're like a dog rolling in grass, you want to soak up that feeling forever. But you're also like, dude, give me some space.

What are we going to do?

The question is thick like peanut butter in the back of my throat. I want to hack it up. I'm not going to, though. She had a rougher day than I did, she deserves time to think. I play with her hair because she likes that. I twirl a soft strand of dark around my finger and pull it close. Breathe it in. Peaches.

She sits up, and I let her hair fall through my fingers. She slowly gets to her feet and creeps toward the hawk.

"Don't," I say.

"Look at those legs." A smile curls around her voice.

I prop myself on my elbows. "Natalie. Quit it."

She lifts her phone, holds it in front of her, maybe as a shield, probably for a photo. She's not acting reckless because she's mad at her parents. This is just Natalie. "You are beautiful, aren't you?" she says, a few steps away from the hawk.

I hold my breath.

My imagination sees the bird launching at her. Natalie stumbling, tripping over the guardrail, and going over the edge.

She takes one more tentative step toward the hawk—she could reach out and touch it, she could hop the rail and jump the cliff—and the bird takes flight, up and over her head.

I exhale as Natalie walks back to me, her smile wide open.

She looks over her shoulder. "It had a wild, hot-feather smell. The smell of flying," she says, her eyes dreamy, as if she could fly away like the hawk, wind rushing under her wings. Nothing tying her down. I'm probably overthinking it. She just wanted a photo of a cool-looking bird. She studies her phone, then shows me her screen. A close-up photo of the hawk's face. Stern, beady eyes.

"Hey—there's this new thing I forgot to tell you about. It's called zooming in." I'm faking excitement. "You could have taken that same photo from here."

She laughs, rolling down to lie beside me. "Who would think a tough-ass wrestler would be such a scaredy?"

"Did you see its claws?" I make a claw with my hand and bring it down over her face. She rolls onto her back and bites one of my fingers.

"Ow." I shake my finger loose from her teeth. "Besides, I'm not a total wuss. I went up to your door, and your mom looked like she was going to take my head off." The words tumble out before I think to stop them.

Natalie sighs and looks up into the tree's canopy of blooms, tinted red by the sunset. "I didn't tell her. She's got a sixth sense for scandal or something. I wrapped the test in toilet paper, wrapped it a ton, like, mummified it, put it in the bathroom garbage. She went in there to clean, like, fifteen minutes after I took the test. Who unwraps garbage from a bathroom trash can? That's nasty. She's demented, actually."

"I have one question," I say.

"Yeah?"

"Where was your dad?"

She doesn't answer right away. She closes her eyes. I watch her chest rise and fall, sync my breathing to hers. I look at her stomach where her T-shirt rides up. Her skin is smooth and flat, the sun lighting up the faintest hairs along her stomach. No sign of pregnancy. Not that I was expecting her stomach to look different. Whatever's growing in there is, like, the size of a peanut. It's weird thinking about it.

"Don't lie," I say.

"He said, 'I don't want to hurt him,' and he walked out to the garage."

My skin tightens over my bones. "He's gonna kill me, isn't he?"

She opens her eyes and rolls toward me. Her eyes make me think of amber, millions-of-years-old amber—magical-old, and mosquitoes trapped in thick sap—and I forget to think about anything for a few seconds. That curved upper lip. I want to bite it. I always want to bite it. My chest flutters.

"He just needs to cool down," she says.

Natalie's got a big family. Seven people. When we first started talking, we bonded over that. Our big families. No one's got big families these days. I mean, well, besides Mormons or whatever. Or people so dumb they don't know how to use birth control. We were using it, by the way. Two kinds. I'm not sure what happened. I guess we could have been doing it wrong. We're the dumb people I'm talking about, I guess.

She's got two younger sisters, Isabelle and Genevieve. Isabelle's wild and never brushes her hair. Genevieve's all quiet and soft smiles, always tugging her sleeves down over her wrists. There are two older brothers, Daniel and Axel. Daniel's cool. He's two years older than Natalie and works as a roofer. He's mellow, smart, content with his existence. Ax is the oldest. He's impulsive and unpredictable. He stole a car at eighteen and had to serve a year in Statesville. Natalie says he came back mostly the same but a little more calculated, like a stalking cat.

So weird to me that Ax is the oldest. The oldest in my family is Dave, and he's got his act wrapped up so tight, it's surprising he doesn't burst. Dave's a stereotypical oldest. A know-it-all, but a good guy. Reliable. Judgmental but fair.

Ax works at the Amazon warehouse in Joliet, rents an apartment with a couple of other guys. He's rough on Natalie's parents, but they don't mind much. When they look at him, they see a kid who's still trying to figure things out. Ax is the only one in Natalie's family who doesn't like me. Well, before today.

"What about Ax? Does he know?"

"Not yet."

"He's gonna kill me."

She laughs. "Why you worrying about my family, Golden Boy? Your mom's gonna kill you."

That's Nat's nickname for me—Golden Boy. Sometimes she says it to tease me. Sometimes she says it sincerely and softly as her lips graze my cheek, my ear, like I'm her treasure.

"I will not be golden to anyone, I'll tell you that. More like lead. Poisonous. Feared."

She laughs again.

"This is serious. Stop laughing."

"Okay," she says, but she's smiling. "They're such hypocrites, though. That's the crazy thing. My mom got pregnant with Ax when she was seventeen."

"Same. I think my mom was pregnant with my oldest brother when she was nineteen."

"You mean Carson?" she says softly.

"Yeah. And it's okay, you don't have to baby me." Carson died in an accident when he was five. I never knew him. To me, he's just a kid I come across in old photos.

"That's weird that your mom was a teen mom. I knew that, but I can't picture it about her. She seems too organized to end up a teen mom."

I want to say, *Yeah, but so are you.* There's no way Nat missed taking one of her birth control pills. She's organized. She's a planner.

"I guess she was different twenty-some years ago. Twenty years is a lifetime," I say. "Do you really think you can have a baby now?"

"Well, it's not fucking ideal, McClane, and I wasn't planning on it, but I am capable." Then, kind of quiet, kind of cruel, she says, "You don't have to stick around."

"I support you. I love you. Whatever you want." Look at that. It came in handy after all.

Her eyes spark with a sudden idea. "Let's jump." She sits and pulls up her top.

"No way, water's way too cold." I coax her shirt down over her stomach, but not before I glimpse her flesh-colored, see-through bra. She rotates through five bras. The flesh-colored one is the plainest, no lace, no push-up, but it's my favorite. "We have to wait till July," I say. I've jumped twice. In August, and during the day, of course. There's a safe place to the right where the cliff face is smooth and tucks in instead of jutting out. First time I jumped was after Hud's mom died. I jumped with Hud. Jack's not into it. Says we're crazy.

She quiets and looks down at her flat stomach. "I don't know if I can wait till July. It's only two months away, but can I do stuff like that in July?" Natalie has never jumped. She says she isn't scared, she's just never been interested. I believe it. She's the most fearless person I know. More than Hud, even. I mean, Hud does crazier things, but with Hud, it's almost like he does crazy things because he *is* scared.

Each time I jumped for a reason, but I loved the adrenaline rush. I'm a chill person, usually. It's just that, sometimes, this insane feeling creeps up on me, and it's like I need to jump out of my skin because it's on fire.

Emotions shift across her eyes, then she's back to business. "You should drop me off. I've got to write a paper."

"We graduate in thirty days. I barely have anything."

"Not all of us took blow-off classes, McClane. Some of us want to learn stuff."

"You're seriously going to be able to write a paper? Tonight?"

"It's not, like, the end of the world. It's just another human being to be responsible for every second of every day."

Even as my stomach twists, I smile. I love this about Natalie. She can make dead-serious shit seem like it's easy. She is the opposite of everyone in my family. They make easy shit seem dead serious.

Natalie is one of the only people I know who doesn't feel sorry for herself. One of the only teenagers I know who doesn't hold a grudge against their parents. She sees them as people, not as a source of cash to harvest. Natalie is the only girl who doesn't bother with drama.

The only girl who would want to keep a baby. Ugh.

Most girls would be like, Fuck no, I'm aborting that blood clot. It isn't that Nat isn't pro-choice, she is. It's more like she likes her parents, wants what they have, and isn't afraid of hard work. Or maybe it's because she believes in God.

Me, not so much. My oldest brother died in a random accident when he was just a tiny dude. If I got to the pearly gates, I'd say, "Why you such a sick fuck, dude? What gives?"

Natalie doesn't mind my lack of faith. She gets a kick out of it. And her God stuff doesn't bother me either. Neither of us feels like we have to be right. And there are things about her faith that I love, that I long for. Ritual. Dependability. Her family bonds are heavy, almost suffocating. I love that.

A text comes through, and I check it. Hud.

Dude, can you pick me up?

Sure. I've got to drop Nat at home first. I'll text you in 15. Good?

Good.

I don't want to give him a ride, but I always say sure with Hud because: One, I have a car and that's lucky. Two, because Hud is owed. By his friends, by his teachers, by the fucking universe. Three, because I can be a pushover. Even when my instinct tells me no way do I want to do that, I go along with it because really, what's the harm?

"Hud needs me to drive him home. You want to write your paper at my house?"

"Nah. Me hanging out in your room would make your parents nervous. I'll do it at home. If Muscles and Dough get crabby, I'll walk over to Olivia's." Muscles is what she calls her mom, Dough is her dad.

She stands and holds out her hand. I take it, and she lifts me up. My chest presses hers. Instant fireworks. I'd step in front of a train for this girl. "You haven't kissed me yet," she says softly. Goose bumps on her upper arm rise beneath my palm. The day's warmth has slipped away with the sun. There is a sliver of red on the horizon, but the lake is all dark.

I thread my fingers through her hair and pull her toward me. When our lips touch, it's raw and electric. Desire jolts through me. Her tongue tastes like mint gum, but I kiss her deeper because I'd rather taste her.

"You really have your shit this together?" I say softly.

Her eyes drift down, her lashes flutter. "I don't think it's sunk in yet. I mean, I feel bad that I let my parents down, but I'm also having sweet thoughts." Her eyes meet mine again. "Like, me and you and a baby."

For a moment, I can't breathe.

I have no sweet feelings, no longing to have a kid. I *am* a kid. I mean, I feel like a kid, regardless of my age and the associated rules—like, okay, I can legally kill a bunch of dudes in the desert and die with a machine gun in my hands but can't buy beer at Walmart, those kinds of ass-backward rules. But, like, I have Legos and Pokémon cards in my room. Sure, they're on the top shelf of my closet, but still.

I envision a kid, a seven-year-old boy who looks like I did at that age. Okay, basically me. I see this kid smiling, a gap where he's missing a tooth, hair messy, holding up his Lego creation, and I have no love for him.

CHAPTER 7

MEG

THE DAY THE POLICE GET INVOLVED, 9:42 A.M.

Two male officers, both very young, stand on my porch. One looks relaxed, maybe a little hungover, and didn't bother to run a brush through his hair. A cowlick on his crown sticks up like a duck's butt. The other guy is a hard-ass, head shaved, puffing up his chest like a bold puppy. He's got a silver band on his ring finger. Maybe he's a hard-ass at work because his wife keeps his balls in the key dish at home. They parked on the street in front of my house. Same place Natalie parked less than an hour ago.

Shaved Head gets right to it. "We got a call about a possible missing person."

"I'm sorry to trouble you. It's probably nothing. It's nothing, I'm sure," I say, feeling a need to reassure them, to come across as relaxed, "but we don't know where my son is. His car is gone, he's not at school, and he's not answering his phone."

"How long has he been missing?" Shaved Head says.

"I'm not sure. I didn't see him last night, but he usually goes to bed later than I do. I can't say if he slept in his bed or not. His girlfriend saw him last night."

"High school?" Shaved Head.

"Oh, right, I'm sorry. He's a senior."

Shaved Head almost laughs at me. Like I'm a naive old lady who doesn't understand teenagers. He tucks a thumb in his belt. "Even the most well-behaved kids skip school at the end of senior year."

"I know. His girlfriend was worried." I can't help but roll my eyes. "I told her I'd call. She did say his two closest friends didn't know where he was."

Cowlick studies the bushes edging my front porch like he's thinking about landscaping. "Odds are, he's fine. Eighteen is legal," he says, and the last part lands strangely because I'm too used to hearing it as a vulgar phrase. "We can gather some information, though, and keep you updated if we hear anything. Mind if we come in?"

Very much I mind. "Sure, come on in."

On my porch, these boys were normal-sized. Sitting at my kitchen table, they're too big. Their shoes bang against chair legs, their belts and equipment squeak with every movement. And they've brought in the smell of outside, worms and dirt, like dogs do.

"As far as you know, he take any drugs?" Cowlick says, his notepad and pen ready.

"No, he's a good kid."

"What all mothers say," Shaved Head responds, leaning back with a smile. I don't like him. I don't like either of them. Seems like they're following a script, playing cops based on their favorite show.

"He has a wrestling scholarship to Indiana University," I say. To prove my point. Kids have to be disciplined and intentional to win a full ride.

"Nice," says Cowlick. "What's his record?"

"This year, forty-three and four."

"Wow. Big guy?" Shaved Head asks.

"No. He's slender, medium height."

They both nod, like they know wrestling. Like they understand records.

They know nothing. They have no idea that his tenth match required stitches along his eyebrow. That his thirty-third match ended with the other kid in agony: a dislocated knee his coach had to pop back into place. They don't know how McClane's starved and dehydrated himself days before meets, used laxatives, and sweat himself sick in a sauna suit in the bathroom stall just before weigh-ins. They don't know that he's double-jointed, and in a sport that involves twisting, it gives him a unique advantage and also puts him at a higher risk of injuries. They don't grasp his devotion. The insight. The reflexes. The calculation. Yes, McClane is easygoing, but there is calculation and planning underneath that easy smile of his.

"Anything going on with his friends or girlfriend?"

"No."

Shaved Head says, "Snapchat gossip? Girl stuff?" Now he's just a cop looking for entertainment.

"No." Although, really, I don't know. McClane doesn't tell me much about his relationship. He doesn't post on social media. If he does, I don't know his handle.

Cowlick slips his notebook into his jacket and stands. "Seems like you've got a good kid. We'll take a quick look in his room to make sure everything seems in place." He heads for the stairs.

"Oh" is all I say, but I want to rewind. Make them ask their questions outside. No, rewind further. Keep the police out of our business. Tell Natalie to chill out. Kids today have no patience. McClane didn't answer his phone immediately, and her response is needing to call the police. Easy, girl. Natalie started rolling this snowball down the hill, and I'm going to end up with a pie-face of snow. "If he knew officers looked in his bedroom, he'd die." My face flashes hot when I say that last part.

"We won't say a word if you won't," Cowlick says from the bottom stair.

"And we've seen it all," Shaved Head says, blocking the hall as he walks in front of me, acting as if his biceps are too big, his arms need more space. He is deliberately walking like a gorilla so I can't rush past him.

"You should see my son's room." Cowlick's voice barely makes it down to us from the top of the stairs. "Toys everywhere. And those tiny craft beads, they're embedded in the rug. You step on one of those beads the wrong way, it takes you down." A chuckle.

Shaved Head places a foot onto the bottom step.

"Please don't touch anything," I say, my voice cracking with emotion.

"Which one is it?" Cowlick shouts from upstairs.

I hesitate. If I don't tell them, maybe they'll leave.

Shaved Head clears the top stair and turns down the hallway.

"Oh, I see," Cowlick says. "The one with the lights on. I love these lamps with the twisty arms. My wife, not so much. Too college-dormy for her."

I thought I was smart getting rid of Natalie, but she guided me right into a trap. She's more calculating than McClane. Police inside my house. Inside McClane's bedroom. What have I done?

"What does he use these for?" Cowlick says from deep in McClane's bedroom.

My pulse pounding, I rush up the stairs. I'm halfway there when I stop. *Don't let them lure you into his room, into more questions.* My hand trembles around the railing. The nape of my neck is wet and itchy. *Don't act panicked and guilty.* I turn, walk down the steps, and do what I always do when I need to calm myself. I go to the kitchen sink and gaze out the window.

——— • ———

Our backyard is the main reason Joe and I bought this house. A full acre dotted with lovely trees. Deep at the end of our yard, the grass ends at a tall aluminum fence topped with barbed wire and guarding a twelve-foot drop to a narrow river. The fence with its barbed wire is a damn eyesore, but it's far enough back to be obscured by the trees, three out of four seasons.

The day we looked at this house, the late summer backyard was stunning and brimming with wildflowers. Purple hollyhocks. Rose of Sharon with magenta centers bleeding out to pink petals. Tall white phlox. Violet butterfly bushes. We walked through the grass, drawn to the back by the sound of the river and a pair of blue butterflies fixed in a dance. It was like walking in a fairy tale. We stood at the fence, watching those blue swallowtails and huge dragonflies flit about the river's surface, the water reflecting sunlight, shimmering and sparkling.

Joe shook the chain links, looked up at the barbed wire, and asked the Realtor, "Is there a lot of theft in this neighborhood?"

"Oh, no," she said, wobbling toward the fence in her heels and pantsuit. "This is a great neighborhood. Maybe to keep the forest animals out? It's beautiful, though, right? Nature up close. You can open the fence there if you want to cross the footbridge to the forest preserve."

The footbridge she was talking about was a bundle of two-by-fours laid side by side. There were no railings, and I'm afraid of heights. I wouldn't dare cross that footbridge. I'd get vertigo and end up in the river. I liked nature, but from afar. I liked looking at the water flowing over rocks and the tangles of tall grass on the other side of the bridge, vines snarling up trees, but I didn't want to be knee-deep in it.

Especially then. I rubbed my hand over the small bump of my belly. I was early in my pregnancy with Jamie at that point.

Our Realtor pointed at the other side of the river. "Look there. The previous owner put steps down that side if you like to fish." My eyes followed her pointing to the wooden steps wedged into the steep bank. No railing there either, but they looked sturdy enough.

Joe said, "I love to fish. Me and my dad, we used to spend a few weeks every summer in Wisconsin."

"Oh?" our Realtor said, not at all interested.

"The stream is nice," Joe said. "Barbed wire seems a little over the top."

"Either way, it's a good safety precaution for little ones," I said. Most people saw barbed wire and thought, *That'll keep 'em out.* I thought, *That'll keep 'em in.* My mom taught me that.

"Impaling them on barbed wire? Oh yeah, great idea." Joe gave me a sideways smile.

I backhanded his shoulder, but I was beaming. I loved the dancing swallowtails and the stream. I loved the yard. I loved the house. Farmhouse cream trim and muted greens. Sunny wood floors. Huge kitchen, and a mudroom with built-in cubbies. Growing up, I never knew anyone who had a mudroom. By the time we were looking at houses, a mudroom became the goal. This small room willing to take on the burden of hiding your filth. I loved the concept.

We were living in an apartment near Joe's parents—our eager babysitters—and wanted to settle into a house before Jamie was born. I was working two days a week at the Art Institute. Joe had started at the brokerage firm. We took the train home together Friday nights, sitting side by side, sharing train-station hot dogs. Joe drinking a beer bought from a beer girl at Union Station. Even though it was cheap beer, watered down and lukewarm, it smelled good. I'd kiss his wet lips for a warm yeasty taste.

The elementary school was a five-minute walk from the house. Scenic Green Lake was a ten-minute drive. Our yard backing up to a thin strip of river and forest beyond was dreamy. A spot of wilderness in the suburbs. Everything about the house in Sugar Glen was perfect.

———•———

One of the officers moves down the stairs, quicker than he walked up. He's speaking into his radio, which squawks sharply. The sound is abrasive, and I shudder.

"Yep, got it," he says, turning the corner. Shaved Head. He's holding the radio to his mouth. The toughness is gone from his expression. He's excited like a kid who's found a fallen baby squirrel in the grass and is thinking he just got himself the pet he's always wanted. "Gibson's in the kid's room. I'm getting the evidence case." He turns to check the kitchen and sees me coming toward him, my face a question mark. "Ma'am, I'm gonna need you to stay down here."

I open my mouth to ask, but he holds up a finger and turns away. I close my mouth. Like a pea-brained fish. A trapped fish, outsmarted and outmaneuvered by a net.

He pushes my screen door open and jogs to his car. Before the screen snaps shut, I follow him out. My ears feel full. My pulse drums in my throat. My teeth chatter, though I'm not cold. It's happening. This is how the unraveling begins. I'm not ready.

Shaved Head digs in his open trunk.

A gray Taurus pulls up behind him in the street, parking against the curb. A young man steps out of the driver's seat in tan pants and a polo shirt, a gun holstered under his armpit. A woman steps out of the passenger seat, dressed similarly, her gun holstered at her waist. I've watched enough shows to know who these two are. Detectives.

Shaved Head closes his trunk and turns to them with a case in his hand. They chat, calm and attentive, then walk up my driveway together. What do they think happened? *Don't say anything. Don't give them anything.* I bite my bottom lip to keep the words in.

The man is young, in his thirties, his hair a mess of loose dark curls, his cheeks ruddy. He looks like a man who doesn't want to give up his weed-smoking college days. Maybe that's part of his trick to putting guilty people at ease.

The woman is my age, ragged, carrying twenty pounds more than she'd probably like. Her hair is in a low, sloppy bun at the nape of her neck. Flyaway hairs frame her face. She didn't bother with makeup. A dark reddish-purple scar crosses the bridge of her nose. It's been broken. Joe has the same exact scar. Her face is flat, but her blue eyes are clear and pretty.

"Hi, you're the mom?" she says.

"Yes. I'm Meg Hart. McClane's mom. He's very responsible, and it's unlike him to not answer his phone. I'm sure he's okay, but I'm worried." I'm trying to strike the right tone. Concerned, but everything's probably fine. Kids can be irresponsible, dumb, even at eighteen. Whatever you found in his room, it's not what you think.

"I'm Detective Ali Flemming." She reaches out to shake my hand, and the smells of eucalyptus and menthol waft off her. She smells like a cough drop. Her hand is as cold as mine when I shake it.

"I'm Detective Drew Becker," the man says with a slight smile. His hand is warm and moist. He smells like mint gum and good cologne. "Let's go inside."

I stand firm. "Can you please tell me what's going on? What you found?" I lock eyes with Shaved Head.

Shaved Head looks to Becker. Gone is his hard-ass demeanor. He's a puppy looking to the alpha for permission.

Becker says, "I understand your concern. Give us a few minutes and we'll be down to chat. While you're waiting, maybe you can call family? Does McClane's dad live here?"

"He lives here," I say sternly, as if I'm offended by the sheer notion of divorce. "He's working."

Detective Becker moves past me. He opens the screen and walks inside like he owns the place. Shaved Head follows. Detective Flemming holds the door for me, says, "We'll be down in a few minutes, Mrs. Hart. If you don't want to call anyone, make yourself a cup of tea. The best thing you can do for your son is to stay calm."

"I appreciate that." I do. It's good advice. I like her. With her broken nose, her blotchy complexion, and her extra weight, she's a woman who's not trying to pull one over on you.

I stand by the door as they walk upstairs. The sound of their shoes hitting each stair is slow and methodical, like hard work. Like a hammer pounding nails into a coffin.

Once they clear the landing, I rush down to the basement.

CHAPTER 8

McClane

25 HOURS UNTIL MISSING

I drive away from Natalie's house, glancing back at her porch in my rearview. I catch a glimpse of her bare calf before her screen door bounces shut. The sky is violet and deep blue. The night is charged, ready to overtake the day.

When I call Hud, it only rings once. "Are you on your way?" His voice is breathy, like he's been running.

"I just left Natalie's. Text me the address."

"I don't know where the fuck I am, Mick." On his end, sirens roll in the distance.

"You in trouble?" Twenty minutes ago, his text seemed casual. Unalarming.

"Nah, I'm okay, I'm okay," but it sounds like he's trying to convince himself. "I'm crossing an intersection but I'm gonna keep walking because this place is suspicious as fuck. Jump on I-55, and when you get closer, I'll tell you the street."

"Just share your location on Snap, and I'll find you."

"Okay. Battery's low, so don't call." On his end, bass is getting louder, thumping the fabric of a shitty car stereo. Here come loose voices, like a car has pulled up next to him and they're talking loud with the windows down.

"You sure you're okay?" I ask again, my own car bumping over the train tracks. I took them slow enough to not catch air, fast enough to rough up my car. I can almost hear Whitney's voice, whiny in my ear: "He's gonna wreck it before it's my turn. I always get everyone's crappy leftovers."

"I said I'm good." Hud's a little annoyed. "Text me if you don't get my location though."

"I will."

At the next stoplight, I check Snap. My phone tells me he's sixty-eight minutes away, Chicago's West Side. It's just past nine. If I pick him up and drive him home, I won't be home till, like, after eleven. It's a letdown, and I'm suddenly exhausted. I'll call him back, tell him I can't, it's too far, or my mom wants me home.

Hud and I are not close enough anymore to stick our necks out all that far for each other. He hangs out with his Shady Grove friends more than he hangs with us. And, really, he can call his dad for a ride. His old man's always home, napping in his chair.

I do what I always do when I'm pissed at Hud. Picture him as a kid.

Hud sitting on the kitchen floor with Whitney, helping her set up the marble run. She's five or six and impatient as shit. He's seven or eight and strangely good with kids. He used to be shiny-apple wholesome, like his mom. When she died, his wholesomeness browned. So even though he's a dick mostly and seems to be sliding toward actual criminal behavior, I try to remember him as that eight-year-old who was nicer to Whitney than I ever was.

I veer onto the ramp, heading north onto 355. Four wide lanes, a straight shot north, no traffic till you get to I-55. You can blow past one hundred here, no problem. I've got Cool Hand Luke's needle pushing ninety.

I've driven to Chicago a bunch of times. Natalie and I went to Lollapalooza over the summer. Jack, Hud, and I have driven to O'Hare to watch the planes take off. We drove to the South Side for a Sox game and to an old neighborhood on the far West Side to pick up a snake for Jack's little brother. But I've never driven alone on a school night, and it's never felt like work.

My phone rings, and I'm hoping it's Hud telling me he found another ride home.

It's my brother Dave. I answer on speaker. "Hey, Dave."

"Hey, little brother. How's it going?"

Mad intense, actually. Nat's pregnant. I've got days to decide on that scholarship. I'm driving to pick up Hud, no doubt somewhere seriously suspicious. "Good," I say. "What's up?"

"I wanted to talk about stuff at home. You got time?"

Dad. He wants to talk about Dad. Relief moves through me like warm liquid. At the same time, I feel excited, nervous. My jaw tenses. I've been desperate to talk about Dad but have also been avoiding it.

Spinning blue LEDs light up my rearview mirror. Shit. I ease down on the brake.

"I'm getting pulled over. Now's no good. I'll call you later." I toss my phone onto the passenger's-side floor. Cop's way the fuck back there, but I swerve two lanes to the right and keep braking. My heart pounds against my rib cage, and I'm holding my breath.

Copper speeds past me, lights on, no sirens. Sweet. Adrenaline shoots through me, and I smile. There is no better rush than getting away with something. I feel like a silverback pounding his chest. I push the accelerator down and swerve back into the left lane.

I'd like to call Dave back, but my phone's out of reach. Talking with Dave will have to wait.

Will I tell him Nat's pregnant? What would he say?

I imagine he might say "Abort, abort, abort," joking like he's talking about a mission in a game. Not to be a dick, though. Just to add levity and humor. Also, he doesn't know Natalie yet, he only met her on a FaceTime call over Christmas, so he might be skeptical. He might say, "You sure it's yours, Mick? Imagine dropping out of school and finding out it's another dude's semen demon. That'd suuuck."

Another set of spinning blue lights coming from behind. I switch into the right lane again. This time, after the copper passes, I stay right. The day going stale, I yawn. I'd rather be in bed. Fucking Hud, man. I don't want to spiral into negativity, so I try to put him out of mind.

I picture Natalie in the passenger seat as I drove her home, her seat all the way back and her bare feet on the dash—those bubblegum-pink toenails. Her singing along to "Suga Suga" by Baby Bash. I used to think it was lame when girls sang along to sexist songs. Like, hello, don't you realize you're belittling yourself? Now, with Natalie, I see it differently. Any song she wants, it's hers. Like, it belongs to her or something, and she makes it her own.

You can do that with just about anything, I guess. Make it about you. Any situation, any song, any story. Make yourself the star of the movie. My mind drifts on that thought as I coast along the highway toward the city lights.

If Natalie's life were a movie, it'd be a creative indie with an uplifting ending. She'd like that.

Oh man, if Hud's life were a movie, it would be seriously messed up. Part drama, part horror—some serious Jordan Peele fuckery. In Hud's movie, I'm the uptight sidekick who's had it too good and finally gets some well-deserved bad luck. He'd like that, actually.

If Jack's life were a movie, it'd be a comedy with a good-hearted message. He'd hate that, but it's true.

If Dad's life were a movie, it would be a two-parter. The first would be a family adventure. That's the dad I remember when I was small. The sequel wouldn't match. It would be an old black-and-white, silent and super creepy.

And if my life were a movie? I consider it. The situation with my dad, the scholarship dilemma, and now a pregnant girlfriend. If my life were a movie, it would be one where things weren't what they seem. It would start out pleasant and sunny, but might end with someone dead.

CHAPTER 9

MEG

THE DAY THE POLICE GET INVOLVED, 10:57 A.M.

I rush down the basement stairs. Joe's home office is in the basement. Joe should have been the first person I searched for after I called the police. No, before that. When Sugar North called and said McClane didn't show up first period, I should have called my husband.

Truth is, Joe never even crossed my mind. Joe and I are no longer like a pair of jellyfish pulsing through the water together. We are separate. I'm an octopus hiding in a crevice; he's a shark weaving through the water above me.

He slips out of the house at strange times. If I ask where he went, where he's going, he gets agitated. Volatile. The less we talk, the more peaceful our existence. It's become habit to avoid him. To pretend he's busy doing the normal things busy people do. I'm good at pretending.

He'll be pissed when he finds out detectives are inside the house. He'll be pissed that I didn't ask him before I called the police. He'll be pissed any which way, but he needs to know what's happening.

He's not down here.

I figured. I mean, with the police walking up and down the hallway, basically stomping, he would have come up to find out what was happening if he were here.

The basement is dim and cold. Even though a plush rug covers most of the floor, it's bordered by exposed cement. Besides his home office, we have a couch and a TV. We used to let the kids have sleepovers with friends down here when they were in middle school. They'd play Xbox and eat pizza and someone would always spill soda on the rug. We didn't mind.

Beyond the couch, the darker half of the basement is for storage. Holiday bins, toolboxes, cans of soup and bags of beans for the apocalypse, bins of toys I'm saving for future grandchildren, and boxes of books.

I move the mouse on Joe's desk to wake his monitor. On the screen is the same document I saw last time I used his computer, a financial report for a tech start-up. He's been down here recently, though, because next to his desk are the kids' memory boxes. They're stacked vertically, one on top of the other. I'm pretty sure those weren't here yesterday. I would have noticed: The boxes aren't small. Each clear plastic bin is the size of a moving box and filled with awards, carefully selected schoolwork and artwork, and medical information worth keeping.

Their memory boxes are usually tucked away in the storage section of the basement, out of sight. But now here they are, and

McClane's is on top, its lid already off. I pick up the paper resting on the top of the pile. It's something he wrote in second grade—one of those fill-in-the-blank profiles.

> *My favorite color is: red.*
> *My favorite toy is: my bike.*
> *My favorite food is: meetballs.*
> *I want to be: a boxer like my dad.*
> *I love: my family.*

His handwriting is barely legible. Recalling seven-year-old McClane, those bright blue eyes, breaks my heart just a little. I wish I could go back, redo moments with him when his little mind was wide open and eager.

A question moves over my head like a spray cloud of toxic bug killer, making me lightheaded, and my smile drops. What the hell did they find in his room?

I leave McClane's second-grade biography where I found it and hustle upstairs. I check the garage for Joe's car. Gone. He must have left the house this morning when I was working with Eileen.

I begin tidying the kitchen, but the police and detectives clomping around in McClane's room set my nerves on end.

I resist the urge to go upstairs. The less I say, the better. I step out onto the front porch and sit, pulling my sweater tight. If Joe comes home while the police are upstairs, he might flip out. That would be bad. Better to wait here so I can intercept him.

Across the street, Griswold meows on his front porch beside a pot of freshly planted petunias, a small American flag stuck in the pot. Carla opens the door quickly, she's still in her fleece pajamas, and Griswold slips inside. She starts to close her door, but stops, noting the police car in front of my house, then me on the porch. She shuts her door, but her face is framed in one of the small sidelight windows edging her door. She's hovering, watching. Carla and I are friends, good for a bouillon cube or a teaspoon of imitation vanilla, but we mostly keep to our own families.

I mentally map out the details of McClane's room, trying to visualize what's where. I was in his room yesterday. On top of his dresser are bottles of supplements with asinine names. Horny Goat Weed. Skull Fuck. Green Bulge. B Kick. All those pill bottles look suspicious, but they're harmless teenage snake-oil silliness. There's a pull-up bar fixed inside his closet door. Some old games on his shelf. Operation. Battleship. Wrestling trophies. Holyfield and Klitschko posters. A pair of Joe's old gloves. Empty Juul cartridges. His bed. His desk. His computer. Oh no, did they find something on his computer?

A car drives by slowly, so slowly it catches my attention. A moss-green BMW. It pulls alongside the curb in front of Carla's house. I know the car. I know the driver.

No. No, no, no. Not now. I stand abruptly and wave the driver away like I'm waving a fly away from my dessert. The car drives away slowly.

I search for Carla's watching eyes in the sidelight window. She's gone. Did she notice the BMW before she walked away?

"Someone you know?" Detective College Boy.

I startle and turn. "Oh, you scared me. What?"

"In the BMW?"

"Oh. Just a nosy gawker. They see the police car and they can't help themselves."

He nods. I think he's agreeing: *Yeah, those gapers are real assholes.* "Would you mind coming in, Mrs. Hart?"

~ My Journal ~

I'm suppost to write in here. I dont know what she wants me to write.

We went to the Memoreal Day parade today. I thought there would be candy but it was a bunch of super old grandpas in convirtables. Boring. Dad felt bad for taking us to the parade so he took us fishing at the creek after. We are not suppost to go down there but dont worry, its safe. He said don't tell mom. When she gets mad she looks like a dragon with lines for eyes. When she gets sad, she looks like a melting dripping face. We didnt catch any fish in the river but we saw the huggest frog I ever seen. It was so big it looked fake. It was noisy too.

After that I built part of my Lego city. There is going be a snake monster in it to chase the people. It's almost bedtime. I don't like to go to bed. In the day I am happy and want to tell jokes. At nite when it's time for bed I want to die.

Jamie's birthday is tomorrow. I'm gonna take lots of pictures with my camera. I hope mom makes a good cake but that it's not a barbie cake or something.

MC, age 7

CHAPTER 10

McClane

24 HOURS UNTIL MISSING

According to the map on my phone, I'm right on top of Hud. I park close enough to the intersection to read the signs. Keeler and Lake. Three guys stand at the corner, all with their hoodies up. One guy wears his pants so low, my headlights illuminate the bare skin of his thighs below his underwear. Dude is seriously hairy. Another guy is waving his arms like crazy. Hard to tell if he's pissed at the other two or just screwing around with his friends.

To my left: two churches, one with a red neon cross. A car wash with no customers to my right. Straight across the street is full darkness under the "L" train. Steel beams crisscross below the wooden tracks all the way down to the cement-and-gravel lot.

During the day, the graffiti along the steel beams probably looks artistic and carefree. Good for those street artists, being expressive and shit. Now it pretty much looks like hieroglyphs painted in blood, a warning that someone's thinking of cutting your throat.

Same with the train. During the day, the "L" train is community, closeness, well-meaning BO, and the notion of heading somewhere for something good to eat. When it's dark, it's more like a stampede of angry horses blowing smoke out of their flaring nostrils.

Now the rumbling is starting, like a low growl. The train is a stop or two away.

I'm not scared, but I'm not relaxed either. I'm actually annoyed. I don't want to be here. Just because Hud came out here and lost his ride, why do I have to pay for it?

I lock my doors and call Hud on my cell. "I'm here. Baptist church direct to my left, car wash and apartments to my right, Green Line station straight ahead. Three dudes standing—"

"Yo, I see you." Hud steps out of the alley behind the apartment building with his hoodie up, backpack slung over a shoulder. It's like he's stepping out of a different dimension into mine.

He tugs at the passenger's-side door, but it's locked. He gives me a pissed-off look—danger and fear flickering in his eyes at the same time. There's something else off about him. His face is pale.

I unlock the doors, and he slides in. A puff of city-garbage stink and deep-fried donuts comes in with him. Also, the smell of weed. Not the good kind of weed smell you get when you step into a party before midnight, but the bad one. Stale weed, party's long over, puke drying on someone's shirt.

He tosses his backpack into the backseat.

"What the hell, Hud? Why you out here with no ride?" My words could sound friendly, but they don't. Annoyance cuts through.

"Leave me alone, Mick."

"I'm not the one who ditched you, man. I'm the one picking you up."

Hud pulls his hoodie down over his forehead and leans against the window, so I can't see his face. Kind of quiet, he says, "I'm not interested in playing Hud's-life-sucks-so-bad to make everyone feel better, okay? You with your scholarship and your girlfriend and your shiny everything. Just fuck off for a few minutes, man."

His words hurt. Piss me off too. I ask a legitimate question like why's he out here with no ride, and he's being a dick. He's rarely a dick, like, directly. Actually, he seems shaken up, so I just stop talking. And absolutely, I get it. He's right. Everyone does that to him. Asks for details about his crummy life so they can make their own problems shrink. Me included. "My bad," I say and drive.

As I swerve onto the entrance ramp to the 290, he turns the radio to heavy metal. Not my favorite but I let it go. I crack my window so the cool air and the rough sound of wind banging against the car softens the steely music. We don't talk. I just drive.

——— • ———

By the time we're back in Sugar Glen, I feel looser. I'm back to enjoying the night. I like being out late, I like the thrill of it, the possibility. The air is brisk. I'm waking up. And I feel bad for Hud. It sucks not having a car, constantly having to ask. He probably felt crummy texting me for a ride.

I go through the drive-through and buy him a chocolate shake and two cheeseburgers. It's a good excuse to turn off the radio. I'm in that in-between place of hating this dude who has become a stranger and also wanting to help a friend who used to be a big part of my life.

"Thanks, man," he says around a bite of hamburger, the food already lifting his mood, chilling him out. "I'll pay you back."

"Whatever. My dad gave me twenty bucks last week, so it's his treat." Dad actually gave me eighty bucks, but that would be an insult. "Everything okay tonight?" I make sure I don't sound annoyed.

He rubs his eyes like he's exhausted, then looks out his side window. "Just some weird shit I didn't want to be around."

"Guys from Shady Grove?"

"Nah, they're cool. I mean, yeah, they were there, but they weren't doing anything messed up. Some of the other people there, though, were just, like, majorly suspicious." His tone is hollowed-out and kind of chilling. "Someone had a gun they kept pointing at people's foreheads and laughing. Just weird shit I don't want to be around." At this last part, his voice has a faraway vibe, like he's seen a ghost.

I want to ask more about the gun, but what's the point? He's out of there. "Your Shady Grove ride still there in the city?"

"Yeah, but they're cool."

"Yeah?"

He's quiet for a while. "They're kind of like family, like anything goes and they'll let it ride. They're like loser cousins who are also just nice dudes."

I know what he means. When Jack and I helped him move his stuff into Shady Grove, the apartment kids were hanging around outside. They were nice, asked us how we were doing, offered us pizza. They had the box sitting on the hood of someone's car. Offered us weed.

"They always have time, which is nice." His tone is light, he doesn't mean it as an insult to Jack and me. "But sometimes they act like scary shit isn't scary. Like, they have different limits for what's acceptable."

I want to ask where they work, what they do. Most of them went to Sugar North and graduated three, four years before us. But I already asked enough, and the answers don't matter. Same about the gun. If I ask more, it would be to satisfy my selfish curiosity.

Hud drops the greasy paper bag between his feet and starts typing on his phone. His messy hair hangs down, and the worry creasing his forehead is lit in blue light.

"They texting you?"

Eyes on his phone, he sighs. "They want me to hang later."

"Just tell them you're puking."

"Huh?" He looks up at me, like he missed half of what I said.

"They're not gonna want you in their car if you're puking."

He smiles, his eyes bright for a second, and he's back to texting. "Nice."

When I pull into his apartment complex, he says, "Natalie mad that you had to pick me up?"

I weave through the lot, driving slowly because it's poorly lit and packed with cars, many of them parked illegally.

"Nah, I was getting ready to drop her back home when you called." My mind drifts back to Nat. What is she thinking about right now? Like, how can she possibly be considering having a kid? Fuck. I should be with her. Hud's dad should have picked him up.

I think about Jack's rip on Hud's dad earlier today. Maybe Hud's dad couldn't have picked him up. I wonder how Hud's dad actually is, like, if he's gotten better or worse. I haven't asked Hud about his dad for a while, maybe this whole year. "How's your dad?"

"Same."

I say nothing. Same is actually worse than worse. You're just constantly waiting, waiting, fucking waiting pulling your hair out waiting for a change until you forget there's an alternative to what you've got going. Like a lobster in a pot of water on the stove that doesn't even realize it's being cooked. I know what that's like. "Same sucks, man. Sorry."

"Yeah, but I don't blame him, you know?" Hud is better than me in that way. I blame my parents for a lot. "So, what'd she say?"

"Huh?" I put the car in park in front of the walkway to his door.

He looks me in the eye for the first time all night. His face cracks into a smile, like he's waiting to drop the punch line.

"What?" I say.

"Did you ask Natalie to prom?"

Oh, dang. My face must drop, because he laughs.

"Dude, you forgot again." He's smiling because it's good to feel like you're not the only fuckup. He reaches into the backseat for his backpack. As he slings it over his shoulder, the glow of the streetlamp catches a dark stain on his knuckles. Could be dirt, could be blood.

"It's all right, Mick. I'm sure you'll be forgiven." His tone still loose, but maybe there's a hard seed of resentment underneath. Like he means *Everything turns out good for you, Mick. Fuck you, Mick.*

What if I told him what was really going on with me? Would

it feel good to put my dark thoughts into words, like sweeping the spiders and cobwebs out of my head, or would it feel like pulling him under and taking away his hope that anyone's life can be good? Or maybe he'd be pissed, like I was trying to undercut his crap life.

I keep quiet and he's out of my car, walking toward his building.

CHAPTER 11

MEG

THE DAY THE POLICE GET INVOLVED, 11:42 A.M.

I follow Detective Becker into my kitchen. His ass is bigger than I expected. I mean, it's not big. He's fit, it's just that he has a round ass where most guys have a deficit.

Detective Flemming stands near my sink, staring out at the backyard like I did earlier. I hate the smell they've brought in with them. Vinyl, metal, maybe gun oil. I've never owned a gun, I have no idea what gun oil smells like, but the particular greasy odor on them is unfamiliar to me, so I'm guessing it's related to their guns.

"Do you have a current photo of McClane?" Detective Flemming says.

"Yes. Yes, of course. Let me get you his senior photo." They follow me to the front room where I was working with Eileen when Natalie rang the doorbell. I pull a frame off the wall and get to work unlatching the glass cover. All McClane's school photos are in this frame, one behind another, kindergarten to senior year. The metal tabs on the back of the frame have been lifted so many times, they're about to fall off.

Flemming lingers at a bookshelf, checking out my books. "Are you a history nut?"

"Art history. I'm interested in people, their creativity, their impact on how the masses think." Oh God. I sound like I'm on a dinner date, trying to make myself seem intellectual. To recover from my fumble, I add, "I like to stay curious."

"In this photo, which one is McClane?" says College Boy. He's pointing to a family photo that's six or seven years old. We have nothing recent. I don't think we've taken a photo together since the older two left for college.

Instead of answering his question, I hand him McClane's senior portrait. The photo highlights McClane's pale blue eyes. He wore a light blue shirt on picture day because he knows that's my favorite color on him. Such a pleaser.

"Are all four kids from the same husband?" Detective Flemming says.

"Yes." I'm used to that question. My friends even joke about it. David and Jamie have straight brown hair and olive skin. Whitney and McClane have black wavy hair and Snow White skin. "My older two look like my husband. The younger two look like me. Although now I have to dye my hair. I use a home kit. Revlon, jet-black purple." I always add that I use a home kit, trying to sound frugal and down to earth. I'm not sure why I feel the need to do that. I am down to earth. And I am so fucking frugal, it's shameful.

"My daughter dyes her hair a blackish purple," says Detective Flemming. "She loves that look."

My cheeks warm, embarrassed to share my fashion sense with the detective's child. Deciding I don't want to sit with them at the kitchen table, our faces close enough to study what's stuck in each other's teeth, I sit on the couch.

"Beautiful family," Flemming says, pulling her gaze from our family photo to me. "What are the kids' names?" She sits in one of the straight-back chairs, relaxing a little. "What are they like?"

I exhale, the tension melting from my shoulders. Talking about the kids is my favorite hobby. "Well, David's my oldest. My most self-assured. At his grandma's sixtieth birthday party, he grabbed the microphone, and we couldn't get it away from him. He was only six or seven at the time, telling jokes and stories. He had the whole room laughing. Jamie's next. She's caring, and she speaks her mind." My words make me hesitate and reflect on what Jamie told me as I drove her to the airport after Christmas. I snap out of it and sigh. "She's also my wild child, my dramatic child. Those two, my older ones, don't live here anymore. Dave's in Tennessee. Jamie's in North Carolina."

I should have called them. Told them about McClane. That's what a normal parent would do in this situation.

"What about McClane, Mrs. Hart?" Becker says.

I exhale. "McClane, well, McClane's easygoing. Hardworking, but easy to be around. Very likeable. Whitney, she's the opposite." I laugh. "She's a good kid, but she's also a teenage girl. Quiet, moody."

The detectives exchange uneasy looks, and my spine stiffens. I reflect on what I've told them. I don't think I've revealed anything suspicious. I've made my family more relatable.

"Thanks for that," Flemming says. "It's nice to get a feel for people. It sounds like you have a lovely family."

I nod, more solemn now. Careful.

"We just need to get a clearer picture," Detective Becker says, pulling out his notepad and sitting down in the other chair. Detective Flemming reaches into the side of her armpit holster and pulls out a notebook. Becker leans forward, pen ready. "When did you first notice McClane was missing?"

"This morning. The school called and said he wasn't there."

Heavy footsteps thud down the stairs. Those first two police officers. My front screen door opens, and they step out. I stand and go to the bay window. Both of them walk down the driveway, carrying black Rubbermaid bins. What did they take?

"The school called?" Detective Becker says.

I'm lost for a moment. I close my eyes and inhale to recall what I'm supposed to say. "Yes. I was telling myself it's the last month of senior year, he probably ditched with some friends. But then his girlfriend stopped by. She was worried and wanted to call the police. I told her you guys wouldn't do anything, he's eighteen, it hasn't been long enough, but that's why I called." I'm talking too quickly. I force a slow breath and sit, easing back deeper into the couch. The fabric exhales scents of vanilla wax and coffee, calming me a bit.

"What's his girlfriend's name?" Becker says. "And his closest friends."

I give them names, taking the time to spell them out.

"What time was it when you last saw McClane?"

"Yesterday, around four or five, I think."

"What did you talk about?"

"College stuff." I picture the hurt in his eyes. Then the anger. Fury, really. This is all my fault. The burden of responsibility is crushing. I struggle to hide my emotions. "Nothing unusual," I say.

"You don't happen to have a phone tracking app?"

"No."

"How many times did you call him this morning?" Becker asks.

"Oh, I didn't. Natalie said she called him a bunch of times. Then she called his two friends. No one's heard from him."

"So you never called him?" Becker says.

"No."

They share a brief look of skepticism. It isn't good. Detective Flemming shifts into a casual posture and smiles like the joke's on me. "But what if he just doesn't want to talk to his girlfriend? Like, maybe they're having an argument. My daughter, she answers her phone for some people, not for others." She gives a head nod toward her partner and rolls her eyes. "He does it too."

He smiles and holds his palms to us, pen in one. "Guilty as charged. When I'm on duty and my wife calls?" He bites his lip, tucks his chin in like he's in trouble. "Don't tell her that." He points to me.

They are suddenly buttering me up, and it's uncomfortably slippery. They don't trust me. Just like that. Because I didn't call him. Shit.

"I didn't think of that. I'll call now."

"Good idea," Becker says.

As the phone is ringing, my face warms. I angle my body toward the front window so they can't see my cheeks redden. He's not going to answer, I'm sure of that. "He never set up voicemail. Kids," I say, my voice thin. The worst thing would be if Joe walked in right now. That would be too much. I put it on speakerphone so they hear the automated voice saying the mailbox hasn't been set up. I look at Flemming, then Becker. Let's get this over with. "What did you find in his room?"

"We'll get to that in a second. Tell us about his girlfriend."

I picture McClane and Natalie together. Over their spring break, I walked into the kitchen and caught him teaching her how to soft-boil eggs. Days later, she was showing him how to make pie crust. They'd made a mess of the flour. Their noses and shirts were dusted with it.

"Natalie?" I sigh. "She's nice. She's normal. Bold." She's loud and comfortable in her skin, like Jamie in that way. I smile. "They have a good relationship."

"Is she maybe a little bossy?" Flemming asks gently. "I mean, she made you call us. She one of those who wears the pants in the relationship?"

"No." I was critical of Natalie a couple of hours ago, frustrated at her demanding nature. Now that Detective Flemming is taking jabs at her, it feels like she's insulting McClane. It's true what they say about family. I can trash-talk my own, but everyone else better shut their damn mouth.

"Natalie's confident. She says what's on her mind. She's mature. Graceful. Exactly how I'd like my youngest to be in a few years." It's true. I would like Whitney to speak up. I worry about her silence. Who has wronged her, why she won't share her burdens. "McClane, he's more easygoing, so yeah, I'd say he lets her call the shots, but they balance each other. He's not a pushover." I picture the nastiness in his expression last night. No, not a pushover.

"Any other girls he's hanging around?" Flemming says.

"No."

"He hang around anyone shady?"

"Not really, no." Hudson. Hudson has become extremely shady. I saw him three months ago and he had that white-trash smell to him. Dirty hair, stale smoke thick in his clothes, glazed look in his eyes. Shady is literally the name of his apartment complex. Shady Grove. Your basic shitty apartment complex for half-functioning addicts or the barely employable. But I wouldn't give Hudson up to these two. I still see him as the little boy who would leave the group playing football out back and come inside to cut cookies out of Play-Doh with Whitney. Now? I wouldn't be surprised if he was cutting cocaine.

"We'll need to talk with other family members who live here," College Boy says. "Your husband. Your daughter."

"My daughter will be home in a few hours. My husband, he works weird hours. I mean, he works at home, but sometimes he works in his car. Change of scenery thing. I work at home too."

I have no clue where Joe is. If he were working, he'd be in the basement. My mind goes back to the kids' memory bins. He never pulls those bins out from the cold, spidery depths of storage.

I want these two gone so I can make a cup of hot tea, wander downstairs with a blanket, wrap my cold soul up with warmth, and sift through my children's childhoods. Their yellowed drawings, their dusted awards, their smooth diaries. I want to steep in their innocence, my innocence. I want my innocence back.

Why did Joe drag their bins to his desk? What is he up to? I'm so curious these days, but asking isn't allowed. Questions make him squirm, and when he squirms, he gets angry.

"Do you have any security cameras?" College Boy asks.

"No. Oh, you know what? There's a camera in the back, but I don't think it's connected, or turned on or whatever. The previous owners installed it." I always forget about that camera because I don't think we've had it turned on for years. Honestly, I'm not even sure it was turned on when we moved in. It was so hectic with the kids being little, and Joe typically took over technology-related responsibilities. Setting up the television, calling the cable company, hooking up the kids' gaming systems, refrigerator repairs. "My husband would be the one to ask about the camera in the back."

"Okay, then. While we wait for your daughter and husband to get home, we'll ask your neighbors. Maybe one of them saw him."

A damp, cold feeling creeps along the back of my neck. Maybe one of my neighbors saw? I shake the thought and return to the question that's most nagging. "Are you going to tell me what you found that required an evidence case?"

Detective Flemming closes her notebook, shifts her weight onto one thigh to stick it in her back pocket, and looks at her partner.

Detective Becker says, "Looks like they found a knife in his room."

"Okay." I'm fine with that. Joe gave him a Swiss Army knife when he was fourteen.

Becker adds, "It was covered in blood."

That triggers worry, but not much. "Maybe he cut himself? Was there blood anywhere else?"

"No."

"Okay, that's good. I'm sure he's fine." I sound like a defensive mechanic. It wasn't me who broke it. That's how it rolled into the shop.

"They found something else." Detective Becker clears his throat. "And, Mrs. Hart," he says, leaning forward, "just to warn you. It's pretty bad."

CHAPTER 12

McCLANE

23 HOURS UNTIL MISSING

In case her brothers are out, I park six houses down from Natalie's. Half an hour ago I was struggling to keep my eyes open with all the driving, but now my skin's buzzing. The grass is damp. Cold seeps through my shoes and socks. The night air vibrates. Maybe it's a Pavlov thing, like my mind associates being out at night with sneaking out with Jack and Hud in seventh grade, diving behind bushes when a cop car drove by. Whatever it is, I'm wide awake.

Seriously, my mind can't even register a baby. It's this abstract thing, like getting old or fighting in a war or having tits. I get it, that those things are real for some people, but those experiences are so far away for me, they might as well be abstract. I've seen people with babies, I just can't imagine it happening to me. So my mind skips the baby. I don't think about it. All I can think about is Natalie.

I've been thinking about Natalie since forever. That's how it feels. I knew I had a chance with her when we talked this fall in

PE, but I'd become obsessed with her a year before that. I kept that to myself, I didn't want anyone to think I was a creep, and it's also hard to explain why I became obsessed.

She had a boyfriend all of junior year. Lars Hansen. Speech team dude, he was in musicals and band. Violin was his thing. He was chill, confident. I mean, he had to be, he played the fucking violin, but not someone you'd think a pretty girl would go for. He was funny, but short and kind of scrawny. I would walk by her locker after lunch to see them together. I didn't have to go that way, I did it more as an act of fascination and self-cruelty. She'd put her hand on his chest and look him in the eye while she talked. He'd get kind of hypnotized, leaning back against her locker like he needed it to keep steady. She looked at him like no one else mattered. She looked at him like she saw some power in him that no one else could see. I wanted that so badly.

I wanted to be with someone willing to tune out the world for me. And I was fascinated by her interest in him. He was chill, but he was also a weird dude. Like I said, scrawny, kind of nerdy. What did she see in him? In this weird way, I was dying for someone to discover special things inside me. Look through me, see my emotional scars and value them as treasures. I sound like a pussy. I know.

I didn't tell anyone about my obsession with her. I couldn't. Obviously. I haven't even told Natalie. Well, not in detail. I told her I'd pass her locker, and she seemed sweet to her boyfriend. She seemed like a cool, interesting person. Genuine. So many girls are TikTok girls, parroting viral videos word for word, acting and singing and talking over each other to hear their own voices. So many kids have YouTube-fried brains, talking so fast they are skittering along the surface like water bugs, they never go underwater where it's quiet and slow. It's not like Nat's abnormal, she's on TikTok too, but she is self-aware, self-regulated. She's the one who can go underwater *and* open her eyes.

Her front porch is dark, but the light above the detached garage is extra bright. Her dad put a floodlight there so her brothers could shoot hoops at night. Darkness pools between the houses. I walk in between her house and her neighbor's, a guy with two pitties. I'd like to say they're sweet, 'cause pit bulls get a bum rap, but they're evil. Truth.

The first window in the back is her sisters'—they share a room. Their light is on, illuminating their silhouettes behind the curtain. I pass quickly. I don't want to be creepy. The next window is dark but there's a cell phone–size glow behind the curtain. I can't help but smile.

I knock, and the glow jumps as she fumbles her phone. Her curtain flies open. Behind the glass, her eyes are struck wide. Her shoulders relax when she sees me. She slides the window up.

"You gave me a heart attack," she whispers harshly. "Why wouldn't you text me first?"

Seeing her flustered, the shine on her forehead, makes me smile harder. She's always in control, so chill. I feel bad to admit it, but I like to see her shaken up. "I wanted to surprise you."

"Congratulations. You scared me nearly to the point of death. What the fuck are you doing? My dad"—she turns her head over her shoulder, even though her door's closed—"my dad is still . . . he's not in a good place." She sighs, tired of speaking carefully. "He might hurt you."

"I have a question."

Her lips part into a small O. Her eyes fill with worry.

"Will you go to prom with me?"

Relief floods her eyes. She laughs too loud, then covers her mouth. "Oh my God," she whispers. "I thought you were going to ask me to marry you." She shakes her head, maybe trying to forget the idea. "Yes, to prom. I mean, I assumed we were going. I'll probably wear the same dress I wore to homecoming."

"I don't care if you wear a garbage bag. Can I come in?"

"No, McClane. No way. You're too noisy as it is," she says, but she's getting a kick out of me.

"I can climb in, just for a little."

"Get the fuck out. This is not a good time. How are you even thinking you're safe here? Like, seriously."

"Let me kiss you." I try to pull myself up, and she slaps my hands.

"Get. Out. My family's gonna kill you."

"How?"

"What?"

"Kill me. How would they kill me?"

Her face slips into an easy smile. She mimes like she's stabbing me over and over, softly screeching the shower-scene soundtrack to *Psycho*.

"They won't. They know they wouldn't get away with it."

She widens her eyes, leans forward, her whole face out the window, and says emphatically, "Out."

Those pitties start barking. Sounds like they're inside their house, so I'm not worried.

"I'm going. I love you."

She smiles hard.

"Good night," I say and blow her a kiss.

She shakes her head and shuts her window before I can ask if she got her paper done.

I'm surprised at myself, at my coping, my chill. I'm already feeling less jittery about her being pregnant. Maybe it's the confidence that comes with cold night air or with a drive to the city to help a friend. Or maybe it's actually who I am. It's actually probably not that.

Those pitties are barking louder, and their chains are clinking. They're out in the yard.

I head toward my car. I'm walking near the street, in the grass, when three guys come out of nowhere. Well, not out of nowhere. They're walking down someone's driveway, their sneakers noisy, their voices scruffy, their hoodies up. I step into the street. My car is maybe twenty-five feet away.

"McClane," one of them calls, his voice charged and loose, rippling through the night like a rock hitting water, sending concentric rings vibrating along the surface. His voice sends chills down my sides. I might be in for it.

CHAPTER 13

MEG

THE DAY THE POLICE GET INVOLVED, 2:38 P.M.

Kiddie porn.

When the detectives said that's what they'd found, my mind went numb like a towel left outside in a cold rain. It took me a few seconds to come around. And when I did, I was clear on one thing. No way would I let them destroy McClane's reputation. Never mind the harm I'd already done to him, McClane's name needed defending.

I said, half joking, "I mean, what are we talking, like, a sixteen- or seventeen-year-old? He just turned eighteen. I know laws are strict, but if he's looking at sixteen-year-olds, those are his peers. You've got to know that, right?"

"We haven't determined the age," Detective Becker said.

"What?" That sounded phony. Give me a photo of a naked girl, I can ballpark the age. "I'm pretty sure I could tell," I said, unable to keep the indignation from my voice.

"We're not allowed to show you."

"You literally took it from my house." I was flat out being an asshole.

"We have to follow department guidelines," Flemming said, apologetic, at least seeming to understand my point. "We can't show you. I can tell you, though, the girl's face isn't in the photo, that's part of the reason it's difficult to tell. Also, it's violent. We have to protect the victim."

"I don't mean to sound harsh, but sexual violence is normal. I mean, it's a normal part of pornography for a lot of people." I wasn't talking knives and on-screen bleeding. I was just talking about the intimation of violence. I'm sure they knew what I meant. "You know what I mean, right?"

These two said nothing. Becker looked down at his shoes. Flemming looked at her phone and sniffed.

"If you can't tell the age, what makes you think the person is underage?"

"Seems to be a young teen," Becker said. "The violent nature of the photo, that's why we're taking it seriously. And we've got the knife covered in blood. These things require us to take the situation seriously."

"I'm sorry we can't tell you more," Flemming said with a tone like an eyeroll. She thought the red tape was bullshit too. They told me they'd be back later to speak with Joe and Whitney, then left me alone with my awful imagination.

———•———

Now my heart is flapping wildly, a big, honking goose trying to flee as a coyote lunges for it. I felt this same exact panic this morning, for completely different reasons. My life is too fucking exciting. Give me boring. Give me a boring life with a boring husband who is so predictable you could set a watch to his bowel movements.

I pace the kitchen, walking through a slice of light shot across the kitchen floor. I can't stop thinking about it: McClane had violent kiddie porn in his room.

Every mother has been a girl who has witnessed a monster lurking inside a seemingly harmless boy. Every mother, at some point, ponders her teenage son and wonders if he could turn into one of those boys, if he could *be* a monster.

So I'm trying out McClane as a monster, seeing if it fits.

I reach for a foul memory from his past. Something circa his obnoxious middle-school years. That one time McClane took a bat to Whitney's shins, then walked away smiling as she cried. It was a plastic bat, but still. I watched through the window, mind blown that my little laid-back McClane, eleven years old, would do that to his nine-year-old sister. The way he walked away from her as she cried, his eyes without remorse, his expression justified, his shoulders relaxed, his gait smooth.

I play the scene over and over in my head. I even play it in reverse, like I'm playing a record back and trying to discern the devil's voice.

At the time, I explained it away. Whitney must have made a snotty comment. She was the sarcastic one, the youngest, perpetually pissed off about being left out. She carried a chip on her small, slouched shoulders. She'd probably said something mean. Or maybe it was McClane's age. Eleven can be tricky. All those hormones bursting from bulbous glands, steamrolling their blood, making them behave unpredictably.

Then again, shitty parents always blame a kid's behavior on their age. Or sugar. Or sleep. Or video games. Shitty parents blame, it's what they do.

I search for the sweet moments too. When he was in second grade and he read *Dog Man* to Whitney every night in her bed. I'd stand in the hallway, listening to them giggle, my heart filling with warm pride. How McClane cried during *The Little Mermaid* because Ursula was such a douchebag. The time I stood at the end of the driveway, watching McClane and Whitney walk to elementary, and a younger neighbor's shoelace got stuck in his bike chain. McClane dropped his bag on the sidewalk and got to work helping the kid. I was halfway to them when McClane stood the kid's bike up and the kid retied his shoe. Problem solved before the needy adult arrived. And last year, when McClane sent Hudson home with a bunch of hoodies, saying, "They don't fit me, Hud. I'm gonna toss them." They still fit.

No, McClane's not a monster. A good boy. Full fucking stop. How dare I even consider it?

Kiddie porn? I doubt it. I'm sure she's McClane's age. But Phlegm and Pecker are laced up so tight, they are going to try to tear apart his reputation.

Damn it, what does his reputation matter when he is gone? I should be focused on the "gone" part.

My phone buzzes with a text.

We need to talk.

I type.

> *Now is not a good time. McClane is gone. Police are involved. Please drop it.*

Three dots appear as I wait for a reply.

> *You started it.*

I type.

> *Please drop it for now.*

My stomach twists as I wait for those little typing dots to appear again, but they don't. My phone is silent.

Joe still isn't home. I need to know why he has the kids' memory boxes out. Honestly, I should put the boxes away in case the police want to tear apart every room. I retreat into the basement. Instead of putting the boxes in storage, I search them. I dig through them like a dog digging for a buried bone. I'm yearning to be close to the kids' goodness, their innocence, but I'm also searching for a clue. How we got from there to here. I get lost in their diaries, their letters, their poems, until the front door shutting yanks me out of my reverie.

I snap lids on boxes, carry them deeper into the basement, and stack them beside the Christmas decorations before I head up.

——— • ———

Joe's car is still gone. Whitney's come home since I've been in the basement, but she's already locked herself in her room. I've let her be, let her have her teenage moody space, let her be quiet, pissy, and distant. Now I need her to be a team player.

I knock on her door. No response. I don't take it personally. She's usually listening to music through her earbuds. "Whitney? Did you see McClane today?"

"What? No."

"When did you see him last?"

It takes a while for her to answer. She's probably on her phone, and she'll answer me when she's good and ready. I bite my lower lip and wait. This is the part of parenting no one warns you about. Constantly having to suck it up. Shut your mouth and wait. Wait on them, yes. But also, wait. Wait. Wait more. Be a doormat, basically.

"Yesterday," she says.

"Can you come out to talk? It's hard to have a conversation through a door."

"Not right now. I'll be out in a few minutes." Which means an hour.

"Whitney, it's—" I'm about to say *important*, but the doorbell rings.

I'm hoping it's someone inconsequential. An Amazon driver running back to his truck, having left a package on the porch. Carla ringing to ask why the police were here, can she help with anything?

It's Detectives Pecker and Phlegm.

"We were down the block when the school bus dropped off. Was that your daughter who walked in?"

"Yes, she just got home, but my husband isn't home yet."

"Any idea where he is?"

"He works in the car a lot."

"Those Find My Phone apps are helpful."

Yes, yes, I know. I should have installed those tracking apps a long time ago. I have been a neglectful parent. Too late now, no one in the house would agree to that. The kids are too old, and Joe is too angry. He likes to be unreachable. Untrackable.

"We're old-fashioned with privacy, I guess."

"We'd like to speak with your daughter. We can talk to your husband later."

"She hasn't eaten yet. Can this wait a half hour?"

Pecker looks at his watch, bites the side of his lip, and sighs. "We need to get back to the station soon for an end-of-day meeting. We'd really like to chat with your daughter today. It will only be a few minutes, we promise." Shark's smile. Phlegm looks tired. Her shoulders slouch.

"Okay, give me a minute to tell her. I haven't told her McClane is missing." My voice wavers as I say this last part. I close the front door on them and run up the stairs. My neck is sweaty and sticky as I knock on her door.

"Whitney. The police are here. They want to ask you a few questions about—"

Her door flies open. Worry creases her forehead. Panic in her eyes. "I haven't done anything illegal," she says. "I only—"

"Not you," I blurt, impulsive and wanting to reassure her. "It's McClane. They have questions about McClane."

Her face softens. Her tension downshifts. "Oh. Okay."

Now I wonder what she would have said if I hadn't cut her off.

CHAPTER 14

McClane

22 HOURS UNTIL MISSING

Those three silhouettes approaching, that reckless voice in the dark calling my name, I'm thinking it's Ax, Natalie's oldest brother. It's got to be Ax. He'll want to use my face as a punching bag.

Electricity shuttles up my spine and floods my head with warmth. I've only fought a guy once, in eighth grade when I had no choice. He jumped me in the hall after last period. Tyler Haptick. Everyone called him Haptics, like he was part machine. Pretty cool last name, even if he was a dick.

I'd pinned him in wrestling practice the day before. I got him good. Trapped him on his stomach, then flipped him onto his back. He writhed like an earwig between my fingers but couldn't move. I guess it pissed him off. Which I understood but also didn't.

Since first grade Dad has been telling me it is a blessing to lose, a blessing to be beaten. It shows you how small you are. The earlier you learn that, the better. There's a freedom there. When you learn it's not about natural skill, it's about preparedness.

I can't reach for my keys, unlock my door, and slip into my car quick enough. There's no avoiding them. If I'm gonna get my ass kicked, so be it. I turn toward them, stepping deeper onto the grass, a softer landing place for my head.

One of them steps forward under the glow of the lamppost.

Oh. It's Daniel. Natalie's nicer brother. The roofer. The one who smokes weed. Super chill, always invites me to shoot hoops. Usually tosses the ball at me as I'm walking up the drive. He still lives in their house. Helps his mom cook. Towel-dries the dishes as she washes.

I exhale into a smile, my muscles loosening. "Hey, Daniel."

He's on me fast. He grabs my shirt collar, shoves me backward, and falls on top of me, landing on my chest. The back of my head hits the grass. He's skinny but still knocks my wind out. I'm stunned for a second, but the grass is wet and cold like slick ocean algae on my neck and on my waist where my shirt rode up, and I'm back to fight or flight. Nothing hurts much. I wasn't expecting it, so my muscles were loose when I hit the ground. I keep my hands free in case I need to block a punch. I'm not gonna hit him. He's been nothing but cool to me this whole year.

"You fucking dick. You ruined my sister's life," he says, his vocal cords strained as he pulls back his scream. A quiet scream is scarier than a loud one. You don't know that until you hear it.

I can't catch my breath, so I'm coughing as I talk. "It's both of us, man. Both. You know I love her."

"Both of us? Shiiiiit. It's never both. You know it." He grabs my shirt, pulls it away from me, then punches his knuckles against my chest. He's hunched over, and his hair falls forward around his face. The lamppost glow doesn't touch his face, so it blends with the night and I can't see his eyes. "You ruined her life, man. She doesn't even realize it." But there's a sad quality in his voice, because he knows these things happen, he knows we didn't do it on purpose. "I don't want to fuck you up, Mick."

I don't know that he could, if we were both giving it equal effort, but that's not the point. His point is, he liked me, and now he doesn't. It hurts worse than if he punched me and left my skin split and stinging.

From behind him, one of his friends laughs, a high quality to his voice. "You look like you're gonna kiss him, man. Your dick is like ten inches from his mouth."

The quiet friend slaps the joking friend and mumbles a few words I can't make out.

Daniel rolls off me. He doesn't acknowledge his friends. He heads for his parents' house and he doesn't turn back.

As I unlock my car, I'm trembling. So much for my confidence and chill. I'm an idiot for pretending this would blow over. Babies don't blow over.

If I got anyone pregnant, I'd be the enemy. But in this case, it's so much worse. Natalie—she's special. Not only to me, but, like, to everyone. Her mom once said Nat's an old soul who was born feeling right.

So I should have known her family would want to rip my heart out. The thing about people, they get fixated on things—their opinions, their routines, what they love, whom they hate—and they can't let shit go.

~ My Journal ~

I've got this big idea. I'll use DNA technology to make creatures that never existed before. Like Pokémon, but I won't keep them in balls because that doesn't make sense, they wouldn't fit. I'll mix a tiger with a flying squirrel and a giant tuna with a pigeon. Stuff like that. I'll have all these pets so I'll never feel lonely. I don't want to take care of my whiny sister. I just want to play with my brother. My pets will know I created them, that I'm in charge, that I'm their master, and they'll do what I want. Make me food. Attack intruders. Give me hugs. Play Nerf Wars. Whatever I want.

    MC, age 8

CHAPTER 15

MEG

THE DAY THE POLICE GET INVOLVED, 3:40 P.M.

"I don't know where he is," Whitney says. She's sitting at the kitchen table across from the detectives. Her shoulders are hunched, and she's trapped her hands between her knees. She's sixteen, stunning with her Snow White beauty—flawless pale skin and dark wavy hair like McClane, swap out McClane's sunny swimming-pool-blue eyes for her cool gray ones—but now she looks like a scared little kid. "Did you try Natalie?"

"We haven't talked to Natalie yet," Flemming says. "The last time you spoke to your brother, what did you talk about?"

Whitney shakes her head, thinking. "Nothing important. I don't know. School. Family stuff."

I set a plate of crackers and fruit in front of Whitney along with a cup of herbal tea. She shoves the plate away. I can't tell if she's annoyed that I'm making her feel childish or if she's annoyed that I'm on my best behavior. I don't usually bring her snacks. I gave up on making her after-school snacks during her middle-school eyeroll days.

I stand to the side, almost behind the detectives, trying to get Whitney to look at me. I didn't get a chance to prep her, to tell her what to say. Please paint our family in a good light. Police are serious. Be a team player.

Kids who haven't spent time with police, they think it's all going to work out. Blow a red light, what a rush. Play with a knife, it's funny. Yank a sign off a public building, what's the worst that could happen? Say a few snarky words to a police officer, no biggie. Kids can't imagine the worst. It's probably better that way.

"Was there a problem at school? Did he mention anything about his girlfriend?" Flemming rests her chin on her palm, trying for casual. "Or maybe something annoying him at home?"

My stomach twists. Did McClane tell Whitney why he was angry at me? I bite my lip to keep myself from interrupting.

"I don't know," Whitney says, her gaze dropping to her lap. She's thinking about it. Her eyes widen for a second, like maybe she remembers something he said.

Becker picks up on it too, but stays silent, and scribbles in his small notebook.

Flemming says, "Even the smallest thing, something that seemed stupid or meaningless, could help us find him."

Whitney looks up at the detectives. "We were just joking around. And McClane doesn't get annoyed. Nothing bothers him."

"What is your relationship like? Is he a good brother?" Flemming asks, trying to sound warm and fuzzy. Chin still resting against her palm, she tilts her head, so her hand cups her cheek.

"We get along okay." She shrugs. "We argue. We joke around. He drives me to school sometimes."

"Has he ever been inappropriate with your friends?"

Whitney wrinkles her nose, as if something smells funny. "Like, asked them out? No. He's got a girlfriend."

"Has he ever shown you any photos or anything on his phone that made you feel uncomfortable?" Flemming rests her palms on the kitchen table, leans toward Whitney, and adds, "Anything sexual?"

"What?" Whitney says, her face pinching in confusion. She grips her knees. "No. What is this about?"

Oh. Now I understand why they exchanged looks when I described Whitney as quiet and moody. Those are the characteristics of someone who could have suffered sexual abuse. They assumed the photo they found was of Whitney. That never crossed my mind—that McClane could have abused Whitney. It still doesn't.

And I get why Flemming is leading the interview too. Questioning a young girl about child pornography is delicate. Having a female cop asking the questions is probably department protocol.

"Has he showed your friends sexual photos?" Flemming says, her voice hardening.

"What's going on?" She looks to me. "Mom?" I shake my head: *I'm confused too, Whitney. Don't go along with it.*

"We found a photo of a young girl, Whitney," Detective Becker says, his first words to her. "She's maybe fourteen. We can't say for sure. The photo was in McClane's room. It is explicit. Violent. I mean, we want to protect you, or whoever. We don't want rumors getting out."

My attention snaps back to Detective Becker. "Excuse me. Are you threatening her?"

"No, not at all," says Becker. "We are trying to protect her, keep things quiet to avoid a blown-up investigation. Our police chief is going to want to dig. I want to give your daughter a chance to protect herself or her friend, explain what this is about."

"You're victim-blaming now?" I say. "Whoever this girl is in this photo, why would she have to explain anything?"

"I don't believe you," Whitney says, staring at Detective Becker. She is cold, severe. There's the Whitney I know. "Let me see the photo. I'll tell you who it is."

"We can't see the girl's face," Detective Flemming says quickly, trying to keep her partner from sticking his foot in his mouth again. "And, I'm sorry, we're not allowed to show you."

"Why are you even talking to me, then? Go figure out who it is." She looks at Flemming, then Becker. Her gray eyes are cold and bright, smooth stones in a cool river. "And, like, if my brother is missing, aren't you supposed to be looking for him?" She stands, her chair scraping roughly against the wood floor, and moves down the hallway and up the stairs.

The detectives don't seem shocked. They seem like this is business as usual.

I am fucking stunned. I mean, yeah, Whitney can be cold. To me. To me, she is. But walking away from the cops like that? She has nerve. I never had the confidence, the naivete, the balls, to walk out of a police interview as a kid. I had chances. I never walked out.

Where did this fight come from? Did she get it from Joe?

Right or wrong, I love her with all my heart. Right now, I'm in awe of her.

CHAPTER 16

McClane

16 HOURS UNTIL MISSING

I startle awake with the memory of Natalie's brother coming at me in the dark. Daniel above me, his eyes cold and mean. In my dream, he's pressing a knife against my neck.

My phone alarm is going off under my pillow. Ripples. School mornings always come too early. I roll out of bed and pull a hoodie on over my T-shirt.

As I swipe on deodorant, Daniel's voice bangs around inside my head. *I don't want to fuck you up.* Pretty much the same thing her dad said. Makes me want to crawl under my thick comforter and bury my head under my pillow.

I knock on Whitney's door to see if she needs a ride, then try her doorknob. She's the only person I know who locks her door even when she's not in her room. Weirdo. I knock hard one more time. No answer. She's already left for the bus with her friends.

I brush my teeth and sling my backpack over my shoulder. Grab a Bang from the fridge, pull my hood up, and step out into the cold. It's barely raining, it's more of a mist, but it's enough that we'll all be sitting in damp clothes during first period. Damn this cold. I should gain weight. I'm still maintaining my wrestling weight. When I'm skinny like this, the cold hurts deep in my bones. Wrestling season is over, I shouldn't still be depriving myself.

In my car, the windows are dewy and beaded. At least there's no frost to scrape. Parking outside all winter long was a bitch, but my parents' cars get priority treatment, even though most days they don't go anywhere.

It's even colder inside my car, which makes absolutely no sense. I crank the heat.

That knife against my neck. He didn't have a knife last night, my brain added that threat like bonus backwash, but his eyes were the same in my dream as they were last night. Cold and mean. Sad, too. I wish they hadn't been sad. Worse than making someone you like angry is disappointing them. Anger is bad behavior on their part. Disappointment is you falling short.

I've chugged half the Bang by the time I pick up Jack. He slides into the passenger seat, bringing in a cold blast of air and the fresh smell of rain, earthworms, and wet dog. He grabs the can in my cupholder and drinks the rest.

"Fucking cold," he says. "I hate the cold. Yesterday was so warm, I thought we were done with it. I had my feet in the lake."

"You sound like my grandma."

"Your grandma says 'fuck'?"

I smile but say nothing. He holds the can up and inspects the condensation dripping down the aluminum. "I bought kiwi last night," he says. "It's good, it's good. I went to Walmart with Johan." Jack's dad's name is John, but we've called him Johan for as long as I can remember. He gets a kick out of it, so we do it to make him happy. Jack's dad is a good guy. Even though he's a cop, he's soft. You know the overweight, kindly cop in a sitcom? That's pretty much Jack's dad. He coached our rec soccer team for a few years. Me and Jack were all right, but Hud was pretty great. Jack's dad would watch Hud break away with the ball, weaving around incoming players, faking them out, and say, "Man, can Hudson juke 'em." Jack and I got a huge kick out of that on the sidelines.

Jack and I dropped soccer, but Hud kept on. He made the school soccer team every year until his mom died. If he would have stayed in soccer, it's likely he would've made the varsity team. Maybe even played in college.

"How was your game?" I say.

"Lit. We kicked. I had a three-pointer so far outside I was practically in the parking lot." Jack loves basketball. He's tall but not graceful enough for the school team, so he plays in the local rec league. What he misses out on in school fame is made up for by not having to wake before dawn for practice.

I'm lucky. My wrestling coach, Rudrick, doesn't believe in early morning practice. But he compensates for that with extra-long evening practices. I'm glad the season's over.

"I caught a sunfish after you and Hud left. Why'd you leave so fast after him?"

I don't want to talk about it. Not that I'm trying to keep Natalie's pregnancy from him, but, also, I am. I'm waiting for her lead. Like, we didn't even talk about how long we were going to keep this quiet. I mean, maybe it won't even happen. Our health teacher told us nearly half of pregnancies end on their own. Where that glob-of-cells baby is like, "Ya know what? This ain't happening. It's not you, it's me. I'm out."

I change the subject. "So you actually fished instead of threading?"

He laughs easy. "Actually."

"Hud called me last night, had me pick him up from some suspicious apartment on the West Side of Chicago. It was kinda fucked-up."

"Huh." Which could mean: *Sounds dope, why didn't you pick me up?* Or just, *huh.*

"I bought him a few burgers and a shake, dropped him off, no big deal." I don't want Jack to feel like he missed out.

I pull into the lot behind Sugar North High. We pass Natalie's car as we walk to the side door next to the gym. Usually when I see her car, I get a jolt of adrenaline and can't help but smile.

Today I have an uneasy feeling, like my future is a slippery fish in my hands, frantically trying to squirm loose, its gills slicing my palms, leaving my skin bloody and stinging.

CHAPTER 17

MEG

THE DAY THE POLICE GET INVOLVED, 6:28 P.M.

When do you know your marriage is over? When the police have already stopped by twice, once because you reported your son missing, and again to question your daughter about the kiddie porn and bloody knife found in his room, but you still haven't called your husband.

That would be a sign.

Funny thing is, even though our marriage is moth-eaten and haggard, a blouse so thin it's see-through, I don't think of it in terms of being over. In a way, I've never had Joe's back more. I've never *had* to have his back more, but that's beside the point.

Point is, I am hanging on to this marriage, this family, this house, whether they like it or not. These things are my history, my truth, my love. Without them, I couldn't breathe.

So why haven't I called Joe? It's complicated. He's unpredictable for the most part, but predictably angry. If I call, if I text, he'll come home and bring his dark-mood cloud with him. It's easier when he's away. The house is sunnier, quieter. Life and all its piddly tasks are easier to manage.

It wasn't always like this. It's only been the past year or two. Maybe three. Before that, I'd look forward to him coming home. I'd make dinner, call him on his drive home, share a funny comment one of the kids said, tell him about this story I fed to Eileen about organ theft and the back-and-forth wacky conversation she and I had about it, tell him what I bought at the grocery store just for him. Usually donuts. He'd tell me the same. He'd make fun of a few guys from the brokerage boys' club who were especially whiny. He'd say he was leaving the teenage slumber-party drama. He was a feminist in that way. He used to be a feminist. I was proud of that.

Joe and I were as solid as they come, sure of our love right from the start. I got pregnant at nineteen, and getting married was the obvious next step for both of us. We married at the courthouse, just the two of us, and had a pizza and cupcake party at his apartment afterward, blasting our song—"This Must Be the Place" by the Talking Heads—and dreaming up our wide-open future before making love on the carpet, the warm aroma of pizza in the air, lemon whipped-cream frosting on our tongues. No regrets about getting pregnant or marrying young or not inviting family and friends. We were both dreamers, free-spirited in our own ways, but strangely pragmatic about our relationship and future family.

I can't put my finger on when his personality started changing. When a transformation happens slowly, you don't notice it. Like putting on thirty pounds over five years. One day you step on the scale at the doctor's office, and you're like—What? When did I get fat? Joe's odd behaviors were subtle at first, and I thought nothing of them. Only now, looking back, are they suspicious.

Two winters ago I was in my pajamas and slippers, washing the dinner dishes before bed when he walked in from the backyard. Leaving the door open behind him, snow gusting in like a cloud, he walked to the sink. He bumped me out of his way and dropped his hands under the running faucet.

"You left the door open. It's freezing. And where's your coat?" I said before I saw the blood. His palms were smeared with it. "What happened? Are you okay?"

"I must have cut myself. Maybe in the shed, I'm not sure." He grabbed a dish towel, wrapped it around his hand, and walked upstairs. At the time, I didn't think much of it. I assumed he was doing some late winter prep in the shed. I shut the door for him and never asked what he was doing. Now that I'm dissecting it, I have more specific questions, starting with how did he not know how he cut his hand?

A few months later, I was making a cup of tea before bed. It was late, I should have already been sleeping. He grabbed his keys and said he was going to the store, he had a taste for chips. I was watching TV thirty minutes later when I heard his car pull into the garage. When he came into the bedroom, I said, "Hey, can I have some of your snacks?" He told me he got distracted and didn't end up buying chips. I should have asked questions. Instead, I thought it was absurdly funny.

"You're crazy," I said endearingly, smiling at him because I trusted him. I trusted who he was. I didn't realize he was literally crazy. When you've known a man for over twenty years, when he's massaged your back as you've delivered his babies, when you've watched him tickle those toddlers and double-knot their shoes and wash their hair and cut their grapes in half and drive them to practice, you trust that man. You don't question. When that man behaves suspiciously, it's not suspicious. It's just a random nonsense moment in a sea of millions of moments that make perfect sense.

———•———

The doorbell rings at seven p.m., and I'm not even hopeful. I know it's those two again. They are like a pair of sticky burrs that has latched on to your pants, pricking your finger when you try to pry them away. They will not be talking to Whitney this time. I will not let them into my house. This is what I tell myself. This is my plan. I am in charge. I inhale. I exhale.

I open the door. Daylight drains from the sky. Mystical blue twilight wicks in. Flemming looks tired. The flyaway hairs framing her face have multiplied. Becker's shirt is slightly untucked and he has that stale end-of-the-day smell. Like pork that's been left out overnight. I'm sick of these two.

"I'm sorry, my husband is still not home."

"Back-to-back meetings all day? Must be an important man," Detective Becker says. "Where does he work?"

"Brokerage firm in the city. He usually works remotely, in coffee shops and in the car. Lot of times when he's working, he turns off his phone." It's true. Joe turns his phone off all the time.

"Which brokerage firm?"

"It's not one of the monster banks. It's small," I say, as if his firm is less greedy than the rest. "Tucker and Westing."

They both wait, as if they don't believe me.

Warmth creeps up my neck. "Do you want me to grab one of his paystubs?" I say, challenging, but laughing a little to show I'm not mindlessly rageful.

"Not necessary," says Becker.

Detective Flemming pulls out her notepad and flips through her pages. "We spoke with the school. The receptionist said that when she called this morning, you told her McClane had an appointment."

Patty. Poor Patty with the shitty job of calling the parents of truants. You didn't have to screw me, Patty.

I laugh as if my blood isn't cold. "I figured he ditched, and I didn't want them hassling him about it. He's a senior. It's the last month of high school."

Becker's smile is thin. "Do you usually lie for family members?"

He says it like it's a bad thing.

"Do you have kids, Detective Becker?"

"Yes."

"They're little, though, right?"

"Yeah. Two and five."

"It's exhausting when they're little," I say. He nods, though I doubt he does much of the work of raising them. After all, the sun's going down, his kids are probably getting out of the tub and in their PJs, and he's still at work. "It takes years off your life, that's what they say, but it's also straightforward. As they get older, they don't need as much. You get better sleep. You barely have to cook for them. But life gets"—I shrug—"fuzzier. More complicated. You don't want to be too hard on them because they are old enough to defy you, disown you."

Flemming nods, straight-faced and thoughtful. She gets me. She mentioned she had a teenager.

"What I'm trying to say is, if you had a senior who had three more weeks of school left, you would not have asked me that."

"Fair enough," he says, which surprises me.

"Your neighbor across the street?" Flemming points to Carla's house. "She was worried about McClane."

"Carla," I say. "Yeah, we've been friends a long time." Our kids are different ages, hers are still in middle school, so we have been able to be friends without grudges or competitiveness. "Her cat likes to watch my bird feeder."

"She let us look at her Ring camera," Flemming says. My chest feels heavy, like I have to belch. "And from her front-porch view, we can catch the bottom half of your driveway." Wow, way to draw it out for suspense, Phlegm. She looks at her notebook. "At eight eighteen last night, a Toyota Corolla pulled out of the driveway. Who drives that?"

"McClane," I say softly, my stomach sour and empty. "The Corolla has been our kids' car. David, then Jamie. Now McClane. It's got over one hundred and fifty thousand miles." Even now, even fucking now in the face of disaster, I am trying to show off my good parenting. Look, I do not spoil my kids. See here, yes, they have a car, but it is shared and old. Sometimes I exhaust myself.

She looks at her notebook again. "Around eleven, a Ford Fiesta pulled out of the driveway. Who drives that one?"

I'm sweating and trying not to show it. "Me."

Flemming nods like she leaves her house near midnight every night too. "Where did you go?"

"Gas station," I say. "The one on 47th and Litchfield."

I remember hearing someone say once that the more details someone adds into their story, the more likely it is they're lying. I feel the back of my neck start to sweat.

Flemming checks her notepad. "It looks like you got home around midnight."

"That's about right. It's a ritual some nights. I bring my hot tea and my calendar. Figure out what I have to do the next day. Scroll Instagram. Relax. You ever do that?" I ask her.

"Not a chance." She laughs. "Once I'm home and in my sweatpants, you have to peel me off the couch."

Becker laughs and bumps her arm. "That's true." To me, he says, "She's a couch potato, but I do that, what you said. Usually when my wife is mad at me because the kids are driving her nuts and I want some extra time away from home. I sit in the parking lot somewhere and scroll the news. I feel bad about it, but yeah, I do that." He presses his lips together, tamping down emotion. Proud of himself for admitting to being human.

"What car does your husband drive?" Flemming asks.

"He drives a Toyota RAV."

She doesn't even have to look at her notepad. "His car pulled out around 11:15, shortly after you. It came back after midnight—close to one in the morning. Any idea where he went?"

I swallow but my throat is dry. "No. You'll have to ask him."

CHAPTER 18

McClane

13 HOURS UNTIL MISSING

We meet at Nat's locker after second period. We have a rhythm, it goes like this: She gets there first. I sneak up, sniff her ear, which tickles her and makes her smile. I kiss her cheek and head to Spanish.

Sometimes I think, how did my life feel full before I met this person? How was there a time when I didn't know she existed? Because now, now she is everything. The most alive person I know. The most interesting person I know. She is the beginning and the end. The life in her fills me up, makes me feel like I could flip cars.

I'm headed there now. Her locker is at the end of the hall. I walk with the crowd. Their heads bounce to their own lonely beat but they're part of the same herd. So much going on in a small space under pressed time. Laughing, sarcastic calls of "bitch" and "goat." Backslapping, girl hugs, fist-bumps, friendly shoulder shoves, handshakes so flimsy that loose fingers barely brush. That one guy grabbing girls' asses, and the girls shoving him away, punching his back. Shared body heat, mixed body odor, someone shouting in your face, sticking their wet finger in your ear. That hyper tiny freshman, Bryce Something, taking the hall like it's an obstacle course, trying to knock into as many people as possible. That friendly dude in a wheelchair, Maxwell Something, who brings out everyone's manners.

Today feels different, though. I am different. I am out of step. My pulse is loud in my ears. Things I don't typically pay attention to stand out: the poster about Spanish literacy testing, the Narcan bag behind glass, the still-life student paintings lining the wall near the ceiling. The theme is "bowls." A bowl of cereal. A fishbowl. A bowl of eyeballs. The paint along the brick wall is thick and glossy. There's got to be at least five coats.

Her dad couldn't even look at me. Daniel hates me. I don't like being hated, not by anyone, especially by people I like, people I consider almost family. How can I fix this?

Natalie's there, twisting her combination lock. Opening her locker.

I try to slip into our pattern. I put my arm over her locker and sniff her ear, but my palm is sweaty, and my hand slips. She catches my slip and squints her eyes, doubtful. I shrug, like, *What are you gonna do?*, and say, "How was the Spanish quiz?"

"For me, easy." She smirks. "For you, it will be 'no bueno.'"

How can she act so normal when the floor is coming apart under our feet?

It makes me think of her house and my house. My parents stay inside, work from home. We don't see my dad's sister or father much. We don't see my mom's parents or brother, like, ever. My parents barely talk to anyone. Mom's gotten stiffer, her smile faker, twitchier. Dad's gone dark and quiet. So many secrets shut tight behind the doors of our house. We do a lot of pretending. Life is messy, and my mom sweeps it under the rug.

Natalie's parents leave their house to work. Her mom works at a nail salon, her dad works on the highway, moving big vehicles. They live in the moment, unafraid of people, unafraid of sharing their thoughts. Her family bickers more, they air their grievances. Everything about their lives is aired out, actually. Their financial troubles and Ax's time in prison ripple in the breeze like damp clothes clipped up on a clothesline, hung out for anyone who wants to see. No big deal, it's just laundry.

Natalie pulls a book from her locker, reconsiders, and shoves it back in. Looks at me. "You're still here?" She lifts an eyebrow, messing with me.

"What are we doing tonight?"

"I work," she says. "Actually, I'm putting in only a few hours to help out. I'll stop by your house on my way."

Huh. She never stops over on her way to work. Like, ever. Must mean she wants to talk. Our vibe is off, and there's nothing I can do about it. Feels like she's the vice principal, and I'm due for an interrogation. My shirt sticks to my back.

Behind me, some guy is shouting. His tone is charged and spitting.

Hairs on the back of my neck prickle. I get that feeling. A fight's about to erupt. I'm not the only one who senses it. The change in atmosphere, time slowing down, every little thing intensifying. Shoes squeak like a car braking. The sharp intakes of breath all around.

I turn toward the fight at the same time as most everyone else. Like we're all pulled by some unseen force, bodies clump together, forming a wall around it. Two guys stand inside the half circle. Something about the back of the smaller kid's head, the twitchy way he moves. Hud.

Hud shoves the guy. He's fast and wild, but the other guy is way big.

I push through people so I can get closer, but someone grabs my arm, holding me back for a sec. I pull free as Hud's shoved against the locker. A fist punches the back of his head on an angle, and bloody spit shakes loose from his mouth. Hud's backpack drops from his shoulder, and he's falling. His hands don't go out. No one's reaching toward him to break his fall.

I bust through the wall of bodies and I reach for him, but I'm a second too late. My fingers catch air.

Hud's head hits the ground. Oh man. He must have been out cold before he fell.

He's on his stomach, his cheek pressed against the floor, blood spilling from his mouth. I'm on my knees next to him, my head hot. "Hud, you okay, man?"

He is not. He is lights out. I don't know what to do, so all I do is guard him from getting stepped on. Teachers are yelling in the distance, forcing their voices into lower, drill-sergeant tones. Hands slap my back and ruffle my hair. The gestures are mostly friendly, I think, but too amped, too aggressive.

I'm yanked backward by my backpack, ripped away from Hud, and thrown onto the floor, my hand sliding in a patch of wet. Spit, probably.

Two men, a security officer and someone in pants and a button-down, most likely a teacher, step beside Hud's body and tip him onto his side. Mr. Ridley marches out of his classroom with his nose in the air and sweat stains under the pits of his button-down, one side coming untucked with his dramatic movements. His voice all muscle and piss, as if he's taking everyone's existence as a personal insult, he yells, "Everyone, get to class!"

Through the empty spaces where their knees and waists and elbows are not, Hud's face is visible. Blood around his mouth like he bit someone. I picture him playing with Whitney when she was tiny, his eyes on her, a delighted look on his face, as if he understood how precious little kids are. The security officer has two fingers on his neck.

Drugs. It had to be over drugs. The only other time Hudson got in a fight this year was because he lifted drugs.

Kids are still standing around, gawking. Mr. Ridley, out of breath, yells again. "Anyone still standing here in ten seconds gets detention."

There is a small puddle of blood on the floor beside Hud's cheek. His eyes flutter.

Between Hud and me is his phone, the screen facing up and shattered. He's going to be pissed. I go to grab it for him, but Mr. Ridley scoops it up and glares at me. Like I'm an asshole who wants to steal it.

"You want suspension?" Ridley doesn't wait for my response. His gaze swoops away to glare at someone else, and I scramble to my feet, taking in the scene before I split. Hud's backpack is a few feet away to my left. Mr. Ridley hasn't noticed it yet because I'm obstructing his view. I take a few steps, grab Hud's backpack, and walk away casually.

I feel crummy leaving my friend bleeding on the hallway floor. I feel triumphant grabbing his backpack for him because if the fight was over drugs, that's probably where they are. Hud doesn't need more trouble.

CHAPTER 19

MEG

THE DAY THE POLICE GET INVOLVED, 8:23 P.M.

None of my kids were born old souls. They were wide-eyed and naive, their feelings raw like the exposed nerve of a tooth. All of them. They were colicky, panicked babies who had difficulty latching on. As they grew, they were sensitive to shirt tags and the toe stitch in socks. Excitable and intense, even McClane. When he was small, especially McClane.

They changed, of course, as they grew. Shed their overly sensitive skins and let other colorful traits rise to the surface like a rash. At sixteen, David was self-absorbed, arrogant, and hilarious. Jamie was happy, bubbling with energy and goodwill, some of it forced. McClane was outwardly easy, but hard on himself privately. And Whitney, now sixteen, is one of those trick puzzle boxes. The outside is smooth, giving no hint to a button or lever, so you simply have no clue where to start. I have told myself for a long time that she is a private person, that's just who she is. It's only now that I'm wondering why.

I hesitate when I'm outside Whitney's closed door. She's touchy. I have to measure my words.

"Whitney? Do you want to talk?"

No answer. She's probably got her earbuds in and didn't hear me. I am opening my mouth to ask again when she says, "No."

"Do you want me to call you in for school tomorrow?" I'd have to speak to Patty, the woman to whom I lied. I picture Patty saying, "Oh, and does this child have an appointment too?" She wouldn't say that, what the fuck does she care, but that's what I imagine. Everyone full of accusations, out to get me.

"Tomorrow's Saturday," Whitney says.

I open my mouth to ask another question. I want to ask if she's in trouble. I want to ask what's going on. When I said the police had questions, why did she assume it was about her? I let my mouth fall closed.

Give her space. Don't push. Don't be one of those parents. You know teens can only handle two or three questions. Ask four, and they erupt. Tune you out. Tell you they hate you. Give her space, and keep your mouth shut.

"How do you think McClane ended up with that photo?" I say. I can't help it. And I'm asking the worst type of question. I'm not asking how she's doing or how I can help her, I'm asking for insight. I'm asking for her to tell me who my son is. I'm asking for her to tell me what I've missed.

I am lost. My judgment and gut instinct have left me these past few years. I wasn't like that in my twenties and thirties. I was an achiever, an easy-talking, big-laughed, crafty-quipped woman who was comfortable wearing red lipstick. Confident in my needs, my wants, and what I had to offer. I smiled easily. I could talk art history or politics or pop culture with anyone. I was opinionated, but lighthearted. I was great in interviews.

Now I am full of doubt. Quiet. I hesitate too often. It's Joe's fault. You think you know someone, deeply and truly, and then they prove you know jack squat. When that happens, it sends seismic fractures cracking along the seams of everything in your mind. You were wrong about this one fundamental thing, and now you question every one of your perceptions. All of a sudden you wonder how much time a person should spend alone. All of a sudden you wonder if you are on the wrong side of politics. You thought you knew the full story, but maybe you don't know enough to have an opinion. You wonder if you clean the toilet correctly. You wonder if you know how to cook a chicken properly, or does the neighbor have a better technique? You wonder if you're the gasbag. If you're the asshole. You doubt your intelligence, your memory, your choices. You keep your mouth shut more often. You retreat into your shell. You wonder if your habits are normal. If you're imagining things. Maybe Joe hasn't changed, maybe you're going crazy.

"Maybe it's not his," Whitney says. I ease into that idea. Yes. Yes, she's right. Of course it's not his. Why didn't I think of that? Oh, thank you, Whitney. You have the confidence in him that I should have.

"Or maybe he's completely fucked-up," she says. My breath catches in my throat. Whitney's never cursed in front of me. "You know he can be selfish and impulsive. He doesn't think." She's silent, then she shouts, "Why are you even asking me? He's *your* kid."

I rest my hand softly on her door. The door is cool against my fingers. I say, "I just wanted to hear what you think." I wait to see if she wants to say anything more. She doesn't.

"If you need me, I'll be in the tub," I say, longing for the days when she needed me. To brush the knots out of her hair. Make her pancakes. Find her sneakers. Find her missing hair bands. Hunt for her lost library book. Buy her bras. Take her out for an ice-cream cone when she was sad. Teach her about makeup primer. Hold her small sweaty hand when she got her ears pierced, breathing in the smell of rubbing alcohol before the pinch.

—— • ——

Our bathroom is roomy, with a triangular tub, a separate shower stall, and a double sink. In the beginning, Joe and I shared this bathroom like two giddy college roommates. I'd be in the tub, and he'd flip off the light switch and turn on the tub's jets. I'd scream, and he'd laugh. Then he'd turn the lights back on, lose his towel, and step into the glugging tub with me.

Was there a deadness in his eyes I should have noticed back then? Some dark nuanced expression I missed? How could he change from that to this?

Now I slip into scalding hot water thick with strawberry-scented bubbles, hoping I can settle my nerves. I picture a pot of boiling spaghetti on the stove, stiff noodles softening. I'm trying to manifest.

Calling the police was a bad idea. I wasn't expecting the suspicion to turn toward McClane and then to me and Joe. I didn't know Carla's

Ring camera could track my driveway. How far will the police dig to find out where I was? Where Joe was?

On my phone I pull up my group chat with David and Jamie. The last time I texted them as a group was to remind them of McClane's birthday. I try not to text too much. I don't want to be a pest.

It takes me fifteen minutes to craft my text. I keep writing and deleting. I decide on brevity. No mention of the knife or kiddie porn. Basically, just checking the box that I've told my other children their sibling is missing and we are following a missing-person protocol.

> Hi, you two. I hope you are both healthy. ♥ I don't want to worry anyone yet, but we're not sure where McClane is. The last time Natalie saw him was last night. I'm hoping he just needed a break and slept at a friend's house. He's not with Jack or Hudson though. Just to be on the safe side, the police are looking into it.

They both respond within minutes.
Jamie texts.

> I just texted him and will let you know if he responds. Have you asked Hud and Jack who else he has been hanging out with? Ask Natalie too. She seems nice. How do you like her? How are you guys coping? How is Whitney? The "police looking into it" seems like it's intense. What

> *does everyone think happened? Did something happen—was there an argument? It will be okay, Mom. I'm sure he's fine. Take a deep breath.* ♥

Jamie is my most emotionally vulnerable child. Says what's on her mind. She is the least secretive person in this family.

She's in North Carolina now, living with three other girls in a small apartment. She works two jobs. One with a small newspaper, another at a coffeehouse. She's progressive to the point of showing up at union rallies. She parties. Girls' nights. Alcohol. Marijuana. She dates, but doesn't have a steady boyfriend. She doesn't tell me most of this, I gather it from her social media posts. I know her more deeply as a person because of her social media. Which is kind of weird, but I imagine that's how it is for most parents. We are lurkers. Fans of our children. Followers, in the truest sense of the word.

I saw her at Christmas, which was four months ago. Other than that, we text or call every couple of weeks.

David doesn't ask how I'm doing. He skips straight to procedural stuff.

> *What do the police think? Who are they interviewing? Are they checking McClane's cell phone? Do they have a call out for his license plate?*

David lists police procedures I should make sure they're following. He's helping in the best way he knows how. Using his expertise.

Dave got a job with the FBI nearly a year ago. And, truly, it's a perfect fit. He has always been a ringleader. Organized, annoyed by people who don't follow the rules, annoyed by dishes that get left unwashed on the counter. He likes things black-and-white. He is squirrelly and energetic like Joe used to be, his eyes sharp with energy, but he's more rule-oriented than Joe.

He can't give us details about his job but says it's mainly computer research. I imagine he's digging up info on fraud and criminals. Exciting, security-clearance stuff. He lives in a small apartment on the edge of Memphis. With the money he's saving on living expenses, he says he'll be able to buy a house in a couple of years. He's not dating as far as I know. He's digging in deep with work. Trying to earn respect the hard way, by doing his job right. That's the cool thing about investigative work, he tells me. It's a no-bullshit job.

I disagree—every job is a bullshit job. But I keep my thoughts to myself. I like to hear him talk. I like to hear all my kids talk. I could just sit, tune out the content, and listen to their voices.

Same as with Jamie, I text David every several weeks. Funny photos. Interesting articles. Sometimes he texts back, sometimes he doesn't. I don't take it personally. He's building his own life, doing what young people do.

I text.

Thanks for the suggestions, both of you. I'll keep you posted.

My bathwater is still warm but my bubbles are thinning. I tip my head back on the ledge and imagine McClane. His sleepy, fairy-tale smile. His pale blue, magical eyes. Smooth skin, porcelain complexion.

Such a beautiful boy. I close my eyes and see blood along his temple and him struggling to breathe as he calls for me. *Mom?*

There's a knock on the bathroom door.

Whitney must want to talk. "Yes, come on in," I say.

"I'm home." It's Joe. My body shrinks lower into the water. His voice is monotone. He sounds dead inside.

CHAPTER 20

McClane

8 HOURS UNTIL MISSING

Did I freeze? Am I the asshole friend? Could I have caught Hud before he fell?

In my head, the fight is still happening. In my ears, Hud's head thuds against the locker. In my chest, the crowd is still yelling and shoving.

I bomb the Spanish quiz. I can't shake the image of Hud free-falling, his cheek hitting the hard ground, bloody spit flying out of his mouth. I turn the quiz in blank.

It's only a quiz, though. Ten points. The worst it could do is lower my grade from a B to a C, and that won't affect college. The only way you get an offer rescinded is if you drop down to Ds or if you get suspended or arrested. Extreme stuff.

In the hallway after Spanish, in between laughter and chatter, I catch shouting and talking about the fight—the kind of loud talking that is meant to be overheard.

Collin T., our best linebacker, is saying, "Yo, you hear Hudson took a beating?"

"Was it Rowly?" says RJ, who's still wearing his football jersey though the season is way over. He wants to make sure no one forgets he's a baller.

"Prolly," Collin says. "Listen up, boys and girls. Drugs? They baaad."

Laughter.

Hud's last fight was with Jay Rowly. The guy's a stoner and a dealer, but he's not your stereotypical laid-back, easy-breezy stoner. This boy is mean. And when he gets in trouble, his mom gets loud. Not at him, at the school. She thinks *this* rule is dumb and *that* rule is assbackward, and I'm in wholehearted agreement about rules being mostly stupid, but there's something about parents who can't sit down and shut up that usually results in them squeezing out loser fuck-trophies.

In history class, I reflect: Am I a loser fuck-trophy too? Same as Rowly? Am I an asshole friend? Could I have caught Hud before his face hit the ground? Or before that?

It's hard to know. I don't think I hesitated, but maybe I did. And if I did, maybe that's the better thing to do. Like, stop and think for a sec. Don't firefighters hesitate a half second before they run into flames? Take a split second to assess and strategize?

It's possible I froze.

A hand smacks my desk. Big, pale, and hairy. Mr. Popeler. "Can you believe it, McClane?"

He leans in, his eyes wide. He's not being a dick. He can be harsh, funny, and unpredictable, and occasionally he comes in stinking of alcohol, his shirt wrinkled and his pockets turned out, but he's not a dick teacher.

I purposefully do not look at that huge mole on his forehead as I shrug.

He waits.

"Sorry, I spaced out," I say.

He smiles knowingly, cutting me slack. "I was saying that all throughout my education, all the way through high school, I thought the pilgrims and Native Americans partied hard and shared this delicious meal and had a smoke together afterward, like the best college roommates." He wants to make us laugh, but we're sick of school. It's the end of the day, end of the year, end of our high school careers. No one laughs. Some kids have their phones out. He doesn't bother yelling at that. He's smart enough to know a lost cause.

He spares me, walks down the aisle of desks, lecturing. "It wasn't until I got to college that I learned Columbus was a bad dude, that I learned about the slaughter and the rape." Popeler's too thrilled by his past ignorance, it's a little creepy. "I read his diary," Popeler says. "Why do the baddest dudes keep diaries?" He's not asking us, he's being profound. "As they say, folks, everyone is the hero in their own story."

Shame warms my cheeks. His words feel like they're meant for me. Hud got his ass kicked, and here I am thinking about myself, what kind of person am I?

The bell rings. I don't need to stop at my locker. I head outside, toward my car. The sun is heating up the lot. I was wrong about this morning's drizzle hanging on our clothes all day. My clothes are dry. My skin is warm.

Nat's car is already gone, which isn't weird. On days she works, she rushes home to eat and get ready. I slide into the driver's seat of my car, throw my backpack and Hud's backpack into the backseat. As I wait for Jack, I text Hud. He probably won't get it, his phone looked trashed, but I text anyway.

> *You okay, man? I grabbed your bag. I can drop it later.*

I go to hit send but hesitate. If he doesn't have his phone, if someone else reads this, I don't want to implicate myself if drugs are involved. No. No, I'm good. It's an innocent text. I hit send. The parking lot is clearing out, no sign of Jack. Did he say he had early dismissal and I forgot? I text him.

> *You coming?*

No response.

I wait five more minutes, then drive home. That feeling, like I'm missing something, like I'm out of step, I'm soaked in it.

——— • ———

I walk in the front door and breathe in the smell of warm tomato sauce. I'm not hungry. I skip the kitchen and head to my room. I drop my bag and Hud's bag in my closet, kick off my shoes, and lie on my bed.

From my bed, there's a view of my closet. Legos and boxes

of stuff I've been thinking about tossing but haven't. Old comics, Goosebumps books, wrestling trophies. The wrestling trophies, they don't mean much. I know the seasons I've done well, I can name the matches, count down the points by move, name the injuries by tendon and phalanx. A gold-painted plastic dude with tight abs will not make me remember more or let me forget.

I stare at Hud's bag. I'm not going to check. If they had a reason to kick his ass, I don't want to know. It's not my business, and I don't need another thing to judge him by. I'm not checking, no sir.

I've played the scene over and over. I don't think I could have caught him. Maybe I'm remembering it wrong for my own sake, but it's already imprinted in my head that way. Like Popeler said, the hero in my own story. Right on, Pope.

Also, I don't think it was Rowly who hit Hud. That dude was big. And when his fist crashed into Hud's head, I caught the flash of a big tattoo along his forearm. Black ink, an image with a face. Last time I saw Rowly, he didn't have any tattoos. Not that I remember, anyway.

A knock at my door makes me jump. "McClane?"

I don't get up. "What?"

"Lasagna's on the counter if you want it," Mom says.

"Thanks."

Her soft footsteps move away and down the stairs.

I can't pinpoint when we stopped eating as a family. I think it was Dad that stopped showing up. His absence was heavy, and sitting down without him was uncomfortable. Or maybe it was me. When wrestling practice stretched later into the evenings, I couldn't make it on time. One less person to wait for gave everyone one more reason to stop sitting together. Or maybe it was Whitney. It's become harder and harder to get her out of her room. She says she'll be out in five minutes, but her five minutes is more like forty-five. It could have been Mom, actually. She's always on her laptop, always working. I'm not sure when she started working so much. Weird that I can't figure out how we got this way.

Dinner is cafeteria style in the Hart Home. Serve yourself. Sit alone. Eat if you want. Don't eat. Up to you.

She might make food for the sake of pretense more than to actually feed us, but I'm not complaining. Well, not too much. At least she makes food.

I slip out of my room, walk down the hall, and hit the bathroom. I flip on the light and fan. I pee and brush my teeth. Natalie said she was stopping by, so, fresh breath and all that.

I step out of the bathroom as Mom comes up the stairs. She might have been waiting to catch me. She does that, I think. Or she has clutch timing. Like Natalie's mom has a sixth sense for scandal.

"Oh, good," Mom says, her eyes light and hopeful. "I wanted to talk for a sec. Did you accept your scholarship?"

"Not yet." I keep walking.

"McClane. Wait." Her brightness dims, like exhaustion is dragging her down. She stops on the landing. "Listen to me. The deadline is soon. Please do it tonight. We can't afford to blow this off."

"Got it." I turn to go.

She grabs my wrist with her cold hand. Her grip is frantic and frail like a skeleton's. It disgusts me. I pull away, and one of her nails scrapes me.

"Ow." What the fuck? I look at my forearm. My skin is raised around the red line where her nail dug in.

"Sorry. I'm sorry," she says. "I didn't mean to scratch you, but you can't slack on this. I cannot do this for you. It has to come from your email." She is anxious, talking fast, total drama. "I don't know what you're waiting for. Maybe you should call David, ask for his advice."

Ask David? Fucking ask David? She's too close, too old, and her voice is too annoying. "Why would I call Dave? What's he gonna do?"

"I don't know. Give you advice."

I'm triggered. A small fire crackles inside my chest. It's the bullshit going down in this house. No one talks about it. I want to tear the roof off this house and scream about it. "I don't need Dave's advice."

"I don't understand what you're waiting for," she says, but I think she knows because she didn't even ask if I want to wrestle. She didn't ask why I'd want to stop. She's got to know. I can't stand how she hasn't asked. I can't stand how she talks about everything but the one important thing. "What are you waiting for, McClane?" she says, demanding.

Her words, her demanding tone, are like lighter fluid, and that small crackling inside me bursts into flames. I get in her face. My words rush out, fast and hot. "What are *you* waiting for? Huh, Mom? What do *you* think's going to happen all by itself?"

She startles, stepping back and shrinking as if I hit her. I've never erupted. I'm ashamed, but it also feels dangerously good.

"What are you talking about?" she says, her face drawn long and tired.

I laugh, and it doesn't sound like me. It's the kind of laugh that makes me think of violence. "Like you don't know. I fucking can't stand living here. You guys make me want to kill myself." I walk into my room.

I'm closing my door when she says softly, sadly, "Natalie's here."

"What? Why didn't you tell me?" Instead of feeling bad for being a dick, I'm triggered all over. Like a gust of wind sending the flames in a dangerous direction. I would hate if Nat overheard me sounding like that, like a bratty child having a tantrum. My parents bring out the absolute worst in me.

"I'm telling you."

"I can't believe you," I say, my tone quieter but still vicious and spitting. I walk past her, careful not to touch her. I can't stand her right now. I can't wait to be free of this house. The vibe here is stale. It's like watching a video of an animal's slow death, sped up. All that dying and decaying on fast-forward. You see the creature stumble and wither on its side. You see the last moment of pain in the creature's eyes before it's lights out, then the flies and rodents come, all of it on fast-forward, night after day after night. Feeding ceases. Bare bones remain, bleached in oppressive sunlight.

But my mind is already leaving her behind on the stairs. It's on to the next thing. The better thing. Natalie. I jog downstairs, shaking off my anger, skipping the last three steps and swiping the ceiling with my fingertips.

~ My Journal ~

I had a soccer game today and it sucked. Brandon kept teasing me. He kept calling me gay. I'm not even gay. Why would he call me that? I was running to set up for a pass and he ran by me and said faggot.

After the third time, I got insane angry and plowed into him. Like, ran so hard I ran him right over. I think I ran right over his face. He actually had a cleat mark on his forehead and his nose was bloody. I was so happy, but mom charged onto the field like a monster, grabbed my ear and pulled me away. She wouldn't even listen. I'm pretty sure she had smoke coming out of her ears so she couldn't hear. She made me get in the car and go home. What a bitch.

I wish dad was there. If dad was there, it wouldn't have ended like that. He's stronger and smarter. He doesn't mind blood since he used to box. He would have talked to me, listened to my side, talked to Coach, and I would have kept playing. I was having a good game too. They wouldn't have scored that first goal without me.

MC, age 10

CHAPTER 21

MEG

THE DAY THE POLICE GET INVOLVED, 9:12 P.M.

Wrapped in a towel, I step out of the bathroom. He's opened the curtains and windows. It's freezing in here, and my skin rises to irritated goose bumps.

Joe lies on his side in the bed, covered with a blanket. I can't see his face. I don't want to tell him. I honestly don't know what he'll do.

I go to close the window, but stop. He opened it for a reason. If I shut it, he may get agitated. Yellow-tinted lights strung outside above the patio cast our bedroom with a soft candle-lit glow.

Now that it's dark outside, my worries grow. Nighttime does that, amplifies things. When one of the kids had a fever during the day, we snuggled and watched movies and ate Popsicles. At night, the same exact fever brought fear of rare-disease death and regret for not going to the doctor when the office was open.

Joe's going to find out anyway. If he doesn't hear it from me first, he's going to be furious. I'm vulnerable in my towel, I don't want him to take it out on me, so I blame someone else.

"Natalie came over this morning. She was frantic because McClane wasn't in school. She said she knew something bad happened. That no one could find McClane. No one could reach his phone. She was going to call the police, so I did. I called the police. They were here today."

He says nothing for a full minute. I hold my breath, shivering in my towel.

Finally, he mutters, "Stupid. You always jump the gun."

"I had to call. Natalie was going to, so how would it look if she called instead of me?" His body is stiff, still turned away from me. "But that's not everything," I say. "They found something in McClane's room."

He sits up and, the blanket falling away, stares at me as if I had grown four more arms. "You let them into our house?"

"They let themselves in."

"They walked right up into his room?" His eyes are cold and dark like slick patches of mud on the sidewalk, waiting to catch you off guard on your night walk. His jaw is scruffy. He could pass for homeless. He swings his legs over the side of the bed. He's sitting, ready to stand. "That seems illegal."

I take a small step back. "They were asking questions. Taking notes. It just happened, them going into his room."

"Calling the police was such a mistake. So stupid."

My cheeks are hot but the rest of me is cold. Anger pumps through me. "You're not listening."

"Let the police in, and now you've invited all sorts of trouble."

My anger boils over. "They found a knife covered in blood," I say through clenched teeth. I take a breath. I hate losing my cool. How does he always trigger my temper? "And child pornography."

He rubs his palms up and down his face, like he's just waking up. He turns his eyes toward me and they soften, shifting to concern. He sighs, exhaling the last of his fury.

"There's a million reasons for a bloody knife," he says, his tone calm and logical. "He's a screwball eighteen-year-old. Maybe he killed a rabbit. Maybe he gutted a fish and got distracted and didn't bother cleaning his knife. You know how easily they're distracted and what slobs they can be. Maybe he was pissed at himself and he cut himself. I did that as a teenager. Everybody's worried about self-harm, but it doesn't have to mean much." He sounds reasonable, and it makes me feel like I'm the crazy one. "Bloody knife is normal. Porn is normal too. Kiddie porn is normal if he's a kid. If he's looking at sixteen-year-olds, that's normal."

"I said the same thing. They wouldn't show me what they found, but they were indicating it wasn't normal."

"That's their job, though, isn't it?" His tone softens. He's back on my team, blaming the police for mistreating me. "They have to trap someone."

My pulse settles. This version of Joe, calm Joe, seeing-the-world-clearer-than-everyone-else Joe, has always made me feel like things will turn out just fine. Like we could be living in a car, eating out of a dumpster, and we'd still find something to laugh about. Head lice and hookworms, maybe. I'm still standing in my towel, shivering from the chill blowing in, my hands squeezing tight where I've knotted my towel between my breasts.

His eyes move from my face to my towel. He looks at me like I'm his prize, not his burden. "Well," he says, his tone cool. "Let's fool around in case our lives are about to be wrecking-balled."

I can't help but smile. That's the Joe I fell in love with. The Joe who jokes in the face of defeat. Cool Joe. He's always had the best "fuck it" smile. Here was a guy who played it smooth no matter what, and I needed that person in my life.

He gave me that same "fuck it" smile as we sat at the bar after his last fight—his third fight after shattering his shoulder. He sipped his beer even though his lip was split and oozing fresh blood and told me he just couldn't get his arm to move fast enough. He smiled at me even though one eye was fat-squeezed shut. "If I miss it," he said, his words slurred, "you could punch me in the mouth to bring back good vibrations? When I long for the good old days, you could kick me in the balls."

We laughed that night. And we cried. But we laughed more. And that became our private joke. Our best joke. Our most supportive joke. Our most loving joke. He'd have a bad day at the brokerage firm, he'd come home bloated, grimy, and pissed, and I'd say, "Would it help if I kicked you in the balls?"

It always worked.

He would either half smile and shake his head or he'd wrap me up into a hug that lifted my feet off the floor for a second or he'd kiss me like he loved me.

I barely had to use that joke. Joe was rarely in a bad mood, rarely temperamental or shortsighted. He didn't get caught up in media gossip or family drama. He was notorious for turning off his phone for an entire weekend. He was unowned. Eccentric. Born here but seemed like he was born elsewhere, on a boat or in a small village by the sea.

I used to wonder if he was that cool as a kid or if it was the boxing that did it to him.

I think it was a bit of both.

Boxing taught him resilience. It taught him to smirk with a mouth full of blood. He knew defeat and humiliation more starkly than most people. He would say, "There is nothing like fading in from blackout on your back, blood filling your mouth, and you hear cheering and the long roar of a crowd, and, just as a bleeding smile breaks across your face, you realize it's for the other guy. The crowd is rejoicing in your loss."

He didn't take it personally. He got a kick out of the beatings. He lived above the noise. He liked shaking the other guy's hand. *I worked my ass off, and you beat me. Next time, brother.*

I want that old Joe back so badly.

I drop my towel, slip under the covers, close my eyes, and pretend that's who he still is.

———•———

I wake up in the night, shivering cold. The curtains billow. Christ, the window's still open. Overnight temperatures this time of year can hover around freezing. I'm naked. Half asleep, I pull on an old T-shirt, cross to the window, and shut it.

A figure on the patio startles me. My pulse pounds in my throat,

I squint my eyes to see clearer. Someone's walking away from the house. I know that walk. Even though his muscles have gone soft, he still has the graceful walk of an athlete.

I watch him until he moves away from the dimly lit part of the lawn near the house and disappears deeper into blackness.

Cool Joe has left him. His murkier half, the half that moves through life like a dark shadow, is back.

His smell lingers on my skin. I press my nose against my shoulder and breathe him in. Clean aftershave, and maybe a little sour-old.

I lie in bed, comparing the Joe out in the yard to the one I had sex with hours ago. Oh God, the sex was good. Even as I've lost Joe, good sex has been the one constant. Even as he has grown distant, my pleasure still comes first. He was the first man I met who was overly generous in bed. If I'm being honest, it's the main reason I married him, and it's one of the reasons I've stayed with him as he's become someone else.

My mind lingers on the sex we had. I'm like a witch trying to conjure that Joe. If I think about him enough, maybe he will come back to me.

CHAPTER 22

MCCLANE

6 HOURS UNTIL MISSING

She's wearing black pants, black ankle boots, and a black top. Polished, professional, and sexy. I could stare at her forever. I would be happy to just watch her exist. Brush her teeth, eat her cereal, write her papers, watch TV. "You look good."

She smiles wide. "You like this look better than my PJs at school?" She's not really asking me, she's teasing.

I step onto the porch and kiss her. "You do rock the PJ look. I like you in bed, so maybe PJs more." She laughs into the kiss. Her teeth move against my lip and I get chills.

We are in step. She is mine. I am hers. Our kiss, our tongues, our hands—everything is in sync. The vibe that was off at her locker has been restored somehow. Maybe it's the trauma-bonding of Hud's fight, maybe it's me feeling more myself right now.

As she pulls away from our kiss, I rub my nose against hers. The soft tip of her nose is cold. "You want me to grab a hoodie for you?"

"I'm good," she says. "Let's go around back."

Where I really want to go is away from here. Get Natalie in my car and drive and not come back. I'm still trying to shake my mom's nagging, disappointed voice, but it's hanging on like a stubborn earworm. What's crazy is that *she* is disappointed in *me*. She's got it backward. Her and Dad are the biggest disappointments of all.

We walk around back. The best thing about this house is not what's inside. It's this huge backyard, the gurgling stream, and the forest behind it. Nat and me, we've spent a lot of time in that forest. We've got a tent back there hidden between a cluster of pine trees. Inside is a cozy nest of blankets I stole from the basement. Nat laughed at how many blankets I'd gathered. She said she never knew a family that stored old blankets in garbage bags in their basement.

We spend time inside my house too. We've made brownies and blue boxes of mac and cheese and watched movies in my room, but mostly, we stay outside. When we're inside my house, the air is static. My parents don't like people in the house. Mom says it's fine, but she doesn't mean it.

We pass the tree that smells like spooge and walk toward the aluminum fence. It's fun how spring comes on fast. Sky to ground is gray and muddy, then you blink and the world is limey green like the Emerald City.

"How's Hudson?" she says.

"I don't know. I can't get hold of him. His phone shattered, then Ridley grabbed it. I saw Hud's head hit the ground. I was right there. I keep thinking I should have been able to catch him."

"I don't think you could have. You rushed toward the fight before

I even knew what was happening, that's how fast you were. I think you got there as quick as you could."

"Thanks." She's not just blowing smoke up my ass, she means it. Her words loosen the tightness in my chest. "So, you okay?" I say, because she doesn't ever stop by on her way to work. Something's definitely up.

"Yeah," she says, shifting her voice toward scratchy and apathetic. "I'm still here."

This phrase, our private joke, lures smiles from both of us.

On cue, I say, "I'm just a fly in the ointment."

"The monkey in the wrench," she says.

"A pain in the ass."

"Now that," she says, pointing her finger at my chest and giving me a poke. "That is true."

There's a funny story to this private joke. The first time we went out—our first official date—we went to Starbucks. When we went to pick up our order, the overcaffeinated old-lady barista said, "McClane! I love that name! Yippee-ki-yay!"

We got back to our seats and I said, "What was up with that? Yippee what?"

"You're joking, right?" she said.

"What do you mean, you're joking?"

"Your parents named you McClane because they loved that movie, right?"

"What movie?"

"Oh, come on," she said. "You're messing with me."

"My parents named me for one of my dad's friends who died in a motorcycle accident."

Her eyes went wide, and she covered her mouth. "Dude. Fucking morbid."

"He was a good guy, I guess. Generous."

"Still."

"What movie?"

"Die Hard."

"Never heard of it."

"Well, it's old, so." She shrugged. "My parents make me watch it every Christmas. It's a terrorist action movie. The reluctant hero is trapped in a high-rise with a bunch of German terrorists, walking around with bloody cut-up feet."

"Wait, why do you watch it over Christmas?"

She spit some of her drink out as she laughed.

So Nat and I went back to her house and watched it. Our first date. Her dad had it on his computer—she said he pirated it years ago. Anyway, it's a great movie. Kind of simple, in a way. I mean, it's old-fashioned and a little boring, but it has some great one-liners. We've watched it a handful of times now. We mimic lines from it. Sometimes she says my name in her best villainous German accent. I love when she does that.

As we pass the quaking aspen, Nat takes a trembling heart-shaped leaf between her fingers, brushes her thumb over it, and lets it go. I've told her it's my tree, that I picked it out, and Whitney named it Earthquake when she was small.

"Tell me what's up," I say.

"My mom wants me to book an appointment with the doctor. She says if I'm serious about having a baby, I need to be responsible."

"That's funny, because you're the most responsible person I know.

You might be the most responsible person your mom knows." I stop and turn to her. "How are you so responsible, anyway?"

"I'm a girl, dummy. We get our period when we're in elementary. All of a sudden, we have to start using a calendar. Being responsible isn't always a compliment, it's not like some worthy value you were born with or you worked hard for. It's more like a trait that's forced on you against your will."

See, she says the craziest, wisest shit. Things that never would have crossed my mind, ever. It's like, all her thoughts are nuggets of gold, and I never tire of panning for them.

"Huh" is all I can say.

"Anyway, will you go to the doctor with me?"

"Yeah, sure," I say, but my mind gets hijacked with images of stuffy waiting rooms, stern, judgmental doctors' faces, cold metal instruments, and girl stuff that I'm pretty sure I'll never be entirely comfortable with. Bloody maxi pads. Baby heads bursting through a girl's legs.

"I'm having doubts," she says.

"Well . . ." I start.

"Just shut up, okay," she says. "Just listen. I need to say stuff. This is me, my life. We both know that. I mean, you might be around for the long haul for the kid's life, you might not, but I will be."

I want to say *I'll be here*, but I keep my mouth shut. My stomach twists.

"My parents. They keep lecturing me about how it goes. They're getting in my head, I guess. I'm all over the place, okay? Like, I'm not myself."

No kidding. Me neither. "Okay."

"I'm just not one hundred percent about everything, okay?"

I think she means she's considering an abortion, but I am so not asking her for clarification. "Okay. I support you."

She stares at me for a few seconds, then slaps my chest with the back of her hand and laughs. "What the fuck is that? Did you steal that out of a greeting card?"

"No. It's pretty much the simple truth."

"Okay, Slick." She smiles and exhales, relaxed again. She threads her fingers through the chain-link fence and looks down at the river. It rained last night, and the river is moving fast and cold. She's quiet for a while. Her cheeks and nose are rosy. It's nice out, the sun is warming my shirt, but the air is cool. "I can never get over it."

"What?"

"That your parents still live in this house."

She's talking about Carson. He died right where we're standing. Little dude climbed over the fence and the barbed wire, tried crossing the footbridge but fell. I guess the bridge was flimsy when my parents first moved in. No railings. Only a simple crossover. After Carson died, Dad built railings and made it sturdy, so we used the bridge all the time when I was in middle school to get to the forest preserve or go fishing on the other side of the bank. We rarely caught anything, but it was still fun to drop our lines into the water and splash around. Especially when we were little and couldn't ride to Green Lake yet.

"Yeah, I guess it's weird. But this is the place where all their memories of him are. I mean, there's that one, the worst one, but also, lots of good ones."

"Seems like a big gloomy cloud over your house."

"I don't know. I never knew him. He's just this kid who had a terrible accident." The gloomy cloud, though, I feel that. But it has nothing to do with Carson.

"Which rock is it?"

"Dave said it was that rock." I point to one of the big ones lining the bank below the bridge. "But who knows? Sometimes he's full of shit."

"Why would he lie about that?"

"He wouldn't. I mean, he told me when we were little. He used to tell big stories, that was his thing." I laugh a little at that, at the stories he used to tell, the dumb things he used to convince us to do. I have a scar on my toe because he convinced me to be part of his circus. He charged the neighborhood kids a buck apiece. I was his knife juggler, barefoot for added danger. I was maybe four or five, and my high-octane brother gave me a knife to flip. Siblings can be such dicks. But also insanely, wildly fun.

I didn't need stitches, but my toe bled a lot. The neighborhood kids got their money's worth. I'm lucky I didn't lose a finger. I miss him, Dave. Jamie too. She was the voice of reason. She was the one who bandaged my toe that day and gave me a Popsicle to shut me up. With them gone, a third of our family is gone. With Dad and Mom the way they are now, that's another third pretty much gone. It's just me and Whit, but she's gotten weird too.

"Was your mom depressed when you were little?"

"Not that I remember, but I was born years after he died."

"You never asked your siblings?"

"No." Was that an early sign of family dysfunction? I thought of our family as happy and connected until recently, but if we were tight, wouldn't I have asked Jamie or Dave what Carson was like and if they still missed him?

"And you've never talked to your parents about it?" Nat says.

"Never. I figured they'd tell me stuff if they wanted. I figured they wanted to focus on looking forward, not back."

I figured my parents were simple and straightforward. That their thoughts didn't go beyond dinner, dishes, bills, work, and *Anyone need anything from the store?* I never gave them a second thought, who they were as people, what were they capable of.

Lately, it's different. I'm not sure if my parents have changed or I'm just noticing weird dynamics for the first time. They seem like they are playing a game. With each other and with us. Like I said, old people have so many weird hang-ups and imagined problems.

CHAPTER 23

MEG

DAY 2, 7:12 A.M.

I wake up like a cat startled by a sudden noise.
Yesterday was all about not overreacting. Yesterday was all about *it hasn't even been a day*. Not a full day.

Now, it's been a day, and a full day feels like dread.

I reach for my phone. No calls.

I close my eyes and all I see is McClane opening his mouth to tell me something, but I can't hear what he's saying because he can't breathe.

I run to the toilet and throw up. I sit on the bathroom floor for a while, sobbing until I'm too exhausted to keep up this charade. It's time to talk to Joe. Tell him about my argument with McClane and what I did that night, where I went. Ask him what he does at night, where he goes. Whatever the consequences may be, I'll take it. I can't live like this.

I walk into the bedroom, resolutely vulnerable, but he's gone. Of course he's gone.

I want to bury myself in the tangle of blankets we slept in. I step toward the bed, but my bare foot lands in a cold puddle.

Water pools on the floor leading to Joe's clothes, wet and muddy, in a heap. Jeans, flannel, mud-dyed white socks. I was hoping that had been a dream, watching him walk to the back of the yard last night.

In my long T-shirt and leggings, a few drops of vomit down the front, I carry his clothes to the washing machine, cleaning up after him. Like I always do.

You can do hard things. That's what I told myself yesterday, but fuck that. Who wants to do hard things? Like it's some sort of badge of honor to have a shitty life you have to wade through like squelching through a mucky, alligator-filled swamp.

Whitney's door is closed. It's Saturday, she's probably sleeping in. I don't bother knocking.

Downstairs, Joe's muddy shoes are beside the back door along with a pair of muddy footprints. The footprints look staged. They're not, I know they're not, Joe is impulsive, not calculating, but that's how his footprints look. Extreme. His shoes are caked in mud. To get that muddy, it takes effort. What was he doing out there?

I wander past Joe's muddy shoes and out the back door. Into the yard I go, barefoot. It rained while I slept. The patio is slick, and the grass is cool and wet. My skin breaks into goose bumps, my nipples rise.

With the rain, the stream is invigorated. No doubt it has risen several feet. On days like this, I picture our sweet little river as angry and defiant, rushing, threatening: *You can't control me. I'm sick of singing for you. I'm done behaving. I'm coming for you.*

The sky is thick and gray, ugly like Joe's filthy socks. Misty drops touch my cheeks. It's drizzling.

I lace my fingers through the barbed-wire fence and stare at the boulder edging the water, the one we tried to remove, but it was too heavy. Joe asked if we should hire a crew. I said fuck it, it's fine, just leave it. And it is. It has been fine, it is fine, but my eyes move to it every time I walk to the edge of the yard.

My mind is untethered and I'm chilled. I need to wrap myself in a blanket and lie down. As I'm walking back to the house, my cell phone buzzes in my pocket. My pulse quickening, I check who's texting. Jamie. Drizzle flecks my screen.

> *Any word from McClane?*

I text.

> *Nothing yet. I will update you if there's any news.*

Jamie texts again.

> *Someone has to know something? Who else can you call? Who should Mom call, Dave?*

Then a text from David.

> *Have they pinged his phone location? Have*

> they found his car? The detectives assigned
> to his case—what are their names?

I text.

> Flemming and Becker.

Jamie responds.

> Dave, maybe you could reach out to them.
> Ask what they are doing to look for him?

I miss having these two around. It's been four months since they visited for Christmas. As they've gotten older, their visits feel more obligatory and restless. Sure, they laugh and go along with the traditions of gift exchange and decorating sugar cookie snowmen, but their desire to escape back to their own lives is palpable, like a fast heartbeat against two fingers, and their hugs good-bye are quick. Each visit is a little different from the last, a little stranger, but still good, I think. I hold tight to the good parts. The times when they have not locked themselves away in their childhood rooms, when they're together.

I lie down on the couch, recalling this last Christmas visit. They slept a lot. McClane and Whitney had just gotten over the flu and were still resting, tucked in bed with their phones. David was swamped with work. The first couple of days, he emerged bleary-eyed from his childhood room only around dinnertime, his hair a mess, stubble along his greasy jaw. When I got up in the middle of the night to pee or get a glass of water, the faint glow of his laptop seeped from beneath his door. Poor kid. When you're ambitious, the pull of work can be strong.

Jamie was the only one with energy and a routine. She took over the kitchen, leaving egg casseroles and plates of powdered sugar pancakes on the counter before settling on the couch to watch movies on her phone.

By Christmas Eve, the house was lively again. McClane and Whitney were back to their hungry teenage selves, eating straight out of the refrigerator, making up for missed meals.

David was buzzing with squirrelly energy. He added windshield fluid to everyone's car and strung up extra Christmas lights out front. When he stomped inside, shaking snow off his boots, cold clinging to his flannel jacket, he said with a grin, "I replaced the license plate bulbs on Cool Hand Luke, little brother. Now the pigs have no reason to pull you over."

Jamie, still wearing her PJs, eating Doritos out of the bag at the kitchen table, made pig noises. McClane, hovering in front of the open refrigerator, joined in. Whitney, sitting opposite Jamie, rolled her eyes.

"You caught up on sleep I guess," I said to David, opening the cabinet and reaching for a mug.

"I guess," David said, but not without humor, snatching a few Doritos from Jamie's bag.

"The question is," Jamie said, pointing at David with a chip, "aren't *you* a piggy?"

David answered her with a hard smile, placing a cold hand on the back of her neck.

Jamie yelped and laughed. "Cold! Get off me."

Grinning at her, he stepped back. "Hey, Mick, let's go for a drive, I'll buy you a slushie."

"I'm not ten, bro," McClane said, holding a slice of white bread in his hand.

"Okay, I'll buy you hot wings."

McClane shut the refrigerator door, his movements loose and easy. "I'm in."

"Nice," Jamie said, standing. "Wings sound good. Let me change first."

"It's just a boys' trip." David winked and turned for the door.

Jamie called after him, joking, "Was it the piggy question? Did I hurt your feelings? I love you, Davie!"

"Yeah, yeah." David gave a small laugh before walking out the front door.

McClane said, "We'll bring you wings." He followed David out, saying, "Yo, we sure it's open Christmas Eve?"

With the boys gone, Jamie said, "Come on, Whitney, let's have a girls' night. Let's watch a super-girly movie like *Fight Club* or *The Raid: Redemption*."

"Never heard of either," Whitney said, grabbing the bag of chips and heading for the couch. "But I'm all over redemption."

They had something special, these four. Something fluid and unguarded—a kind of camaraderie I never shared with my brother. They teased each other, sure, but their jokes were laced with affection and ease. On this occasion, I kept quiet, making myself a cup of tea and soaking in the warmth of their interactions. Listening was a pleasure in itself.

I wake up on the couch when the doorbell rings.

I didn't mean to fall back asleep. My skin feverish, I'm caught with part of my mind still in a bad dream: McClane's limp gray body being dragged from a river onto the shore by officers. As they drag him, his body and sodden clothes cut a path through tall grass under the ugly morning sunshine. Near the silty riverbank, a construction vehicle sits on an incline, its engine steaming against the cool air. The vehicle is hitched to a drag harrow. The chain mesh spikes of the harrow glisten with mud.

I shake off the dread of how specific the dream felt. Feels. That's not what happened to McClane. It's from that news story I heard about the missing Missouri woman—they pulled her body from the river near the southern tip of Illinois.

The doorbell rings again.

Dalí's melting-time clock tells me it's 12:13 p.m. I slept the entire morning. I'm appalled at my indulgence. Who naps the morning away when their child is missing? Time is rushing away from me. I am behind.

I picture Eileen singing *Come on, Meg*, as I've sung to her countless times. It's Saturday, so I'm not expected to work. Still, I should email my team, apologize for missing yesterday's meeting. Do I tell them McClane's missing? No. They'd have questions I'd have to answer.

The doorbell rings again. I yank my blanket off as if I'm ready to perform. At least I changed out of my vomit-stained T-shirt and stepped into pants and a sweater.

The doorbell rings again. Oh, hold your horses.

It's Carla, my neighbor from across the street. Her eyes are tired and full of worry. Her messy bun is floppy and way off center. She's holding a rectangular green plastic Tupperware. Her watery eyes search mine. She wants me to invite her in. She wants a hug. "Oh, Meg. Any news yet on where McClane is?"

I shake my head.

"What can I do to help?"

"There's nothing I can think of right now. I'm sure it will turn out okay," I say, and wonder why I'm intent on pretending.

"The police stopped by my house yesterday but didn't give me any details." Her voice tight, she's aching for details.

"We don't have any yet."

"I gave them my Ring camera footage. I hope that helps."

If this house weren't oozing with filthy secrets, it might have. She's sweet to think we are a wholesome, buttered-popcorn-and-game-night type of family.

"How is Joe holding up?" Before I can answer, she says, "You know, I haven't seen him in a while. I don't think I've seen him since last summer."

That's because he's only on the move after dark. "You know, same ol', same ol'. I should be going."

"Oh, of course. Oh!" She realizes she rang my bell for a reason. "I made you muffins. I've got sourdough in the oven too. I'll bring it by when it's ready."

"The muffins are plenty. Thanks, Carla." I close the door slowly on her.

She's a good neighbor. She's given me zucchini and tomatoes

from her garden. I've given her bags of clothes my kids have outgrown. Easter dresses. Name-brand swimsuits. Church clothes. We haven't needed those in ages. That was one of the first things to go. We stopped going to church long before we stopped eating dinner together. Not that I'm implying our Godless life led to our downfall. But it's an impressive feat for an entire family to get their asses out of bed and to church on a cold weekend morning. It requires discipline and a teamwork attitude. One mutinous child and the whole pious affair falls apart.

While I'm waiting for my coffee to brew, I stuff a muffin in my mouth. Banana walnut. I'm suddenly ravenous, realizing I haven't eaten since yesterday morning. I devour three more muffins, gulping them down too fast, barely tasting them.

My phone vibrates. Five new texts and a voicemail have come through during my nap and chat with Carla. All from friends who saw neighborhood posts or heard through their kids: McClane is missing.

Is it true? What can we do? Is there a search we can join? They're already hopping in their cars, asking where to go.

The thought of responding exhausts me. They are my friends, but I've fallen off get-togethers and basic communication recently so they don't know the full story—what's been happening with my kids, with Joe. Even if I was comfortable explaining it, which I'm not, that would take more energy than I have left.

But there's one text I can't ignore: Deb, Jack's mom.

> *Jack said Natalie's freaking out. She told him McClane's missing. Me and John want to help.*

John's gonna put in a call to the Sugar PD, and he'll call you soon. It's going to be okay, Meg. Love you.

John's a cop. Works up in River's Edge, forty minutes away. His go-to joke is he doesn't want to live among his "clientele." But John and Deb are good people, so I listen to the voicemail he left shortly after Deb texted me.

"Hey, Meg. John here. I can't get anything from Sugar PD, but no search is being set up. That's a good sign. It means they've got a lead they're following."

Yeah, but the lead is us. The muffin is turning pasty in my mouth. I reach for my coffee and sip, forcing it down.

John's still talking. "I'll keep pushing them. Maybe this squeaky wheel will get some oil. Deb's in Minnesota with her mom, but she's on her way home. She'll come by tomorrow. You call me at any time. It's gonna be okay, you know that. This is McClane we're talking about. He's a good kid. These kids, they can just be stupid. This is one of those times."

His tenderness undoes me. My jaw trembles. I exhale hard, trying to find calm in myself.

I don't want Deb rushing home on my account. I start texting this to John when the doorbell rings again. Carla's not going to let up, I guess. She wants to dip her toes into our tragedy. Bathe herself in gratitude that she is not us.

But no. It's not Carla.

Here are the two detectives, standing on my porch, rain misting their hair, looking tired and disappointed.

"Have you found him?" My voice is barely a whisper.

"Not yet," says Detective Becker. "Can we come in, Mrs. Hart?"

I don't want them here. They were supposed to help, but they have only attacked my son and my family. Projection is a convenient police tactic.

I nod and let them follow me to the kitchen. I sit at the table with my coffee.

Detective Becker sits. His expression is weathered. I have an urge to cheer him up, apologize for his bad feelings. I bite my lip. Detective Flemming stands, studying Joe's muddy shoes but saying nothing. Her expression is bummed, but curious. The scar across the bridge of her nose is purple this morning. Maybe it's the cold.

"You found something," I say. "Tell me."

"The last missing persons case I worked, it was a missing teenage boy," Becker says, laying his palms flat on the table. "The mother was calling me around the clock, wondering, did I hear anything? Anytime I knocked on her door, she teared up." He leans forward. "You're not like that, Mrs. Hart."

Last night these two hinted at their attack on me and Joe. Now they're going to dig in. "I'm trying to remain calm and trust that things will sort themselves out. Would it be more productive if I were hysterical?"

"No, it's just that people can't usually control their worry." He drums the pads of his fingers on my table. Detective Flemming gazes out the back door. It's almost like she can't look at me. Like we were besties, and I've let her down. Kissed her boyfriend or something.

"What are you not telling me?" I say.

He leans back now, getting comfortable. "I was going to ask you the same thing."

They couldn't possibly know about my argument with McClane two nights ago, and they couldn't possibly know what happened afterward. There's no way. I shake my head. I wait them out. It's not easy. I count. Everyone is silent until I reach seven.

"You never mentioned your oldest son. Carson?" Becker says. "And that he died here at the house."

And so. The other shoe drops. It's a stupid saying, really. It doesn't carry dread. No one's life is going to end with the drop of a shoe.

The saying should be different. Something like: The grizzly bear finally escaped his cage. Now there's a saying that conveys someone's in deep shit.

To be honest, I've been waiting twenty years for this. For the accusation. Carson's death being someone's fault. That person being me, his mother. His ultimate guardian. The accusation never came. I expected it. Maybe even wanted it, at least for a year or two.

Now that I don't want it and I didn't expect it, here it is. Like a bear's massive paws crushing my chest.

I feel faint and grip the edge of the table so I don't go down. My fingers are numb. My nose is cold. "Why would I mention him? He's a private memory, a source of heartache, and none of your business. He died when he was five years old. It was accidental."

"Your neighbor mentioned Carson had developmental delays as a kid," Becker says.

What the fuck, Carla? Is that why she baked me muffins this morning—because she blabbed to the detectives yesterday, flaunting the most tender details of my life?

"As a parent of little kids, it's hard as it is," Becker says. "I can't imagine that, that extra strain." His voice is a mixture of honest-to-goodness empathy and devious calculation.

As if a "difficult" child is easier to kill.

I swallow my rage. It's dry and I almost choke on it. "He got past the fence," I say, my jaw tight, my tone more defensive than I'd like. "He fell off the footbridge and landed on a rock. Died of a head injury. How could that have anything to do with McClane being missing?"

Becker raises his eyebrows as if to say, *It has everything to do with McClane being missing. You are the type of person, the type of mother, that lets bad things happen to her children.*

"That must have been painful." Flemming's voice is soft and sympathetic. My jaw softens. "I can't imagine staying in a house where my child died," she adds.

"Me neither," I say, unoffended and in agreement. "It just happened. It was too overwhelming to move when I wanted to. Once life became bearable, I didn't want to move anymore. I didn't want to lose the good memories. Also, I didn't want to uproot my other children." That's the truth.

She pulls a chair out gently and sits beside Becker. "I can understand that." Her eyes are moist with empathy. Yesterday I thought she was stoic and sturdy. Today I see she's temperamental, like a child. Sweet one moment, nasty the next. Giving you a good hug, asking if she can watch *Squid Game*. Then yelling that Tess's mom lets her, and slamming her bedroom door. She's about to say something but stops. Then says it anyway. "Is there anyone you can think of who would like to see you suffer? Anyone who would want revenge?"

The question throws me off-balance and sends shivers up my spine. Yes, I can think of one in particular.

Becker huffs and leans back in his chair, like he's annoyed with his partner because she's going off script. Flemming leans forward, making it clear she couldn't care less. Their tension calms me a little.

"Well, my husband was a well-known boxer," I say. "Even though this was two decades ago, jealousy lingers." I can spot the jealous type right away. They hold their smile a beat too long. They wonder why you got lucky. Why was your husband asked to be involved in the ribbon-cutting ceremony at the new gym? Why did your family get seated at the local restaurant quicker than theirs? I never liked the small favors, honestly, but it was easier to accept them graciously than refuse.

"Anyone you can single out?" she says.

"No," I lie. My nerves are frayed. The detectives have gone from criticizing my lack of hysteria to blaming me for the loss of my first child to suggesting that Joe's long-past success has cursed us. "And if you have no news on McClane—" I close my eyes, and instead of seeing McClane's body, I see Carson's, limp as a doll, his blood spilled on the boulder, the river meandering along lazily as if nothing's happened. "Please don't come here unless you have something."

Detective Becker stands. "Oh, I meant to ask before." He raises his eyebrows like if there's a victim here, it's him. "Have you called your parents?"

I'm startled by the question. "No."

"Don't you think they'd want to know McClane is missing?"

"Why, so they could have one more thing to worry about?" Exhaustion tugs at my shoulders. "My parents are in their seventies.

They've had a shit life. They sit with their troubles, share them like drinkers share a bottle of whiskey." That's honestly a great line, I should feed it to Eileen. I can't stand myself.

He holds my gaze and says, "We paid them a visit." My skin grows icy. Muscles in my legs tremble.

These suburban detectives are smarter than I could have imagined. Smarter than the magnitude of unsolved crimes would lead me to believe. They are smarter than me. "We met your older brother, Nathan. Seems he has similar challenges as your oldest child, Carson. Your parents told us about his history, how hard it was for you growing up with him as a brother. They told us about his friend's accident."

My idiot parents. They have no sense of self-preservation, no suspicion of authority.

And Carla, that backstabbing bitch. She must have tipped them off about my brother too. No way the cops would've dug that deep that fast—it's barely been a day.

"Get out," I say.

The detectives walk calmly to the front door. I follow them, hating their squeaks and shuffles, hating their dirty smell. Pigs. They literally smell like pigs. I can't wait to slam the door shut after them. As they step out, an SUV pulls into the driveway. Joe.

"Oh," Detective Becker says, looking back at me as if he can't believe his luck. "Our timing is good for once."

CHAPTER 24

MCCLANE

4½ HOURS UNTIL MISSING

Most of the teachers at Shaw Elementary have cleared out, so the parking lot is nearly bare. Two girls who could pass for early middle school are slumped on the swings in the playground, their feet on the ground and barely rocking themselves as they scroll their phones.

Jack's playing three-on-three on the court next to the playground. I park next to the court and watch their game for a minute. I recognize most of them, they're good guys. I don't know them well because they're usually at the Y, playing ball, but I've hung with them at parties this year. Senior year has been smooth in that way. People who were only faces in the school hallways for three years have finally become cool acquaintances. Through the smoky haze, overheated body-packed bedrooms, and flowing alcohol at Rick Halloway's mansion on Friday nights, we've finally connected. Rick's parents are fully negligent and leave him home alone for weeks on end while they vacation in Bali and Antigua. His dad's a private pilot. Dude's got an airplane hangar instead of a garage.

I call to Jack. He says a few words to the guys on the court and jogs over to my car.

"Hud got shit-kicked," I say.

"I heard. I messaged him but haven't heard back."

"His phone got toasted."

"You driving to his place now?"

I nod.

"Give me a sec." He jogs back, talks to his friends, slaps hands with a few of the guys, and grabs his drawstring bag. His friends keep playing as he heads my way, limping the slightest. He slides into the passenger seat, the smell of sun and his sweat filling my car. I don't mind.

"Dude, why you always play here?"

"It's the only court that's walking distance from my house, man."

"Those little girls on the swings, man."

He looks over his shoulder at the swings. "Oh, come on. Don't ruin it. This is my court, man. This is my place." He's getting emotional, pushing his hand through his hair. "I don't want my favorite place to be all mashed up with little girls on swings, bro. Don't fuck me up."

I laugh because he's easy to ruffle. Sentimental. Like, he means it about this being his court. Jack is pretty much the best person to fuck with.

I pull out of the parking lot and weave through the subdivision toward the main streets. Jack connects his phone to my stereo and plays "Die for You" by the Weeknd. I'm sick of this song, it's overplayed, but I don't dislike it as much as he likes it.

After a bit, I say, "I saw Hud go down."

"Really?"

I play it over in my head. "His head hit dead hard. Definitely a concussion. Bad one." Now that I'm thinking about it, he could have bleeding in the brain. They should have taken him to the hospital, but I don't remember hearing an ambulance. "Did you hear an ambulance?"

"I was at the dentist, man."

That yanks me out of my head. Total whiplash. I bust out laughing.

"What?" he says. "Like you don't go to the dentist? My mom makes me appointments twice a year. My grams says, 'Whatever you do, take care of your teeth.' Lady knows what she's talking about. She's got no teeth. Grams can't eat a damn drumstick. That's sad, bro. No drumsticks, can you imagine? Like, seriously?"

Listening to Jack talk, it's the best.

"You accept your scholarship?" he says.

"Already told you. I don't think I will."

"It's, like, eighty thousand dollars over four years, son. Kids our age are signing up for ROTC, taking a shit roulette bet, just to pay for college. How can you turn that down? And forget the money. You're good. To be born with talent, it's like, how can you waste it? Hide your light under a bushel and all that? It's, like, spoiled." The way he says *spoiled* makes my stomach feel queasy. He can't hide his jealousy. He's my best friend, but would probably give up our friendship for a basketball scholarship. If he could move with Durant's grace, fast-twitch muscle and all that, what wouldn't he give up?

"I don't know. I mean, what does it matter? I'm not good enough for the Olympics. I'm only good enough for college wrestling, that's it. I'm not sure it's worth the risk of a lifelong injury."

"Shit, son. You sound like an old man. 'Lifelong injury.' Who says that? And what the fuck is 'only good enough for college wrestling'? You are one spoiled little bitch." He's not angry anymore, he's cracking up. He's on a roll with his ranting, he's having a good time. "Maybe I can take your scholarship, make a wig out of your hair, lose fifty pounds, wear your tight one-piece. Fuck, I'd wrestle naked for eighty grand." A thought strikes him, and he looks up at the ceiling of my car. There's a burn mark there from Hud fucking around last year. "Now I'm trying to think if there's anything I wouldn't do for eighty grand."

It's a great invitation for a joke. He's basically asking for it, but I don't have the energy. "Yeah. I need to give it some thought. I don't know." Which isn't true. I do know, I just haven't said.

It's my dad. It's all about my dad.

He's gotten weird over the past two years. Not funny-weird or oddball-weird. Scary-weird. Like his brain goes offline. He gets this blank expression, his eyes dark, his face slack, like there's no one home in there. He does strange things when his eyes go blank. Leaves at night on foot, comes back hours later, filthy and stinking. I don't know where he goes. I actually don't have the guts to follow him. That sounds bad. Like I'm a coward. It's the truth, though. I want to know what he's doing but I also don't want to know. Once you know, you can't go back.

I can't pinpoint when he started to change. I've been focused on my own stuff. Like, I'm eighteen, I'm supposed to be focused on me, right? Figuring out what I want to do with my life and all that.

It wasn't until a couple months ago that I connected his creepy behavior to his concussion history. You know when footballers get too many concussions and it can lead to aggressive behavior? Poor impulse control? Violence? Suicide? He's got that, I think.

Actually, it wasn't me that connected the two. It was Mom.

A few months ago, I walked in from practice and went to grab a Bang from the refrigerator, as I do, and Mom was standing behind Dad near the sink, saying, "Football players and boxers are at the highest risk."

"Risk of what?" I said. Whitney looked up from her Pop-Tart at the kitchen table and gave me a death stare. Like speaking was risky. Dad stood at the sink, staring out the window, holding his mug midair.

"CTE," Mom said. There was a beat of heavy silence, and then the explosion. Like a grenade.

Dad threw his mug so hard against the sink basin, ceramic chips ricocheted back up and landed across the kitchen floor. "Don't call me crazy," he said, his voice held tight by gritted teeth. "It's you. It's you. Everything wrong with this house is you." He stomped out to the garage and left.

"Well, that didn't go as I planned," Mom said, surveying the multitude of broken shards across the floor, one sliver caught in her dark hair.

"What did you expect?" Whitney said. "You word things wrong. You say the worst things at the worst times. And he's not wrong about you." Whit stomped upstairs.

"What's CTE?" I said.

Mom smiled a funny smile, her face got blotchy, and she shook her head, the sliver of ceramic holding tight to her hair. She didn't want to talk. She turned away from me and started picking up chips. "When I break something, I clean it up. When he breaks something, I clean it up," she said, her voice cold.

I should have told her she had a chip in her hair. I should have helped her clean up, but in that moment, I hated all of them. I got back in my car, drove to the lake, and, in the parking lot, searched *CTE* on my phone.

I don't think I would have connected his creep factor with CTE, I still don't know if that's his problem, but now that Mom's called it out, I can't disconnect the two.

I have to admit, connecting them is a relief. Like the feeling of having a word on the tip of your tongue. You can't place it, you're reaching for it, and suddenly it slides into your brain smooth like butter. If there's no explanation, then he's just fucking psycho. Blaming all his strange crap on boxing is a relief.

I mean, he's not always fucked-up. His mind is clear sometimes, and we talk. In those moments, everything seems okay. I think, *Well, maybe he's getting better.*

Most of the time, though, he's not himself. Like someone put electrodes to his temples, gave him a jolt, and all his neurotransmitters froze. I can't stand it, the way he is. And no way could I stand it if that happened to me. If that happened to me, I'd choose death. It sounds spoiled, like Jack says, but it's the truth. I'd seriously rather die.

Wrestling isn't boxing, I know that. I've only had two concussions, and they were minor. Still, I had to follow recovery protocol—sitting in my bedroom for a week, no lights, no screen, no reading, just me and my thoughts—and the last time all I could think of was my dad and his concussions. CTE isn't some intangible thing. It's real and weird and can't control its temper and says off-the-wall garbage and walks naked in the backyard.

Contact sports used to shimmer and pulse with vitality for me. Now they have a nursing-home vibe: stale air, the cringy small talk of afternoon talk shows, someone arguing with themselves, a beeping sound that a nurse turns off—oh well, bradycardia isn't that big of a deal—the smell of unwashed hair and urine, canaries trapped in a glass box, making nests for babies they will never have.

I swallowed Mom's seed of doubt months ago. It settled in the pit of my stomach and sprouted. Now it's overgrown, and it's too big to ignore.

I could never again compete like I used to. Go all in. The doubt would whisper things in my ear during meets. I'd hesitate. I'd blow it. I kind of hate Mom for giving me that doubt. Sometimes I wish I never heard her say CTE. Sometimes I wish I thought Dad was crazy just because he was crazy. He could be. He could just be fucking psycho.

Point is, I can't take that scholarship.

And I'm not sure what my parents will do when they find out.

~ My Journal ~

Stupid Elsa Middleton. She took a photo of me during study prep class and it looked like I was picking my nose. I wasn't, but it looked like it. At lunch, she ran from table to table in the cafeteria, showing everyone, as if it was the most important thing ever. Like she won the lottery.

People were sticking their fingers up their nose at me the rest of the day, actually picking their noses to make fun of a picture of me that only looked like I was picking my nose. How does that make sense?

Stupid Elsa with her smelly braids and her fat boobs. Her and her stupid friends, always watching those YouTube improv shorts, laughing like they're being recorded, like they're in a movie. They are idiots. Always out to trick you and trap you.

MC, age 11

CHAPTER 25

MEG

DAY 2, 1:48 P.M.

Which Joe are they going to get? Even as he walks from his car to greet them, even as he makes eye contact and shakes their hands, I wonder. He shakes Flemming's hand first. Nice touch, to not come across as sexist. Even as Joe says the correct words, "Do you have information to help us?" Even as he strikes the correct tone, worried yet stable, I don't trust he can conceal his dark half.

I've picked his behavior apart, carefully, intently, like peeling the papery, dry skin of a garlic clove. I've put so much effort into trying to figure out what happened to him, but I've been wasting my time. What does the cause matter? It's the effect you have to live with.

Becker and Flemming ask me if I wouldn't mind waiting in a different room. My skin itches with worry. I tell them I'm going to call my parents, and that I'll sit in my car.

The cushioned seats in my car are cold and smell of wet dog

even though we've never had a dog. I have no intention of calling my mom. I back my car out of the garage and park in my driveway, so I'll know when they leave.

Since I killed one of my children, it's plausible I killed another. That's the assumption the detectives are going with. They're assuming a lot. They're assuming I killed Carson. They're assuming I killed Carson because he reminded me of my brother and I was scared for my other children. It's not a bad assumption. They really dug deep. Made connections no one made before.

Growing up with Nathan was scary. My first memories are kindergarten age. I would jolt awake in my bed, struggling to breathe, a pillow smashed in my face, his knees bony and heavy on my small shoulders. He thought it was funny. He would always pull the pillow away before I passed out. Before he'd leave, he'd smile and say, "Don't tattle, or I'll kill Mom." His tone was casual and nonthreatening. When you're little, the line between joking and serious is magical and mysterious. I thought he must be joking, but I didn't want to find out.

At the public pool in the summer, he would hold me under for too long. It would look like we were playing, but my lungs were stretched and my heart was pumping with terrorized adrenaline. I had gone so long without tattling, it didn't even cross my mind anymore. This was what it was like to have siblings. Like, at night, you take a bath, brush your teeth, read a book, and hope your brother doesn't try to kill you.

I was eating dinner at a friend's house when it clicked. My ten-year-old friend held up her plate and asked her fourteen-year-old brother to drop a pickle wedge next to her hot dog, and he did. I was appalled by her trust and I was appalled that he did it without an evil *I'll get you later for having the nerve to ask me for something* sparkle in his eye or a feigned punch to make her flinch. He forked a pickle from the jar, placed it gently next to her hot dog, and went back to eating his own hot dog.

The realization clicked like *Tetris* pieces locking in: Siblings weren't a dangerous part of every kid's life. My brother wasn't normal. Something was wrong with him. Later that night, I told my parents, "He doesn't belong here. He belongs in a place for people like him."

With their loving eyes full of ache, my dad bit his lip and my mom said, "We can't do that to him. He's our child, same as you. We'll make sure you're safe."

I hadn't been safe for as long as I could remember. I rode my bike to the hardware store, bought a bolt and a padlock for my bedroom door, kept the key around my neck and tucked under my shirt. That key made me feel safer than my parents ever did. They weren't bad people. They were simply unequipped for what life dealt them.

I was scared of my brother until the day I moved out. I'm still scared of him. My kids have never met him.

My oldest boy, Carson, was sensitive, excitable, and peculiar. A wobbly little toddler who liked playing with my hair when I read him books. He liked holding a strand between two fingers and rubbing it like he was rolling the end of a joint. He liked eating macaroni three times a day. He refused to drink milk and would only drink juice. He was neat with his toys, picky with his food, and messy in the bathtub. He'd chew on the soap and scoop water out of the tub and onto the floor. He shared his Matchbox cars with his little brother, David, but not his trains. He'd pet David's head and say, "Good boy." Funny, and sweet.

He also liked to dig along the windowsill for dead houseflies and pull off their wings. He stared at things—his toys, the grass, bugs, people walking their dogs—intently. It was peculiar but not alarming. He didn't talk much, but the pediatrician assured us that wasn't uncommon. When three-year-old Carson ate the neighbor's goldfish, the pediatrician said it was unfortunate but not quite worrisome due to his young age.

When it's the first kid, you don't know what's normal and what's not, especially when they're young. I told myself, little kids are weird. I'd see kids having temper tantrums at the grocery store or headbutting their sibling or knocking things off shelves. They're all weird, I told myself. He'll grow out of it.

When Jamie was born, Joe's sister brought Carson and David to the hospital to meet their baby sister. Carson walked up to Jamie's bassinet, went on his tiptoes and peered in, and gently put a pink cat stuffie by her feet. Sweet. Gentle. Then he looked at Joe and said, "She's not coming home with us, is she?" We laughed. Kids say the darnedest things.

The summer before Carson started kindergarten, I set up a toddler pool in the backyard. Carson was five, David was four, and Jamie had just turned two. I stepped inside the house to get my camera—I was in the cold whoosh of air-conditioning for three seconds—and when I stepped back out into the heat and scorching sun, my vision went dark at the edges for a moment. I squinted against the sun to check the pool. Jamie was gone. I looked left and right, then back at the boys. David was playing with a plastic boat. Carson was standing in the pool, hands on hips, triumphant, and gazing down at the water.

My heart stopped. I knew. I just knew.

I ran to the pool. Carson had Jamie's small body trapped under his foot. She was face down, arms flailing, his foot on her back. He had this curious expression, as if she were a bug and he wanted to see what would happen if he plucked one of her legs. I knocked him over and pulled her out. She was coughing, she vomited, but she was okay.

I told myself he deserved another chance. He was little and he'd made a mistake. I had a talk with him about how babies are fragile, and living things need air to keep living.

Weeks later it was just after dawn when a noise woke me—the squeak of a mattress. I walked into Jamie's room and found Carson in her crib, straddling her small body and smothering her with one of his stuffies.

After, when I had Carson and David settled in front of the television, I brought Jamie into my bed. With her warm, wet cheek against mine, I rocked her back to sleep.

When Joe woke, I told him what happened in whispers as Jamie slept between us, snoring softly.

"Christ, it's like your childhood all over," he whispered. "It's like karma."

"Karma? For not letting my brother kill me, I'm owed bad karma?"

"No. I don't mean that. I'm just waking up. Sorry. I mean, do you think it's genetic?"

"What does it matter the cause, how are we going to deal with it?"

"What can we do?" he said. "We just keep our eyes on them."

Our eyes meant *my eyes*. Joe still slept like a baby at night. I slept on Jamie's floor, in fits and starts. Every time my eyes would close, I would tell myself, *Do not let your guard down*.

I quit my part-time job at the Art Institute. Carson started wetting the bed and sucking on Jamie's pacifiers. He wasn't ready for a full day of kindergarten, and I wasn't ready for having to constantly explain his behavior, so I signed him up for another year of preschool.

When Carson was home, I would not go to the bathroom unless I brought Jamie. If Jamie waddled out of my line of sight, for even a moment, I'd have a sudden panic attack that had me gasping for air and left the taste of Nathan's foul pillow in my mouth.

Every second of every day was exhausting. I got UTIs from having a full bladder all the time. I went on antianxiety medications to manage heart palpitations and hyperventilation.

Joe and I fought a lot. I was tired and grouchy and had too much responsibility. Joe told me I just needed to relax a little. I told him to fuck off. So many times.

Then Carson had his accident. He was gone, and I stopped having heart palpitations and UTIs. I slept through the night. Night after night after night.

Jamie doesn't remember her near-death. She was only two. I've never told her the story for fear it would mess with her head. She might ask if she was held underwater too long, if oxygen deprivation could have affected her brain. Grades never came easy to her. Sports never came easy to her. I don't want her to blame one thing on the other.

And it's not only Jamie I never told the story to. I never talked about Carson's dangerous side to any of the kids. Talking ill of a dead child is like punching a puppy.

I have asked Jamie if she remembers him. She's said maybe, but maybe only because she's seen photos or because Dave has told stories about him.

Being nearly murdered by our older brothers, Jamie and I share a trauma bond. Then again, is it a bond if only one of you knows about it?

———•———

Flemming and Becker walk out the front door of my house, and I step out of my car to meet them.

I search their eyes, trying to discern what Joe told them. They give nothing away. They are more professional than I guessed when I met them. Yesterday I figured Flemming for a tired middle-aged woman who couldn't wait to retire. I made Becker out as a former weed smoker turned mid-thirties suburban man with nice hair and a round ass his kids probably like to whack. I didn't think a place like Sugar Glen could churn out brutally clever detectives. I mean, how many missing persons cases can there be in a suburb of only forty thousand people?

It's possible this is a naive question. I live in a safe upper-class neighborhood, but there are seedy apartment complexes and river-bordered industries. Maybe there are drug deals and death deals done under that huge bridge in the dark or down by the steel plant. Just because I haven't heard of the missing persons cases and the murders that happen here doesn't mean there aren't any. It only means my local police department has a good PR team and my town newspapers are understaffed.

If I'm going to have a chance with these two, I have to think smarter. I stand straight, convince myself I am not the criminal they think I am. Convince myself I want them to dig deep to solve this and I am going to make sure they are doing their job. In fact, I am going to help.

"The knife you found," I say. "Right away you assumed McClane had hurt someone. Could it be McClane's blood?"

They look at each other briefly. I can't read their exchange. Are they deciding who's going to answer my question or are they registering that I'm asking a good one?

"We submitted it to testing," Becker says plainly, no traces of the taunting tone he'd given me before his interview with Joe. He's more serious and thoughtful. "We submitted other items belonging to McClane for comparison."

What other belongings? His comb or a sock from his dirty laundry basket? His pillowcase? I want to ask, but I'm distracted—what did Joe tell Becker that subdued his mood?

"We'll know on Monday," Becker says.

"What about McClane's friends?"

"We've talked to Natalie Marin and Jack Latner," Becker says. "We'll talk to Hudson White next. I guess McClane was stressed about a wrestling scholarship. He was going to turn it down."

"Oh." It comes out like an unexpected hiccup.

Of course. Of course he didn't want to wrestle anymore. It's stunning that I missed it. I was so caught up in Joe's nonsense, it made me dumb.

They tell me they'll be in touch, and they walk toward their shared car.

I want to ask about the kiddie porn but I'm tired. I'm tired, and I hate them. I hate how they're unearthing our secrets. I hate how they've turned on me. How they are so convinced. And I hate Carla for siccing them on me. When you share private, sensitive information about your child during a tender moment with a friend, you don't expect that friend to spill it to the police. The fucking nerve.

After they drive away, fury propels me down my driveway and across the street. The sun glares, mocking the street's quiet peace. Two doors down from Carla's house, two children doodle with chalk on their sidewalk. In the other direction, a worker slathers asphalt on a driveway, absorbed in mundane routine. How dare everyone carry on as if the world isn't crumbling to pieces? I hammer on Carla's door with the edge of my fist.

As she opens the door, her face slips into an empathetic smile. "Meg," she says warmly.

"What the fuck, Carla? Painting me as a monster, then baking me your guilt-muffins to make yourself feel better?"

"What?" Confusion pinches her features. "What are you talking about?"

"Telling the police Carson had developmental issues *just like my brother*. What is that?"

"Only because they kept asking. They asked for all these details about Carson—"

"Bullshit." I cut her off. They wouldn't fixate on Carson without a nudge.

"Honestly, Meg. It's not, it's not cool—you coming over here and yelling at me." She inhales sharply, trying to compose herself. "I know you're stressed," she says, reaching out to touch my forearm. "But there's no excuse to blame me for—"

"Blame?" I say through clenched teeth.

That's all I've ever felt. My son's accident—blamed on the mother, of course. My brother's violence—my fault for provoking him. Joe's messed up. I must have not been able to help him how he needed me to. McClane's disappearance. Who's to blame?

I can't stand her warm, moist fingers on my forearm. I flinch from her touch and shove her shoulder back so she can't touch me.

Her foot catches on the welcome rug—smiling sunflowers—and she stumbles backward. I expect the wall behind to catch her, but it's inches too far away, and she falls back in slow motion. Slow is good, I think, at least she won't hurt her back, but her ass hits the ground kinda hard. Her head bumps against her foyer table, setting the legs wobbling, and her key bowl tips off the edge. The ceramic bowl strikes her head with a *thud* and shatters on the floor.

"Meg?" she says, confused, as blood seeps into her eye from the gash above her brow.

"I'm so sorry, Carla." Blood slips down half her face. It was such a minor injury—why is there so much blood? "I'm really sorry. What can I—"

"Get out," she sobs, her body shaking on the floor.

CHAPTER 26

McClane

4 HOURS UNTIL MISSING

Hud's apartment complex looks like a slum set in a postapocalyptic sci-fi movie. Crap-brown aluminum siding. Six tall units crammed together and crowding out sunlight. Narrow stairwells with flickering lightbulbs and an elevator right out of a nightmare.

Train tracks to the east, the river and steel factories to the south, and everything worse to the west. The neighboring city, Hellenbrook, is a casino town. When we first got our licenses, we went there. It was depressing as shit. And that's not an easy thing to do, depress a bunch of sixteen-year-olds on a joy ride. So we say Shady Grove is the gateway to Hell. We've gotten serious mileage out of that joke.

With all these people stacked vertically, the parking lot is always crammed. I drive around for a while before I find a spot. We step out of the car, shut the doors, and it hits me. "Oh man. I forgot his backpack."

"No big deal, Mick," Jack says. "We'll swing by your house for it after. We're just checking on Hud, that's why we're here."

We are here for Hud, but there are other reasons too. Selfish reasons. If I'm worrying about Hud, I don't have to think about my scholarship. I don't have to stress about Natalie. Hud's problems add levity. He's right about that. How people want to dig into his sad life to make their own problems smaller. Seriously, though, if Hud knew Nat was pregnant, he wouldn't mind me using him as a distraction.

Three guys stand against the building, smoking marijuana, looking sleepy and homeless. One of them has this mustache and long beard that makes you wonder if bro is vibing that look to add humor to the world or if he takes himself seriously. They could be Hud's friends or not, I don't recognize them. The door is propped with a brick.

"S'up," one of them says.

"S'up," Jack says as we open the door and step into the cement stairwell. It smells like pizza, smoke, and vomit, and the light's flickering.

I'm walking behind Jack. "S'up," I say and laugh.

"What, bro? Just trying to avoid getting murdered." He flinches at something up in front of him. "Aw, shit, look at that fucking spider, man." He hugs the railing as we pass a brown recluse in the corner.

I laugh again. "Who's gonna mess with you? You're the goat. That's why I brought you. To be my bodyguard."

"Fuck off," he says, but it's lighthearted. He's not insulted by me poking fun. He knows he's jumpy, he knows he can be a wuss, and takes a sort of pride in being the butt of the joke. Hud says Jack is comfortable in his pussiness, and it's true. Sometimes Hud is dead-on. Jack says, "Fucking light's glitching. Feels like we're in the Matrix.

Yo, did you ask Natalie if any of her friends want a prom date?"

"Sorry, I forgot."

"Dude, it's coming."

"I've got you. I'll ask."

"Like, just a friend thing." He's starting to huff as we corner the third floor. Hud's on six. "No hookups. I mean, I wouldn't mind a hookup, obviously, but I don't expect that."

"I get you."

"What does Natalie think of you going to college with her staying here?"

"I dunno." I don't know, but now I'm thinking about the baby. Like, logistics and stuff. I'm trying to visualize how that would work, her visiting my dorm room with a baby and all its food and diapers or whatever.

"Is she planning to visit on the weekends?"

"I guess." I'm imagining her and the baby sleeping over in my dorm room. It doesn't seem like that would work. Would my roommate be cool with that? Is it allowed, even?

"Where are Natalie's parents from?"

I laugh. "Dude, what are you even talking about?"

"Just giving you a 'How well do you know your girlfriend?' quiz. You failed, son." His turn to laugh.

"Laugh all you want. Those are just details. We are connected. Like, deeply."

"I don't need the sloppy details, bro."

But it's true. We *are* deeply connected. We are in deep shit too.

——— • ———

Jack and I step out of the stairwell. Hud's door is the first to our right. I go to knock but it's cracked open. The TV's on loud. Jack gives me wide eyes. Like, what is this, a horror movie? What are we walking into?

"Hud? Mr. White? It's McClane Hart and Jack Latner. Door's open, so we're stepping in."

No answer, but like I said, the TV's on loud, so they might not have heard. We walk down a shotgun hallway to a kitchenette attached to a small family room. Jack's breathing heavy behind me.

Hud's dad is in a recliner, watching *The Mandalorian*.

"Mr. White?" I say.

He flinches in his chair and spills his can. "Jesus, you scared me."

"Sorry. The door was open. We're just looking for Hud."

"He's not here. Went with some friends, I think."

"Mr. White, is Hud okay?" I say. "He got hurt at school today."

"Don't I know it. They had me pick him up." I wait for him to give more information, but he stares at the TV. "This Baby Yoda," he says. "He's cute. You watch this show?"

"I've heard it's good," I say.

"I watched it," Jack says. "First season is the best. I like Mando."

Mr. White turns his head toward us, looks at Jack and me, really looks at us, like he hasn't seen us since we were in elementary. His eyes look glassy. "Who was it that hurt him? Was it Bitty or Rowly?"

"I'm not sure." I should know. I was there. I think back. Longish hair, black-and-red flannel. Black tattoo on the dude's wrist—an animal's face, big ears. A cat, maybe? A donkey? "Did you hear who it was, Jack?" I say.

"No."

"Bitty should know better," Mr. White says.

"Do you think Hud should have his head checked at the hospital, Mr. White?"

"I had to listen to the vice principal give me sympathy. It was shit. Hud came home. I fell asleep. When I woke up, I heated up some frozen burritos, went to see if he wanted one, and he was gone."

I'm not sure if he heard me about the hospital, so I say, "Maybe he should get checked out for concussions or whatever."

"Nah, he'll be okay. He's tough. He's small but tough."

That's true, Hud is tough, but I don't think your personality matters when it comes to head injuries. I'm not gonna say that. Maybe Mr. White's got an issue with health insurance or bills that would prevent him from taking Hud to the hospital even if he wanted to.

"Thanks, Mr. White. We'll shut the door on our way out," I say.

In the stairwell, heading down, I say, "That's weird, though, right? That we don't know who knocked out Hud? Guy had long hair."

"Bitty or Row. Both those dudes have messy brown hair. Could be AJ." He's listing off the guys on drugs who are not chill stoners. Guys who deal or are hooked and come off as pissy, guys who are looking to work out their personal problems with their fists. Guys who fit that description *and* manage to show up at school here and there—those guys you can count on one hand.

"One of those guys have a tattoo on their wrist? I remember black ink on his wrist." I'm jogging down the cement steps, relieved to be out of Hud's apartment. It's a different type of depressing than my place. More like, Hud's never getting out of there.

"Maybe it was a bracelet," Jack says.

"Bracelet? What? No, man. It was a tattoo. I think it was a cat or donkey."

"Bro, who gets a donkey tattoo?" Jack says, his tone amused and curious, like he's gearing up to go down a rabbit hole. "Was it Eeyore?"

"Who?"

"Eeyore. The donkey from *Winnie the Pooh*. Yo, but why was their door open? That was creepy, right?"

"I don't know. Not really. 'I like Mando.'" I mimic him, laughing. He laughs too, and our voices echo off cement walls. He jumps down five stairs to the landing, lifts his chin, and shouts, "Mando! Mando!" just for the echo.

Outside, we're headed to the car and I turn back to those dudes leaning against the building. "You guys know Hudson White?"

"Yes, sir," says the one in the middle. "Dude is fucking legend."

"What do you mean?"

"He's a good guy," the one wearing glasses says. Calm, sincere.

I nod and ask the middle guy, "Why is he legend?"

"Fucked around with a scary dude. Probably gonna find out," says the one in the middle.

"Who's the scary dude?"

"Gangster, bro. Vice Lords."

Other guy on the end, the one with the mustache, exhales whatever he's smoking and laughs. "It's on like Donkey Kong."

CHAPTER 27

MEG

DAY 2, 3:24 P.M.

I step off Carla's porch, my stomach sick and the sunny day vibrating with unease. A battered two-door, its tire wells gnawed by rust, pulls in front of my house and Whitney steps out. I thought she was in her room. The car speeds off before I can catch a glimpse of the driver.

"Whitney?" I call. She turns and waits for me. "Where'd you go?" I say.

Now that I'm close enough, I notice her face—her glassy eyes, her trembling lower lip. "It's on the news now," she says, her tone cold. "My phone is blowing up. Everyone from school is texting me. People I don't even know are texting me."

I haven't even thought to turn on the news. "What are they saying?"

"Don't worry, nothing about what they found in his room," she says coldly. "Yet." Her gray eyes lose their icy sharpness and grow curious. "Why were you at Mrs. Heely's?"

I picture Carla, her forehead cut open, blood streaming into her eye. My heart flutters. Afraid I've messed up, I replay what happened at Carla's. No. It was an accident. She knows that. When she calms down, she'll realize.

"It's nothing important. Who drove you home?"

She shakes her head, annoyed, and stomps into the house.

"Whitney?" I turn to go after her, when my phone vibrates in my pocket. A text.

The police want to interview me tomorrow.

My heart picks up extra beats. My fingers bang out a text quickly.

We need to meet tonight and plan what you'll say.

Another text comes through.

I can't meet tonight.

I text.

Meet me at the gas station on 47th and Litchfield at 9 pm or I'll come to your house.

I stand in the driveway, heart thumping while I wait for a

response. I wait minutes before the response comes.

Okay. 9 pm.

I'm going to need some coffee. It might be a late night.

——— • ———

Joe's sitting at the kitchen table. His presence is startling, honestly. I've gotten so used to his catlike behavior—his slipping silently away, his absence.

He dips a cookie in a glass of milk and shoves it in his mouth. He's so focused on his cookie, he's like a little kid. I want to protect him, tell him whatever it is, it's okay. I have an urge to use our most sacred line, our private joke. I consider saying it—"Do you want me to kick you in the balls?"—to make him laugh, to break the ice. The two of us could use a good laugh. It's been a long time.

The thing is, I've run out of humor. I gulp down a glass of water. "What did the detectives say?"

He doesn't answer. I wait, listening to his loud chewing and nose-breathing. I want to scream and rip my hair out, but I've gotten good at waiting. I've gotten good at faking calm. I've gotten so good at faking calm, I have become a calmer person. It's like a thick coat of shellac around my heart, separating me from my emotions. I can sense my emotions like the rumble of a freight train miles away on a silent snowy day, but they can't touch me.

He dips another cookie in his murky glass of milk. I give up on him answering. I make coffee. My stomach is sour, and I haven't eaten since I stuffed Carla's treasonous muffins in my mouth. I force-feed myself a bowl of cereal.

I put my bowl in the sink and leave the kitchen with my coffee when he says, "They didn't ask much about McClane, but they think you know more than you're saying."

I stop in the doorway, waiting for more. Always at his mercy. "And?"

"They wanted to know about Carson." His tone is soft, confused and sad. "They asked about your brother too. They met him today. He's on their mind."

"What else?"

"Seems like they think you killed Carson," he says thoughtfully. "I'm not sure how they'd prove that."

Even though I already knew what they thought, my knees go wobbly. I lean against the doorway. "What did you tell them?"

"I told them you didn't," he says plainly. "I told them you love your kids. I told them you sacrificed your well-being for Carson's. I told them how you used to read him all those books about filling people's buckets with kindness. Books about siblings. That one about the older brother letting his little sister come into the blanket fort he made. You must have read that one a hundred times."

His words take me by surprise. I can't believe he remembers. I can't believe he has my back like I have his even though our relationship has gone dark and distant. It takes me so much by surprise, tears slip out. Without my consent, without my knowledge, I am silently crying.

"I told them you never let the kids meet your brother. I told them you were careful." He stuffs a mushy cookie in his mouth. With his mouth full, he says, "Weird that I haven't seen your brother in decades. I wonder what he's like these days."

He stands up and heads out to the garage. No explanations. His switch flipped, I guess. On the table, cookie crumbs and small milk puddles wait for my tidying. I don't know how he doesn't see the mess he makes.

It's true about my brother. The kids have never met him. They've asked. They don't even know where my parents and brother live. I've never given the address, in case they get too curious. My parents have spent plenty of time with my kids, but always here in my house.

Like I said, my parents are good people. Exploitable, but good. They are still protective of Nathan, so I doubt they told the detectives about how dangerous my childhood was. But the big bad thing Nathan did, they couldn't sugarcoat that.

———•———

Nathan and Adam met in swim lessons when they were both nine. My mom and Adam's mom, Anne, became best friends. Nothing bonds two women more intensely than facing the same overwhelming challenge.

Adam received the diagnosis that my mom never sought for Nathan. Mom thought a diagnosis would be bullshit, that doctors would blindly throw a dart at a board and pick whichever known condition landed nearest to Nathan's behavior. She was convinced Nathan's behavior was beyond the bounds of any recognized medical condition, and that a diagnosis would hinder his future. Adam's mom thought it would get Adam the help he needed. They were both right in their own way, and neither woman judged the other. That's another thing about mothers in impossible situations. Their deep expertise in shitty complex scenarios makes them incapable of passing judgment.

Adam and Nathan had a weekly playdate. Their moms had a playdate too. I think the moms enjoyed it more. They laughed more than their sons. They sat on the couch in the living room while their sons played video games in the back room. Anne was the only adult invited into our house.

I found their conversations fascinating. Standing on the fifth stair, barely breathing, barely moving because I didn't want to creak the step, I'd eavesdrop.

Anne and Mom would gossip about teachers and share rude comments strangers had lobbed their way at the grocery store or the dentist—humiliating moments and parenting fails. They were each other's only friend, so they would also share husband stories and recipes and makeup tips. Aching for validation, I was always waiting for Mom to relay how Nathan had nearly drowned me or how she caught him trying to suffocate me. I'm not sure if she ever shared those stories, but I never heard her recount them.

Anne once said, "I love that child to death, but I pray every night he dies before me. Because with me gone, who would take care of him? Who would understand the nuances to his triggers? Bill's fucking useless." She laughed, but the sadness in her voice was heavy. "I try to see it another way, I try to pick apart my logic, but I can't."

Adam did die before his mom. Nathan killed him. They were

both seventeen when it happened. They were playing *Mario Kart* and fighting over who got to drink the last Orange Fanta, and Nathan smashed Adam's head against the fireplace.

Anne didn't fault my mom. She didn't fault Nathan. She insisted against pressing charges. She said she saw it happen, and it was an accident. She lied. She wasn't there. I was.

Anne stopped coming by, but only for my mom's sake. Anne didn't want to trigger Nathan. Anne and Mom still met for coffee, but not at the house. As far as I know, they still meet.

My parents and Nathan live in that same house I grew up in. It's about an hour south of here, in Wayfield. The house is small and old and surrounded by ten acres, a barbed wire fence all around. That fence cost three times as much as the house.

CHAPTER 28

McClane

3½ HOURS UNTIL MISSING

"I'm calling Hud 'legend' from now on," Jack says.

"He'll love that," I say. We're joking because the alternative is to wonder if getting knocked out by a gangbanger was the end of it or a taste of what's to come.

"I can't go back to Hud's tonight. I'm reffing a game." Jack is a ref for the seventh-grade rec league at the Y. He loves it. He has the most hilarious stories because seventh-graders are insane. If he ends up as a cop like he plans, he's gonna be one of those rare clutch cops who gets a kick out of kids.

"I might go back," I say.

"Don't go back there alone," he says in his enthusiastic, dramatic way—shit cracks me up. "Those kindhearted stoners could turn into low-key Dahmers after dark."

"Low-key Dahmers? Now I'm going for sure."

"Shut up, you're not," he says.

"We'll see. Plan on tomorrow for sure, though."

"How'd that asshole with the tattoo get into school anyway?" Jack says.

I think about it. "He could have come in with the crowd before the first bell. Hid in the bathroom till second period."

"That's a long damn time to hide in the bathroom, bro."

I drop Jack at his house and head home. After that argument with Mom, I don't want to run into her. I feel bad for upsetting her, but I'm sick of this family's crap. Hopefully she's hiding at her desk or grocery shopping or whatever. When she's out of the house, when he's out of the house, I breathe easier.

Dad's car is gone, but Mom's car is in the garage, so I skip the kitchen and head up to my room.

Near the top landing, if you look left, you're looking square into the bathroom. The door is open now, and Whitney's doing her makeup at the mirror. Hips pressed against the vanity, her face so close to the mirror she could kiss it, she lines her eyes with black. She calls them smoky, I call them racoonish. She's dressed like she's going out. Short jean shorts over ripped black tights, a green crop top, heavy black boots.

How skimpy she's dressed, how attention-seeking, well, it gets under my skin. I'm protective but also annoyed because, dressing like that, it just seems dumb. Naive. A bad idea. Obvious. It's so obvious.

Also, ugly.

It's not my business, I know. I've been schooled before. Jamie reamed me over and over until I learned to keep my mouth shut.

Whitney started wearing makeup in seventh grade. She wore this sky-blue glitter shadow over her whole lid. I'd say, "That's nasty,

Whitney. Why would you think that looks good? It looks phony. Guys don't like that."

Jamie shut me down. "You sound like an idiot, Mick. Why are you assuming she's wearing it for guys? Maybe she doesn't care what guys think. Maybe she's not trying to get guys. She's in *seventh* grade. She's wearing it for herself. She doesn't exist *for* guys."

If I mentioned Whit's outfit now, I'd get the same shutdown. If I say, "Guys are going to get the wrong idea with those jean shorts and that half top," she'd say, "That's on them, not on me."

She'd be right, but also, let's be real.

I'm not a dick. I'm not sexist. I don't think I'm better than her. She's smarter than me, we both know it. She's my equal. And *that's* why I'm going to be fucking honest.

"What up, Gothic? Where you going on a school night looking like the green Wicked Skank Witch of the West?" I stop on the second stair to the landing, put my hand on the railing, and wait.

"Wouldn't you like to know?"

"Duh. Why else would I ask? How many more hours you gonna be in the bathroom, drawing rings around your eyes?"

"Another hour, at least. Use the one downstairs. Or use Mom and Dad's."

"I need the shower," I say. The downstairs bathroom doesn't have a shower. "And no way to Mom and Dad's. I don't want to come across something that ruins my opinion of them."

That gets a slow glance my way and a smile. Her eyes are lined in thick black. If those are sultry smoky eyes, I'm high. "Yeah?" she says, holding her eyeliner close to her eye. "Anything weird I'd come across could only improve my opinion of them."

I play along. One pro of having siblings is fun at your parents' expense. "What? You don't love being a part of this family? You don't feel loved enough? We all love you, Gothic."

That gets a small huff of a laugh. She goes back to lining her eyes. "Correction. Mom loves the idea of this family. Dad loves nothing. Jamie loves her friends. You love Natalie. David loves himself."

I walk up the last two stairs, clear the landing, and lean my lower back against the railing so I'm facing her again. "Well, that sounds well thought out. Dare I say rehearsed to yourself in front of your mirror with your door locked." She doesn't look my way, she's applying more liner, but the side of her mouth curls into a smile. "You're totally Mom's favorite, Whit." I'm teasing, but I'm being honest too. Mom feels most in tune with Whitney. She reminds her of herself. Secretive and clever. Plus, Whitney's the baby. I mean, c'mon. All parents love the baby.

She slips her eyeliner away into her makeup bag. Finally. No more of that. She pulls out a tube of lipstick and turns to me. "You're the favorite, Mick. She tells anyone she can about your full ride. She'd run out in her PJs to tell the garbage man if she could time it right."

That wipes out my easy vibes. My lower back stiffens against the railing. Man, that wrestling scholarship is waiting around every corner, ready to jump out and spook me.

Whitney says, "Also, to show off how hip she is for wearing a long T-shirt as PJs."

"She is proud of that." I laugh. "But I'm pretty sure she talks about David's hot-shot job with the FBI more than my wrestling. She was telling me again today." I lift my voice to sound like Mom. "Call David. Ask David. David knows."

Whit thinks about that, puckering up for the mirror and applying lipstick. She smacks her lips together and studies herself in the mirror. "David knows nothing. He's seriously messed up. You know, he hasn't texted me back in months."

"That's weird. He texted me last week. Called me last night, actually." I should call him back, but I'm not up for serious talk.

She looks at me, a small crease between her eyebrows. She's a little sad, but more resolute. The lipstick color is normal, at least. Soft pink, like a seashell. "He's a dick, Mick. Our brother, he is an actual dick." Her face is serious. She means it.

That's kind of sad. I mean, yeah, he's got an ego. He's a know-it-all, but I don't think of him as a dick. I have good memories with him. Playing dodgeball in the driveway. Sledding down the big hill. Playing his games, being in his circus. He was on the bossy side, rounding us up, giving us jobs, but he made sure we were okay. He made sure we all had fun.

I like when Whitney's light and funny better, so I say, "Hey, you know who isn't Mom's favorite?"

We say it at the same time—"Jamie"—and that gets a smile from Whitney because Jamie's clutch. She's just a good person. Freewheeling. Says stupid stuff, has no regrets. Her lack of discipline, her weight, her lack of worries annoy Mom. Jamie's that kid in school who was on student council and journalism club because she wanted to be, not just to pad her college application. Got to admit, though, her do-gooder vibe, her stick-up-for-the-underdog MO used to annoy the hell out of me. God, she used to drive me nuts.

"Actually though," I say, crossing my arms in front of my chest. "Where you going?"

"Actually though. None of your business."

It comes to me. "Hey, did you hear about Hud getting in a fight?" Whit and I have such different lives, sometimes I forget we go to the same school. Maybe she heard who punched him.

"No," she says, her forehead creasing, her eyes full of worry. Whit loves Hud. She still thinks of him as that boy who was always good to her when I was telling her to get lost. "What happened?"

I don't want to worry her. "He's fine. It was a low-key throw-down. I was just curious if you heard who did it."

"No. I didn't hear." It's weird she didn't hear about it, but also not weird. Different grades have their antennas tuned in to distinct frequencies of gossip.

"He's fine," I say. Whit can be anxious, so I change the subject. "Where did you say you're going again?"

Her face melts into a sly smile. "I didn't."

"Don't tell me you're going to a party on a school night."

"I'm going to sell my body and do coke with a bunch of strangers, whom I will also be sharing needles with. Maybe some witchy, murdery stuff too. You wanna come?"

"No, but have fun with that." I drop my arms and push away from the railing.

"You think I'm kidding," she says, capping her lipstick and dropping it in her makeup bag.

"I know you're kidding." I start down the hall toward my room.

She steps through the door frame, tilting her head. Smirking. Curious. "How?"

"Because you're the smart one. Have fun at coding club, dorkwad."

"Whatever you say," she says, and I shut my door behind me.

~ My Journal ~

I'm so pissed at Jamie. She made me look like an idiot. We were at the 7-Eleven, drinking our slushies on the curb, laughing about brain freeze. Kristin and her dyke friends came out of the 7-Eleven eating sour gummies and Mike and Ikes—what insane person actually eats Mike and Ikes?—walked by us and called me a perv. Kristin's a fat pig. Frizzy hair, squinty eyes, ugly little mouth, no tits.

Before I could do anything, say anything, Jamie stood up and said don't call my brother names, bitch.

Kristin got in Jamie's face and said, I'll call him a pervert because he is a pervert. Which hurt, got to admit it. She pushed Jamie, and Jamie fell backward, her slushie flying everywhere. Jamie's hands were all cut up and bloody and she had bits of gravel lodged in her skin. Slushie all down her shirt and sticky on her legs. She looked up at me and said, I think I'm good to walk home.

Mom would probably be so mad if she found out Jamie picked a fight with those girls. But that's how Jamie is, always spouting off whenever she feels like it.

I told her she should have kept quiet. Let me deal with it.

But I'm bigger than you, she said. It's true. She's tall and kind of chunky.

So? I said.

And you froze, she said. You didn't say anything.

I would have. You should have let me.

She should have let me take care of myself. She always thinks she's right. She's a good sister but sometimes she annoys me. Dad says sisters can be annoying sometimes. That's just how it goes.

MC, age 13

CHAPTER 29

MEG

DAY 2, 8:45 P.M.

You want to know what was on that video I sent. Of course you do.

Let me set the scene. Picture a wealthy person's patio, late at night. Picture beautiful landscaping, accent lighting, all of it classy and surrounded by a privacy fence. You hear the trickle of a waterfall over a rock fixture. You hear the patio door slide shut, and a man walks into view. He's wearing a linen button-down, cargo shorts, and Crocs. He's in decent shape. He likes steak and whiskey but his cocaine habit keeps him trim. Like his landscaping, he is well-manicured. Salt-and-pepper hair and a fashionable close-cropped beard. He's fifty-six and wealthy enough to retire, but the wealthy never have enough money.

He sits down on a rich man's comfortable outdoor chair, sets his whiskey down on the table, and says, "Thursday nights have become my favorite night of the week. Get over here."

A woman comes into view. Her back is facing the camera, and you can't see her face. She's dressed like she's out for her nightly walk with her neighbor. Gym shoes. Shorts and a T-shirt, an open sweater jacket. She kneels down in front of him, unzips him, and gets to work. He doesn't even bother caressing her hair. He grabs her hair and forces her head toward his crotch, forcing himself deeper into her throat.

The man doing the head-pushing is Vincent, Joe's boss. The woman doing the work, her knees getting scraped against the stone, is me. You knew that back at *open sweater jacket*, right? Here's what you don't know. What you couldn't possibly guess.

I did it for Joe. Sounds like a load of bull, I know. But believe me, if you met Vincent, if you had to listen to this guy for five minutes, you'd know. I was taking one for the team. Big-time. This was not a passionate blow job, if such a thing exists. It was work. A filthy job, like unclogging the drain with your bare hands, spidery webs of slimy hair clinging to your skin. It was an *I would rather be doing taxes* blow job. It was an *I would rather be bagging a full season of dog poop in the yard after the snow melts* blow job. It was a fucking sacrificial blow job.

Joe wouldn't see it that way. Then again, Joe had checked out of the world of responsibilities entirely, pretended the bills paid themselves, the food arrived on its own—dropped gently onto our porch by a stork, maybe.

———•———

It's 8:50 p.m., and I'm parked at the gas station. I'm watching people walk in and out. I'm watching people stare at the digital display tick away their money. I'm watching a car emerge from the car wash like a baby's head crowning. Those big floppy brushes are twisting, beating their hundreds of bristles against the car. What crazy person goes through a car wash late at night besides someone who ran down a jogger and needs to wash away the evidence?

I drop my head against my headrest and think back to how the sequence of events led me here. The night it started, so many months before I recorded the blow job, I went down to the basement for batteries. It was January first. I always change the smoke detectors and carbon monoxide detectors on New Year's Day whether they need to be changed or not.

Joe wasn't at his desk. I accidentally bumped his mouse, and his work email popped up on his screen. He had dozens of emails that hadn't been clicked on yet. I clicked on one that said *Urgent*, dated December 18.

> *Hey Joe, I'm waiting on that report. We'd like it to go to production by Monday, so we can publish on January 3. Thanks, Vincent.*

I clicked on another, dated December 20.

> *Just checking in, Joe. Haven't heard from you. Called you yesterday, it went to voicemail. Let me know if you need anything. —Vincent*

I clicked on the next, dated December 22.

Hi Joe. I'm assuming something's happened. You're sick maybe. I hope everything is okay. I'll go with Liz's report for the January 3 email series. Call me when you can. No worries. I put you down for sick days. The office will be closed for the holidays. See you back in January. —Vincent

In the emails Vincent comes across as a reasonable boss, a good boss, but I know the guy. We went to dinner with him a few times. I've been to his house. I've helped his sinewy blond wife make mojitos. Vincent was frequently keyed up on coke. When they were in-office before the pandemic, Joe said Vincent would chew someone out with his door purposefully open to induce fear.

That New Year's Day, I read through all Joe's work emails. It looked like he hadn't opened his inbox for three weeks. Which was weird. He had been spending time in the basement, maybe four hours a day, and he was spending another three or four hours in his car. I'd assumed he was working, like me.

I marched up to our room, ready to bust him.

He lay in our bed, our comforter mummying his head and body, sleeping. His bare feet and calves, uncovered, hung off the bed. My fury dissolved. Something was wrong. I knew. I just couldn't put my finger on it. I still couldn't. *Be kind.* I sat in bed next to him and spoke gently, "Hey, Joe?"

"What?" Grouchy.

My words light, tolerant, I said, "I saw that your boss has been emailing you."

"You're spying on me?" Pissed off, but still under the covers.

"No. I was getting batteries. I bumped the mouse, saw your screen."

Agitated, he said, "Do you want to know when I go to the bathroom too? No wonder Whitney locks herself in her room."

My head pulsed hot. Here I was, trying to be nice—tolerant—and he's turning this around, making it my fault? My voice escalating, my skin itchy, I said, "That's not the point. The point is, are you going to turn in your report?"

"No."

"Why not? What happened?"

"Leave me alone."

I took a breath, forced compassion in, let it settle like a feather on top of glowing-hot coals. My voice calmer, I said, "Why won't you talk to me? Tell me what happened?"

"Nothing happened."

"So you're just not going to work?"

He said nothing. I waited for five minutes, ten minutes—cycling through emotions. Anger, bitterness, confusion, sadness, compassion, empathy, frustration, anger and bitterness again—before I noticed he was snoring.

Down in the basement, I emailed Vincent from Joe's work account.

> *So sorry, Vincent. Yes, we're sick. We're okay now.*
> *I'll get you that report by Monday. Thanks, Joe.*

The thing was, we were still paying off David's and Jamie's student loans and we still had two car payments and our mortgage and all the rest of the standard bills. Joe's paycheck was twice mine, and we couldn't lose it. I spent the night going through Joe's files. I took his old reports, plugged in the new data, and used Eileen to rewrite sentences, make things gel.

By dawn I had a decent report. Nothing to brag about, but passable. My body threatening flu symptoms, I hit send.

A half day later, Vincent responded.

Looks great, Joe. Glad you're back.

It went on like that for months. I did my job during the day and Joe's job at night, working like the elves while the shoemaker slept. I wasn't a happy elf, delighted to make the sleepy old shoemaker money. I was a sick, angry elf, resentful as fuck, tempted to defecate on the shoemaker's desk or dump a cup of ice-cold water in his mouth while he snored. But we were on this ship together. If the shoemaker sank, I sank too.

When they were little, I read each of my kids "The Elves and the Shoemaker." I remembered it as a story of generosity and kindness. The moral was to help someone who was down on their luck, and good karma will boomerang back to you. The elves witnessing that sad old shoemaker and wanting to help. The shoemaker and his wife getting back on their feet, being able to buy food and pay their landlord. Then, sneaking a peek at the elves after midnight, finding out those elves worked in their underwear, and realizing they could repay them with new tiny outfits.

Looking back on it now with fresh eyes, that shoemaker was a dick. Reaping rewards night after night. Getting rich off the blood and sweat of anonymous mystery workers. That cobbler might have been lazy, he might have been senile—after all, he couldn't muster the energy or know-how to make a single pair of shoes anymore—but in the end, he was mostly a dick.

Because when the shoemaker sees it's these little naked elves who have made him rich, he doesn't give them a cut, he doesn't give them a room, he gives them an outfit. And those elves, they're so used to servitude, they're truly happy to have clothes. They don't think to ask for more.

I'd write a different ending. The elves kill the shoemaker, stab him with their leather-poking needles, and sew his eyes shut in symbolism. Old man was blind to their suffering.

By mid-March, I was dangerously sleep deprived. I was cold-sweating all the time, and my right eyelid was twitchy. I was working two jobs, half-assed at both. Joe never mentioned our conversation or his job. He was so much worse than I'd imagined.

Vincent stopped by one morning when Joe was gone. I made him a cup of tea and we sat at the kitchen table. I was nervous as hell. I was nervous he came to fire Joe, to say his reports were inadequate.

He told me he knew. He said I shouldn't have to stretch myself so thin, shouldn't have to stress so much. We could work something out. My limbs softened under his generosity, on the promise of relief. He stood, walked over to me, unzipped his pants, and held his dick out like he was a waiter showing me their featured marbleized ribeye.

I was so shocked, I did what I always did: took the path of least resistance.

After he finished deep in my throat, he said, "I'll keep Joe on for now. You don't have to work his job. Renee has girls' night on Thursdays at eight. Park down the street and meet me around back."

So the story goes. The elves got propositioned by the landlord. And those elves thought, sucking that dick won't be so bad. It will be so much quicker with less carpal tunnel pain than working with leather all night long.

Seven blow jobs under their tiny belts, and with the elves exhausted from their never-ending compromises, they had a thought. It was so obvious, they were kicking themselves they hadn't thought of it five blow jobs ago. They would blackmail the landlord.

So I set up my camera. I recorded Vincent and me. The next morning, I sent him the video and a text message.

Shame if Renee found out.

When I hit send, I hadn't known McClane was missing.

———•———

There's a knock on my passenger's-side window. I unlock the doors, and Vincent slips into the front seat. "I can't believe you sent me that video," he says, seething. "That was really messed up. You are messed up."

"Me?" I laugh. Of course he would think his behavior was reasonable. "I was sitting in my kitchen, fretting about my husband, and you put your dick in my face."

"I thought you liked it." Most repeated statement by assholes everywhere.

I give him the most *that's bullshit* stare ever given.

He's twitchy and flustered. "Those detectives are coming to my house tomorrow. Becker and Flintstone."

"Becker and Flemming."

"Right. Flemming. I have to tell them I had nothing to do with McClane."

How did they know to contact Vince in the first place? The only thing I can think of is they were able to see the history of my phone's location. Did they get a warrant? Christ, I should have already called a lawyer. I'm overwhelmed by the urge to smash my head against the steering wheel.

"I'm going to tell them the truth," he says. "We were having an affair."

"An affair?" I laugh. "More like extortion."

His left eyelid twitches. His palm scrubs his jaw. "Whatever. Anything is better than being suspected of foul play in a missing persons case."

His words hit me like a slap on a cold day. I don't want to be in my car, talking to this asshole. I don't want Joe to find out how he's staying on the payroll. I don't want to be scheming against the police. I don't want any of this. I just want McClane back.

"Just tell them I stopped by your house because I was worried about Joe. He's been acting strange."

His face turns stony. "They think I did something to your son, Meg. They mentioned a bloody knife. They think you and me did something bad to your son. I cannot afford to get caught up in this. I'd rather lose Renee."

I need to take a bat to his confidence. "My face is not in that video. Yours is. Maybe I'll send it to everyone in your company. You won't just lose Renee."

"You wouldn't."

"You doubt what I'd do? How low I'd go? You, of all people?"

He makes a fist with his right hand. He wants to pound the dashboard but he bites his bottom lip instead. He stares me down, his eyes cold. If he could get away with it, he'd kill me.

I don't flinch. "Get out of my car. Don't tell them about us or I'll send the video. Every single person at your company. Everyone you know." I throw my head back and exaggerate an orgasm expression with sound effects. Such an obnoxious thing to do. I didn't know I was capable of acting so juvenile. I'm giddy. Back to serious and stone-faced, I say, "Out."

He stares at me, angry but curious, like he's trying to understand who he's dealing with. He steps out. I expect him to slam my passenger door, but he closes it quietly and walks to his car.

Shoot. I don't know what he's going to do. That didn't go how I needed it to go. He took my threat seriously, but he was too calm there at the end.

I drive away fast, afraid he might follow me and try to run me off the road. My skin prickles with heat. I'm taking the side streets at fifty miles per hour. I really don't want Joe to find out. Yes, I should have thought of that before. But when you perceive the ceiling crumbling to pieces, you only think about the next few seconds. You only think about what's in front of you. In my case, it was a dick-ticket out of pulling all-nighters and working two full-time jobs. I was exhausted and not thinking clearly.

Take me back five years when Joe and I were a team, and I'd

never imagine I'd do something like this. But that's life. You don't sign up for half of the things you end up doing.

Take me back five years, and I was proud of the career Joe had built. He kept the post-boxing—sunglasses and gloves—deals going for a bit, squeezed in side jobs, and took the broker tests. He landed at a firm and worked his way up to a six-figure salary. My salary was barely half his, but it didn't matter because we were a team.

Now I resent his climb. He didn't even have a college degree, how did he work his way up to six figures? I could do his job. I *was* doing his job *in addition to mine*. Now the upward mobility of his career looks less like hard work and more like a free pass into a club smelling of gym sweat, cigar smoke, and stripper perfume, everyone patting each other on the back for being born with a dick. It's going to be okay, I tell myself now. I breathe deep and blow it out like I'm trying to blow out a cake full of lit candles in one shot.

"It's going to be okay," I say out loud to myself. These are words my mom said frequently, and she was almost always wrong.

I turn down my street. Two cars are parked in front of my house. One is a police car. No lights, no sirens—the cars are sitting dark.

Detective Flemming is helping someone out of the police car. Blanket wrapped around their bare shoulders, their naked legs and bare feet ghostly in the dark. Short hair disheveled.

My stomach turns like a puppy chasing its tail, anticipation rising in my throat. McClane? Oh my God. Did they find McClane?

I slam my car into park in the middle of the street, leaving the engine running and the door flung open as I run toward them.

"Mrs. Hart?" A voice calls out only feet away, her shoes pounding in my direction. Caught in a fugue, I strain to place her voice. Who is she? More footsteps pad toward me, hurried and heavy, along with the clunky sound of equipment being carried.

"Did they find McClane?" the woman demands, thrusting a microphone in front of my open mouth. It bumps against my front tooth as a harsh light blinds me. "Is that McClane?"

A man's scolding voice says, "Why didn't you ask for the public's help in finding your son? Why have you stayed quiet?"

Reporters. Their vehicles must be parked on the other side of the street. I was so focused on the police car, I hadn't noticed the reporters.

I push the microphone away, flail my arms as if fending off swooping bats, and make a break for my house. Two police officers charge past me, heading into the street to hold back the reporters, yelling to give us space.

I rush toward Detective Flemming and the person she's guiding to my front door, cocooned in a heavy blanket. Dark hair, pale shoulders marred by scrapes and blood, a muddy handprint along his back. My heart leaps—McClane? Gratitude swells within me.

Then I realize. Oh. It's Joe.

CHAPTER 30

McClane

3 HOURS UNTIL MISSING

Someone opened my windows while I was out with Jack. Mom, I'm sure. She likes to let in the fresh air. I like the windows open too, but it bugs me that she was in my room. I imagine her snooping through my things while I'm stuck at school or out with my friends. Can't wait to get out of this place.

I lie on my bed, breathing through the irritation, and try to clear my mind. I think about Natalie. How her skin feels silky and firm under my fingertips. How her laugh is so free and wild when I kiss her neck. And her smile. She smiles like she's got a joke for you that you're gonna love. That she admitted she's freaking out makes me love her more. Makes me feel more normal, too. No one likes to feel alone in their crazy.

Outside my window, in the driveway, Whitney is calling to someone. I can't make out what she's saying, but her tone takes me by surprise. It's playful, confident, bitchy even, and so different from how she talks at home. A car door slams, and the engine's whirr recedes. I don't bother looking out my window. No idea who picked her up. I care a little, I mean I don't want her to end up dead in a ditch, but she's her own person and, like I said, she's smarter than the rest of us. For real, though. Always, she just knows things.

Like, this one summer before sixth grade, this new kid who moved in at the end of our street kept ringing our doorbell in the morning to play basketball. I kept turning the dude down because I wanted to watch cartoons. One time when I flopped back down on the couch as far apart as I could get from Whitney, she said, "You should be nicer to Tyler B."

"Why, so you can have the remote to yourself?"

"No. Because he's got a harder life than you."

"What do you mean?"

"I don't know. I mean, he's gay. That's got to be hard."

There were absolutely no signs Ty was gay. Dude came out sophomore year. Whitney called it when she was, like, nine.

Crazier than that, she knew random stuff about people when she was even younger. There was this girl who moved in across the street when Whit was five or six, like, real young. Whitney and the girl, I can't remember her name, seemed to get along. Jamie said, "Whit, that's so cool you'll have a friend to walk to school with as you get older."

"I don't think they're gonna stay living here."

"Why?" Jamie said. "Did she say they were gonna move?"

"No, but her dad isn't that good. I think they'll move."

The dad seemed fine to me. To Jamie too. Guy mowed his lawn

and got his mail like any other old guy on the street. Looked normal. Wore shoes, clothes without holes. Shaved.

Sure enough, they didn't make it a year in that house. One day, they were just gone. The grass got long, the FOR SALE sign went up.

I used to think it was freaky how Whit knew things. Now, I get it. She's got serious intuition. She picks up on things other people miss. And by other people, I guess I mean me. I miss things.

More noise outside my window. Someone's garage door is opening, and a car's engine hums. I roll onto my side and prop myself up on my elbow so I can see out my window. Mom's car backs out of the driveway, and she's gone too.

Sweet. There are few things better than being home alone.

I head for the kitchen. My muscles feel loose and primed, and the urge to sprint a mile or drop for push-ups hits me. I shove the vibe away. I need to eat. I need to chill.

Lasagna sounded sad and stale when Mom told me it was waiting in the kitchen hours ago. Now it smells and looks delicious. No one's touched it. It's perfectly hard and crusty around the edges, soft and stretchy-cheesy in the middle. It's still the slightest bit warm. I scoop a huge plateful, pour a tall glass of milk, sit at the table, turn off my brain, and shovel it into my mouth.

———•———

I'm licking my plate clean when I notice Dad outside by the shed. When did he get home?

I open the door and step out. He's shoveling debris into a garbage bag. I stand there, holding my breath, waiting for a sign that will reveal his state of mind.

He drops his rusty shovel, ties the bag, and stands up, his hands pressing against his lower back. Something about getting old makes people touch their lower back. That won't be me. No, sir. I've pretty much decided I'm not growing old. I'll off myself before I become wobbly, achy, and chronically pissed off.

He notices me. "Oh. Hey, Mick." His face is bright, his eyes are clear. I exhale.

"Hi, Dad. There's lasagna on the counter if you're hungry."

"I saw, thanks. I need to wait a bit. Just cleaned up a bunch of dead mice." He peels off his gardening gloves.

"From the shed?"

He nods. "The traps I set in the fall."

I wasn't planning on asking him, but the words fly out of my mouth. "Hey, what do you think about that scholarship from Indiana?" My chest goes tight. I immediately regret asking.

He shrugs and tosses his gloves on the garbage bag. "If you want to keep wrestling, if you want to keep putting in the time, you can't beat a free ride." He looks deeper into the yard, all the way to the fence, sizing up what else needs to be done. "But if you want to focus on school and have your weekends free, that's valid. Up to you."

That's the dad I grew up with. The good one. Emotions well up, bigger than expected, like wild waves before a storm. I shut them down.

"Was it hard letting go of boxing?"

He shrugs again. "Well, the decision was made for me, so there was nothing to fuss about. And all that work in physical therapy, I had time to get used to the idea. I had time to realize I was at the mercy of my body. I tried to go back to it, but my shoulder wouldn't cooperate."

"You still miss it?"

"I still miss it." He walks up to the patio and pulls out a chair at the table. I think of sitting down at the table too, but I stay on my feet.

He says, "I miss the precision and mechanics of it—placing a punch in a vulnerable spot. I miss fighting back. I miss the hard physical work. I miss the violence." He looks back at the shed, at his shovel and the garbage bag in the grass. "Without fighting, life feels more two-dimensional, but I'm okay with that." He looks at me patiently, waits to see what I want to talk about. When he's calm and clear, he usually stays that way for a bit. Still, I don't trust his calm. I've been burned too many times. I exhale and try to relax.

"If I quit for good, I wonder if I'll miss it like that."

"You might, but you can replace it with other things. That hard-work mentality, the idea of picking yourself up when you fall, fighting back, taking a stand. You can get that mentality from other things. You know what I miss most?"

"Your back against the ropes?" He's told me this a bunch of times, especially in these last few years.

"Yep. Those ropes, pressing against my back, all scratchy and rough." He closes his eyes, tips his head back. A smile creeps up along his face. His arms are loose at his sides, his legs stretched out and crossed at the ankles. I don't see him like this often, and I want to savor it. I'm tempted to pull my phone out and take a video. I know it sounds crazy, but part of me worries this will be the last time I see him this loose.

He says, "The ring itself, too. The chalky stretched canvas of the mat. The smell of the mat—like a gym locker room—moldy and sweaty, but still I miss it. They clean the blood up after each fight, scrub the mat with the white foamy stuff, but I swear I could still smell it. Blood from yesterday and last week and last year and ten years ago, and what almost felt like blood from millions of years ago, even though that's impossible." He opens his eyes and looks up at the sky. Finding some thought funny, he smiles wider. "This is crazy, but if I accidentally bite my cheek while I'm eating and I taste my blood, that's when I miss boxing the most. Like, I miss the coppery taste of my own blood."

"That's gross, Dad." I have no love for the gross stuff. Someone getting their skin split? Yuck. The smell of the other wrestlers' BO? Not a fan. I'm really not a fan of BO. Except Natalie's. If she works out and doesn't shower, I fucking love it. I could stick my nose in her armpit and fall asleep.

"Hey, you asked." He gazes out at the yard, eyes touching upon each tree, like each one brings him a different memory. I have that urge again, to record him. I can't remember the last time I saw him this relaxed.

I think of him flying kites with me in the wide-open grass behind Shaw Elementary, going on bike rides—riding all the way to the train tracks, fishing in the river with him behind the house, laughing when we caught giant frogs.

I think of him when his eyes go dark and cold, fucking lights out, and his mouth turns down as if it's too heavy for him.

How can those two people be the same?

I mean, I know people have all different parts to their personality,

I'm not an idiot. I'm the same way, bad and good, brave and weak, mean and kind, but fuck, how can a person have the extremes he has? If it's CTE, that's actually so fucked-up. If it's not CTE, then it's even more fucked-up.

"I'm worried about concussions," I say. "Like, what Mom said about CTE?"

He's staring far away, like all the way back at the forest, like he's looking at where Nat and I put our tent.

"Fuck her," he says. My thighs prickle with cold, and my throat thickens from the gluey milk I drank. "She tells herself crazy stories."

I don't ever feel like sticking up for my mom. Until now. Until he's pretending like his messed-up behavior is somehow her fault. My tone matching his, cold and stiff, I say, "You don't realize you've changed?"

His eyes turn to me, and man, if looks could kill. His eyes—small and cold—drill into me. Chills spidering up my spine, I take a step back.

"I'm fine," he says, mean.

I walk back into the house. I don't bother saying anything more. You can't talk with denial.

It sucks because he's usually in a crap mood. So when he is finally in that rare good mood, that's the only time I can talk to him. Problem is, if I raise the subject, the subject that needs to be raised, I'm gonna put him back in that crap mood. Lose-lose. Always lose-lose.

I should have just asked him about the dead mice.

CHAPTER 31

MEG

DAY 2, 10:04 P.M.

Joe's teeth chatter. His forehead is bleeding, his palms are blood-smeared. His face, his hands—they're streaked in mud.

"Oh my God, what happened?" I say, touching his arm, his neck. His skin is cold against my fingertips.

He says nothing. He has that stare. No one's home.

To me, Flemming says calmly, "Let's get him settled first." Something about her is not quite right. I mean, in addition to her guiding my bleeding, incoherent husband into my house, she's changed. I can't put my finger on it.

"Right. Okay," I say. "In the tub."

Flemming helps me walk Joe up the stairs and into our bedroom. It's such an invasion of privacy that this cop is in my bedroom, my undone bedroom. At the bathroom door, I say, "I've got him."

"Okay. I'll wait downstairs. Take your time." She goes.

I run the water warm and help him in. He lets the scratchy wool blanket fall onto the floor, revealing his nakedness. It's a shock. I mean, I can't believe he was outside and fully naked. I have so many questions. He's passive now and lets me rub a washcloth across his back, clean his hair. I tell him what to do, and he does it. It's been a long time since I cared for anyone this intimately—when they're naked, when they're incoherent. The last time was probably when one of the kids was young and had a high fever.

"I don't understand," I say. "What happened?"

He stares at the tile wall, as if there's something there to look at besides aged grout and the early invading speckles of mold. He used to be my equal, my partner—now he's my most difficult child.

It serves me right for marrying someone unconventional. Someone who thought outside the nine-to-five, who resisted a typical life, someone who loved the feeling of life coming at them fast and didn't mind losing a bit of blood for it.

In my twenties, everyone congratulated me on Joe, as if I birthed him or conjured him. My friends and coworkers thought it was cool he was a boxer, he was a free spirit. When you're young, it's fun to stand out, show you're different from the rest of them.

But eccentricity doesn't age well. When you're older, you are desperate to fit in. Be careful to tuck in your shirt, zip your fly, wipe the food off your chin. Say the wrong thing, and people wonder if you can take care of your kids. Say the wrong thing a dozen times, they sell your house and put you in a home with doors that lock from the outside.

So it serves me right. I chose him. I chose interesting. Well, how do you like that interesting now?

I blame myself. For everything, really. It's the woman's fault.

What her kids do is her fault, what her husband does is her fault. If she wanders outside her box, she gets what's coming to her. If she gets curious and hungry and eats one fucking apple, all of mankind will suffer for eternity.

Okay, so I'm being facetious. But truly, I am to blame for pushing away McClane. I am to blame for not realizing he might not want the scholarship. I am to blame for not addressing Joe's behavior. Joe's enigmatic fucking behavior.

But I did not harm McClane. All I did was get into an argument with him. All I did was piss him off. Piss him off so bad, he told me he wished he were dead. Which is alarming, but also not. I've raised a pack of kids, and anything alarming that can be said or done, they've said and done. Alarming becomes normal.

McClane was furious at me and needed to get away. That's what I assumed. Yesterday I worried he wasn't answering his phone but didn't think there was reason to panic. Also, I was overwhelmed by what they found in McClane's room. I was preoccupied with keeping my indiscretions secret. I was so focused on keeping my family's secrets, I didn't mull over all the awful things that could have happened to McClane. Now, though, now I am properly fucking panicked.

"Joe, listen to me." Kneeling beside the tub, I squeeze his shoulder. The bathwater is almost to the overflow drain, and his skin is warming. I shut off the water. "Do you know where McClane is?"

He says nothing. Just stares that nursing-home stare.

Irritation prickles to the surface of my skin. I don't want to be here, kneeling on the hard tile, my clothes wet and clingy, begging for answers. "Joe, where'd you go tonight?"

He says nothing. He has been dark, he has been strange, but

he's never been caught outside naked by the police.

"What about last night?" I say. "You were outside last night too. Through the bedroom window, I saw you walking away from the house."

"I tried moving that boulder," he says slowly, in a daze. "I haven't done that for years." Oh. Strangely, it makes perfect sense. After Carson died, Joe would go out at night after the kids were asleep and try to pry that boulder up with a shovel. He could never get the thing to budge. In quiet voices, Joe and I discussed hiring a crew to move it, but we could never pull the trigger. Bringing in a landscape crew to remove it felt garish. Talking logistics and price over the phone would have cheapened our loss in some way. Better to keep our struggle private.

McClane going missing and the police being in our house dredged up memories of Carson for Joe. The last time police officers were in our house was when Carson had his accident. It makes sense Joe would go pry at that boulder again after all these years.

But the important question now, the *only* question now, is: Why did Joe leave the house shortly before midnight on the night McClane went missing?

"Joe, where did you go the night McClane went missing?" It hurts to ask. "The detectives said you pulled out of the garage late that night?"

When they told me Carla's camera caught our cars leaving that night, I didn't mention it to Joe because I didn't want to make him mad. And I didn't ask where he went because I was scared of his answer. I didn't want to know. I still don't want to know.

"Where did you go that night? Joe. Answer me."

His eyes are glazed, like he's running a fever. "I didn't mean to."

"What do you mean? What did you do?"

A knock on the bathroom door makes me jump. "Give me a minute," I shout over my shoulder. Jesus. So like a cop to say *take your time* and not mean it. "Let me get him dressed. Wait downstairs."

In case Flemming has her ear against the door, I whisper it when I say, "Did you hurt him?" And now that I've said it, emotions rise to the surface in a rolling boil. Through gritted teeth, I whisper, "If you hurt him, I will—" I stop. What would I do? Leave him? Kill him?

I expect him to say nothing. I expect him to maintain that tired, faraway stare, but he shakes his head, looks down into his filthy bathwater at his scraped hands, and says, "Idiot." His tone is sad and angry at the same time. I've been there before, called myself an idiot. My heart opens with empathy. Poor Joe. "Idiot," he says again. "Trash, all dressed up. Your crazy has ruined us all."

My skin bristles with irritation. He's talking about me. Joe, you're an asshole. My wet clothes are clinging to my skin, my head is burning up, and I'm sick of his bullshit.

Flemming's waiting downstairs, probably listening as carefully as she can for an argument. I walk out of the bathroom so I don't slap him.

My phone vibrates in my pocket. Jamie.

> *What's going on, Mom? I know you're under pressure, but you have to update us.*

She's right. I've been too silent. I opt for transparency, albeit limited. I can't burden her with the details about Joe.

Standing at the top of the stairs, I text.

> *One of the detectives is here. She has been questioning me about Carson's death. The detectives seem to be more focused on pinning blame than helping. I'm going to talk to her now.*

Jamie texts.

> *That's awful, Mom. I'm sorry. They should be working to find him.*

David chimes in.

> *What do they think you did?*

——— • ———

Downstairs, Detective Flemming is sitting at my kitchen table, two of my mugs steaming on the table in front of her as she talks on her cell. "I hear you. I'll pick up a pizza on the way home," she says. "I've got to go now. Bye."

"Your kid?" I say.

She lifts her eyebrows and slips her phone into her pocket. "They are always hungry." She's wearing jeans, an evergreen hoodie, and old sneakers. That's what looked off about her. She's not wearing her detective outfit. No gear, no gun, no notepad.

I sit across from her. I didn't change out of my clothes, so my long-sleeve cotton shirt and my jeans are soaked and suctioned to my skin in all the uncomfortable places. Chest. Thighs. Stomach. I shiver.

"The reporters are gone, but they'll be back," Flemming says. "They'll be asking you about your neighbor tomorrow."

"What? Which neighbor?"

She gives me a knowing look. She types on her phone, then holds it up to my face.

A tabloid's online story features a chilling image of Carla Heely, her expression distressed, her black eye starkly evident.

Honestly, it looks *bad*. The skin below her eye is a dark, sinister purple. Her brow bone is a sickly yellow blue. Blood, not yet wiped away, smears her forehead, adding a raw touch.

Below the photo is a caption: *Carla Heely told the* Glen Sun *Meg Hart is responsible for her injury.*

That can't be good.

I hope the reporter from the *Glen Sun* caught Carla off guard, maybe while she was heading to her car or after being cornered in the grocery store. After nearly twenty years of friendship, I'd like to believe she wouldn't betray me so easily. At least, I hope she hesitated.

Her black eye is striking. "Do you think that's makeup?" I say.

Appalled by my question, Flemming lets her eyelids fall shut for a few seconds.

"I didn't punch my neighbor," I say. "She touched me, I pushed her away, and a bowl fell on her head."

Flemming tilts her head and squints her eyes, interested. She's about to ask a follow-up question, then sighs instead. "Well, she hasn't filed a report yet." Flemming shrugs like I might get lucky.

"Anyway, your tea bags were on the counter. We could both use it."

She pushes a steaming mug in front of me and tells me how she came upon my naked Joe. She was driving back to the office to fill out paperwork when the call came through. There was a car up by Breakneck, its engine running, lights on, and clothes on the street, a naked male standing close to the wooden fence at the cliff. When he didn't respond to their questions, the two patrol officers thought he was a jumper, and one of the officers tackled him. They put him in the backseat of their squad car. He sat there on the plastic seat, wrapped in a blanket, while they ran his plates and dug around in his car for his wallet. They ID'd him. Flemming heard it on the radio and told them to meet her at my house.

"What does he have?" she says.

"Joe was a boxer. Did you know that?"

She nods. "Head injury?"

I shrug. "CTE, maybe." Chronic traumatic encephalopathy. It's a type of neurodegenerative disease you develop from repeated concussions, which makes boxers and footballers at risk. It starts with a bit of memory loss and can progress to depression, aggression, explosiveness. "I can't get him to go to the doctor."

"That sounds like a lot of walking on eggshells." I can't tell if she's being empathetic or manipulative, but it doesn't matter. I answer honestly.

"Not eggshells." Eggshells would be easy. You can slip on shoes and stomp over them. This is like walking on rocks. Every step holds the risk of twisting an ankle or taking you down. "It's the helplessness that's worse than the disease. You look up a health condition online, and you read this clean list of five or six symptoms. I think doctors are describing who they see, and they maybe only see a percentage of what's out there. You never read about the weird stuff. You don't ever read a symptom like 'Person scatters birdseed around the toilet every morning or drops quarters down the garbage disposal.'"

She squints, and the lines edging her eyes pop. She doesn't get what I'm saying.

"People with brain problems do weird things that aren't on the list," I say.

The internet is this bustling, bright neon hub of connectedness, but when you're typing in these off-the-wall symptoms, the internet might as well be a tattered Confederate flag blowing in the wind—irrelevant, disconnected, disdained, useless. Or maybe that's me. I'm the tattered Confederate flag.

"Isn't there anyone who could talk him into a doctor? Family? Old friends?"

"There's no one." I feel this truth like a deep cold ache in my bones. You're on your own, and no one's got your back. No one wants your trouble. They'll help if they have to, if others are watching, if Jiminy Cricket is sitting on their shoulder, screaming in their ear, but they don't want your crazy.

Community is dead, friends are weak, and blood is so thin, it's nearly invisible. It takes a village, my ass. The village is full of zombies, confused and bumping into each other.

No, we are on our own, stranded on this island of mental illness. Doing the same things over and over each day, disoriented from the sun, slowly losing track of time and of what life is supposed to be.

Everyone preaches empathy and support. *Oh, you're depressed? Take time for yourself. You are worthy. It's not your fault. It's a disease.*

Like multiple sclerosis. Like cancer. You wouldn't blame someone for cancer, would you? You deserve mental health days. We don't discriminate. Talk therapy works! Medication works! Take time to work out what works for you. Hooray for mental illness!

But no one wants it up close. Up close it's like, *Shit, man, you are really nasty. Brush your teeth. Pull up your pants. You are as embarrassing as bad gas. Why are you blowing your money on gambling, you deadbeat piece of shit? Quit it with the temper tantrums. Why can't you just be normal for, like, two seconds?*

Joe's family doesn't want to hear about it. They want to hear everything's good, maybe a funny story about the kids, maybe a normal-type problem like you had the worst luck at the DMV, you know, just to make yourself seem down to earth, but they do not want the real deal. They love Joe, they know he's not himself, but they are overworked, overbooked, familied-out, and buried in bills. The Joe Project isn't some one-off favor like bringing over a casserole, the Joe Project is one of the never-ending kinds, and no one wants to sign up.

"I don't know what to say," she says. Her tea is gone. Her kid is waiting for pizza. I'm thinking she's going to say *Well, I should get going*, but she doesn't. She says, "Where did he go the night McClane went missing?"

"I don't know. He wouldn't hurt McClane, though. He lives for his kids." I don't know if this is true. I don't know what's what anymore.

"You said you went to the gas station on Litchfield and 47th the night McClane went missing. I looked through the footage at the gas station. You weren't there."

I'm tired. I drink my tea and try to think up some other excuse. I think about what Vincent will tell Flemming and Becker tomorrow. I think about how much I don't want Joe to find out what has kept him on the payroll. Then I think of Joe as he is now, upstairs, mind-fucked. I think about how I can best help McClane. Flemming and Becker are too suspicious of me and Joe. They need to focus on finding McClane.

Fuck it. Fuck me. Fuck whatever Joe thinks of me. He was arrested for being naked and incoherent at Breakneck, and I'm the one worried about self-image?

I tell her everything.

CHAPTER 32

McCLANE

2 HOURS UNTIL MISSING

If I stay away, they'll say, "See, he's a coward. He'll split the second things get hard."

If I go to her house, they'll say, "He's disrespecting our feelings. Cocky asshole."

I don't want them to think any of those things about me.

I stop at the grocery store to buy flowers. Nat likes white daisies. I drive to her house with the cellophane-wrapped flowers on the passenger seat, my window down, and the radio blasting. Imagine Dragons. Everyone says they're sellouts. I don't get it. They make songs so solid that movie producers and car companies are begging and bidding. How does achieving success make them sellouts? They're only hard workers with a bit of talent. Same as me working my ass off in wrestling and getting offered a scholarship. There's nothing sellout about it.

Okay. Lame comparing myself to a famous band. I'm just trying to keep my mind busy so I don't psych myself out, really. I'm trying to think about anything but walking up to Nat's front door. Anything but coming face-to-face with her pops.

I'm on the west side of town. It has a dustier feel to it, less manicured. More like an old Western town. That's an exaggeration, but that's how it feels to me. More free. More Wild West.

I shove the accelerator down and blow over the tracks. All four tires catch air for a beat and even though everything is fucked sideways, I can't help but smile. No way you can't smile with all four tires high. They bump down, and I smile harder. How do other people resist flying over these tracks? I'll never know.

Sunset is coming soon, but it's not here yet. Sky is tornado yellow and gray, like it's cooking up an epic storm. Her garage door's up but no one's around. Her mom's compact is in the garage, her dad's Ford Ranger is parked on the curb. I park behind her dad's truck, but give him a lot of space so he can't accidentally back into my front bumper.

Her neighbor with the pitties is out front, carrying a recycling bin, a cigarette dangling out the side of his mouth. See, like a Western. Glass bottles clink inside the bin as he walks. He gives me a squinty look, like, the nerve of me, parking near his house.

I roll up my window and grab the flowers. I tell the guy, "Hey," and walk up through the grass, headed for her front porch. Someone's grilling chicken and doing it the right way. Smells juicy and seasoned. I can't remember the last time my dad pulled out the grill.

I thought the coast was clear but here comes her old man. Dough. That's what they call him. It's cool, actually, a good nickname for a doting father and husband, but right now, I don't think he's feeling pliable.

"Hey, Mr. Marin."

He keeps his jaw tight and eyes fixed on the street as he rolls his garbage bin down the broken driveway. He's short and thick. Strong. Forearms like a cartoon. Forehead scarred, like there's little bits of gravel underneath his skin. He keeps rolling the bin, like he's going to ignore me, but he can't. He shakes his head, turns, and drops the front corners of the bin. He's a dozen feet away from me, his fingers still wrapped tight around the handle of his garbage bin.

"You're a boy," he says, stony but calm, eyes set on me. A chill goes through me. My jaw trembles, so I clench it. "You don't get it," he says, "what it takes being a father." He looks at his neighbor, who's setting his clinking recycling bin down by his mailbox, and his lip curls up on one side, snarling, doglike. "Being a mother, there's no choice, so they do it because they have to. They have to feed it, and their instinct is strong. Even if they don't want to, they know they have that responsibility." His eyes swing back to me. "Being a father, you have to choose every day. Every day you have to choose to stay. You are an accessory. The kids don't need you much. She doesn't need you. Once she has the kids, she doesn't need you. I mean, she needs you to go to the store and work, but she doesn't need you. Not really."

I keep my eyes on him, show him I can take his old-man lecture. My jaw is tight, but I can take it. And here he goes, still fucking talking. "So you're the odd man out, and still you have to choose to stay. Some days that choice is easy, you don't even think about it. Some days it's hard." He shakes his head. His eyes soften like he feels bad for me, like I'm pathetic. "You're not cut out for it, McClane."

It's like I'm talking to my mom and she's telling me how Dave knows everything. *You should ask David for advice. David got himself a good job. David knows something about that. Call David.*

I'm a pussy. I go along with whatever's easiest. Picked up Hud 'cause I didn't want to say the word *no*. Couldn't break up the fight because I hesitated. Couldn't catch Hud's head before it smashed on the floor. Dang. I hate that her pops is calling me out. I hate that he's right about me. I'm not cut out for a lot of things.

Adults are good at making you feel less-than, and that's about it, to be fucking honest. I want to bite back. Better yet, I want to keep calm, show him I can take his bitching and keep my head straight because I'm tougher than he thinks. It feels like a hot desert storm gusting inside my head.

"Maybe you'd be up for it in ten years," he says, "but not now." Old man still has gas in the tank. "Not coming from that family, mom and dad work from the couch, scholarship opportunities, only working in the summer when it's warm out." Him taking my whole life, my hard work, and turning it into a pathetic joke is like a punch to the chest. "You're a good kid," he says. "But it takes strength to stay, and you don't have it."

Stay cool, I tell myself. Don't take his bait. "Sounds old-school, that mindset," I say. "Sexist, like. Why would staying be work? Maybe you had a hard time staying, but that's not me."

Muscles ripple under his cheek, then his face loosens. He nods, smiling sadly. "Maybe. Maybe you're right. What you said, it sounds like the right thing to say. You can't relate to what I'm saying because you're above it. Mighty big of you." Him not disagreeing feels like he's humoring me, like he knows I'm talking bigger than I am.

"Talia's in her room," he says. "You can go in the side door. Don't ring the bell, you'll piss off her mom, and I'll pay for that." He tips the garbage bin and wheels it down the driveway. He doesn't walk back up the driveway. He gets in his truck and starts the engine. Dude always keeps his keys on the passenger seat. If someone steals his truck he gets a new one is his thinking. He drives away slowly, like he wants to show me he's chill as fuck.

I lean against the siding beside the side door and breathe. My lungs feel cat-scratched, and the cool air burns my insides. My eyes sting. If I walk in now, I might cry on Nat's chest. She doesn't need that.

I should have said more. I should have kept my mouth shut. I called him self-absorbed and sexist. Basically proving his point that I'm a *boy*. He took me down in the most calm, thoughtful way.

I open the screen door and step into the kitchen. Dark and still, the refrigerator clicking. Some component's been broken for months, but it still works. A thick aroma, garlic and tomatoes, hangs heavy in the air. Probably coming from that covered pot on the stove. The Marins' kitchen is small and lived-in. Herbs on the windowsill, family photos on the walls. Cluttered, but clean. I step through the kitchen and down the dark hall, hoping I don't run into anyone until I get to Natalie's room.

A bell tinkles in the next room. Tyson rounds the corner and spots me, which immediately pisses him off. He runs up to me and starts barking. Back tense, tail stiff, he eyes my shoes and ankles like they have teeth. The little shit starts growling.

~ My Journal ~

Dad took me to a fight. This is the third time he took me, but this time was different. I went before with him, when I was in middle school, but I was just a kid then.

This time I could hear skin splitting. I didn't know that had a sound. It's like a pound with the slightest hint of a rip, and it makes you think of stitches. Front fucking row. His buddy got us the seats.

It felt like the whole arena, the crowd, the refs, the fighters, were one living thing, pulsing to the same heartbeat. Like a hydra moving through water, life eternal. That we were connected to each other through the smell of sweat.

He said, you know what was a great feeling out there?

When you won Golden Gloves, I said.

No, he said. It was getting knocked out and coming to, the lights fuzzy and drippy, the crowd roaring like a train barreling in the distance, faces wobbling, then falling into focus. Realizing I got knocked out and the crowd was cheering and laughing.

No way, I said.

Yes way, he said. I figured, if I could handle this, there's nothing I couldn't handle. Getting so up close with the darkness and surviving it, I felt bulletproof.

And the ropes, he said. Your back to the ropes, kid. That shiver up your spine—the good kind. Everything is stripped away. It's your energy versus his. Who wants it more, who trained harder, who feels the ropes pressed against their back more.

Damn. Got to say, my dad is the fucking goat. Made me want to be up in the fight, my fists scraped raw and bloody, my back against the ropes.

MC, age 15

CHAPTER 33

MEG

DAY 2, 10:42 P.M.

I tell Detective Flemming that McClane and I had a fight that night, so I thought he was staying away to get back at me. That's why I wasn't worried about him being missing that first day. That's why I lied to the school about him having an appointment. That's why I hadn't called him before I called the police. I only called the police to get Natalie off my back.

I didn't mention the argument that first day because I was ashamed. What parent pisses their kid off so much they say they wish they were dead?

I tell her I am desperately worried now.

I tell her more. I go back further. Months further. I tell her about finding out Joe wasn't working. I tell her about my arrangement with Vincent. I tell her that the night McClane went missing, I recorded a video of me and Vincent—and sent it the following morning. I don't use the word *blackmail*.

Flemming nods as if my decisions have been logical. She is calm, quiet, and empathetic. Her expression is familiar. Too familiar. She is giving me the same face I give to Joe.

It hits me. For the first time, it hits me. It should have hit me before. I am an idiot. I have been living in a Wacky House of Mirrors in my mind.

Up to this point, I would have defended my choices. All it took was someone to give me that look, that look I give Joe because he's so far gone, for me to realize I have blown a mind gasket.

What was I thinking? Where is my dignity? How did I end up like this?

"My parents, they were good parents," I say. "My brother, he was a mess, a monster, but my parents were kind and calm. In the face of the shit life they were dealt, they held it together. When I was younger, I kept a list of all the things they did wrong and how I was going to do better. But really, I've done so much worse."

"I get it," she says. "Everyone wants to do better than their parents did. Or at least as good."

"It was time for someone to break the cycle of good parenting." I laugh. I'm exhausted. My life has tied me to the bumper and driven me down a dirt road. Honestly, I have tied myself to the bumper. My skin still burns with shame from telling Flemming about Vincent. A pang of regret thumps my chest, but I talk myself out of it. Her knowing the truth is better than her thinking I conspired to hurt my son.

"How did you know Vincent was involved?"

"We pulled your call records and location history."

"What about McClane's phone? Can you see his location history?"

"His last location was local. Either his battery died or he turned it off."

I let out a single moan like a whale crying out for its missing calf. I wipe my eyes and say, "Can we be done now?"

"Not yet."

This takes me by surprise. We have picked through my flaws and poor choices the way I examined Whitney's head for lice in the fifth grade, dissecting every square inch of her dark roots against her white scalp and picking the little crawlers out with my fingernails. What haven't Phlegm and I covered?

"We have some new evidence."

"New evidence? Why didn't you mention it right away? What is it? The knife? Something about the porn? Something one of his friends said?" I wait, my back stiff. I'm holding my breath.

She stares at me, deciding her next move. She sighs and pulls her phone out and starts typing as she says, "We've talked to Natalie and Jack. We haven't talked to Hudson yet. We don't have news on the knife or illicit photo. We're not focused on that right now."

"What? Why not?"

She looks up at me, turns her phone to me. "Take a look."

I don't want to. Whatever she wants me to look at will be bad. My stomach is already lurching, threatening to pitch whatever's there into my throat. I don't want to look, but I do.

There's the tinkling of wind chimes and the ruffling of leaves. A soft breeze. The video was taken outside.

It's a woman, bending over to pick up a tennis ball. She's young, wearing jean shorts and a skinny tank. A yard full of grass in the near distance.

The footage is clear but low quality.

"I'm just so tired," the woman says, but she doesn't sound tired, she sounds furious. Seething. Brimming with hate. "I can't do this anymore. I don't want to do this anymore. I hate this. Truly. Hate." This sounds like a woman who's about to jam a knife into her own throat. Or someone else's. "He's too fucking hard."

A man walks into the video, and I recognize his tattoo—a cartoon shark on his shoulder. Oh. Oh God. That's Joe. A much younger version of Joe. He's wearing a tight T-shirt and he doesn't have an ounce of fat on him. He's all muscle. So that young woman with those skinny legs and tight ass must be me. I barely remember looking like that and I definitely don't sound like myself. I sound vicious. A truly terrible person. But now all I can focus on is my tiny ass. And those legs. Oh, what I'd give to have that body back. "I don't want him," she says, *I say*, the words gravelly and cruel. "I am a shit person. I wish he were gone." The woman in the video—me—I'm talking about Carson.

Flemming pulls her phone away, stops the video.

I'm at a loss for words. I can't recall saying that, and it's shocking how hateful I come across. But that's me. It's not fake. I struggled when they were little. I didn't sleep much. I was always worried Carson would kill Jamie.

The footage must be from our backyard camera. Where did she get that footage? Did they find it when they were searching our house for evidence that first day?

"I don't understand. Where did this come from? Why are you showing me this?" My thoughts are frantic, scuttling like hundreds of ants when you wreck their nest, scrambling to save their eggs, their home, grab everything dear to them before it's stolen. "Wait, are you even looking for McClane?"

I search her face. She searches mine back. She's looking for my reaction to the video. "We are doing that too."

"People have bad days."

"People don't wish their children gone."

"You think I killed Carson."

"Carson died *hours* later," she says slowly, gravely. "*Hours* after you said you wished he were gone, he was dead."

I shiver. "I never even spanked my children." Muscles tighten along my jaw. "Leave. Just leave."

Flemming looks at me, waiting.

"Leave!" I scream. "Leave! Leave! Leave!"

She leaves. Gets in her car and drives off to get her teenager a pizza.

My teenager is missing.

I walk up the stairs. My heart so heavy it's in my stomach. My cold wet clothes weigh me down, constricting me like sausage casing. Why would Becker and Flemming go looking for an old video? They must have spent dozens of hours searching through footage to find that ten-second video of me being a shit parent.

That video. There was something *wrong* about that video. It wasn't fake. I don't remember saying those awful things, but I believe I said them. There's an unsettling feeling, though. I can't put my finger on it.

I turn the corner to walk to my bedroom, and Whitney's standing in her doorway. Her eyes are full of emotion. Fear, disgust, sadness, anger.

"Whitney" is all I say. I'm exhausted.

"I heard."

"I'm sorry, honey."

"The way you were talking about Carson," she says, shaking her head. "The way you sounded. It was bad. It was, like, like, I don't know."

"I didn't."

"Where's McClane, Mom?"

"I don't know. They're two separate things."

"Are they?" she says. Her bottom lip trembles, and she slams her door shut before I can see her cry.

In our bed, Joe is curled on his side, snoring softly. I strip off my wet clothes. I'm trembling. Shivering because I'm cold, yes, but more because I'm scared. I snuggle up to his body, spooning him. His body stirs awake. His skin is radiating heat. I wish he could take care of me like he used to. I wish things could go back to how they used to be. He'd come home from work with fast food, and the kids and I would be obnoxiously happy that he was taking care of us.

"Did you give those detectives footage from our backyard camera?"

"What?" he says, groggy. "I don't think so." His voice sounds sluggish and uncertain. "I mean, I might have a flash drive from that camera in a junk drawer somewhere, but it would be decades old. Why, what do they have?" he says, but he's barely interested.

I'm too exhausted to explain and too humiliated to retell the things I said on that video. "I just want McClane back." Tears stream down my cheeks and onto his shoulder. "I miss McClane."

"I'm sorry," Joe says, his voice shaky because he's crying too.

I'm afraid to ask what he's sorry for.

CHAPTER 34

McClane

1½ HOURS UNTIL MISSING

I turn her doorknob and the door opens, letting Nat's music escape her room. I don't recognize what she's listening to, it's one of those soft, emotional songs. Shoving Tyson aside—he's nipping my ankle—I step inside her room as her sister comes out of the bathroom in a towel at the end of the hall. I don't think she sees me.

Nat's lying on her bed looking at her phone. She's not wearing a bra under her T-shirt, and the way her breasts slide toward her armpits and ripple when she moves flat out mesmerizes me. I could stick my nose in her armpit and lay my cheek against her tit and stay there forever. It's where I want to be, like a dog wants to curl up head to tail.

Even her room is hypnotic. She has these soft pink curtains that transform the lighting in her room to pink, and being in here is like crawling inside a sweet watermelon.

She notices me and laughs, her mouth and eyes wide. "What the fuck, Mick? Why didn't you text?"

Her question throws me off. I don't know the answer. Then I do. "Seriously, I was so focused on your parents, what I would say to them, I forgot." I'm still in a daze.

"Are those flowers for my mom?"

"Shoot. I didn't think of that. Should I go give them to your mom?"

She laughs. "Lock the door."

I do as she says. I lean over to kiss her, and she slips her hand around the back of my neck. She pulls back, smiling. "You're sweaty."

"I told you. I was nervous to talk to your parents."

"Did you see them?"

"Your dad."

"What'd he say?" Her eyes are wide, full of humor. Even now, with everything she's going through, she is chill. I don't know how she does it.

I sit on her bed, my back against the wall, putting some space between us, and think about it. What the hell did he say? His words are kind of a blur, but I sure remember his sentiment. "He basically called me a pussy."

"Pft. No biggie. He thinks he's tougher than the rest of us. He basically calls all of us pussies. Especially Ax."

"This felt like a biggie. It was a beating, and it kept going on and on. He'd stop talking for a sec, then launch back in."

She smiles wide. She loves when I talk about getting my ass handed to me. After wrestling meets, she likes to hear about my wins, how I took down the other guy, but she *loves* hearing about my losses. She says she likes the way I tell a loss. She likes that I don't try to play it off or give excuses. I think of another comparison she'll like. "Picture that scene in *Avatar* where the blue girl tells Jake he's stupid. It was exactly like that. Your dad kept calling me a boy."

"Sounds about right."

"It was humiliating, actually." Sharing it, though, airing it out, that he kept calling me a *boy*, dulls the sting. "I also might have called him sexist."

"Pretty sure my mom's called him worse. He'll get over it."

"It was heavy, though. You know?"

She leans forward, grabs my hand, and yanks me to her. Slips my hand underneath her T-shirt. With her skin so squishy, my brain goes soft, and I go hard.

"*This* is heavy, McClane." I love how she says my name.

"Yes." I go for her mouth and she pulls back, her lips curling slyly.

"What else did you want to tell me about your conversation with Dough?"

"Who?"

She laughs, pulling me down beside her, and kisses me. Her lips are wet. My hands move quickly over her breasts, along the curve of her waist, her ass, back to her breasts.

My worries about her parents melt away. My tension about the pregnancy loosens. It shouldn't, but it does. I love that she makes me feel sleepy and wide awake at the same time.

"Wait, wait," she says. "I love this song."

I forgot she had music on. All of my mind is consumed by her skin and her smell.

Her smell is a mixture of everything in her life. Her mother's homemade cooking, the starchy real estate office she works in, her peachy shampoo, the soft plastic smell of the squishy toys and gel pens on her desk, the almond oil she rubs on her cuticles. Her body is like a country, and no matter how much time I spend exploring it, I will never be satisfied.

Her small hands flutter away from my chest to her phone. She turns up her speaker. It's "Calm Down" by Rema and Selena Gomez. She lowers her mouth to my ear and says, "Vibes," along with Selena and she laughs, her hot, moist breath tickling my ear. She props herself up on her elbow. Her eyes lit like sparklers. "This is a great sex song."

"Any song is a great sex song." I pull her back down and kiss the corner of her mouth.

She pulls away. "What about 'Peanut Butter Jelly Time'?"

"Perfect sex song. It's about lube." I kiss the inner corner of her eye, by her nose.

She laughs under me, and her hand smacks my chest. "What about 'We Are the World'?"

"Another perfect sex song. It's about love and connection." I kiss her neck, where her clavicles meet. I bury my nose there and try to breathe her in.

"What about Weird Al? 'Eat It'?"

"Oh, come on. You set me up for a slam dunk."

She giggles. I pull her shirt up and slip my tongue around her nipple.

"Anything's a sex song to you."

"Yes, that's what I said."

My lips move down her stomach, breathing against her skin as I go. I pull her shorts down halfway, just enough for me to flick her with my tongue. I always imagine my tongue licking a small, slick button, and once I lick it enough, I win the video game. She can't resist me.

She moans and moves under my mouth, lifting her hips toward me. There's nothing hotter than her pushing her hips toward my mouth and her hands in my hair. She tenses against me, pulling at my hair, pulling me closer. Her breath catches and she says, "Get inside me. Now. Without a condom."

"But—" I start.

"No condom. I want to feel you."

We've always used a condom. We've never considered not using a condom. But I guess she's thinking since we're already screwed, what does it matter?

I'm hard. I've been hard since I walked into her room. I pull her shorts off in one sweep and slide inside her slowly. My mind explodes.

Her calves clench against the back of my thighs. "Stay in, stay there. Just stay." It's so hard to stay still. My hips want to smash against her. I ache to go deeper, but I resist. It's torture, and it's exquisite.

Skin to skin, she grinds against me, her breath catching more until she bites her lip and whimpers through her orgasm. "Okay." She sighs. "Okay, do whatever you want."

Inside, she is soft and squishy and ridged and solid all at once. Best. Thing. Ever. I feel invincible. I could cure cancer. End world hunger. Make all the idiot leaders agree. Isn't sex without a condom the best thing there is? Yes, they all say. Yes. Yes, it is. Let's stop fighting. There is absolutely no reason for fighting. I could lift a car off a cat. Talk that homeless man into cleaning up. I will never be sad or pissed off again for the rest of my life. My family is great, my parents are fine. If I die tomorrow, I will die happy.

I thrust a few more times and pull out before I explode.

"That was nice," she says and turns away from me, backing her bare ass against my hips. More exquisite torture.

I wait for her to say more. I wait for her to tell me what she's thinking about. To tell me more about how she's falling apart like she told me this afternoon.

A small snore escapes her mouth, and I smile. Here I thought she was quietly stressing out and worrying, deciding what to share, but she's sleeping.

That feeling of ecstasy is slipping away from me, and I want it again already. I could have sex with her all day long, every day. We could make tons of babies and work stupid jobs and have sex over and over every day and we would be happy. Stupid and poor and happy. I think that's what I want.

I prop myself up so I can see the curve of her face. Her jaw, her big earlobe, her one eyebrow higher than the other. I love that. She's got a scar along her clavicle. A pale, slick mark where her little sister whacked her with a tree branch when she was younger. I feel no stress about the scholarship or about Dad. He's a good guy, my dad. I'll just hold on to the memories of who he was five years ago and forget this nursing-home version. I can do that, no problem. I'll take Whitney out for pizza this weekend. Do some yard work to help my mom. My life is perfect. My life is easy. I'm, like, at one with the universe and all the wonderful helpless living things within it.

My phone, lost in her sheets, buzzes with a text. I feel around for it and come across a wet patch of my spooge. I wipe it up with my shirt. I find my phone and open my messages.

Hey, can you meet me?

CHAPTER 35

MEG

DAY 3, 7:48 A.M.

Enough of this bullshit.

I get out of bed and throw the covers off in a panic. The sun is beating into my bedroom. My naked skin is damp and hot, almost feverish.

McClane's absence is a pain in my chest. The ache of a broken heart. Something about him was *Aw, shucks. I'm sorry. I'll try to do better.* His smile was easy, his light blue eyes sparkled. He was someone you could count on, lean against. Like a tree. Christ, me and my fucking trees. But truly, he *was* like that quaking aspen—shimmery leaves reflecting golden bits of sunlight. He was golden. *Is*, goddamn it. He *is* golden.

I need to take control. Make a move. His absence is a tuning fork vibrating my teeth—a cold nerve pain—driving me crazy.

Beside me, the bed is empty. I pull on my robe and wander the house, searching for Joe.

Joe's gone. Of course he is. My man of mystery.

Whitney's door is closed. I don't knock. I don't know what to say to her. Also, I don't want to wake her. It's Sunday.

Flemming was right—they're back. Three news vans are parked out front, and their crews, in jeans and T-shirts, lean against them, smoking in the street. And something new—a dozen teenagers sit in the grass on the parkway, clutching teddy bears. I search for Natalie, Jack, and Hudson, but they're not here. These teenagers in my front yard are strangers to me. Are they even friends with McClane? Which one of these attention whores had the sick idea to pop a squat in front of my house and hold a fucking vigil? He's not dead, assholes. Please let him not be dead.

Why aren't Jack, Hudson, and Natalie here? Why haven't they called? They should have. I mean, Jack and Hudson are the kind of boys who wait around for things to happen, for others to take charge or give them instruction, but Natalie is annoyingly proactive. Why isn't she here? Flemming mentioned she spoke with Natalie and Jack but hadn't talked to Hudson yet.

It's time someone did.

I get dressed, pull my hair back into a bun, slip on my sneakers, forgo makeup, and grab my keys. I back out of my driveway, my pulse quickening as reporters swarm my car. I should talk to them—that's what people who need help do. If I give them McClane's story—this lovable, beautiful good boy, his future bursting with potential—it would draw public interest and might help locate McClane quicker. If these reporters see how panicked I am, how sad I am, how *normal* I am—just like them—maybe they will try harder to find him.

Suddenly, a palm presses against my window. My pulse spikes. A face lowers right next to my window, her eyelashes spidery, her lipstick glossy pink, her teeth ultra white. "What happened to Carson?" she says, her breath fogging my window.

Then, against my passenger's window, someone's knocking—a man with days-old scruff in patches along his jaw. He says, "Did McClane have an accident like Carson?"

Someone aims a camera in front of my windshield. Behind the camera, her hair is wrapped up in a shiny green scarf, her mouth chewing gum. She shouts, "Why did you assault your neighbor?" My breath stuck in my chest, my skin adrenaline-slick, I press the gas pedal hard. Their hands smack against my car. They are shouting.

"Fucking lunatics," I say aloud, watching them grow small in my rearview. Giving them an interview would be a mistake.

———•———

The parking lot at the Shady Grove apartment complex is crowded, cars bumper-to-bumper and double-parked. Build a six-pack of high-rises but only half the necessary parking.

After circling the lot twice, I give up. I park illegally against an orange-painted curb and a fire hydrant. I haven't been here since the day Hudson and his dad moved. McClane and Jack helped with the moving. I didn't want to intrude, handle their dishes or bedding, so I dropped off donuts and coffee-in-a-box. That was Jamie's suggestion. Which reminds me.

I text Jamie and David.

> *Still no word from McClane. I'm sick with worry. Did he mention anything to you in the past few weeks? Anything you can think of at all might help. And do either of you know where we kept the footage from the backyard camera? Dad mentioned a flash drive.*

My questions about the security footage are irrelevant. I know that. Still, there's a nagging feeling about the video Detective Flemming showed me, and I'm hoping David or Jamie will mention something—anything—that shakes loose what's bugging me about that video.

I don't wait for their responses. It's early. It's likely they're both still sleeping.

I climb the cement stairwell to Hudson's apartment, not too worried about getting attacked because it's seven a.m.

The front door of their apartment is an inch open. My heart races, and I pull out my phone. Something's happened. No one leaves their door cracked open in an apartment building. I dial 911, my finger hovering over the call button. But I don't press it. If they are drugged out of their minds, I don't want to get them arrested. I shove the door open with my sneaker and call out. "Hudson? Chase? It's Meg, McClane's mom. I know it's early, but McClane is missing." The hallway is an obstacle course of shoes, plastic soda bottles, a delivery box torn open the wrong way, a fork, a dog leash. They don't own a dog.

I step down the hallway, scared, bracing myself. Preparing for the worst. A dead body. There will be a dead body.

"Hello?" I say. "It's Meg Hart. I'm sorry to barge in so early, I'm worried about McClane."

There's a body on the sofa. It's Hudson. His hoodie is pulled all the way up and he's face down. There's no blood, but he's not moving either.

"Hudson. It's McClane's mom." His hand is down by his side. I touch his wrist, looking for a pulse. Just as I relax at his skin's warmth, he flips fast and swings to hit me. If he got me in the stomach or leg, I would have gone down, but he hits my forearm, so it only hurts like hell. I scream out and step back. "Don't hurt me."

"Oh, shit. Mrs. Hart?" His voice is raspy. "Oh man, I'm so sorry. Oh man." He buries his face in his elbow like a little kid.

"I'm fine, Hudson. I'm totally fine." My words spill hot and fast. "It's my fault. I walked in. The door was open, and I was worried something bad happened, so I walked in. It's totally my fault. Is your dad home?"

"I don't know. Maybe in his room." He sits awkwardly, unsteadily, maybe a bit hungover but also trying to be polite. He drops his arm away from his face, letting his hands fall into his lap.

His eye. It's worse than Carla's. It's my turn to flip out.

"Hudson! What happened? Your eye. Who did that to you?" Please let it not be Chase.

"Some assho—" He stops. "Just some guy. I'm fine, Mrs. Hart." He looks up at me for the first time. His cheek is creased from sleeping hard on the couch. "It happened at school a few days ago."

I'll never get used to seeing Hudson's life like this. I still remember him as that skinny, happy, bright-eyed kid who'd tell us funny stories about the turtle he and his dad rescued off the street during their bike ride, the teacup pig they saw outside the hardware store, the potato shooter he built with his mom.

He'd be in our house, out in the yard, then back in. The boys were always moving fast, rushing in and out as they hatched goofy plans. Whitney would cry because she wanted to play with the big kids, and McClane would say, "Go play with your own friends."

She would cry harder. "But I don't have any friends." McClane would shrug and walk outside. Hudson would stop rushing, open my art cabinet, and grab the plastic toolbox filled with Play-Doh. He wouldn't talk her out of crying, he wouldn't say, *Of course you have friends, I'm your friend*, or, *What about that new girl across the street?* He would just open the toolbox and start playing with Play-Doh, talking to himself about what he was building and all the cool colors until she slipped up beside him like a curious kitten. He'd line up his creations in front of her, and she'd join, completely forgetting her sadness. And pretty soon she'd be laughing and telling him stories as if she were the babysitter.

I loved seeing Hudson at our house. He was the old-soul child I never had. The one who was comfortable in his skin, confident in his words. He never doubted himself, because he was simply good. When you're that good, there's nothing to doubt.

But he and his dad crumbled after Lorraine died. No one could sweep them up and glue them back together. I should have shaken Chase, told him to pull himself together for his son. I didn't want to impose.

McClane and Hudson's friendship has withered, and Hudson is so different now. Still, if he knows something, he'll say.

The mess that started in the hallway settled in this room. You can't take two steps before you meet garbage in any direction. Papery ice-cream sandwich wrappers with chocolate goo slick on the inside. Beer cans. Crumpled paper towels. Empty bowls, metal spoons glued inside them with dried milk. Shiny white garbage bags, as if someone considered cleaning up, then forgot.

"Hudson, have you talked to the police?" I say.

"Yeah, they were at the school. I'm suspended."

"No, I mean about McClane."

"What?" He's confused. He doesn't know.

"McClane is missing. Since Friday, he's been gone. He's not answering his phone."

Hudson's eyes go from confused to worried. He rubs his forehead. "I haven't had a phone since Thursday. Since that guy decked me. It's busted. I haven't seen McClane since, since, the day before. He gave me a ride, uh, I think it was Wednesday night." He looks even more worried.

"I'm scared, Hudson. If you know anything that could help, please tell me. Did he say anything the last time you saw him? Anything unusual?"

He thinks about it. "No. I mean, I don't remember what we talked about."

I'm so embarrassed to say this, to this boy. This young man who used to be a boy. "The police will come by today. They're going to ask you about a few things they found in McClane's room. It kills me to say this, they found a knife. It was covered in blood. And they found child pornography."

Hudson's eyes light with recognition.

"What is it?" I say. "What do you know?"

He shakes his head, squints his eyes, looks at the floor.

"Please, Hudson. I need to know what's going on with McClane so I can help him." I'm talking too fast, rushing him. I sit in the ratty recliner, and the smells of body odor and beer waft from the fabric. "I don't want anyone to get in trouble." My voice cracks. "I just want him back." My back trembles. My fingers tremble. I need to slow down. I need him to understand.

"The police, they aren't even looking for him. They're investigating him like he's a criminal. They're investigating me and Joe." Hudson looks up at me through glassy eyes. I catch his gaze and hold it tight. "They're going to find out in the end, so please, as painful as it might be, tell me what you know. You know something. The police will be able to tell. Whatever trouble McClane is in, just tell me."

He breaks his gaze, tips his head back on the couch, and closes his eyes. I watch his chest inhale and exhale. "That photo. It's not his. It's not mine either," he says quickly, defensively. "But it's not his."

Relief floods through me. I knew McClane would never do anything like that. Even if I doubted him for a minute, considered it, I knew that photo and knife were out of place. Because McClane always left his door open. He had nothing to hide. Ever since he was little, he left his door open when he left the house.

As calm as I can manage, I say, "Tell me about the photo."

Hudson pushes his hands through his hair roughly. "I was at a party with some bad people. Like, really bad. This guy was telling us about this girl he, like, had access to. I, well, I completely lost it. I grabbed a kitchen knife, put it against his neck." He blinks his eyes, squeezing out a small tear. He swipes it with his palm. "I didn't hurt him. I wanted to. I didn't. I just threatened him, nicked his skin. I grabbed the photo, I was going to bring it to the police maybe, but I got scared. This guy, he had someone seriously scary come to my school, threaten me, knock me out. McClane must have taken my bag," he says, thinking it through. "I thought the guy who hit me took it, but McClane must have grabbed it." He sighs. He looks up at me. "I've never called the police, what do I say?"

"Ask for Detective Flemming."

He nods.

I nod. I want to thank him, but it feels cheap. McClane's innocence comes at Hudson's expense. "You're going to be okay. You have time to do anything, be anything, go anywhere. You don't have to be responsible for your dad. You don't owe him that. The only thing you owe your dad is your effort to be happy. There's nothing tying you down."

He looks at me straight, vulnerable, eyes glassy, and he huffs a laugh. "I'm tying me down," he says. "I can't get away from myself."

——•——

Walking to my car, I check my texts. Both of my older kids replied. David's text:

> *Dad turned off the backyard camera ages ago.*
> *Dad and I fast-forwarded through the footage*
> *once. Nothing interesting there. Why?*

In spite of the stress and worry, I smile. It's so like David to enjoy fast-forwarding through security footage, eager to catch someone doing wrong. Even as a small child, he was a vigilant tiny cop. Joe and David were such a pair. Oh, the seemingly boring activities they would make entertaining.

Then Jamie's text:

> I'm coming home. I booked a flight. Arriving at O'Hare at 6:42 p.m. I should have booked a flight yesterday. I'm sorry I didn't, I wasn't thinking. Don't worry about picking me up. I'll Uber. Try not to worry, Mom. I'm sure he's okay. How is Whitney doing?

I smile again. This time as tears slip down my cheeks. It's so like Jamie to offer comfort and concern. Of course she booked a flight. Of course she's apologizing she didn't do it earlier. I can just see her wearing too many hats for some fledgling newspaper or nonprofit, pouring her energy into a hopeless cause. I used to praise her generosity. She used to give her toys to her friends, and I would compliment her. I was in awe of her, really. I should have told her to protect her reserves, put on her own life vest first and all that.

I am texting in the group thread when my phone rings. I recognize the number. I answer my phone as I get in my car. "Did you find him?"

"We haven't found him yet." The voice is deep, authoritative. Becker.

I start my car and back out too recklessly for the tight condition of this parking lot. I nudge someone's bumper, then peel out. "The kiddie porn and the knife aren't McClane's."

Becker waits a beat, in case I want to say more.

I do. "Hudson says he'll call you today, he'll explain. I'm leaving his apartment now. Please call him if he doesn't call you. They're not McClane's." I shudder. Cold races up my spine. He's still missing. It's all the same. He's still missing.

"Mrs. Hart. The video of you has been leaked."

"Wait, what?" Which one? Pretty pathetic when you don't know *which* incriminating video of you has been leaked.

"The one my partner showed you. It's on YouTube. The media may reach out, so you should talk to your family and be prepared for what may come."

As I drive, I replay the video in my head: a much younger version of me saying I'm sick of my kid, I want him gone. It's bad. My voice is gravelly and cold, and angry sunshine washes everything out, making the whole thing seem like a faded, yellowed photo you'd find in a haunted house. It's ominous, for sure, but it's a distraction. Why can't Becker and Flemming see that? McClane is missing, and they keep talking about a stupid ancient video.

"What may come? I don't care what may come. I care about now. McClane being missing. Did you hear me about the knife and photo? They're not his. He did nothing wrong."

"Yes, I did. I know."

Phlegm and Pecker spent all of Day One vilifying McClane, recklessly trashing his reputation, and now he's saying *Yeah, I know*. Fuck that. The police, once they show up on your doorstep, they press their shoe into the muddy parts of your life, squishing back and forth and stomping around, spreading muck everywhere and making a mess.

"You know?" I say, irritation clawing up my neck. The sun beating through my windshield is too white and fuzzy in my eyes. "You wasted so much time trying to pin blame on my son instead of trying to find him. All you can say is you know? That's it?"

"That's not it," he says. "We need to talk. Can you stop by the station now?"

CHAPTER 36

McClane

40 MINUTES UNTIL MISSING

I'm still in the grips of ecstasy, so I don't think twice before I respond.

Dude. Yeah, I can meet you.

Tomorrow's Friday. Even if I stay up all night, I'll be all right. I'm still high and I'm not coming down anytime soon. Not all the way down, anyway.

I look over at Nat one more time, think about waking her. Her shoulder's irresistible and soft. I want to squeeze it. I want to kiss it. Bite it. Instead, I get dressed and pull on my hoodie. I climb out her window and drop into the grass while pulling the window shut behind me. So slick, I'm practically Spider-Man.

I'm halfway to my car when I see the floating glow of a cigarette by my rear bumper. His tight jittery posture gives him away. Her oldest brother, Ax.

I pause for a sec, then keep walking toward the front of my car. I keep my breathing slow and my stride casual, which is hard work.

"I heard," he says and blows smoke. Who smokes cigarettes besides the elderly?

"You slash my tires?"

He laughs. "Nah, I'm happy for you."

"Shut up."

"Serious. This baby will take the magnifying glass off me. I love it. Perfect Natalie, smart Natalie, all knocked up. And you're not even trying to convince her to scrape it out."

I want to shove my forearm against his chest, against his neck. Maybe that's what he wants, so I don't. I walk around the front bumper to the driver's door.

"No, really," he says. "I appreciate you." He pounds his fist against his chest. "So, no college, no wrestling? Bet you'll miss wearing that leotard, huh?"

I get in my car and drive away, hoping to roll over his toes, but he steps away from my car in time.

So much for curing cancer. So much for solving world peace. Rage burns from deep inside and rises to my skin. My jaw hurts from keeping quiet.

It's true, what they say. The people who care about you are harder on you. Her old man and Daniel, they were disappointed and worried for her future and frustrated. Axel thinks it's funny. Her parents are smart; how do they not see their oldest son is a total dick? So weird how people can be smart yet completely blind when it comes to the ones they love.

I study my rearview to make sure he's not following me. The thing about Ax, he's like one of those people you seesaw over. You think, he's okay, he means well, he's coming around. Then you're like, no way, that is one seriously scary dude.

I blast the radio, roll down the windows, and try to get that feeling back that Nat gives me. It's out of reach. Gone.

I look back in my rearview. Headlights swing in from a side street, coming up behind me, but I don't think it's him.

Cool night rushes in, beating on my face, cooling down my hot head, evening me out. With that night air blowing in my window and the party smell of pizza sauce and yeasty warm bread oozing from the pores of my car, a thought crystalizes in the center of my mind. We should get married, Nat and me. Yeah, why not? I have to live in the dorms first year, but second year we could get an apartment, take turns with the baby while the other drives Uber and I go to class. It could work. I am not high on the idea of a baby—a little McClane, as Nat thinks—but I am not repulsed either. I could do it. I could do it for her. Change diapers and feed the little squirmy, slimy thing bottles and stuff. It could work. Being with Nat, living with Nat, sleeping with her soft skin against mine, that would make it all feel right.

I park in the Denny's lot. I text.

Hey. I'm here.

Same. I'm at a table.

I walk into Denny's. He's sitting in a booth, facing the door. He sees me walk in and smiles huge. That smile, that wattage, gives me back some good vibes.

"Dude, what's up?" I say, sweet serendipity back in my voice. I drop my keys, phone, and wallet on the table and slide into the booth across from him. I toss my hoodie down on the seat beside me. "Why you in town, man?"

My brother, Dave. I haven't seen him since Christmas.

CHAPTER 37

MEG

DAY 3, 9:39 A.M.

Detective Becker wants me at the station.

He can kiss my ass. He spent two days dragging McClane's character through filth, making me question my own child's goodness. Becker didn't bother apologizing, didn't bother acknowledging his mistake, didn't bother acknowledging how much time he wasted not looking for my son. So let him wait.

I'm not sure I can ever forgive myself for doubting McClane. Whitney will never forget me standing outside her bedroom door, asking her who McClane is.

I pull into my driveway, maybe running over a reporter's toe, ignoring the dozen teenagers sitting in the parkway, ignoring the sign they aim at me that reads WHERE IS MCCLANE? and shut the garage door. Smothering my rage, I walk calmly through my house, searching for who is left of my family. Whitney is gone. Joe is gone. Thank God I don't have to hold it together for anyone.

My muscles coiled, I walk outside to the shed, open the door, and grab a shovel. I march toward the house, raise the shovel over my head, and smash the camera mounted high beside the back door. I beat the shit out of it good. That superhuman strength that comes with an emergency situation, the kind of vigor that they say overtakes a mother when her child is trapped under a car and adrenaline explodes into her veins, that's the kind of strength I unleash on the camera. It shatters, flinging small, dangerously sharp pieces across the patio. Stupid backyard camera has survived and stayed sturdy and vigilant all these years while everything else has fallen apart. I dent the wood siding pretty good. My lovely house I've cared for so well, invested so much of my time and vitality beautifying, I've defaced it.

I drop the shovel and fall into a lawn chair. Tears cloud my vision. Snotty, salty tears slip into my mouth.

Where the fuck is McClane? I picture the most terrible things happening to him. I picture him getting tied to a fence in the middle of a nowhere road. I picture him getting tortured. I picture someone smashing his face with a brick. I picture him jumping off Breakneck in the dark, hitting a jutting rock.

Oh God. Have the police searched Green Lake? Have the police searched anywhere?

Useless police. They've been about as helpful as a gaggle of teenage gossip queens at a slumber party. Which one of them leaked the video? Becker, or one of his underlings? Someone who hates his mother. Some rookie cop who hates women because he isn't getting laid because he's a dweeb *and* an asshole. You can get a girl if you're a good-looking asshole or you're a sweet dweeb. But you can't get laid if you treat people like shit *and* you have no game.

Maybe the leak will help me. No doubt they're going to treat me like a criminal. But the leak will end up keeping me out of trouble. That's how it works on TV anyway. Police leak a video, tamper with evidence, and lawyers can't use it anymore.

And maybe it won't be that bad. Maybe mothers everywhere will sympathize with my mental health. They will say, *I get it. I've wanted out. I've wanted to walk away. I've wanted to take back having kids. It doesn't mean I'd kill them.* Mothers will recognize a witch burning at the stake and they will rescue her from the fire.

My arms are sore but they feel relaxed and rubbery. My rage is gone. I pull myself out of the lawn chair and walk the yard. I ignore weeds that need pulling and focus on my children's trees. I always gaze upon them from the kitchen, but it's been a while since I've seen their leaves up close.

I go to Jamie's willow tree. Its long, flexible switches sway slightly in the easy breeze. A tree with roots spreading wide, unafraid of taking what it needs. Regardless of what happens, Jamie will be okay. She has made a family out of friends. She has a support system and a passion for helping people.

I walk to Whitney's honey locust and touch an irresistibly long thorn. It's stunning and it hurts. Hopefully Whitney won't be like that. Hopefully she will let people get close to her. People who are not drawn only to her beauty but intrigued by her mind.

Pathetic, isn't it? Personifying these trees, making them fit my children's natures. I can't help it, though. The similarities are uncanny. Then again, we bend our reality. Make it fit. Maybe that's what I'm doing.

What is it about the video that seemed off? I can't bear to

open YouTube to watch it again, to see how many views it has.

How would I even find it on YouTube? If Becker leaked it, what would he have titled it?

Bad moms. Asshole mom. Another Karen mom temper tantrum. Parenting fail. Dangerous parent. Caught on tape. Son dies in suspicious accident same day mom says she doesn't want him. Mom has temper tantrum, boy dies hours later. Parenting a difficult child. Parenting a dangerous child.

How does our backyard camera even work? I don't remember ever watching any videos it captured. Honestly, I thought we turned the damn thing off shortly after we moved in. I don't even know how it worked or where it stored video data. Joe was the one who took care of those details. I wish I'd paid more attention.

I try to replay the video in my mind, but all I can focus on is Joe's stupid cartoon shark tattoo. I used to love that tattoo, but now I hate it. That cartoon is a joke I don't get anymore, and the joke's on me.

I walk to McClane's quaking aspen. The small heart-shaped leaves quiver in the barely there breeze. All those leaves trembling simultaneously, so light, so in sync, it's dazzling. Shimmery. Like McClane.

I wonder how Natalie is holding up. It's Day Three, after all. I call her, and it goes to voicemail. I don't have her parents' number. I've never met her parents.

My phone buzzes in my hand. A text from Jamie.

What's going on? You haven't responded.
I'm freaking out. Please respond.

I'm sorry, Jamie. Nothing has changed.
I'll see you when you get here.

I read the previous texts in the thread to check when her flight leaves. I read David's text, asking about the security footage. Jamie and David, they are so different. Their responses are so different. She is panicked and emotional. He is calm and tactical.

I make my way to David's tree, tucked farthest in the back, beyond McClane's. I smile. David's ash tree stands proud and strong and tall. From my kitchen window, I can only see part of it. Up close, I take it all in. Hands on my hips, I tilt my head back and look up at how big it's grown.

Huh. There's a branch up there without leaves. I walk around and find another thick branch without leaves. Now that I'm walking around, seeing the whole thing, it's ragged all over.

I thought it survived ash borer untouched, but I'm wrong. Ash borers were a big thing ten years ago. These big beetles, native to northeastern Asia, came to the US, hidden in wooden shipping crates. They began infesting ash trees around the country and made their way to our neighborhood. Most people's ash trees died. We only had this one ash, and it looked okay, so I thought we got lucky.

Shame. It's rotting from the inside out.

It looked healthy from the kitchen window. Looking at a thing from the wrong angle can misrepresent reality.

What has eluded me about the video comes into focus. Just like that. I didn't know what felt off, and now I do. I run back to the house.

On my phone, I open YouTube. It only takes a few tries before I stumble upon the video of me and Joe.

I press play.

You think it's painful reliving your mistakes in your head during the night. That one stupid thing you said, that one cruel thing you did but you didn't mean it, you didn't know in the moment it was cruel. Or maybe you did. You toss and turn and replay it, cringing at yourself, wishing you could take it back.

Imagine that one mistake you made caught on video, shared with anyone who was bored and wanted to be entertained. My stomach sours, and I'm trembling with shame.

I look up at what's left of the busted security camera. Then back to the YouTube video on my phone. Up at where the camera was. Back to my phone.

It's the angle that's off.

That video camera is (was, before I smashed it) beside our back door and above it, so the video should be shot from above, looking down. But the angle of this video I'm watching is straight on. No, that's not exactly right. It's aiming slightly *up*. Someone's taking this video. Someone was standing inside the kitchen with the glass door open.

David took this video.

CHAPTER 38

McClane

25 MINUTES UNTIL MISSING

I sit across from my older brother in a booth.
    Dave's touching everything on the table. Adjusting it, setting it right. Salt. Pepper. Wire basket of creamer cups. His coffee mug. His fingers move quickly, gracefully. He's always been like this. Like an addict itching for his next fix. Fidgety, but not annoying. More like fascinating. My dad's that way too. Both of them are tightly wound, squirrelly, strong, and have quick reflexes.

Dave, he's sure of himself. Unflinching and straightforward. He sees the world in black and white. His for the taking.

He wouldn't have let Hudson drop to the floor. He would have moved fast to break up the fight. And when Mr. Ridley told the kids to get to class or they'd end up in detention, Dave would have ignored that crap. He would have stayed to help Hud. He would have helped the teachers and security carry Hud to the front office. And the crazy thing is, in the end, the teachers wouldn't yell at Dave or give him detention. His certainty commands respect.

I've always wanted some of that certainty.

I'm not saying I want to be Dave. It's good to be me. I mean, I like my life. Nat chose me, my friends have my back, people admire me, all that, but it would be cool to not question myself. It would be cool to move through the world like you were born for it.

I would seriously love it if Ax did in fact follow me here. If he walked in through the front door of Denny's right now, wanting to start shit with me, I would be chill because Dave's got my back. Dave would have my back even if I was at fault. And even though he's average height and build, he can be intimidating. The way he takes up space, and those small cold eyes that buzz with confident energy, you just know he's going to take things too far.

"Why you in town, man?"

"Just passing through for work, little brother," Dave says, talking fast. "When we've got a carrot, we end up working weird hours. It's late, I didn't want to wake everyone up. I figured you'd be up, though." Maybe he took amphetamines or caffeine pills. It's a long drive, I'd do the same.

"I have no idea what that means, when you've got a carrot."

"Just work stuff." He smiles, cool. "I got you a coffee, a water, and an orange soda." He points to each, like he's an actor in a commercial. "I was bored." He laughs.

"Thanks." I take a few big gulps of the orange soda. I was thirsty and welcome the sweetness, but now I've lost the taste of Natalie. I wipe the condensation from the glass on my jeans.

"Remember when my friend Stevie drank a two liter of orange soda?" His eyebrows lift.

"How could I forget? He was puking orange, spraying it out his nose." I nod at him. "You told him to do it. One of your circus acts."

"Ah, yes," he says theatrically. "Dave Hart's circus. The circus with heart."

"You know what I remember more?"

"What?"

"Your friend Nick eating a sixteen ounce can of mushrooms."

"Yeah, he puked too." He laughs. "There's a theme here with my friends and puking."

"No, man. The theme is you can be really fucking convincing. You told them both to do it." He busts out laughing. He likes that. "So, how's the job going?" I say. "You headed back to Memphis tonight?"

His eyebrows twitch. His eyes are intense but he's still smiling. "Job's been crazy. We're doing important work, you know. We work a lot of paid hits on the dark web."

"Wait. What?"

"Paid hits. People who go on the dark web and hire a hitman to kill someone."

"How much?"

"Usually start at a thousand."

"I can't imagine risking life in prison for a thousand dollars."

"'Cause you're not crazy, man." He laughs. "We go bust this lady who has a hit out on her husband. They toss me a bulletproof vest, we get into a van, and we roll in. I expect we're going to the hood, but no, it's, like, this mansion." The way he's talking, it's like someone popped the cork on a champagne bottle. He's talking fast, and dude's got a lot to say. "Bitch is super rich and entitled. She can't believe she'd get in trouble for hiring someone to kill her sugar daddy. She's appalled we'd bust into her house, she looks at us like we're roaches. Old dude is super nice, too. Tells us about his old man who used to play for the Sox."

"You must see the weirdest shit."

"On God, man."

I have this itch to tell him about Natalie, about wrestling, about my scholarship, but Dave wants to talk. And that's good too. Listening to him talk, listening to his stories, keeps my worries away. He's a great storyteller. He makes shit up and adds it into the story, but it's fun as hell.

He goes on, "So then they put me on really heinous shit. Sex crimes. Kids. This one lady, she has two kids, right? One's seven, the other is not even a year old. These two boys. She's selling them for sex, thirty bucks for thirty minutes. I'm watching a video of this—"

"Wait, wait. I actually don't want to hear about it."

"Yeah, okay. I get it. But the thing is, we got her. We took her out."

"What happened to her kids?"

"No fucking clue, man." He shifts back into his seat, annoyed by my question. As if I missed the punch line of his joke. "All I know is they're better off now that she's gone." He leans forward, switching gears, and breathes in. "Hey, I've got my gun in my trunk. I should take you shooting. You ever been?"

"Once with Jack and his dad. Shooting ranges are closed by now, though."

"Right, right, right," but he's talking so fast it sounds like *ririright*. "Hey man, I ever tell you about the time Carson and me rode our Big Wheels down the Gleakers' sledding hill?"

"No, I don't remember anyone talking much about Carson."

His eyebrows pinch. His eyes grow muddy, then they clear. It's like a storm cloud moves over them real fast before it's back to blue skies. "Dude woke me up at like six in the morning, opened the garage, and we rode out like two tiny cowboys. He was five, I was four. We drag our Big Wheels up that big fucking hill. We're at the top, like two sherpas at the top of Mount Everest, looking down on everyone and what we've accomplished." He smiles. "Carson doesn't say a word, just gets on his trike and starts down. Instead of waiting to see what happens to him, I've got no fucking patience at four, right? I go down right after. The snow had a layer of ice from overnight, it was cold as hell, and we cruised all the way out to the edge of the pond. No shit. Our Big Wheels stopped right at the edge of the pond, my front plastic tire on the ice, cracking it. Crazy shit. We went home, he made us pancakes and hot cocoa. Played *Mario Kart* all day. What a fucking day. Mom and Dad never knew."

How does a five-year-old make pancakes? I can see two little dudes making hot chocolate, but I can't see a five-year-old standing on a chair flipping pancakes over a fire. Dave embellishes, it's his thing. I'm used to it, so I don't call him out.

"I miss that little dude," he says, his eyes wet. Dave's other idiosyncrasy is he's comfortable crying. I admire that. Dave lives in the moment all the fucking time.

"I wish I knew him," I say. It's true, but I don't feel strongly about it. Only strong feeling I've got is I've got to piss. My soda's gone, and I never pissed after sex. "Hey, I've got to use the bathroom." I go to grab my phone and keys.

"Dude," he says like he's about to launch into an argument. "You leaving or just going to piss?"

"Just the bathroom."

"You can leave it. I won't hack your phone, man."

I smile and head for the bathroom. I pass a few tables of guys coming off second shift. We're near the steel factory. I pass a table of high school girls I don't recognize. A few couples. Denny's is kinda busy for this late, but Thursday's close enough to Friday.

I think about my last conversation with Whitney as she stared at herself in the mirror, pressing her lips together to smear her lipstick where she wanted it. *David knows nothing. He's seriously messed up. You know, he hasn't texted me back in months.*

Shame that Whitney thinks Dave's a dick. I'll tell him to text her. She's probably still awake.

I push open the bathroom door. One guy washing his hands, two guys at the urinals. One guy has his pants down at his ankles, his bare ass out. Never seen that, and I cannot wait to tell Dave. He loves obnoxious stuff like that.

I step to the urinal farthest from Bare-Ass Pisser and unzip.

~ My Journal ~

Senior year, this year. It's September 17. Leaves turning yellow and orange, like everything's starting to burn. Homecoming is next weekend. I take these walks at night. Sometimes I can hear the football game happening a mile away. The announcer's voice, deep and techno-God-like, the soft hush of the crowd roaring a mile away.

Other nights, it's quiet. There's just that one owl hooting in the massive evergreen at the end of my block. I walk and breathe in everyone's bonfires in their backyard. Everyone is so close with their family, burning marshmallows and shit. My parents feel like aliens to me.

I can't wait to get out of this place. I'm going places. I'm going to do bigger things than my dad and mom. They are small-minded. Mom with her art history degree, Dad a failed boxer turned brokerage hack. They are both pathetic. They are both cold statues in their own way. I walk and I walk at night and I listen to the girls jumping on their trampolines in their backyards and talking too fast on their phones. Most of the girls in this neighborhood are even stupider than they used to be.

MC, age 17

CHAPTER 39

MEG

DAY 3, 10:48 A.M.

Sugar Glen's police station is only five minutes from my house, but I've never been inside. I park my car and walk up to the large glass doors.

Joe's been here. When Jamie got in trouble for pulling down a street sign on a Friday night, Joe was the one who went to the police station to sign her six-month probation agreement. He joked about it when they got home. "First one in our family to get fingerprinted," he said, laughing.

"Who else?" Jamie said, beaming.

That was a Jamie-ism. *Who else?*

The last time she said that to me was on the way to the airport. She was giving me a summary of Christmas vacation at our house as she saw it.

"McClane seems good but quiet. Same with Whitney. I can't believe she still locks her door even when she leaves the house."

Jamie laughed. "What do you think she's hiding in there? A baby?"

Despite my worries she was hiding something, I laughed.

"Dave seems off. Too intense about his work," Jamie said.

"That's his personality."

"No, it's more than that. Seems like he's on cocaine or something."

"What?"

She shrugged. "Dad seems weirder and quieter. Where does he go in the middle of the night?"

"I think he likes to drive. He doesn't cause trouble for anyone, though."

She laughed. "I'm telling you, things are not right. I'm worried something bad is going to happen. Why are you making excuses for everyone?"

"What else can I do?"

"Something besides making excuses."

"Why do I have to do anything?" I said it in a confident tone, but the sentiment was immature and spoiled. Why me? Why do I have to be the one?

She laughed again. "Who else is there? *Who else?*"

As I step up to the thick glass doors, an officer in uniform steps out, holding the door open for me. Inside, I take in the wide reception area—brick interior, low lighting, long front desk, a heavy door to the far right, a half-dozen small rooms to my left. Doors wide open, each room is identical with a small table and three chairs, the space small enough you'd have to round the chairs carefully.

I head for the receptionist. After beating up the backyard camera, my hair is sticking out of my ponytail and my eyes are red and glassy. I look like I was driven here in the back of a squad car.

"Can I help you, ma'am?" says the young woman at the counter in uniform, stoic and cool.

"I need to talk to Detective Flemming," I blurt. "My son is missing. He's been missing for three days."

She nods. She's not picking up her phone yet. "What is your name?"

I soften my approach. I need to talk to Flemming. I need her to answer a few questions, and I need to see her expression when she answers so I can get rid of this nagging suspicion. "Oh, right. My name is Meg Hart. Detective Becker asked me to come in. Flemming is his partner."

"Okay, I'm glad to help. I'll give them a call." She picks up the phone and conveys my information to another receptionist. "Someone will be out to talk to you in a few minutes. Have a seat, if you'd like."

I pace the area, checking my phone. Rereading the texts I've received from Jamie and David in the past three days. Thinking about the questions David should have texted me but didn't. The worry he should have expressed but didn't. His questions were all procedure.

> *The detectives assigned to McClane's case—what are their names? Have they pinged his phone location? Have they found his car?*

Why has David been the only one who's not worried? My stomach is tight. My chest flutters with uncertainty.

It's the pressure, that's what's screwing with my thoughts. David is worried, of course he's worried, but he's also a problem solver, a doer. His questions came from a place of expertise. He's helping in the best way he knows how.

But is he?

That YouTube video isn't from our security camera. It's from David's camera. We bought him a cheap digital camera for his fourth birthday. It kept him busy for hours on end. It was one of those gifts we congratulated ourselves on for years after we bought it: *Boy, that kid sure got our money's worth.* He loved that camera.

It's possible the police came across a flash drive from David's old camera in our house while they were collecting evidence. It's possible, yet David's texts are like insects crawling chaotically in my mind, each cold, clinical word irritating and itchy, making my skin crawl.

I don't want to doubt David. I don't want to wonder if he's not the person I thought he was. I doubted McClane, I entertained the notion he was cruel, violent, and criminal, and I don't know if I can forgive myself.

Detective Flemming walks out from the door on the right to greet me. "Thanks for coming in, Mrs. Hart." Calling me Mrs. Hart feels off. Twelve hours ago I told this woman I've been blowing my husband's boss. "I know Detective Becker asked you to come in, but we're in the middle of something. I'd like you to wait in one of our offices." She points to the tiny rooms behind me.

I don't move. I don't want to be trapped in a small room for God knows how long. "Where did you get that video of me and Joe? It wasn't from our backyard camera. Did you find a flash drive in my house or did it come in anonymously?" Please let her say she found a flash drive in my house.

"I'm not sure where we got it," she says, but she's lying. Flemming is meticulous. She would know.

"You received it anonymously," I say, my voice thin and strained, my statement full of dread, my heart heavy. My warm, sweaty skin goes cold. I shiver. My teeth chattering, I search her eyes for an explanation. "If you receive evidence anonymously, don't you question it? It would be obvious to question it."

Her eyes, typically exuding calm, are skittish like a cornered cat. She doesn't like being caught. She's not used to it.

"You thought you just got lucky?" I say it only to make her feel stupid.

"We are in the process of reviewing all our evidence in your son's case," she says, though her voice is less certain.

"What about Carson? How did you find out my oldest died? And my brother?" I thought Carla tipped them off about Carson and my brother. When she said she didn't bring up Carson, I assumed she was lying. "Did you find that out about Carson on your own or did you receive a tip?" I want Detective Flemming to say *We did our detective work. We found everything out on our own.* Then this idea David is involved in some strange and confusing and awful way can evaporate. I can tell myself I considered it briefly, only because I was under immense strain. I considered it briefly, this crazy idea, then threw it away.

She hesitates. Glances over my shoulder, considering something. If she'd found these things out on her own, she'd say so.

Emotions rise inside my chest—a tsunami of conflicting feelings—and my jaw trembles again. "It's David," I say, my words shaky, weepy. "My other son, David. He has McClane. I don't know why. I don't understand."

For a moment I try to convince myself David and McClane are just having a good time. Catching up on brotherly stuff. Maybe camping in Tennessee. Unplugging. McClane's pissed at me and needs a few days to calm down. Or maybe McClane finally took my advice and reached out to David, asking for his opinion on the wrestling scholarship. They've discussed the pros and cons, and they're spending a few days together to let the right choice settle.

I'm trying on these ideas, hoping one will fit, but I'm too fat for them. This is not a brotherly trip off-grid. There is no benevolent reason David could have sent the police that video. He did it to blindside me, to hurt me. I don't understand it, but nothing else makes sense.

If David thought I killed Carson, why wouldn't he ask me about it?

I know the answer to that. Same reason I don't ask Joe about what's happened to him. Why I don't press him about his behavior. A conversation would be painful and confusing. It was honestly easier to blow his boss. It makes no sense. Yet it does.

"David has McClane," I say again. "I don't know why he'd do this, he's a good boy. He must be—" I say, getting choked up. "I don't know."

I truly don't know. Unwell? I never pictured him that way. He always had his shit together. Confident, a know-it-all, a little arrogant. I try to picture it now. What would unwell look like? You don't want to picture your child that way, but I let in those possibilities like a flash flood. I picture him mumbling racial slurs in grocery store aisles, slut-shaming a girl in a parking lot, stealing a blanket from a sleeping homeless man, accidentally not accidentally jabbing a small guy with a pool stick at a bar as they pass behind him on his backswing, no reason, just to be a dick, forcing himself on a drunk girl in the backseat of his car.

I can't picture any of it. I mean, my mind *is* picturing it, but it doesn't seem like David.

Flemming is silent but surprised. The way she leans slightly forward, the curiosity in her eyes, suggests she never considered David. Why would she? I didn't either.

"You have to find David. He lives in Memphis. He works for the FBI. He's an agent." When I say the last part, my heart flutters. Every time I've said that last part, peoples' eyebrows lift and they nod in respect, and it makes me proud I had a part in who he's become.

Flemming isn't everyone, though. Her eyebrows lift but that's it. No nod. No smile. Maybe she wants to look out for fellow law enforcement, not see him get dragged into trouble. Blue Lives Matter or whatnot. Or maybe she likes the juicy idea of a rogue FBI agent.

A staticky squawk comes from the device clipped near her shoulder. Someone giving a code. It makes me think of a hospital emergency alert.

She takes my elbow and turns me toward the entrance doors. "I'll look into your son, David. Listen, I have to attend to another matter. Would you like to wait in one of our offices or go home?"

"But you guys told me to come in."

"A few things have changed." She says softly, "It's best if you go home. I'll come by later."

"What? What's changed?"

"Listen, Meg," she says, and her expression changes. She's familiar again. Empathetic, almost like a friend. "Go shower, wash your hair. Call a lawyer. There's enough evidence to arrest you."

"What? For what?" I truly don't know what. Not because I'm a perfect, law-abiding citizen but because there is too much wrong. Arrest me for Carson's death? For McClane missing? For blowing Joe's boss to keep the paychecks coming? "I don't understand. What could be more important right now than you looking for McClane and David?"

From over her shoulder, a door opens and a woman's scream fills this empty stale place with a spark of echoey rage. "It's her fault!"

CHAPTER 40

McClane

7 MINUTES UNTIL MISSING

You know that feeling you get when the party's over? Someone's flipped on all the lights and everyone's features have lost their sleek mystery and people are funneling toward the front door and it's suddenly too quiet—but you still didn't say what you were dying to say to that one person? I have that feeling.

Dave's got to get back to work, but I haven't told him about Nat being pregnant. And I've got so much I need to say about Dad. And I want to hear what Dave's got to say about my scholarship. He'll have a strong opinion, and I'd like to hear it. My stomach twists. Syrupy soda on an empty stomach didn't hit right.

When I walk out of the Denny's bathroom, Dave's at the counter next to a smudged display case of stale desserts. He's laying cash on the counter while the woman behind the counter is punching in numbers on her register. I head to our table, slide back into our booth, my hand squeaking on the vinyl seat. I sip my coffee. It's bitter, cool, and leaves grit on my tongue.

Panic startles me. My wallet. Keys. Phone. Fuck, they're gone.

Dave's probably got them. I check under the table anyway. The carpet is thin and dark reddish brown, good for masking dropped items, so I search carefully. Nope.

I turn, and Dave's behind me, his eyebrows pinched. "What's up?"

"Do you have my stuff?"

"What stuff?"

"My wallet, phone, keys. Even my hoodie's gone."

"No, man," he says coolly. "I got up to pay, like, one minute ago. I was going to grab them but figured, I'm right fucking here. You look on the seats?"

"Yeah, I looked on the seats and under the table." I feel exhaustion hit me, like walking into a wall. If I've got to wait in the DMV line again, get all my cards new, buy a new phone. Shit. I don't want that work.

"Let's ask the busboy," he says, calm and with a plan. "There he is." A few tables over, the busboy is clearing a booth, setting plates into a rectangular bin balanced against his hip. Dave walks over, shoulders back, chin up, like he's got everything under control. He always does. It's not like I need help here, it's not like he's doing anything special, but I'm feeling tired and a little nauseated, so his composure makes me breathe a little easier. The busboy—he's a man, actually—is not startled when Dave taps his bicep with the back of his hand.

"My brother went to the bathroom and now his wallet is gone," Dave says.

The guys at the nearest table watch my brother, interested. They're my dad's age and wearing brown canvas jackets, their knuckles stained filthy.

"Which table?" the busboy says.

"There." Dave points to where we were sitting.

"No, I didn't take anything," the busboy says, his expression flat. It's the expression of someone who's too familiar with getting hassled. "The drinks are still there, see? The glasses, the mug. All there. No one cleaned up."

I step to the side so Dave's not blocking me. "Thanks for your help, man. And no worries," I say to the busboy. "Dave, it's fine. All replaceable."

"It's not fine," he says, calm yet firm. "Someone stole from you. It's not fine."

It actually is fine. All my stuff's in the cloud. I've got an extra set of keys at home. Not much in my wallet besides my license, school ID, and bank card. I can get new cards. But I'm lightheaded, so I don't feel like telling him. I don't think I ate enough today. It was a crazy day, with Hud getting his ass beat and talking with Hud's dad and fighting with my mom and getting my ass handed to me by Nat's dad and Ax being a dick. God, what a day. I didn't eat breakfast or lunch either. I only had that lasagna. Sweat is breaking across my forehead.

Dave looks around, chin up, fidgety, and heads to the front counter. I trail behind. "Dave, it's fine, man. We have another set of keys to Cool Hand Luke and my phone, man, it's all in the cloud." I laugh, trying to bring him back, but it's a flimsy laugh.

The woman at the counter is scrolling on her phone. Dave drums his fingers on the glass counter, and she looks up. Lifts her eyebrows instead of saying hello.

"You have cameras in here?" He looks up at the corners of the ceiling. He points to a white round thing on the ceiling that looks like a light fixture.

"What do you mean?" She slips her phone into her back pocket.

"My brother's wallet was stolen a few minutes ago. He left it on the table while he went to the bathroom. I was up here, paying. Do you have in-house cameras so we can see who took it?"

She shifts her weight. "We have cameras, but I honestly have no idea how I'd get that footage. It gets sent to corporate."

"Can I speak to your manager?"

"You're speaking to the manager, sir." Respectful but firm, like she's had a lot of practice saying that line.

"I'm with the FBI," he says, his voice like a sudden gust. "I'd like access to those cameras, so my brother can get his personal effects back."

She nods a few times. "All right. Why don't you give me your number." She pushes a pad of paper toward Dave. Sets a pen on top like she's acting. "I'll talk to corporate about how to get the footage first thing in the morning, and I'll call you."

He writes his information down on the pad of paper. "Hey, thanks. Sorry if I've offended you, I'm just worried about my little brother here. I'll look forward to your call."

"Oh, of course," she says, friendly and eager. "I completely understand your concern." That's the type of accommodating response Dave always gets. Which is kind of funny. It's, like, the bigger the dick you are right off the bat, the bigger the apology you give, the bigger the understanding. What about just not being a dick in the first place? Like, Hud's rarely a dick, and no one gives him the understanding he deserves. Reminds me of what Natalie says: "The guy who talks the loudest is always the biggest baby." It's funny, but Dave's not the type who would appreciate that comment.

He heads for the door, and I'm relieved to finally get out of here. I feel crappy and can't wait to crash in my bed. Dave reaches for the door, then stops and turns. His voice booming like a WWE announcer, he says, "I'm with the FBI. I'm reviewing the camera footage tomorrow." He is broadcasting to the entire restaurant. Like we are acting in a movie. It feels so cringe and dramatic. "If you want to avoid prosecution, bring the wallet and phone forward and we'll be on our way, no trouble. You have my word."

Then I realize. He's joking. He's got to be joking, acting insane to make me laugh. If I didn't feel nauseous, I would bust up laughing.

"Did you check your backpack?" one of the waitresses says, a challenge in her voice. She's my age. She's got a tray under her arm.

"Excuse me?" Dave says slowly, and I realize: He's not joking about any of this. I shrink a little.

"You should check your backpack. Maybe you have it and you jumped the gun." She holds his gaze.

Someone mumbles a few words at the table nearest to the door, a group of high school kids, and the rest of the table laughs. I don't recognize them, but they could go to my school.

"Dave, let's go," I say, and now I'm annoyed. I want to be home in my bed. I feel like I could puke, I don't want to stand around while he goes on. He's being dramatic, and that reflects on me. Who is he to make a big deal about my stuff when I'm telling him to quit it? He was the one who said he'd watch my stuff. It's his fault, and now he's blaming all these strangers. "Dave. Let's go," I say again. "It's not a big deal, man."

Dave ignores me and the waitress. He looks around. "Last chance," he says. A few people look over. Most are back to talking and eating and not taking him seriously.

"Let's go," he says, and pushes through the door.

I follow, but I'm dragging. It's like I've got Benadryl running through my veins. "I feel like garbage. Call Mom or Whitney. They'll pick me up."

His eyebrows harden, and he frowns. "Fuck that, man. I'll drive you. I can spend the night and visit."

"I thought you had to get back."

"It's okay, man. I can make time."

He unlocks his doors, and I get in the passenger seat. I close my door and press my forehead against the window. The cool hardness feels good on my skin, but I still feel nauseous, like the ground is pulling away from me and starting to spin. Drunk, almost.

He drives out of the parking lot and heads toward Route 43. The trees are tipping sideways, so I close my eyes.

"Hey, Mick," Dave says. "I need to tell you some stuff. I'm not sure you're gonna believe me." His words are pulling away fast, falling under quicksand.

"I'll believe you," I say. Or maybe I don't say it, I just think it. Then it's lights-out.

CHAPTER 41

MEG

DAY 3, 11:04 A.M.

Interested, I turn toward the commotion. Misery loves company. Someone else's shit is hitting the fan, and I'm here for it. I'm completely shocked to find the petite furious woman is pointing at me. Becker is there, his hand on her arm, trying to keep things under control.

"It's her fault," she shouts, but her voice breaks into a cry. She looks at Becker. "I need to talk to her."

"Who is that?" I say.

"Natalie's parents," Flemming says. *Parents.* Just as I'm looking for the other one, a man walks up behind the angry woman and stands at her side. He's stocky and dressed for a beer in the yard with neighbors, wearing flip-flops and shorts and a shirt with the sleeves cut so he can show off his muscles. His hand is on her back and he's talking in her ear. Natalie's parents. I've never seen them before. "Natalie's missing," Flemming adds.

"What? When?" I say.

"Since yesterday," Flemming says. "I need you to leave now."

That doesn't make sense. It's David and McClane. I don't understand why David's taken McClane, but I know it's David. How could Natalie be involved?

"I want to talk to that bitch," Natalie's mom spits. It's like lightning striking. Shocking. It makes the hairs on my arms rise. I'm threatened, I want to flee, I want to come across as taking the high ground, but also I'd like to throw down. Just a little bit. Because this is Natalie's fault. I have no proof of it, but I feel it in my bones in this instant.

Joe taught me how to fight. I've never thrown a punch outside of sparring with Joe, but now I want to. Becker's talking to her. I can't hear what he's saying, but his grip on her is tight.

"I saw that video of you," she says, her accusation sharp. "You're an evil bitch. Where's my daughter?" Natalie's mom wails, her tone both strong and broken. The intensity of her desperation makes me feel for her. We are connected, the same. Our children are missing. We have matching holes in our souls. Now I want to embrace her.

She shakes free from Becker's grip and runs at me, closing the space between us.

I'm not ready for it. My feet are deadweight. I'm frozen. I can't punch. Not in the moment I need to.

She's a few steps away—I'm going to get tackled—when Flemming steps in front of me and takes the hit meant for me. Flemming stumbles back, but she's still on her feet. Joe always said it's more impressive to be able to take a hit than to give one.

Becker rushes from the side, taking Natalie's mom down. It

happens fast. Even with that round ass, he can move. He's got her on her stomach, one hand behind her back, and now Natalie's dad comes in like a thick piece of furniture from behind and knocks Becker down.

The woman behind the desk side-hurdles it like a cowboy and she's drawing her gun and shouting for backup. Flemming's got her gun drawn, aimed at Natalie's dad, she's screaming "Freeze!" in the lowest, strongest voice I've ever heard. *Freeze? They really say freeze?* The door to the right opens and a few husky cops barrel through, moving awkwardly, their gear squeaking and clanging.

Natalie's mom and dad are on the ground, crying through their words, but staying still.

Gun still drawn and pointed, Flemming nods to me. Her eyelid is fat, a horizontal cut below her eyebrow, and the white of her eye is bloody. "Go," she says.

I should already be gone. She shouldn't have to tell me to leave, but it's all happened so fast, and it's hard to look away. I pull the thick glass door open and run to my car. My heart is twitchy with adrenaline. I'm grateful Flemming stepped in front of me, that she wants me to wait at home, but she's also a threat. Flemming and Becker, they're going to arrest me.

I can't afford to be stuck in a jail cell. I can't count on their help. I need to find David.

CHAPTER 42

McClane

MISSING

The acidic smell of puke is everywhere. I feel its grit inside my nose, but I don't remember throwing up. My eyelids are heavy, swollen shut. I'd say this is a bitch of a hangover, but I didn't drink. Must be the stomach flu. Last time I had a stomach bug I was in middle school. That time it came on fast too.

Under my palms, the ground is sweaty and cold—tile. I push myself up, and my hand slides against a slick puddle. I don't have to take a guess what that is.

I force my eyes open against the light. I'm on a bathroom floor, next to the toilet. The light is dim, but it's still too bright. My orange puke is on the floor and splattered on the walls. I've never been in this restroom. It has that careless public-bathroom stink to it. Stale water and strangers' skin. Three pubic hairs are plastered to the base of the porcelain bowl near the floor.

That does it. I grab the moist rim of the toilet and pull myself up to heave into the bowl.

I drop to the floor like I'm an old man and roll onto my back. My mind is foggy. I'm in a dreamy-sick purgatory, fuzzy and untethered, and weird thoughts pop up. Prom is coming. One week, three weeks, something. I should order Nat's corsage. And a tie to match her dress. I've slacked on that stuff. I should clean my car. She loves the yeasty pizza smell, though, so I shouldn't clean too hard. I'd smile if I had the energy.

I've got to get Jack a date. He wants to go with Olivia. I should get off my ass and go talk to Olivia. My list of *should*s is pathetically long. What a crappy friend I've been. He's stressed about it, wondering if he's going to his senior year prom or not. He can be awkward around girls, I should help him out. I'm gonna be a better friend. To him and to Hud. When I get home, I'm gonna do good for my boys. Whitney too. I owe her. I picture her as a little kid, sitting at the table by herself, taking a stand against eating cooked carrots. I picture her in middle school with her sky-blue eyeshadow and strands of her black hair dyed lime-Kool-Aid green, tinkering with robotic components.

Someone's knocking on the door.

"I'm sick," I say.

The door opens a foot. Dave's assessing the damage. He laughs a little. "Way to destroy the bathroom, little brother," he says, but his tone is kind and calm.

"Where are we?"

"Motel. You got too sick. I had to pull over." He sounds tired.

We were at a restaurant, I think. Yeah. I push through the fog in my mind. Denny's. We were just at Denny's. He was amped up, squirrelly, talking fast. Someone stole my phone. Now he's talking slower.

"Call Mom to pick me up," I say.

"Hang on." His footsteps fall away, and a bit later—five or twenty minutes, I can't tell—he's back at the door. "Here. Drink some water so you don't get dehydrated." I sit up and lean against the wall. It's a process. He hands me a bottle of water, and I drink. Small sips.

"Did you call Mom?"

"Not yet." He's thinking. "Why don't you get in the shower. Rinse off your clothes, and I'll put them on the vent to dry."

That seems reasonable. I mean, my clothes are covered in puke. I can't get into anyone's car like this. Even if it wasn't reasonable, I'm pretty sure I'd agree. When you know you're sick, you follow instructions. "Okay."

"You need help standing?"

"I got it." I get to my feet. My shoes are gone but I'm wearing my socks. I step in the shower, turn it on, and tilt my face up so the spray hits my face and clears the smell of puke from my sinuses. My knees are weak, though. I reach out, slide my hands down the shower walls till I'm sitting in a puddle of warm water. Strings of mucousy vomit glide by.

Dave mumbles something.

Brain fuzzy, muscles weak, I say, "Huh?"

"I'm just cleaning up your puke, man. It's like Stevie down the block all over."

"Huh?"

"The orange soda puke fest."

Oh. Right. "Thanks." My clothes, soaked and pasted to my skin, weigh me down. "Is Mom coming?"

Sounds like he's moving a towel around, wringing it in the sink. The faucet is running. "I need to tell you some stuff."

"Dude, I feel like I got run over. I don't want to riff."

"I know," he says. "Just listen to me. My work—it's really opened my eyes. It's like I'm finally thinking clearly for the first time."

Nausea rolls over me. I want to be home. I want to crash in my bed. "Mom's coming though, right?"

Something smashes against the mirror—his fist, I think—and glass rains down into the sink.

CHAPTER 43

MEG

DAY 3, 11:55 A.M.

The sun is an ugly bright, making me nauseous. On my way home, weaving down side streets, I pull over to throw up on the grassy parkway in front of a stranger's house. Not much comes up. I stand in the grass next to their garbage cans, bulging with black bags, and look at their house: doors closed, curtains shut. No one watching me. Is their house healthy or sick like mine? The garbage bags sigh a rotten-sweet smell.

I think of McClane's body cut into pieces, stuffed inside black garbage bags. No, Natalie's body. I throw up again.

I wipe my mouth with my hands, wipe my hands on my jeans. My skin is pasty and hot-flashy. I get into my car and blast the air-conditioning. I pull out my phone and text Dave.

Why are you doing this?

I delete it.

> *Are you with McClane?*

I delete it.

> *I know you think I killed Carson. I didn't.*

Delete.

If I have learned anything in the past year living with Joe, it's calculation. Strategic texts. Keep it ambiguous. I don't want to provoke David, especially if he's not feeling like himself.

> *Call me, please. I'm worried.*

I read it five times and hit send.

I try to wrap my mind around Natalie being missing but can't. She can't be involved in this. Maybe she's missing because she's searching for McClane. She can't be with them. That doesn't make sense. McClane was missing a whole day, maybe two, before Natalie went missing.

McClane's either conspiring with David or he was taken against his will. In either scenario, David wants to wreck me. It hurts like the worst heartache. I gave my whole life to my kids, planned my career around their needs, swept aside dreams of travel and frivolity, lost years of sleep and health. I worried over their stresses, rejoiced in their joys, carted them around to friends' houses, school activities, sports, doctors, dentists, tutors, in an effort to enrich their lives and make them feel whole and healthy, to make them feel safer than I felt as a kid. For what? For them to hate me so completely. How is it possible to put years of work and love into parenting, yet fail at it so grandly?

I ignore the reporters, pull into my driveway, push the button, and the garage door opens. Joe's car is gone.

Joe. Last night he was naked and out of his mind at Breakneck, maybe thinking of killing himself. So where the hell is he now? I imagine him sitting at the posh Starbucks in quaint downtown Sugar Glen, working on his laptop and sipping an Americano, maybe writing his manifesto.

I would laugh if I weren't so empty.

I close the garage door, sealing myself in darkness. My mind swirls in confusion. I've never felt this disoriented, this full of self-doubt. Even the quiet dark of my garage feels untrustworthy.

On the passenger seat, my phone buzzes, jolting me. Oh God, is David texting me back?

No. It's Deb, Jack's mom.

Hey, Meg. I'd like to help. I'm heading over to you.

Shit. Worried she's already on her way, I frantically type a reply.

No. I won't be home. I'll call you later.
You can come over tonight. Thanks.

I sigh and walk into the kitchen on old-lady feet, my tongue sour with vomit. I lean down and drink straight from the faucet. Wiping cool water from my cheek, I take in my tidy white kitchen. Everything is in its place, as it always is. But now, it feels like a lie.

I open the dishware cabinet, lift a handful of porcelain plates, and throw them across the room. When they hit the floor, the sound is not a high-pitched shatter, but more like the heavy, low banging of many hammers. A few plates shatter into larger pieces, slingshotting themselves down the hallway. One plate doesn't break but wobbles along its edge until it loses momentum.

I pull down the bowls, throw them down.

Next, the mugs.

"Mom!" Shouting from the hallway. My face is hot, and tears blur my vision.

It's Whitney. Oh. The cars were gone, so I thought I was alone. I forgot about Whitney. Which is a detail she'll probably repeat casually, with a laugh, to her therapist or to a friend over a cocktail, when she's older: "I was the forgotten child."

She's barefoot among the broken dishware in her cutoff jeans and half top, her bra strap showing, her dark hair cascading down her shoulders, her toenails each painted a different bright metallic color. She wears no makeup on her face. Her complexion is flawless, her eyelashes are thick and long. Such an effortless beauty.

Her hands are clenched in fists at her sides, her body tense and braced for bad news. "Is he dead?"

"No," I say calmly, as if this shattered mess isn't mine and I just stumbled upon it. "No, it's not that. I don't know, but—"

"But what?"

I turn toward the kitchen window, searching for the ash tree. I only see a small section. From a distance, it looks healthy, thriving. I can't believe I missed it. How could a good mother miss it? Easy. A good mother would not have missed it.

"I think McClane is with David," I say, but that's not what I mean. Saying what I mean will be stepping over a line. Saying what I mean, well, I won't be able to take it back.

Whitney tilts her head ever so slightly, like a curious dog. Her fists are still clenched.

"David has McClane." I sigh. "I think David is not well and he took McClane. Abducted," I say, but the word sounds strange coming out of my mouth.

She unclenches her fists and nods thoughtfully, unsurprised. Which surprises me. A chill shivers across the back of my neck. I study her more carefully. Her serious, calculating eyes. Her delicate fingers. She's rubbing her thumb and forefinger together like she's rolling a joint. It's a habit of hers when she's thinking. Carson did that too. It doesn't make sense that she's calculating, that she's thinking. I just told her something unimaginable.

"Let me grab my laptop," she says. "Meet me in the car." She turns away and rushes down the hall.

"What? Why?" I stand there among my broken dishware like a fool, like an old woman who has gained no wisdom, who has learned nothing. Who has aged ungracefully, stupidly, uselessly.

"I know where he is," she says, breathless as she runs up the stairs.

CHAPTER 44

McClane

MISSING

I shiver. Not sure if it's because I'm sick or because Dave just smashed the bathroom fucking mirror. "Did you hurt your hand?" I say, my voice shaky.

He's silent for a few seconds. "I'm fine, man," he says, kinda quiet. "Fine. I'm fine. Not a scratch, actually." He's perking up, sounding impressed. "Whoa. I'm, like, bulletproof." He laughs a little.

Nausea picks up again, small huffs sighing across my head. I'm still sitting, shoulders hunched, in the tub. It'd be great if the water was warmer, but my arms are too heavy in my soaked shirt. I tilt my chin up to let the spray catch my face. The showerhead spawns another showerhead. There's two. I blink a few times, and my vision clears. "But why'd you break the mirror, man?"

"I told you. I'm finally seeing things clearly. Everything, it's connected like the threads holding a sheet together. Five hundred count, bro. Five hundred. The stuff I've seen, man, you can't imagine.

You can't trust people. They do the most terrible, filthy things. No one is who they pretend to be." He sighs. "When I was little, I had this camera. Dad would download my photos and videos onto a thumb drive for me."

I let water fill my mouth and let it pour out. I don't have the energy to spit. So. Tired.

"It's the weirdest thing how it happened," he says. "It was fate, really. It was fate I stumbled upon that thumb drive. It's all connected, Mick. Everything is connected." He's getting energized, talking faster and louder, and it's an assault to my brain cells. "All these terrible things I've seen, there's a reason. One thing leads to another, everything touches. This case I was working, then I lose my keys and I'm looking everywhere, tearing apart my apartment, and I find this old dusty thumb drive."

I reach through brain fog and try to grasp what he's trying to explain, but it's too slippery. He says things are connected, but these things are years and miles apart.

"I knew what it was when I found it," he says. "At the time, I thought, well, no big deal, I'll look at that drive later, maybe, for old time's sake, but this voice in my head told me I had to look at it now. It was important. It was connected. All these strings, they connect everything."

If I had energy, I'd laugh. I'd say, *Dude what the fuck are you talking about? Why you talking so fast? What's the rush, man?* But I'm drowsy. I barely shake my head.

"So I stayed up all night going through these videos and photos," he says. "Most were of Carson. I took so many videos of that kid. He was always doing things to make me laugh. It was like I was his favorite person in the whole world. I think I was." He's getting choked up, overwhelmed with emotion, the opposite of me. I'm blank like a steamy, fogged bathroom mirror. The only thing I'm feeling is lost. Lost in time and place. "There was this one video though, it was Mom. She was talking to Dad, telling him—" He's seriously choked up. He takes a few fast breaths. "Telling him she wanted Carson gone. She couldn't stand him."

Water spraying weakly on my face, in my eyes, my mouth, I say, "He probably did some stupid little kid thing, and she got pissed."

He pounds his fist against the door, and I startle. "Carson died that same day, Mick. The same fucking day. That shit doesn't happen on accident. She killed him, man. She killed my brother."

Through the fuzziness, panic rises, and an urgent thought: I've got to get out of here. I grip the edge of the tub and struggle to get my feet under me. My wet, heavy clothes pull me down, but I manage to stand. Getting up was exhausting, I need a break. I need to just stand here for a sec. "C'mon, Dave. That sounds crazy. You misunderstood somehow. She wouldn't do that."

"I'm not crazy," he screams, so loud. Even though I'm out of his reach and I'm numb, I flinch a little. I turn toward the shower curtain and flinch again because the shadowy shape of him stands inches away, facing me. "She killed him," he says. His breath comes fast, quick and angry.

Panic grips my mind, tries to slap it sober, but I'm too numb. My heart beats slowly. My limbs are rubbery, and my eyelids droop. I'm silent for a while. He's silent, but he's there. His silhouette is unmoving. His breathing slows, but it's still too loud and full of emotion. What's he waiting for?

My knees tremble. I want to turn the shower hotter, but I don't have the energy. "I think I need to go to the hospital." My vision smears, like windshield wipers against hard rain. "Can you bring me to the hospital?"

"You don't need to go to the hospital," he says, but his words sound underwater. "We'll talk when you wake up."

Fuck. I think I'm in trouble. "Dave? Did you drug me?" I say, then I'm falling.

CHAPTER 45

Meg

DAY 3, 12:32 P.M.

Of course Whitney knows where David is. She is my quiet, moody, but clever child. She is always thinking. Always watching. As the youngest, she was left out of the fun, told to scat, so she trailed far enough behind to go unnoticed. She picked up on the older kids' moods. When their auras shifted darker, she kept her distance so their nasty fun wouldn't be at her expense. When their hearts and words were light, she took a chance and tried to prove herself worthy by performing funny or daring antics. She'd crawl into the storm grate. Crack an egg against her forehead.

Once she realized they weren't worth her sacrifice, she withdrew. No longer aching to be part of their fun, she wanted to be superior. Smarter. Unreachable. She read. She took programming classes because they told her girls weren't good at that stuff. Defiance became her strongest motivation. With her fawn-like limbs, her porcelain skin, her long dark hair, and those slate-gray eyes, she seems more magical creature than human.

I brag about Dave's job. I brag about McClane wrestling. I don't brag about Whitney much because it would be obnoxious to brag about Whitney. She is too smart. Too beautiful. I wonder if she knows that.

As we're driving away from our house, she tells me to stop the car. The reporters are gone, maybe on their lunch break, but the adolescent vigil is going strong.

"What?"

"Stop the car, Mom." She opens the door before I shift into park. She stomps up to the group of teenagers, kicks a teddy bear across the lawn, and screams, "He's not dead, you needy assholes. He wouldn't want you here. Get the fuck off my lawn." She gets back in the car, her wild hair caught in her mouth, and mutters, "Idiots. He'd better not be dead." This last part comes out wobbly. I'm not sure if she's saying it as a prayer or a threat to me.

I keep my mouth shut and give her time to cool down as I drive. She sets my Google Maps to Memphis, Tennessee, no specific address. Says she's working on that.

Eventually, she asks, "So, he sent that video to the police? That old video of your temper tantrum?"

I'm about to dispute "temper tantrum," but my ego has dried up like cracked, scorched earth. There's no point. "I think so. I think he thinks I—"

"Killed Carson," she finishes. "Because in the video you basically said that, that you wanted him gone."

"I didn't mean it. I was exhausted. He was exhausting. It's hard to explain. He was dangerous for Jamie, so I could never look away. Me saying all that, it was just a heat of the moment thing, like when you tell McClane you hate him."

"I'm not McClane's mom. I didn't decide to be his sister. But whatever." She sighs and sets her laptop down by her feet. "So Dave came across this old video, maybe stumbled upon it for the first time. Anyway, he sent it to the police so you would get in trouble."

God, I still don't want to believe it. "Let's just say he sent it, yeah. Why would he involve McClane?"

She leans back and puts her legs on the dashboard.

"Please don't do that. If we get in an accident, you'll snap in two."

"Don't get in an accident, then."

My nerves fray. I breathe deep, try to calm myself. I keep quiet.

"He took McClane to draw attention to you," she says, impatient, like it's all so obvious and I'm dumb. "Your kid is missing. So then, what happened to your other kid? You obviously have serious problems," she says. "I mean, your brother was violent and unpredictable. He literally killed someone."

Panic grips me, and my fingers tighten around the steering wheel. "How did you—"

"There's this thing called the internet. C'mon, Mom. Living with you and Dad for sixteen years, you think I wouldn't know about your brother?"

I squeeze the steering wheel tighter, angry at myself for not being careful enough. I never wanted my kids to know their blood relative was capable of murder. I thought it could confuse them, make their teenage brains wonder what horrific potentials they had pumping through their veins. Joe and I only talked about my family with our door closed. Even then, we whispered.

Whitney's legs stretching straight onto the dashboard are like tiny needles under my skin. I try to stop looking at her bare feet on the dash, but they're so pretty, each toenail painted a different color. Metallic yellow, metallic green, metallic purple. I can't imagine painting my toenails that sickly yellow. Young girls can get away with so much.

"How would he convince McClane—"

"Maybe he *took* him. To get the police involved and invested," she says confidently, as if she's got it all figured out. "To get the police to dig into your history. To *hurt* you."

"I don't know that David would—"

"You're his mother," she snaps. "You don't see your kids as they are. You see them as you want them to be."

"We're talking about your brother, not some criminal."

She sighs and looks out her window. I glance down at my phone on the console between the seats, checking for texts. I sent David another message before we started driving.

I need to talk to you. It's important. Please call me.

He hasn't called or texted.

"We've seen Dave only once this year," she says, as if this settles an argument.

"Why would that matter?"

"At Christmas, Dave seemed off. You didn't notice?"

"No," I say, but my tone is weak.

"Of course not, he's perfect." She's trying to pick a fight. Keeping my eyes on the road, I bite at the skin along my thumb. Jamie said the same thing on our drive to the airport. She said he seemed intense, like maybe he was using cocaine. Sure, he slept a lot those first couple of days. His mood fluctuated from sleepy to hyperproductive. But the kids, they are always going through a new phase, a different phase. Their transforming personalities and new habits have become a constant.

"He's always been a know-it-all," Whitney says. "His way was the best way, he had the best idea, he talked the loudest. Sorry, but it's true," she says. "Having a conversation with him was occasionally fun but also felt pointless. Like, he's never going to consider what I'm saying."

I try to keep my voice calm. "But what does this have to do with McClane?"

"It doesn't. I'm trying to give you a feel for how," she says tentatively. "How someone like him could head down the wrong path."

She knows more than she's told me. "McClane has been *missing* for *three days*, Whitney. Please, tell me what you know."

She exhales. "I saw something on Dave's laptop. He left it open on his bed when he went to the bathroom. Over Christmas. This was when he and Jamie were visiting. I walked by his room, and it caught my eye. The format of the page, the text—"

"I'm not following. What page?"

CHAPTER 46

McClane

MISSING

Before I open my eyes, I'm aware of four things. One: My head aches. Like dehydrated-hungover or ran-into-a-tree-trunk ache. Two: I'm naked. Three: I'm lying in bed, which is so much better than the bathroom tile. And four: Mom's here.

I'm not a mama's boy, not at all—there is constant tension between Mom and me lately—but it is a relief to hear her voice as my mind pulls away from groggy sleep. It means Dave called her, and this story I'm telling myself, that Dave drugged me, is just that—a story. I was sick, so my mind made shit up. Mom's voice means everything is okay.

But now that her voice is coming into focus, it sounds cold. "I can't do this anymore," she says. "I don't want to do this anymore. I hate this."

I turn toward Mom's voice and open my eyes. It's not her. Dave's sitting on the other motel bed, his legs crisscrossed like he's a kid, with his laptop open. Oh. The video he was telling me about. That's what he's watching. Everything is not okay. My hand goes to my forehead and touches the goose egg there. Right. I passed out in the shower. Dave knew I was going to pass out because he drugged me. He was there to catch me, but not before I knocked my head. Everything is so far away from okay.

"Can I see?" I say, my voice raspy from my Olympic-level puking.

He looks over at me, his eyes sparking with nervous energy and emotion. "Yeah. Yeah, of course."

He turns his laptop to me and presses play. He keeps talking, narrating the video to me. That annoyed the fuck out of me when we were kids. I'd be watching a show, and he would talk to me the whole time, so I couldn't even take it in. On the positive side, I've perfected the art of tuning him out.

The video shows the back of a woman. She's young, wearing shorts and a tank. It doesn't look like Mom. This woman is younger and skinnier, but it's her. Her posture—the slump of her shoulders, her chin tilted up, and how she holds her hands on her hips—gives her away. That's her angry stance. She's standing on our patio, looking out into our backyard.

The quality of the video is crap, faded and grainy, but it's good enough to see what's what.

A man walks into the video, and I recognize his tattoo. The cartoon shark on his shoulder. Dad. A tighter, younger version of Dad.

My mind is foggy, and this video is so old—the effect of both those things is disorienting.

"I don't want to do this anymore. I hate this," she says. It's Mom's voice, but it's not. Mom's always been annoying, but in an energetic, get-your-shit-done, don't-screw-up, bright and sunny way. Here, the bright, sunny energy is stripped away. "I don't want him," she says. "I am a shit person. I wish he were gone."

"See," Dave says. "I told you. I fucking told you." Eyes bright and cold, he's triumphant. "Carson died the same day. Tell me that's not suspicious, Mick."

"It's suspicious," I say. My brain fog is thinning a little. My goose egg throbs to a quick beat.

"Fuck yeah," he says, punching the air like he just scored at the buzzer and his teammates are about to pick him up and carry him around on their shoulders. This is his response to a horrible, depressing video? Fuck.

Yeah, Mom can be too much, too in your business, too uptight about money, too worried about stupid stuff, like the neighbors are having a party for the Fourth of July and we're not, so we should do *something*, but she's fairly typical mom material. She takes care of us, worries over us, tells us to put away our laundry, pesters us to eat our vegetables—fucking still—to take our vitamins—still—get enough sleep—still—work hard in school. That's just so far away from killing her own kid. Lately, she's doing a terrible job of dealing with Dad's problems, like, seriously pathetic. At the same time, I don't know how she'd fix him, so I get why she pretends there's no problem.

"It's creepy and it's real sad," I say, my voice dry and scratchy, but confident. "But it's a coincidence. She didn't kill him."

His eyes narrow and harden. Dude's actually pissed at me for saying Mom didn't kill her kid. "Your problem, Mick, is you're too trusting."

No shit, I want to say. I trusted you. But my twitchy stomach tells me to keep my mouth shut. I roll away from him.

"I mean, of course you are." His voice softens a little. "You haven't seen what I've seen. People are scary motherfuckers. All of them."

Sunlight flows into the room through a heavy wool curtain. It's the golden orange of afternoon. Seriously? I slept the whole day? My pulse speeds up, and I have this weird feeling. Like I'm lost and missing out. I mean, I'm missing school, yeah, but it's more than that. There's something about losing a whole day that's alarming.

There's something about this situation that's alarming.

"Where are my clothes?"

"Oh," he says. "I found a laundromat a block down. They're drying."

"What about my shoes?"

"In the car."

"Can you call Dad?"

"Not yet. We need to get their attention."

"If you want Mom and Dad's attention, call them."

"Not them."

"Who? Who are you talking about?"

"The police."

"Why?"

"So they can connect the dots."

I sigh. He said that before—*connecting the dots*. That what happened was fate. That he was thinking clearly for the first time. He sounds crazy. I think he is crazy, but he's still my brother. We can work through this.

I roll back to him. He's staring at me. He looks lost, like he's waiting on me. Like I'm in charge. I'm naked, no shoes, recovering from puking and hitting my head, and I'm in charge? I say, "What do you want to happen?"

His mouth turns down at the corners. His eyebrows do a weird thing where they're both anxious and sad at the same time. "She needs to pay."

I shiver. "Man, that's just crazy."

His face twitches, and he closes his laptop. His lower lip juts out.

My skin feels irritated, and my gut feels loose. I might not be done in the bathroom. I hold my stomach and moan. "I don't feel good, Dave. Can you get me something to eat?" I say, my words slow and labored. "My throat hurts, my stomach hurts. I feel real sick, man. I'm going back to sleep." I close my eyes. I let my breathing slow. I let my mouth fall open.

I have this urge to ask him how hard I hit my head. All this worrying about CTE has made me paranoid about head injuries. Now is not the time, though. I keep my eyes shut, like I'm sleeping.

He paces a bit. His shoes creak as he walks. He stops.

My mouth open, I breathe heavily, slowly.

He paces more. Near the bedside table, he pulls a cord and fumbles with something. A few minutes later, the door opens and shuts.

I wait a few seconds. I get up slowly and peek out the window. He's in the parking lot, standing beside his car, his laptop and the motel single-button phone in his arms. He puts both in the passenger seat and gets in the driver's side. I wait for him to drive away.

My legs are weak. Even if I'm not done puking, I need to eat. I look around the room for my clothes, my shoes, his bag.

Nothing. There's nothing here. Panic digs its nails into my chest. *He took the motel phone. He took the fucking motel phone. You should be panicking.*

I'll walk out naked. Someone will help me out or call the cops. Either way, it's better than being trapped.

Am I trapped, though? I'm having a hell of a time reconciling the brother I've known all my life with this brother—this person who might have drugged me. He wouldn't trap me, though. He wouldn't hurt me. I must be confused.

I check the bathroom. Nothing in here.

I get down on all fours, the grainy carpet digging into my knees, and check under the beds.

His backpack.

Inside are a bunch of crinkled papers, along with my keys, phone, wallet, and hoodie.

I'm sweating, like, profusely. Partly because I feel sick, partly because I'm nervous he's going to open the door, but mostly because he stole my stuff. *He* stole my stuff and accused the busboy and the manager and *all* the people in the restaurant of stealing my stuff. I'm stunned. I sit my bare ass on the carpet, too shocked to care.

Snap out of it, Mick. You have to push past the fog.

I turn my phone on, and I'm confused by the date on my home screen. It's Saturday? I met Dave on Thursday night. I lost a day and a half?

Snap. Out. Of. It.

I work as fast as I can. I go into Snapchat and turn on my location. I hide my Snapchat icon in a folder so he can't find it. I turn my phone on Do Not Disturb. I text Natalie.

I'm in trouble. Come get me. Check Snap. Don't text me—

Footsteps outside the door. A key card sliding in. I don't bother finishing my text. I hit send and delete the thread. I throw my phone back in his bag, shove it under the bed, and lurch toward the bathroom.

The front door opens when my hand touches the bathroom doorknob.

"Hey, Bare Ass," he says, lighthearted.

"Hey," I say. "Did you get me food? I feel like I'm gonna pass out."

"Not yet. I forgot my bag."

"Oh," I say. I hope I shoved it under the bed far enough. I hope he won't know I looked through it. What would he do if he knew I knew he stole my stuff? "I'll be in here for a bit in case I puke again."

I close the door and kneel in front of the toilet, shivering and slick with sweat. Waiting for him to ask if I rummaged in his bag, waiting for him to explode. Instead, the front door closes. I sigh, relieved, but only for a second.

I meant to text more. I meant to tell Nat to call the police. I meant to tell her to call my parents. I meant to tell her Dave could be dangerous.

CHAPTER 47

MEG

DAY 3, 12:34 P.M.

I don't understand what she's telling me. How could something she saw on David's laptop over Christmas be connected to McClane being missing now?

"I'm trying to tell you," Whitney says, annoyed. "Quit interrupting me and listen." She sighs. Calmer. "Just listen to me, okay? He was on 8kun. It's an unregulated message board. There's lots of normal stuff there. People who like anime, people pirating movies. But there's bad stuff too. People into child porn, all that."

"He's—"

"No, he's not into that. I saw his tripcode and left his room before he came out of the bathroom. Later, I checked his posts. He's, like, big into retribution. Against parents, against mothers, against women."

I'm dying for details, but I'm also terrified. "So, you could pull up what he wrote and—"

"I'm not reading it to you. It's bad. I mean, not all of it. He posted things about his job. He talked about how he was on 4chan and 8kun before they—"

"What are those again?" I've heard of them, but I don't grasp.

"They're anonymous message boards. Like Reddit, but with much less moderation. You can post without an account and stay anonymous."

I don't understand this language of internet locations and anonymity. I don't think I need to, though. "How did you find those message boards in the first place?"

"It's easy. You just need a Tor browser to access some of them, but others are on the regular web. People talk about the dark web like it's mysterious and illicit, but it's just a different way to access certain sites."

I'm barely following. "When did you start doing this?"

"Since forever. I don't know. Middle school."

I bite my lip and stare straight ahead at the highway. I was the mom who collected phones at night and had everyone's Wi-Fi shut down at ten p.m. I thought I was keeping my kids safe.

Sensing my tension, she says, "I like anime, Mom. I have lots of friends on Discord. I post fan fiction on a few boards."

"Okay, thank you for sharing that." I force a slow exhale, preparing myself for worse. "Tell me what you found on David."

"Well, I mean, he posted his thoughts about random stuff. I mean, with his job stuff, he bragged about his security clearance, how he took down some child abusers. He posted more about the women abusers, the meth moms who sold their infants' bodies by the hour." My skin is crawling. That he was exposed to the worst human behavior in his job. That Whitney read details, that she's talking about them so casually. I squeeze the steering wheel to stay present and alert.

"The moms who would drug their middle school kids and sell them for sex. The moms who kept their toddlers in the trunk while they partied, their preschoolers starved in their basements. He posts on a bunch of, well, like, women-hating boards."

She's saying he's an incel without saying the word. I can't stand the word. It makes my skin shrink. It's overused, overdiscussed. That they're all sexually frustrated misogynists who think they are owed a motherly cook, a fuckdoll, a bangmaid. Heat spreads all over me, and I feel nauseous. That's not David. It can't be. You can't end up a woman hater if you have sisters, if your father wasn't one, can you? Joe used to treat me well. We used to be partners, not perfectly equal, but we would fill in each other's gaps.

"Maybe he just got unlucky," she says. "Like, maybe he fixated on one case, obsessed over this creepy, terrible woman, and then he fell down a dark hole. Somewhere inside that hole, I think he associated that woman with you."

"No. How could that happen? I'm nothing like that."

"Maybe he found the old video. The way you sounded, I mean, it was freaky. It sounded like you wanted your son dead. And then he was dead. That's, like, some serious coincidence," she says, her voice wavering with uncertainty.

I swerve onto the shoulder, my tires kicking up dirt and gravel. My skin is muggy, my vision is closing in. "I need a minute," I say as I step out and walk directly into the balmy forest. When all the greens become shadowed and the temperature dips, when I'm deep enough, I scream. I scream and moan, hands on knees, hunched over like I just puked.

Behind me, Whitney says, "Don't freak out, it's just me."

I wipe my eyes. "You said message boards are anonymous. How do you know it was him?" It's my one hope. That she's wrong.

"Are you joking? I'm, like, skilled, Mom." She laughs, trying to lighten the mood. I appreciate her effort, but I am empty. I stand there, my face heavy, thick forest sighing around me, the smell of pine needles reminding me of a candle. That may be another sign of what's wrong with me. Real things remind me of the fake things fabricated to mimic real things.

"Why didn't you tell me?" I say, my voice wet.

She shakes her head a little bit, as if it's a stupid question. She looks so grown. "Why would I go out of my way to hurt your feelings?"

I almost laugh. I want to say: *You hurt my feelings all the time, kid. Your locked door, your bitchy comments. Why not do it this one time when it matters?*

My expression must be on point because she gives my question more thought. She shrugs and says, "Being a misogynist isn't a crime. It just makes him an asshole."

CHAPTER 48

McCLANE

MISSING

Dave's still gone. I'm still naked and worried but feeling less pukey.

There are two bottles of Coke in the mini fridge. I'm not sure if Dave put them there or the motel put them there as a tempting extra charge. I didn't see Dave bring any bottles in from the car. Then again, I missed a lot when I was unconscious. Like, a day and a half.

I am fucking parched. Puking-up-a-lung-and-not-drinking-anything-but-shower-spray-for-half-a-day parched. And my body's aching for calories.

I grab one of the Cokes and inspect it as if it's poison. I'm being paranoid. I mean, he's not actually trying to kill me. He's unstable for sure—he stole my stuff and lied about it, which is crazy, and he drugged me to kill time—but he wouldn't kill *me*. I slowly turn the cap. It clicks when the seal breaks and hisses as carbon dioxide escapes. I drink both bottles.

What did he do while I was out cold? Watch me sleep? Run errands? Binge TikTok? He didn't strike me as messed up over Christmas. Then again, I wasn't trying to head-shrink him.

My belly full of sugar water, I lie on the hard mattress under the starchy covers and review our interactions.

About every other week he texts me. Since he graduated college two years ago, he texts. He's sent me some seriously obnoxious memes and Reddit posts. Stuff that was offensive but also funny or interesting, so I focused on the funny or interesting parts instead of the offensive ones.

I didn't think much of it. I figured Dave got a kick out of sending strange content to shock me. Kids at school do that all the time, seek out the weirdest shit on their phones and share it. Doesn't mean they're crazy. Doesn't even mean they're cruel. They're just goofing around.

I feel lightheaded. My blood sugar is spiking. I should have stopped at one soda. I consider wrapping a sheet around my waist and walking to the front desk. I really should, but getting up takes energy.

The door opens, and Dave walks in, bringing with him the smell of greasy french fries. He drops a paper bag on the dresser.

"Can I have my clothes?"

"Still working on it."

You know when you're at the eye doctor and the dude is switching the lenses, saying, *Which is sharper, one or two? A or B? Now which looks bolder, three or four? B or A?* And you're thinking, *Dude, they all look the same.* But they don't actually. Dude is changing up the slightest thing, making the world a touch dimmer or the slightest bit fuzzier. That's how I feel right now. A new lens just clicked into place, and Dave looks different. Like, actually.

I always considered his eyes energetic and jittery with bright ideas. Now they strike me as unstable and cold. Even the sweat on his brow takes on a sleazy sheen. Dude has been sending me obnoxious videos and memes for, like, two years. I never realized he was an asshole. Whitney did, though.

How could Dave be reading me Percy Jackson when I was eight and laughing at all the right parts, and years later, he's laughing at rape jokes? If people can change like that, what's the point of trusting anyone?

I shiver. Chills wrack my body. My limbs are heavy and numb, like they aren't attached to my torso. I close my eyes and open them slowly. Everything in the room looks blurry.

"Dave?"

"What up?"

"How did you drug the Coke bottles? They were sealed."

He tosses his backpack on the bed, sets down his laptop. "Syringe," he says, like it's business as usual. There's no triumph in his voice, no disappointment.

"Why keep drugging me?"

"I told you, man. I need time to pass. I need the police to connect the dots. I need you to sit tight."

Oh. That's right. He did tell me that. I didn't know he needed to kill *that* much time. I didn't know he was *that* crazy.

A shot of panic sparks in my chest.

Natalie. She's probably driving here now. I need to be awake when she gets here. I try to let the panic do its thing, wake me up, but my body's like a slab of meat. My fingers tingle. I fight against fatigue, but it's an undertow pulling at my legs, at my center.

I should have walked naked to the front desk when I had the chance.

CHAPTER 49

MEG

DAY 3, 2:30 P.M.

We're driving again. I'm driving, she's in the passenger seat. Whitney told me who she thinks David is, but all I want to do is go back to who he was.

"I believe you." I sigh. "But most of my memories are of him as a kid, and most are good."

She's looking out the window, her earbuds pooling in her lap. She's listening to me.

"Remember when he used to pull you around the snow in the sled?" I think he was twelve or thirteen, which would have made her four or five. "He'd run through the snow as fast as he could, and you'd be laughing and screaming."

"He liked controlling me."

"Why do you have to spin it that way?"

"I'm not spinning it. That's the way I remember it. Sometimes I'd be laughing, but sometimes I'd be screaming 'stop' and he wouldn't."

"Then why did you keep getting on the sled, day after day?"

"I was in kindergarten. I just wanted to be included. I'd do whatever they told me."

I had invited her to a lighthearted volley, but she keeps spiking it. There's no point to keep setting her up for the slam. I bite my lip and look ahead at the long stretch of highway before me, contemplating how well I know my son.

He was closer to Joe. He gravitated toward his dad, like a lot of boys do. Joe went on the Boy Scout outings. Joe took him to boxing matches, to car shows, to football games. David didn't ask me for much. It didn't bother me at the time because I had smaller children who needed things from me. At the time, I appreciated his lack of wanting.

Still, I know my son. I've watched the scenes of his life play out, revealing his bright spirit.

I picture David as a little kid at Joe's mom's sixtieth birthday party. White lights twinkling in a dark room, jazz turned down low. David's eyes sparkling brighter than the lights when Joe's brother said, "Hey, little man, what do you want to tell Grandma on her birthday?"

David leaned toward the microphone and said earnestly, "Well, I'm glad she's still alive."

That got a roar of laughter, and Dave's face lit up like he'd discovered anything was possible.

"Anything else you'd like to say?" Joe's brother said.

David leaned in again, this time wrapping his small hand above Joe's brother's hand. "My name is Dave and sometimes my dad calls me Davie. Yesterday, my dad and I were fishing behind our house and a grasshopper jumped right into my dad's eye, it was like he got shot with a Nerf gun, and he fell back and slid down right into the river. He looked exactly like a cartoon; you would not believe it."

Smiles from friends and family, along with laughter in all the right places.

David ended up leading "Happy Birthday," clutching the microphone tightly in his palm while the waiters rolled out the cake, candles flickering in the dark mahogany room. Helping his grandma blow out the candles, delighted to share the spotlight with her.

After that, we called him MC.

~ My Journal ~

My eyes are wide open. I'm seeing clearly for the first time. These women, they have kids so they can have their Mini Me. Small people who will touch them and need them and fulfill them. This job has pried my eyes open. I didn't want the curtains drawn back, I didn't ask for it, but here it is. I am one of the few, one of the chosen who sees how it all goes down backstage, how the gears turn. I am one of the few who have seen how disgusting people are, how heinous people really are. It is painful to witness, it is a curse, but it is also a privilege.

And then, can you fucking believe it, when my mind was wide open and ready for it, I came across that video. Any other time, I would not have understood. It happened at the perfect time. Everything just fell into place, happened because it was supposed to happen. I saw that video, and now it all makes sense. This feeling inside my chest my whole life, hard like a corn kernel, then seeing the video added the heat till the kernel fucking popped. And now, my chest is loose, like I'm a different person, like I've changed, like I'm fucking enlightened, redeemed, born again, but, see, now there's this different tightness. Hate. Resentment.

She pretended to be so good for so long, she fooled her own self into believing it. She thinks she's a good mother, good person, good little worker and homemaker, but she killed my brother. She killed my favorite person in the whole world, yanked him right away from me, and left this gaping, bloody hole in my heart. How could a person kill their own child?

I was never supposed to find out. No one was. But fate wanted me to punish her. I got this camera when I was 4. It was a little shit camera, not much space, 50 megabytes maybe. When I was sixteen and had long since forgotten about that little plastic camera, Dad came across my photo file on his PC and downloaded everything onto a thumb drive. I tossed that little lozenge of data into my junk drawer, and when I moved, dumped my junk drawer into a Ziploc, moved it to my sock drawer.

Yesterday, I needed to reset my phone and remembered the last time I used the tiny pointy end of a safety pin in my mom's sewing kit. I don't keep safety pins anymore, but then I remembered that junk bag. I was pretty sure there was a safety pin in there.

As I was looking through the bag, I came across a bumble bee trapped in a marble my dad bought me from a museum. And my first-class Boy Scout pin, and my water rescue badge, and a book of matches from my grandma's house, so I was getting all nostalgic and shit and I came across that thumb drive and wondered if there were any photos of Carson on it.

It might take a long fucking time, but people will get what they deserve.

MC, age 24

CHAPTER 50

McClane

MISSING

The doorknob's rattling.

"Natalie?" My tongue heavy, I struggle to call her name. My eyes feel swollen shut.

"No, man. It's me."

I force my eyes open. My brain is like a wet dog, damp and thick. I have this lost, Rip Van Winkle feeling.

Dave drops a shopping bag on the crap carpet by the door and tosses his backpack on the other bed. His movements are excessive, agitated. Pulling the curtain aside, he sneaks a peek out the window. Dark out there. He lets the curtain fall closed. Peeks out again. Paces. "We got to go," he says, frantic.

"I'm naked," I manage. Every word takes effort.

"Here. They're right here." He picks up the shopping bag and throws it at me. My reflexes are snail-slow, so it hits me in the face. It doesn't hurt much. My skin is kinda numb.

"You're a dick, man. You know?" My words slur. "I can't get dressed. I can barely move."

He stops pacing and blinks a few times. His head is still and his eyes blink too fast, and the combo strikes me as alien. Not human. That would explain a lot. My brain thinks this is funny, but the humor doesn't make it to the surface. My mouth is flat, my eyelids low.

"Sorry. I'm stressed. It's making me itchy." He reaches back with both arms, pulls his shirt off, and tosses it on the bed. "I can't think straight. There're two cops parked across the street."

Maybe Natalie shared my location with the cops. That thought squeezes my chest with worry. I want the cops to help me because Dave's messed up. Still, I don't want to see his face slammed against a cop car as they snap cuffs on him. He drugged me, he lied to me, he's not right in the head, but he's still my brother. Years of good memories with him are tattooed on my brain. Sure, the color's faded with time, but they're permanent. And seriously, I keep thinking he'll snap out of it. I keep thinking maybe he is snapping out of it. Of course I'd think that, I've known him eighteen years. He's been the same person for eighteen years. The last thirty-six hours is temporary. The brain wants to trust eighteen years more than a day and a half.

I lift my arm, and it barely moves. You know when you slept on your arm so hard you cut off the circulation, and now it's this slab of meat that doesn't feel like it belongs to you? It's like that.

"I hear you, Dave. I get that you want to leave, I do." My voice has an underwater quality. "Thing is, I can't pick up my arm. It's like all my circulation is cut. What drug did you give me?"

"Roofies," he says casually.

Date-rape drugs. Shivers crawl over my neck like ants on my

skin. I picture what it's like to be a victim of date-rape. Waking up in a strange place, puking or feeling like you can barely move. Your memory is fuzzy and you have the strangest feeling of lost time, but underneath the heavy, drug-sick stupor, you know you've been violated. Your skin is torn. The pain is raw and fresh.

My jaw aches with stiffness. That Dave has roofies and is comfortable using them on me makes me wonder if this isn't his first time. Seriously, I can't bear to ask.

"Good thing you didn't kill me, right?" I say, trying to sound sarcastic, but I only sound slow.

He doesn't catch my tone. He grabs the bag, takes out my filthy sneakers, a new shirt, and sweatpants. He rips off the tags and says, "They don't kill you, they only knock you out. You wake up well rested."

My teeth chatter but my neck is hot and itchy, and I'd like to beat his ass. "Fuck your well rested. You saw my puke all over the walls. I can barely move. You should take some right now, so you can feel well rested, so you can fucking think *straight*."

"I'll get you dressed." He is completely out of touch with how pissed off I am. He helps me sit, and I watch him. I study him like he's an exotic, poisonous snake. His movements are still restless. His facial expressions are stiff, he keeps pushing his jaw forward and side to side, but his eyes soften. They are calmer, like stagnant, muddy water. He helps me get both arms into the shirt. It's such a completely fucked-up feeling to not have full control of your limbs. I'm able to stand but he squats down and helps me get the pants on. "Little kids deserve a better life," he says. Shit, it's like he's on another planet.

"They do," I say, exhausted by him. "But we're not little kids, Dave."

He stands up quickly, goes back to the window. "Fuck. They are still motherfucking there." And he's back to pacing.

"What day is it?" This drugged feeling, it's just this overwhelming sense of being lost and misplaced in time.

He looks at me like I'm an idiot. "Saturday. Close to midnight, so almost Sunday. We got to go, man."

I've been gone two whole days.

———•———

I can barely move, but he's agitated and determined, so I do what I'm told. He helps me with my shoes, ties them, double-knots them. From his backpack, he pulls out my Sugar Glen North hoodie and helps me into it. I'm about to bring up the crap he pulled at Denny's, accusing the whole damn restaurant of stealing my hoodie, but I'm exhausted, and what's the point?

Dave walks me out the door. The air is heavy and humid and thick with wet cedar. The smell flips a switch in me, and my brain thinks: vacation. Either someone got a fresh batch of mulch or I'm not in Sugar Glen, Toto.

I was thinking I'd yell for the cops once we got outside but they are way the fuck across a four-lane street. They're both in their cars, and I'm not even sure their windows are down. If I scream for help and they don't hear me, Dave might lose his shit.

I get in the front seat of his Dodge Charger slowly, like I'm nursing the tail end of the stomach bug and I'm not sure if my asshole is my friend or not. I pep-talk myself. *It will be okay. Don't drink or eat anything he gives you. And when you get your muscle function back, you can run. Easy. Or knock him down. You will be okay.*

I lean my head against the window because the cold glass feels good. Also, so I don't have to talk with him anymore. He drives past a gas station and a Taco Bell. I'm starving but there is no way I'm putting anything in my mouth that goes anywhere near his hands. He turns down a dark street, forest on both sides. He slows and parks. Tiny alarms buzz along my neck. "Why we stopping here?" My limbs are still numb, and if I have to run this second, I'm in trouble.

"Hang on," he says, looking in his rearview, his face stiff and still. Headlights pull up slowly behind him. Probably those cops. Thank you, God. Not that I want Dave dragged away in cuffs. Like I said, I don't. I just want to go home. I don't want to be the scapegoat for his crazy. I look in my side mirror but all I can see are bright lights.

Dave sighs, turns the car off, and pulls the keys out of the ignition. He pops the trunk before he steps out.

"Oh, thank God, it's you," she says.

CHAPTER 51

MEG

DAY 3, 3:22 P.M.

We stop at a gas station off the highway. Whitney's hungry, and I have to pee. With the heat coming off cars and trucks, the heavy afternoon sun, and the thick smell of diesel hanging low, it feels like summer.

I told Whitney about where the porn and bloody knife really came from. She was unfazed. She already knew they didn't belong to McClane. She is a more solid person than I am. Her head is screwed on better. Her feet meet the ground more firmly. Or maybe she has a smaller imagination. Fewer nightmares.

When I told her they belonged to Hudson, she was relieved his intentions were noble. She has a soft spot for the kid. We all do.

When I come out of the gas station and into the bright sunlight, Whitney's sitting cross-legged in the passenger seat, laptop on her lap, a grocery bag of snacks and energy drinks spilling open on the floor.

She's got an open bag of Fritos on the dashboard, an energy drink in the cupholder, and a Twizzler in her hand. She is self-possessed, at ease, and in her element.

I open the driver's-side door to grab my purse.

"Did you punch Mrs. Heely?" she says.

"Do you think I punched Mrs. Heely?" I say, curious as to what she thinks I'm capable of.

Whitney shrugs. "She's saying you gave her a black eye."

"I didn't."

She squints her eyes, thinking. "You should stop, like, interacting with people."

"Or maybe I don't interact enough." I stare at her bag of chips.

"What?" she says, defensive, like I punched her too. "I can't think straight with low blood sugar." She grabs the edge of the Frito bag and holds it out. "Want one?"

I shake my head.

"Okay. You win, I guess." Calm, but still easily annoyed by her mother.

I dig my credit card out of my wallet.

Her annoyance evaporates. Her eyes grow wide and mischievous. "Aren't you curious if I've found anything?"

"Have you found anything?"

"I don't have his phone location, but I see his laptop. It's on a road outside of Memphis, not a highway, but a two-way road about an hour from his apartment. My guess is he left his laptop in his car on the side of the road. Wherever he is storing McClane is a walk from the car." She looks up at me, sees the drawn horror on my face, and says, "Sorry. I shouldn't have said that. I didn't mean to sound creepy."

I turn away to fill up the tank, then turn back. "Do you think McClane is in on it?" The question has been bugging me, and Whitney seems to have all the answers.

"No." Her tone is calm, matter-of-fact.

"How can you be so sure?"

"Mom. No offense, but you're losing it."

"Of course I'm losing it. How can I not be?" My lower lip trembles. "I can't trust my instincts anymore." They've failed me so spectacularly. First with Joe. Then Dave. I thought a person was one thing, but they're another. I used to be confident in my intelligence, in my common sense. I've turned into a mouse of a woman. The type of pathetic, weak-shouldered, flimsy-looking woman I used to feel sorry for. I'd think, how can you be in your forties and look like a gust of wind will knock you over? You've come this far in life, what are you so scared of?

But now I know better. I know how complicated situations can get. How a strong woman can be hollowed out so slowly she doesn't notice. Look at how water carves out rock.

"Fair," she says. "I trust my instincts, though. So trust me. McClane is obsessed with Natalie. Obsessed and happy. Even with his anxiety and his dumb wrestling-exercise habits, he's happy. He's not fixated on you, and he's definitely not thinking about Carson." She stops, looks through the windshield at the trucks parked on the other side of the gas station. She's thinking. She turns to me. "Yeah, he's totally solid, Mom."

"Thank you." I reach over and grab a Frito. She's right, eating is not wasting time. Gas is glugging into my tank, so we're stuck here for a few minutes anyway. She holds up her energy drink, and I take a sip. It's way too sweet. Watermelon or something. I make a sour face, and she smiles.

My phone rings, setting my heart flapping. I pull it out of my back pocket, check the number, and exhale. "It's only Dad," I say, and she nods. I walk to the back of the car for privacy.

"Hi," I say.

He's crying. I roll my eyes. I actually roll my eyes. I am so tired of his up-and-down. Of all the changes I expected as we aged—the compromises, the fatigue, the kids pulling us in different directions, the kids stealing our attention, the boredom, the erectile dysfunction, the bickering, the financial problems—I never imagined this. The goddamn drama.

"It's okay, Joe. We're okay. I'm with Whitney."

"I got home, and dishes are broken everywhere. I th-thought," he stutters. "I don't know what I thought."

"I'm sorry. That was me. I had a temper tantrum." Whitney's words. "I lost it. The stress of McClane being gone, it just . . . it took me. I'm sorry. I should have warned you." I am sorry. I'm not all that sorry for breaking the dishes, but I'm sorry I forgot to give him a heads-up.

He cries harder, tries to slow himself down but can't.

"Listen, Joe. Me and Whitney are going to find McClane. We're taking care of it. Go lie down and take a nap. Wait—" Flemming said she's coming by. "Now that I'm thinking about it—you should leave the house, so you don't have to deal with those detectives. They're coming by this afternoon."

"Why are they coming?"

"I don't know." It would be too much for him to learn they're coming to arrest me or him or both.

"It's my fault," he says.

"It's not your fault."

"Listen to me!" He screams so loud, I pull the phone away from my ear. The weird thing is, my emotions barely flinch. They've been tugged and yanked and cut and burned so many times by Joe, they're dull. I glance at Whitney through the back window. She's focused on her laptop, typing away.

"I'm listening." I pull the nozzle out of my tank and seat it in the kiosk.

"You're always talking, talking, talking, making coffee, working, doing dishes, making food, running here and there, and you never listen."

I want to punch back, *Yeah, because you checked out*, but I keep my mouth shut because he's still crying.

"It's my fault," he says quietly, sniffling. "I left it open."

Had I not watched the leaked video on YouTube, I would have had no idea what he's talking about. But I watched it today and it's etched in my mind, so I know. I know exactly what he's talking about. I brace myself for the inevitable surge of emotions, a dam splintering and ready to burst, but it doesn't come.

"That day," he says, "that day you were just, you had hit a wall with him, and I could tell you were done. I was going to lose you. The kids and I, we were going to lose you. You were tired in such a final way. I was trying to hold things together, but I was overwhelmed. I was working in the yard and I wasn't thinking straight and I left it open."

I sigh. I rest my forehead against the back of the car. Sunbaked metal warms my skin.

"I didn't mean for it to happen," he says. "But also, maybe I did." He's crying hard, breathing fast like he's going to hyperventilate.

"You didn't mean it."

"I told myself it was an accident. At the time, I convinced myself no one was to blame, it was just a tragic accident, but I've been thinking about it lately. Since those detectives asked me about Carson, I've been thinking about it. Why didn't I say it was an accident back then? Why did I keep it secret? What if I meant to do it?"

I think it's the CTE making him question himself—these strange neural wires short-circuiting and burning out frayed, crispy ends, making his reality like a house of horrors with distorting mirrors and jump scares. Strange how the past is coming at him uncertainly.

My head against the glass, I feel lightheaded. The crazy thing is, he doesn't even know. About that video. He doesn't even know about the video that captured the day he's remembering. And he doesn't know about David. He doesn't know how much Carson is at the center of this.

Flemming and Becker asked him about Carson yesterday. That's all he knows—that the police think I am responsible for Carson's death. I can't tell him about the video or about David. He couldn't handle it.

"I'm a terrible person."

"You're not. It was an accident. I could have done the exact same thing. You lost yourself for a moment, you made a mistake, and I forgive you," I say, but I don't know that I do.

"Come home, Meg."

"I can't. Whitney and I are looking for McClane. Go stay with your dad or your sister for a few days."

"I don't want to," he says, his voice unstable. *He* is unstable. But his situation has been unstable for a long time now, so what's another day of putting off another talk? We've done it so many times before.

"Then go stay at a hotel so you don't have to deal with the police. They said they'll be coming by. Stay away from the house till we can figure this out."

"I want you to come home." The yearning in his voice rubs against my mind like sandpaper, grating my delicate tissue. My skin grows hot and itchy. I hit my head against the window. I want to be driving on the highway already. How much time is he going to suck up? How much more time will he use up but not get better?

"I'll call you tonight." I hang up. I told him to leave the house. I told him the cops were coming. What he does next is on him. I slide into the front seat, my emotions evaporating like sweat stolen off my dewy skin by the blast of air-conditioning. I've had so much practice ignoring my feelings these past few years. Pretending.

"Everything okay with Dad?" Whitney says, eyes curious.

"Yep." I take another sip of her energy drink. Still sour, but it's growing on me. "Tell me how to get there."

CHAPTER 52

McCLANE

MISSING

"Where's McClane?" Natalie. Her voice is my favorite sound in the universe—deep like a cave yet soft and velvety, bold yet kind—but it's the worst thing to hear right now. Sick panic floods my head.

I should have known it would be Natalie. She's reliable and good and she loves me. She would come right away when she saw my text. I should have known. It's just that my neurons are shorting out, so my thoughts aren't linear and productive. My mind is swimming through a thick undertow.

I open my door and step out. "McClane!" She rushes toward me. I back up against the car so her momentum doesn't knock us over. She wraps me in a hug. Pulling back, she holds my face in her warm hands. Her citrusy perfume fills my senses, overtaking the wet smell of cedar from the surrounding forest. Her nails graze my skin, giving me the chills. "Everyone is so worried about you. The police asked me a million questions. It's crazy. I thought you were in trouble."

"It's not safe," I whisper.

"What?" she says. "You reek. Did you puke?" she says, laughing, not getting it.

Dave is at the back of his car, beside his open trunk. "How'd you find us?" he says, his tone cool and calculating.

"Snapchat location," she says, still cheerful and unaware.

I want to interrupt this conversation before it starts. I don't want him knowing I know he stole my phone. "Dave. I'm gonna go home with her."

"That's not the plan," he says.

Emotions rise up. I've always looked up to him. But he's let me down *hard*. Like, push-me-off-the-roof hard. Which he actually joked about doing when we were kids and goofing around on the roof, but he never did. This is not his fault, some switch has flipped inside him, it's not really him anymore, but I hate him. I do. "I don't want to be part of your insane plan."

"What's going on?" Nat says, pressing her palm against my chest—her hand is so familiar, so much like home, it's burning a hole in my shirt and making my eyes tear up. Her lips turn down and her eyes tighten.

"No one wants to do the hard work," Dave says. "But it's got to be done. It's important work." He's calm again. His voice is casual, and he's sure of himself. He has moved back and forth between agitation and self-assuredness so many times in the past few days, it's disorientating.

"I'm going, Dave."

"I don't think so."

"What are you going to do, drug me again?"

"Nah." He reaches into his trunk and pulls out a gun. Panic rushes my head like a brain freeze, and my feet are heavy. Nat's palm squeezes my shirt, pinching my chest hair.

"Are you serious right now?" I scream, my voice cracking as I cry. "What are you going to do, shoot us?"

He holds the gun comfortably at his side. Too comfortably. His mouth twitches into a brief smile, then it's gone. "No, just her."

I wasn't expecting that. I wasn't expecting any of this. I step in front of Natalie. From behind me, her nails dig into my arms. She grips my arms like the roller coaster's about to drop. "Leave her out of your crazy shit. You have to leave her out of this. I swear to God, Dave." My voice sounds vicious, but tears are sliding down my cheeks. She's tugging at my arms, my clothes. I think I might fall, so I press my palm against the car to keep steady. I can't run, but I can tell her to run. I should tell her to run.

He laughs. "I'm your brother, man. Brothers are important." He unlocks the safety. The click is like the only sound in the world. I can't breathe.

"Fuck you, Dave. Fuck you so much. You're not my brother. You're someone else. You're crazy."

His mouth turns down. He steps toward us. "Natalie. I won't hurt you if you listen to me, I promise. Sit on the ground."

"I'll listen, Dave," she says. "I'm doing it now." She lets me go and steps back. The shuffling of her shoes against the pavement is soft and feathered.

"Nat," I say, pleading.

"See, Dave," she says. "I'll sit, so don't hurt us." She's thinking she can talk him through this—his confusion—just like she talked her friend out of swallowing half a bottle of Tylenol last summer. She's assuming that beneath his troubled heart he's a good guy because he's my brother and I've told her he's a good guy. She doesn't know what he's done. She doesn't know what he's capable of. Neither do I. That's why I didn't tell her to run.

"Put your hands behind your back, Mick." He pushes the gun into my side. I don't feel the metal or grooves through my hoodie, but the knowledge of it makes my guts feel liquid.

I do what he tells me. As he yanks the tie tight around my wrists, I say, "Just let her drive back home, Dave."

"I checked your Snapchat. Don't fuck with me." He spins me to the side and knocks me down.

I can't put my hands out. My knees hit pavement a moment before my forehead hits. Pain tears across my head. I'm on my stomach, hands trapped behind me.

Natalie screams. She's not right next to me, she's maybe twelve feet away. I don't know if she's running or he pushed her. I listen. Tearing fabric, sneakers sliding against gravel, grunting—they're all sounds of a struggle. I pull my wrists apart but I'm not strong enough to snap the tie. I try to leverage my body against the car to stand, but I slip and fall. Pathetic. I am fucking pathetic. I will never forgive him for making me this helpless. My head feels sick. My stomach feels sicker. I dry-heave a few times, my body shaking badly.

When my body calms, Dave and Natalie are quiet. Crickets chirp in the grass beside the road.

The trunk closes. Dave's footsteps close in on me. He kneels on my thighs, grinds his knees into them, and zip-ties my ankles.

"Did you hurt her?" I say, my throat raw, my voice breaking.

He doesn't answer. He pulls me up by the back of my shirt and shoves me into the backseat.

CHAPTER 53

MEG

DAY 3, 5:45 P.M.

You've seen the post on social media. It goes something like this: Your wife has been kidnapped and you're driving to rescue her. It's a warm night and your windows are down. Do you listen to music on the way, yes or no?

Yes, we have music on. Whitney's playlist. I'm not enjoying it. It's not that I don't like her music, I'm just barely listening to it. I don't think she's enjoying it either. But, yes, we're listening to music. To pass time, to keep the mind occupied and numb. Like eating cold cuts in the back room at a dead person's wake. Like letting your dog lick cheese spray off a Popsicle stick as the vet puts a needle in his hind leg to sedate him before cutting off his balls.

Whitney tells me we'll be there in an hour and a half.

We pass baby goats munching grass. We'd usually coo and laugh over a thing so precious. Now we say nothing. It's the same with the unhinged apocalyptic road signs. Ordinarily we'd scoff at the JESUS IS COMING. READ YOUR BIBLE sign. Now, we stay silent.

I keep going back to Joe. I keep asking myself if what I said was true—that I forgive him for Carson.

I can't conjure Carson's voice anymore. I can't remember if he had a sparkle in his eyes. I can't visualize which baby teeth were lost. I can't evoke the smell of his hair. I don't know what his little toes looked like. I can't remember his laugh. My mourning for him was raw twenty years ago, an aching, bleeding wound that wouldn't heal for so long and perpetually oozed, but then it did heal. Now my feelings for Carson have scarred over dozens of times. The scar is a little more sensitive than my other parts, but mostly it's numb.

Joe was a good dad to the other kids.

It's not like he pushed Carson off the bridge. It's not like he lured him to the farthest stretch of our yard with candy and locked him on the other side of the fence. He was just careless and forgetful leaving the gate open. It was an accident.

I consider my conversation with Joe earlier. *What if I meant to do it?* he said, tears thick in his voice.

Even then. Even if it was only a half accident. I can imagine him feeling overwhelmed, like he was losing me, and being frustrated with Carson, and impulsively, carelessly leaving that gate open. Like *Hey, you want to fuck yourself up, kid? Have at it.* I can imagine it because I've been there. I once let Whitney ride down the big snowy hill on a sled by herself even though she was too little to avoid a crash if she needed to. She was nagging and whining and pouting, and I was trying to juggle her and McClane in the cold and I had to pee.

I finally said, "Okay, have at it, tiny menace." And she rode down and was fine and happy, and we went home and peeled off our snow gear and had a peaceful day. But it could have gone a different way.

I forgive him. I can get past this. We already are past this.

What I'm worried about is how little he knows about how he's still getting paychecks, about his own neurological condition, and about David. There are so many terrible surprises. Little gifts to unwrap with different poisons inside.

Same with Whitney. So many awful things for her to find out.

Strangely, we're getting along easily right now. The gravity of this situation has diminished all her other grievances with me.

"Whitney, there are some things I should tell you." She'll find out anyway. And with the gravity of this situation, maybe she'll forgive me for the other news I'm about to drop.

"Whitney?" I touch her leg.

She pulls out an earbud. "What?"

"The video Detective Flemming played in the kitchen?"

"Where you sounded creepy?"

"Uh-huh. It's out there for anyone to see. You should watch it before everyone you know sees it."

"I've already watched it. Someone from school sent it to me."

Of course she has. She's one step ahead. Always.

"Aren't you worried what people will think?"

"Not really. It won't go viral." As if I were trying to go viral. "It's not as interesting as you think," she says. "There's no kid in the video. You sound like some tired, angry mom being dramatic. Middle-aged women do that on TikTok all the time, looking for sympathy for their super-hard lives. It's unoriginal." Shame burns my skin. I want to crawl into my shell and hide, but I'm also relieved. "As for it being connected to Carson dying," she says. "People my age are skeptical of that stuff, video dates, deepfakes." She pops her earbud back in.

I touch her leg again. "There's another thing I have to tell you."

She huffs, annoyed.

"I don't want to tell you this, but I don't want you to hear it from someone else."

"If it's about you cheating on Dad, please don't."

"What? Wait. I wasn't—" I close my mouth. Of course that's how it would look to her. And how does she know everything anyway? "It's not like that. I hate Vince."

"Oh God!" she screams. Startled, I swerve out of my lane and back. "Don't say his name, you're going to make me puke." She pulls her hoodie over her head and turns as far away from me as possible.

"I have to. I have to tell you. You have it wrong. Dad wasn't working and I started doing his job and Vin—his boss—found out and he, like, well, he blackmailed me. I was worried about being able to pay the—"

"Quit it, Mom. That's actually so much worse. Shut up or I'm going to jump out of the car."

My skin is so hot I want to strip right out of it. *That's actually so much worse.* It can't be worse, though, can it?

"I'm shutting up. Don't do anything crazy."

"'Don't do anything crazy,'" she mocks me, keeping her hoodie covering her face. "You're the crazy one," she says, her voice steady now. Calm and quiet. "The other day you were wondering if McClane, like, molested me? Actually? You're blind to Dave's self-righteousness. You are just, I don't even know how to describe how fucked-up you are."

I take a few breaths, thinking about her words. "I think you're doing a pretty good job."

As I press a little harder on the gas, bringing it up to ninety-five, my cell rings.

CHAPTER 54

McClane

MISSING

My mind is like an industrial toilet stuck on flush. These tail-chasing thoughts, loud and urgent, go around and around and around. I can't think straight, and I can barely catch my breath.

Did Dave kill her? He couldn't have killed her. That would be too insane, too fucking barbaric, even for someone who's going a little crazy, right? Right? *Right?*

I froze. I should have done something different to help Natalie. I could have helped Natalie. I could have caught Hud before his head hit the hard floor. Still, Nat's got to be okay, right?

I am a pussy.

Never mind that my mind has been cotton-candy fuzzy, sticky and air-whipped. Never mind that I could barely control my muscles, I should have helped her out of this. I should have used common sense. I didn't see any of this coming. Actually. Every fucking thing that has happened since I sat down at that Denny's booth with Dave—I saw none of it coming.

That I couldn't see it coming doesn't make me feel better. It makes me an idiot.

I have looked up to Dave since I was too small to reach the faucet handles. Now I wish the asshole was dead.

"Quit crying back there," Dave says to me. He says some other stuff too, but I block it out. I don't care what he has to say. And he talks so fucking much. His chatter is incessant. You think he's finally done talking, but wait a beat, two, three, here he goes again. More to say. He is background noise. Background garbage.

Still, she's got to be okay, right? I scream, and it sounds animal but pathetic—an injured goose or a rabid possum.

I'm on my stomach in the back, my nose pressed against the seat, the smell of factory-made fabric and fast food in my throat. With my arms pulled back, my chest aches and I can't get a good breath. I'm choking on my own mucus.

Then I hear it. Banging against the backseat near my head. It's coming from the trunk. Natalie? Yes, of course, it's Natalie. Of course he didn't kill her. Why would I even think that?

I am so relieved, so happy, I'm laughing. Crying-laughing.

Thank God. We're going to be okay.

Guilt rushes in. I feel shitty for even wondering if Dave killed her. Which is crazy. I know. He has done very bad things in the past few days. We are bound, and he has a gun. I know I'm not thinking straight. I know.

I try to stop the rushing thoughts, the venting, the second-guessing, the backtracking. All the emotions. Wiping my forehead against the seat, I clear my vision. It's wet and blood-smeared. My forehead is oozing.

Get her out of this. Think. Quit being the asshole.

I need Dave to untie my wrists or my ankles. I need his help. I need to convince him I can help him. I need to satisfy this crazy itch he has and help him get what he wants. She's banging against the seat again, and my chest is bursting. I want to touch her, hold her, help her. But instead I focus on breathing slower and I replay snippets of things he's said to me over the past forty-eight hours. At Denny's. In the motel room. Him showing me that old video of Mom.

Right from the start, he was trying to tell me about his job busting abusive parents and about Carson. I wasn't listening. I was thinking about what I wanted to tell him about my life, about the scholarship, about Dad. Now that I'm paying attention, what he wants seems clear. He wants to bust my mom for Carson's death. He wants to protect little kids. *The kids deserve better.*

My approach has been all wrong. I have been treating Dave like he's reasonable. But my wrists and ankles are zip-tied. My forehead is bleeding. He drugged me.

I don't know much about mental illness other than your basic depression or anxiety. What's happened to Dave is bigger and stranger. He's more than a danger to himself.

The Dodge slows, rolling over dirt and pebbles on the shoulder, and comes to a stop. My stomach twists with fear. I should have been talking to him instead of wasting time in my head. He shifts into park.

I tip my head to the side. With my cheek pressing against the seat fabric, my one eye stares at the back of his hair. "Tell me more about Mom."

He sighs. Twists the keys out of the ignition.

"I watched the video." My voice quivers. "Tell me more so I understand. I want to understand."

"You wouldn't listen. You're trying to trick me. Just like Mom."

"I'm listening now. I'm listening. I'm fucking listening, Dave."

His head falls back against the headrest and his hair bounces over the top. His hair has been so familiar all my life—in the sleeping bag next to me, on the couch pillow across from me while we played *Fortnite*—and now it seems so foreign. "I think it might be too late," he says.

"Put me in the passenger seat and tell me your plan, man," I say, my words rushed, tumbling. "It's never too late."

"Sometimes it is." He opens his door, letting darkness and humidity seep in, and he steps out.

"She's pregnant, Dave. Me and her are having a baby. You said you need to help the children. They deserve better."

It's dark, but my vision adjusts. I pull his features out of the darkness. He's standing beside his door, looking down at my face. He tilts his head. "Better to not be born at all." He shuts his door.

"Don't hurt her," I call after him. "Don't hurt her, Dave. Dave?"

The trunk clicks open. Creaking, shifting, so I think she's getting out. They're talking. Her voice is calm. She's still thinking she can talk to him. I can't make out their words, but I can hear their voices getting farther away. They're walking somewhere.

"Natalie? Natalie!" I scream as they move farther away. I writhe like a suffocating fish, kicking at the door, and I scream long after my throat feels clawed. The door doesn't open. The windows don't break. I can't do shit. All I manage to do is fall onto the floor, racking my balls on the middle hump and tearing muscles across my chest. Fucking face down on the floor, my wrists trapped behind. Useless. Devastated.

Dad was wrong about being beaten. Yeah, okay, it's a good life lesson if you fail sometimes. You get knocked out in the ring or pinned in a wrestling match, sure, okay. You learn to get back up, you learn those beatings are minor and survivable. Those losses are like hairline fractures, they heal. But your psyche being annihilated? There's no insight to glean.

CHAPTER 55

MEG

DAY 3, 6:02 P.M.

My cell rings again. Please let it be McClane. I glance down at the number.

Flemming.

It's a risk answering. It's a risk answering on speakerphone. I do both. "What?"

"No one's at your house, Meg."

"I'm looking for McClane. This whole time, you haven't looked."

Silence for a few moments. "I talked to the FBI satellite office in Memphis."

"Okay."

"Turns out Dave was working on a particularly disturbing case. His supervisor, an older guy, ended up in the hospital, a heart-related event. This guy, he was out for four months, then he died." My skin prickles. I'm feeling cornered. "There was another guy working the case with Dave," Flemming says. "This guy took a leave of absence for cancer treatment—his colon. Another team member was in and out with a back injury."

"What are you telling me? David killed off his team?"

"No, no. That's not what I'm saying. Not at all. I'm saying Dave ended up working this case alone, mostly from home. Through these odd circumstances, he fell through the cracks." I picture him falling through cracks between deck planks and being trapped beneath, peering up with his jumpy eyes. "He stopped checking in at work," she says. "He, well, we're looking for Dave. We've got this under control."

"Do you, though?"

"Where are you, Meg?"

"I'm talking things over with Whitney."

"Okay. I need you to head back to Sugar Glen now."

"Yes, ma'am."

"Meg." She sighs. "There are two things I need to tell you."

"Go ahead."

"Natalie's parents say she's pregnant."

"It's not related," I say. "Natalie being pregnant."

Detective Flemming sighs. "Natalie's car was found on the side of the road in Missouri. We found McClane's phone near her car." It's like diving in freezing-cold water, I can't breathe. "Natalie found McClane's location on Snapchat. We checked it right away when he went missing, but he wasn't posting his location then. Are you there, Meg?"

I clear my throat. "I'm here." My voice sounds small.

"The second thing is about one of the cases David was working." Flemming pauses. "This woman, Angie Giano—"

I recognize the name immediately and hang up.

Whitney pulls her hoodie back. In my peripheral vision, Whitney's staring at me, jaw slack in shock, waiting for me to say more. "Mom! Why'd you hang up on her?"

"I wasn't ready for it."

"For what?"

Whitney obviously didn't recognize the name, which doesn't surprise me. She doesn't listen to the news. I'm not ready to tell her what I remember hearing about Angie Giano.

"What weren't you ready for?" Whitney says again.

"Whatever Detective Flemming was going to tell me."

Whitney's silent for a bit. "Why didn't you tell her what I told you about Dave?" I don't have a good answer for her. "You don't want them to know," she says, more to herself. "You don't want their help."

"What good have they done? They don't want to *help*. They're only looking to trip us up."

"Mom. What do you think Dave and McClane are doing? Roasting s'mores?"

"I don't want him to end up in legal trouble."

"Mom."

"Let's say McClane is fine. Let's say Natalie is fine. Let's say I can help Dave. I don't want to dig a hole for him to fall in. I want to pull him out."

Whitney's silent for a few seconds. "Then you should turn your phone on airplane mode so the police can't track you."

"Right. Good idea. Thanks."

CHAPTER 56

McClane

MISSING

That first time I talked to her in gym class. I think of that. Of her amber catlike eyes—mischievous and confident. Of her mouth curling into a crooked smile so easily. Later, how she got a kick out of me when I'd say a few sweet words to her mom or when I said I never saw *Die Hard*. Her eyes would go round and her mouth would fall open and reveal her pretty pink tongue, then her mouth would settle into an old-soul smile. Pure goodness. I think of time with her in our tent in the forest behind my house, tangled in our nest of blankets and—not the sex, though the sex was phenomenal—just staring into her eyes in the dark and listening to her tell me stories. Of holding her close, skin to skin, pulse to pulse, and feeling calm because I knew I was capable of giving and receiving love. That I wasn't scornful like my parents. She kept my mind healthy, my heart golden.

My face wet with tears, I kick at the car door again. Not knowing is harder. Not knowing if you should fight for your life or give up. If the girl you love needs your help or she's dead. If you need to live or want to die.

I can't tell how much time passes before the door opens and he drags me out and shoves me onto the ground. My forehead hits again. There's pain, but I'm numb thinking about Nat.

"No wrestling moves," he says, his voice slow and muddy. "I don't want to use it, but I will." His gun. He's talking about his stupid gun. He thinks he's a cowboy because he has a gun. He thinks he's tough because he has a gun. If he didn't have that gun, if I wasn't drugged, I'd beat his ass. He knows it.

I'm not going to stand for him. I'm not going to walk for him. I'm not going to make this easy.

"Get up, Mick," he says, no anger in his voice, just this deep fatigue. I lie there.

"Or what? You'll shoot me? Go ahead," I dare him, my voice deeper and more gravelly than his.

He holds his gun behind my ear. "Don't you want to see her?" he says, kind of sad, and I can't tell what he means.

I can barely get the words out. "Did you kill her?"

"Come see," he says. I don't know what to think. If she's gone, I'm done. I'll tear his eyes out and kill myself. "Just get up," he says, and he sounds like a kid asking me to go along with his game even though he knows it's stupid. For a moment, I'm positive she's alive.

I get up and go along with it. I let him steer me into the forest, his gun at my back like he's a fucking cowboy. Air is still swampy, but the temperature drops a few degrees. Gun moist and cold against my skin, he aims me around towering oaks and fat cypress trees.

UPSTANDING YOUNG MAN

Mosquitoes buzz at the gash across my forehead. The ghostly glow of moonlight filters through the dense canopy, pooling here and there. Twigs snap beneath my feet, and the sound is jarring because the forest is quiet. No wind rustling trees. No birds calling. Only dead silent, the air soupy decay.

We keep walking. I start talking about Natalie. Everything I can think of about her. That she's the beginning and end for me. The best person I've ever known. How she tunes out everything around her when she looks at me. It's like she's dropped into this time and place from a completely different time. How that sounds phony, but it's true. She is like a god to me. That if he hurt her, I will kill myself.

He keeps taking deep breaths, like the sound of my voice is a fist around his balls squeezing tighter with each word I say.

I tell him how I looked up to him. I waited for him to come in my room first thing in the morning and last thing at night just to tell me stuff, everything, anything. I waited for his praise. I watched his football games. I watched them fasten pins to his Boy Scout sash. I watched him and Dad drive away, going to watch another fight in the city. I thought if only I had the confidence he had. I tell him he is the biggest fucking letdown.

Up ahead is a structure. I wouldn't call it a cabin. It's so much shittier. As we approach, toads croak. Getting louder. We must be approaching water.

Acid creeps up my esophagus. Terror snakes up my spine. That vibe I had for a second back at the car, like he only wanted me to play along with his stupid game and then I could go on my way, that vibe is gone. I am trembling. "What? What are you going to show me?" Tendons in my neck hurt. I stop outside the door. Tears fill my eyes.

He nudges me forward. I step back. He shoves me inside and I aim toward the wall so I crash into it instead of falling onto my face again. My cheek hits, and a numb tingly feeling washes through my head for a few seconds.

Blue moonlight falls in through a single grimy window and lands across the room on Natalie's wet eyes. She's sitting with her knees up, her arms pulled tight behind her back.

Relief floods through me. I feel bad I assumed he killed her again. Which is crazy, I know. Mad-ass crazy. He has steered me with a gun pressed against my skin, and I feel bad? Fuck. This is how someone *goes* crazy. The drugs, the vomiting, the time blindness, the dehydration, the hunger, and me thinking Natalie's dead and then thinking she's alive and dead again and alive again. Drugging me and lying to me and teasing me and tricking me. Is he oblivious to how scrambled my mind is?

Maybe he's doing this on purpose. Messing with my head. Maybe this isn't about Mom and Carson, maybe he's trying to wreck *me*. Crack my mind into pieces like that mug Dad threw into the sink.

CHAPTER 57

MEG

DAY 3, 7:37 P.M.

My fingers are tight on the steering wheel, my spine is erect. My mind is simulating a wild range of scenarios. I'm planning for the worst, but pep-talking myself for the best.

Whitney tells me we'll be there in twenty minutes. We are about an hour north of Memphis now. Dense hardwood forest. Lots of bald cypress and swamp tupelo. We're off the highway now, so I've got my window open, and there's not a lot of traffic. Smells of cedar and cypress are thick. Hawks soar over treetops. The sky is fading to soft peach. The sun will set soon. I have a flashlight in the trunk. Bug spray too. I have a sweatshirt. A few bottles of water. Not much else.

Looking at her phone, Whitney says, "Everyone's sending me links to Facebook posts about Carson's death and about your brother killing his friend. 'Death follows the Harts,'" she says dramatically. "Maybe you'll go viral after all." She tosses her phone down by her feet.

"It's kind of amazing," I say.

"Going viral?"

"You. You found him faster than the detectives. You're resourceful. Book smart too, but clever and intuitive and, well, I'm grateful. I don't know what I would have done without you."

"Break the rest of the dishes. Keep breaking stuff. Your Dalí melting clock, maybe."

"I need to frisbee that clock out the window." I laugh. She laughs too. Our laughs feel inevitable, like we are heading toward danger and we need to give life the finger.

Whitney's laughing turns into crying.

"It's okay, kiddo. It's going to be okay."

"I've known for months. I've been tracking him online, gathering dirt on him so I could convince everyone he's an asshole. I didn't think to help him. And now, McClane . . ." Her words trail off as her crying intensifies.

"It wasn't your job." I reach over and pat her leg. She lets me. She rarely lets me. "Like you said, being an asshole doesn't make someone a criminal. This type of thing, no one ever sees it coming."

We settle back into silence, music on low. Evening is coming, and the air is getting wet and cool. Everything is coming at us fast. The air, the bugs. We're getting closer to finding them. I've been in a fluctuating state of panic for days now, and my body feels weaker. Old. I feel old. And I smell bad.

Whitney's breath catches. She clears her throat. "I thought you were cheating on Dad because he's gotten weird. I thought you abandoned him."

"No. I was trying to"—I was going to say *compensate for him*, but that's giving myself too much credit. I barely tried communicating with him. I settle for the truth—"keep his paychecks coming."

"God, Mom. Stop mentioning his paycheck. It's so cringe. We could have moved into a smaller house. You say it like you had no options, like you had a gun to your back." She shakes her head. "You know Dad's going to find out. Did you think no one would find out?" she says, baffled.

I wasn't thinking much, to be honest. "When your world feels like it's falling apart, you're not always thinking clearly."

"I guess," she says, mostly blowing me off. "It's not going to go well."

"I know."

As a parent, that's the moment you remember. When the child becomes the parent, and the parent becomes the child.

"There's his car," she says, her hand flying onto the dashboard.

I slam on the brakes and pull over onto the dirt shoulder in front of his car. Without saying anything else, we both get out and walk to his car. All four doors are locked. It's empty. Nothing in the front seat besides coins on the floor, a fast-food drink in the cupholder.

"The windshield is dusty," she says. "Like the car's been sitting here for a while."

"Can't be that long."

A blanket in the back and a crumpled fast-food bag on the floor. A wrinkled straw wrapper. The slick silvery inside of a granola bar wrapper. Looks innocent enough, but my stomach is churning because it's all very real. His car, parked here on the road. Even though Whitney said it would be here, I thought she might be wrong. I look toward the forest. The underbrush is dense. I look for shoe prints in the dirt at the forest line. There's nothing. No trace of anything.

Whitney's fiddling with his trunk.

"What are you doing?" I say.

"Making sure no one's in the trunk." How could she think of something so grotesque? She's prying the edges of his trunk with a crowbar.

"Where'd you get the crowbar?" I say. Birds call high in the trees, like they're screaming.

"Your trunk." She catches its sweet spot and the trunk pops open.

I hold my breath and step back, worried we'll find something gruesome.

We don't. But we also kind of do. Here's a shovel, shiny and new. A half-used roll of duct tape, its edge crumpled and worn. An open bag of zip ties. An old backpack, streaked with dried mud. A blue tarp, neatly folded and sealed in its plastic. And, beside it, so small I almost miss it—a tiny, tangled gold chain. A bracelet. I search my memory, trying to picture Natalie's wrist. Did she wear a bracelet? I can't remember.

Whitney unzips the backpack. My eyes linger on the bracelet.

"His laptop's in here, but there's nothing else."

I tear my eyes away from the delicate chain and head back to my car. I grab my sweatshirt, tie it around my waist, slip my phone in my pocket, and pick up the flashlight. The sky is growing fiery, dark shadows are stretching out from the forest. It will be dark in an hour.

Whitney walks toward me, looking lost.

"Here, take my keys," I say, handing them over. "Stay in the car."

"What are you talking about?" she says. "I'm going with you."

"No. I need you here in case I need help. If I'm not back in an hour, call Detective Flemming. My phone is charged, so you can track me." I open the Find My app on my phone. "I shared my location. Accept it." Annoyed, she pulls out her phone and accepts my request. We're finally sharing our locations. Ha.

She gazes back at Dave's car. "You should take the crowbar. Something to—"

"No. This is David we're talking about."

"I know," she says. "But do *you*? Do you know? What's your plan, Mom?" Her eyebrows knit in frustration as her eyes tear up. She pulls her hair back, drops it, pulls it back again. Shakes her head. "This is serious. This might be so serious. What is your fucking plan?"

To sacrifice myself. That's my plan. Dave wants me to suffer. I owe him that. I failed him when he needed me most. I was too deep in my grief for Carson, I didn't think about what David needed. Now I am.

"To find them," I say. "If I find them, everything will be okay."

A tear drips down her cheek. Gently, I press my palms to her cheeks and kiss her on the forehead. I can't remember the last time she let me touch her face. I can't remember the last time she let me kiss her. She's always yanking away, turning away. "You have given me so much," I say. "You have no idea."

"You need a better plan, Mom." Her bottom lip trembles. Her eyes are wet. "Mom? Listen to me."

A faint noise rises in the distance. We both hear it and tilt our heads like retrievers. Sirens. They're far, but it won't take long. A few minutes.

"Tell them I went that way." I point across the road to the forest.

"Tell them we saw movement over there." I rush toward the trees beyond Dave's car, with no idea if it's the right way. There's no time to search for footprints. "Don't tell them all the bad things about him. He can recover."

"Mom, no," she yells.

"Go back in the car so they don't run you over."

The temperature drops by a few degrees the instant I cross into the forest. I run straight, lifting my feet so I don't twist an ankle. Branches scrape my arms, stab at my neck. I don't have enough time. How did the police know? How did they get here so fast?

With the trees and brush a thick barrier of insulation against the sound, the police sirens dim a little as I run deeper into the forest.

I'm cracking branches, breathing hard. I'm too loud. I stop for a second to take in the sounds. Nothing but deep forest, cool and dark. Small animals rustling leaves, the faintest trickle of water, birds calling overhead.

Oh. Of course. Whitney contacted them. She's going to point them in this direction too. I have even less time than I thought.

CHAPTER 58

McClane

MISSING

You picture yourself as the hero.
You're cruising in your car with your windows down, summer air thick and sweet, and on the breeze, you catch the panicked sound of little kids screaming. Not that fun-screaming sound, this racket is charged with terror. A group of them, elementary kids, races along the edge of a pond, back and forth, like ants. You swerve your car and take the square curb on a slant, drive through the grass like a rebel, throw the car into park, and jump out.

"He went under and didn't come up," one of the girls tells you, her face sweaty and filthy. You hand her your phone, say, "Call 911," and you splash into the water, the mucky bottom slurping and tugging at your shoes. You dive under, opening your eyes against the murk, and feel around for a limb. Sixty seconds later, you come up with the kid's body in your arms. You CPR the kid, he coughs up water, the ambulance arrives. Bam, you're the hero.

Or. It's late, and you're walking home from your friend's house. You pass the neighborhood park. Creaky swings, a rusty merry-go-round, a plastic spiral slide so narrow it bruises hips: all of it surrounded by clusters of trees. Against the slide, dark shadows move. Not kids, no, but adult silhouettes. You think, oh, teenagers macking. They're not old enough to drive, so they've got nowhere else to fool around. But then you hear small huffs of screams, most of them trapped screams—sounds you understand in the dark basement of your heart are violence mingling with sex. You come up on the guy, you do it brave Marty McFly style, grab the asshole by the stretched-out collar of his T-shirt and knock him out. She looks up at you, her cheeks shiny with tears, the whites of her eyes still fearful, but she breathes in, and it sounds like relief. Bam, you're the hero.

You've thought up so many scenarios, at the Taco Bell parking lot and the stairwell at school and the mall with a shooter. These fantasies are embarrassing, self-indulgent, and pathetic—sexist even—but they're important to you. They reveal the hero lurking underneath, waiting for a chance to show his strength and goodness.

But this, here, when it counts, when it is all that matters, all that daydreaming is for shit. You cannot get out of this. You never planned for the nuances of lingering sickness and dense brain fog. You never imagined the mental arm wrestling, the moment of inevitable compassion for your enemy that makes you hesitate. And you never imagined how disabling being bound would be.

In all the scenarios in my head, I've always been the hero. But these are the real headlines:

Selfish Idiot Gets Girlfriend Pregnant and Lures Her into Mess with His Psycho Brother.

Confused Boyfriend Hesitates, Too Big of a Pussy to Save His Pregnant Girlfriend.

Dumbass Accidentally Calls His Girlfriend to Meet His Women-Hating, On-A-Rampage Brother.

Dave left the door open, and he's standing outside. Moonlight hits the top of his boot. I can't see any more of him, but I can picture him. He's leaning against the front of this shit cabin. Slipping a nicotine pouch in his lower lip, reaching for a moment of calm. Trying to slow his pulse and let the sweat along his forehead cool.

Natalie tugs quietly at the zip ties. We are both bound the same way, with zip ties around our wrists behind our backs, around our ankles, and with one ankle chained to a heavy piece of wood about twelve feet long and bolted to the wall. We're chained at opposite ends of the plank so we can't reach each other. It's stupid that plastic zip ties can be such a complete trap.

I breathe slowly. My mind is clearer than it was an hour ago, but I'm still a little fuzzy. "Dave?"

He ignores me.

"Dave? Seriously?"

I can almost feel his sigh. I wait, giving him time. I listen. Crickets and cicadas doing their thing, punctuated by an owl's hoot. Smells like moldy clothes. Damp earth. The forest doesn't breathe cool breath. It's more like the fetid breath from a drunk standing too close on the "L."

"Dave! Seriously?" I scream. "You chained us up, Dave? What's your plan? This isn't you, Dave. This isn't you."

His body fills the doorway, and he screams, "Shut! Up!" Veins bulge from his neck. His chest moves up and down. The switch comes so fast, it's startling. He chills out, forcing a half smile. "Sit tight, man. Why can't you sit tight?" His voice is almost calm, but there's a pleading there.

I don't get who he is half smiling for. I don't get who he's trying to appear calm for. I say, "You. Chained. Us. Up."

"No one has any patience anymore. Just sit fucking tight." He slams the door. Outside, here come the sounds of a fight. Rocks thrown, punches thrown, cursing and screaming, but he's the only one out there. He's kicking trees and throwing punches. Nat and I listen, like him punching a tree is going to give us some necessary insight. There's no insight, obviously, he's just melting down. The forest recognizes his tantrum as well, and the birds chirp again, unimpressed.

"Natalie." My voice trembling with emotion, I can barely say her name. "I'm sorry. Does anyone know where you went?"

"I didn't know," she says, dazed. It's dark, so I can't make out her expression. I can barely see the whites of her eyes. All we are is our words, our voices, scratchy from screaming. "I saw your brother, and I relaxed. He's your brother," she says, her voice small and full of questions. She doesn't understand. Even after the cruelty he's shown her, she's confused.

"How could you know?" I say. "I didn't know either. I still don't know." I mean, I don't know what he's capable of.

"The gun is our biggest problem," Natalie says, coming out of her daze. "We have to figure out how to get that away from him."

Through my tears, I smile at her silver-lining thinking.

"Don't give me your sad story, Golden Boy," she says, the slightest bit of humor there. "I know you wanted to be the hero, but forget about that."

Her words melt the ache in my heart. She knows me. I'm tormenting myself, and she doesn't even blame me. Dead serious, I say, "Will you marry me?"

"Fuck off with that too. Tell me everything that's happened."

She knows exactly what to say to keep me grounded. I tell her everything, starting with the text from Dave and meeting at Denny's.

~ My Journal ~

I don't understand why this is going wrong. I'm doing all the right things. I am protecting the vulnerable. I am standing up for those without a voice. I am an instrument of retribution. I am fucking noble. Why is this going so wrong? Mick doesn't respect me, I can see it in his eyes. He says one thing but thinks another. All I'm trying to do is show him how his mother is a monster, and I swear to God almighty, he's looking at me like I'm the monster.

It's the slut. She's got him brainwashed. He's so whipped, he is neck-deep in his own ass. It's not his fault, she's hard to resist. Her skin is smooth, and her ass is round and tiny—I could fit it in one hand. I might have to do something drastic. I might need to be a hero. I need him to see. Only way someone can see what's underneath the surface of the water is if you shove them under and hold them down. Baptize them, make them born again.

This isn't how it was supposed to go. I wanted to explain to him what it's like. I want him to understand. I lost my whole world when I was only four. She took him from me.

MC, age 24

CHAPTER 59

MEG

DAY 3, 8:26 P.M.

Angie Giano.

Ever since Detective Flemming said her name, I wanted to repeat it.

Now that I'm away from Whitney and surrounded by tall cypresses, long shadows, and barmy mosquitoes, I keep saying it. I'm huffing it as I run.

"Angie Giano," I tell the forest. In response, a bird, high above, shrieks.

The Missouri woman's body washed up on the Ohio River shore in southern Illinois. Notorious for being the most polluted river in the US, the Ohio flows out of Pennsylvania mostly southwest and empties into the Mississippi River in Cairo, Illinois.

Sharp pain slashes at my forehead, and my hand flies up. It's wet, and I pull my hand away. Blood. I ran into a stray branch. Lucky it didn't jab my eye. *Lucky*. Ha! I don't feel lucky.

I glance up. The burnt sky is broken to pieces by the canopy of trees. Dark gray is overtaking fiery orange. It's dark in the forest. No God beams shining through, kissing moss with magical light. Pretty soon the sky will be dark too.

Before I hung up on her, Flemming said David was working on Angie's case. And Whitney said David wrote on message boards about a woman he was investigating, that she did the most heinous things to her child. Sold her child. Tortured her child.

But that's not what the reporter said about Angie the morning McClane went missing. They said Giano was tortured. They made her out to be a victim. "Police would like the community's help. If you have any information." They would discover it in time, though. If she did horrible things to her child, evidence would come to light.

The deep ache in my heart wants to know. Who killed her? I mean, if this Angie Giano was wrapped up in heinous activities with other criminals, it's probably one of those people who killed her.

But what if it was David?

Even if she deserved it, even if she tortured her child. If David is capable of something so final, I won't be able to pull him out of that hole. I wasn't ready to hear Flemming tell me David killed her, that's why I hung up.

I should have been asking questions about his job right from the start, about his boss, his team. But I didn't want to annoy him, and honestly, my mind has been in tangles over Joe. I neglected David when he needed me. Yet again.

I trip on a mess of dead branches and fall forward. Pain shoots up my wrist, but it's brief. I get to my palms and knees and sit back, checking if my bones still feel intact. Falling gets harder on my body with each decade. My right knee stings. My jeans are torn, and I'm bleeding. I get up, look around for a clue, a disturbance in the brush, anything, but it's all the same in every direction, trees and shadows. I listen for human sounds. Nothing. My arms bristle at the cool air. There is so much forest. I'm an idiot for thinking I could possibly find them. Just like Joe said. Still, I keep running.

Memories from David's childhood gust through my mind. I grab hold of one: the kids' backyard circus. Dave, Jamie, little McClane, and a half-dozen neighborhood kids.

From my room on the second floor, I waited for toddler Whitney to wake from her nap while I folded clothes on my bed. I had the window open and heard the kids laughing and bickering. I couldn't make out their words, but that was okay, I didn't need to hear them. The cadence of their voices conveyed what I needed to know. That they were being kids. That no one was hurt. That they were getting along, or figuring it out at least.

I glanced out the window. A few were cartwheeling in the grass, a couple were lying down, but most of them were listening to the ringmaster, David. At ten, he was the oldest and a natural manager. He wore a purple cape and two studded costume bracelets.

Eight-year-old Jamie was in her bathing suit and a pair of cowgirl boots, twirling her rubber-tipped silver baton.

Three boys who were David's age built a balance beam out of cinderblocks.

Jamie's friend had her dog on a leash.

McClane, four years old, stood beside David, holding a small and shiny thing in his hand. A knife? No, it couldn't be. They were wacky little kids, but they weren't insane. Still, I figured I should go check on them.

From the next room, Whitney's crying burst like a siren, and adrenaline shot up my spine. I dropped Joe's shirt in a crumple and headed for Whitney, forgetting all about their circus.

I always thought of David as the ringmaster, the creative mind, the person who brought the neighborhood kids together.

I'm trying to view him as Whitney does: manipulative, a bully.

I go back further and try to remember David younger. He was four when Carson died. I can't remember David at five and six—those years were a blur.

After Carson died, every morning I woke up thinking I could not wait to go back to bed. Getting up to feed David and Jamie was painful, keeping them entertained with toys and television was painful, existing was painful. I only looked forward to the night when I could close my eyes and make myself go away.

I was depressed. Everyone forgave me for it. They let me soak in my depression. They thought it would be good for me. I lost a young child in a tragic accident, I should grieve hard, so I could pull through and come out the other side.

But what about my two living children? What had it been like for them at that young, impressionable age while their brains were making important connections? To have a mother so miserable, shuffling through life like a lost kitten, her mind and soul empty, barely capable of conversation.

I sleepwalked though my days for two years. My next pregnancy was a blur too. Morning sickness and fatigue set to the backdrop of depression.

It was when McClane was born that I snapped out of it. Holding this warm, helpless newborn, his eyes squinty and angry as he cried because it was all so bright and raw, I got that jolt of dopamine or adrenaline or oxytocin, and it flipped my light switch back on.

Basically, I had the opposite of postpartum depression. I had a postpartum coming back from the dead. Even with the exhaustion and the sleepless nights, I clawed my way back.

Brand-new life motivated me. New life was helpless and fresh and bright-eyed, and it kept the depression away. And when I started to slip back, I told Joe I wanted to try for another. We had Whitney.

Some would argue it was a bad reason to have kids. To stave off depression, to find a bright spark in a dark, painful life. But I think it's a good reason to have kids, as long as you're prepared to nurture them, teach them, and be present. I came back to them. Eventually, I came back.

But maybe I was gone too long for David. For several years of his young life, I was a ghost, living alongside him.

My shoe catches another tangle of branches, and my foot goes through. I throw my hands out, thinking I'll fall forward, but queasiness flips my stomach because I'm still falling. Pain lights up my right shin as it's sliced, and the arches of my feet burst with pain as they hit a rocky bottom. Pain flares at the back of my head too, bursting toward my ears, and my vision dims. The flashlight inside my drawstring bag hit me.

Crickets chirp above my head. Damp earth surrounds me in

all directions, the smell of decay and earthworms close. I breathe. I talk myself out of panic and confusion.

Like a pathetic, frantic mouse, I've fallen into a trap. Literally. I'm in a well-shaped hole, water in its base. My shoes are submerged. Forest floor at my hairline, I can't even see aboveground unless I look up.

CHAPTER 60

McClane

MISSING

An entire day has gone by.

The lower back pain is intense. If this is what old feels like, I'll pass on that shit. We've both pissed ourselves. The smell of urine dominates the outside odors of cypress and cedar.

Dave has been gone since last night's temper tantrum. And now, the setting sun coming in through that one window next to me is amber with the faintest hint of crimson. Which reminds me, I'm probably coming down with a bladder infection. When I pissed my pants, it burned. I don't want to die young, but I'm serious about passing on growing old.

Everything aches. Long hours of standing with our wrists bound behind our backs, our chests extended, is worse than my most grueling workout. I'm dumbfounded by the pain. My thumbs even hurt. We've talked about how much time has passed. It's been about seventeen hours. Seventeen hours bound in this shithole cabin.

In those long hours, we've loosened the twelve-foot plank from the wall. That motherfucker was bolted tight, but we've stood on it and rocked it and pried at it with our fingers. We didn't feel the slightest give until hour ten. But since, it's come loose, and in another hour we'll be able to pick that plank up and walk out of here together.

Our fingertips are bloody. I keep getting charley horses in my palms. For Nat, cramps keep tensing her calves. We can take breaks to sit, yeah, but sitting is actually more uncomfortable than standing when your ankles and wrists are bound. We can lie down to take a break, but it's difficult to get back to standing, and we don't want to make ourselves vulnerable. We've discussed this.

I'm not drugged anymore, but I feel off. Like I'm losing it. I'm exhausted, nauseated, and a little delirious. Almost like being drunk. Not the tipsy warmth that makes you feel loose and invisible. The oh-shit-I-drank-too-much drunk. Jumpy too. A strand of my hair falls against my forehead, and I flinch. Shadows skate around the edge of my vision. I flinch at those too.

I'm out of it, ragged but overreactive, and my limbs are weak. My knees have given out a few times. Natalie feels it too from the lack of sleep, though her knees aren't giving like mine because she hasn't been drugged and puking. Dryness claws at my throat.

We keep prying at the wooden plank.

As if she can read my negative thoughts, she says, "The police are looking."

"Yeah, but why would they look into my brother?"

"I don't know, but they're looking."

"Three days, Nat. I've been gone for three days. After forty-eight hours, they give up a little."

"Is that for real, though, or, like, from movies? Besides, I haven't been gone long. They probably just started looking for me this morning. My parents would have expected me to be home for church." More thoughtful, she says, "Me being gone has to change their minds about what they think happened to you."

She didn't tell anyone she was coming to pick me up. When she read my text saying I was in trouble, she thought I had gotten myself into trouble. She figured telling the police could get me in trouble *legally*, so she didn't tell anyone where she was going. She told her parents she was sleeping over at a friend's.

"They're never gonna assume it's Dave, though," I say. "My mom's probably telling the police her son is FBI, and they think that's the shit." Shadows dance to my left, and I flinch. "He stuck a syringe in a plastic Coke bottle to drug me. How insane is that? He gave me roofies."

"Stop it," she screams. "Stop it. Stop!"

I'm quiet. We're both quiet.

She makes a weird, strangled noise. Then she's screaming.

I go to reach for her but forget I'm bound. The plastic ties cut against my raw skin. "What is it? What's going on?"

"Get it off," she screams, her voice shredded, her body jerking and twisting. "There's a spider on my arm. Get it off. Get it off!"

I can't see the spider. I can't help her. Her hair is flying, she's like a dancing mop. She's losing it, just like me. I try yanking at my zip ties again, but it only chafes the raw skin.

"It's okay, Nat. It's just a bug. You're gonna be okay."

She stomps over and over, eventually settling down. She falls to the ground, crying weakly.

"Did you kill it?"

"Yeah, but it was a brown recluse, I think."

"I am such a shit boyfriend," I say, trying to make her laugh.

"You really fucking are."

"I would so love it if your dad could lecture me right now, tell me I'm only a boy."

Her shoulders tremble and her head lowers. She's sniffing, trying not to cry.

"Hey," I say, my voice strong, movie-star quality. "You okay?"

She huffs a small laugh. "Yeah, I'm still here."

My voice scratchy, I say, "I'm just a fly in the ointment."

"The monkey in the wrench."

"A pain in the ass."

"Now that," she says, nodding her chin at me because she can't point. "That's true."

"Natalie," I say, pleading. "I love you. I will get us out of here."

"Maybe I'll get us out of here," she says. "Or maybe you can do one of your wrestling moves to get us out of here."

An idea smacks me. It might actually work. I don't know why I didn't think of it hours ago. Thank God for Nat. She is logical and always has a plan. Thinking when I'm not. Holding it together as I'm losing my concentration. "I think you just got us out of here," I say.

I was so focused on Dave. Stupid Dave. What's Dave gonna do? How can we get out of these zip ties when they're behind our backs? When your hands are bound in front of you, it's a different story. You can scrape your hands against anything. When they're tight behind your back, you are helpless. My mind has been like a radio tuned to static and with the volume cranked up, so I couldn't think about much besides Dave. What I needed to do was think about myself. What I can fucking do.

"What do you mean?" she says.

"Natalie. I can—"

The door opens, and Dave walks in. His mouth is drawn down, his eyes are stony. He doesn't look at me. He looks at Natalie.

"What are you gonna do, Dave?" I say, my voice scratchy and low.

He ignores me, takes keys out of his back pocket, and unlocks her ankle.

"No. No. Dave, leave her alone. Let's call Mom. Let's tell her we know what she did."

He ignores me, shoving the keys back in his pocket and aiming his gun at her. "Out. Let's go."

"Take me," I plead, my voice cracking. "I want to talk with you. I need to talk to you. Same as you need to talk to me."

"Sorry, man. You're too far gone," he says, tone stagnant as swamp water. "Got to rip off the Band-Aid. It will hurt at first, but you'll thank me later."

CHAPTER 61

Meg

DAY 3, 8:38 P.M.

Did David set this trap? I don't bother entertaining the idea. There are so many crazies in the world, why would it be David who set this trap? No, it wasn't David. That fall could have killed me, so it can't be David.

My skin stings in so many places, and there's a twinge in my back, warning me it might seize up like an engine without oil.

I rub the burning out of my hands, shedding stuck pine needles and smearing blood. I put my hands on the ground above me and try to push myself out. I don't have the upper body strength. I try again and fail. Desperation reaches into my chest and squeezes my heart. My breathing is shallow, and my pulse races.

I tilt my face to the sky as if I might find answers there.

Orange light is faint above the canopy, but down here below the trees, it's dark. I check my phone. No service. I pull the flashlight out of my drawstring bag and sway its beam, lighting up the forest floor, searching for anything that could help me get out. Nothing, but there are two other small piles of brush a dozen feet away in opposite directions. More traps, I bet.

Swooping the flashlight down at the water swallowing my feet, I catch sight of my jeans, blown out at the knee and torn down my bloody shin. I can't gauge how badly I'm cut. The sting is raw, but it's a secondary problem. I need to get out of this hole.

When I fell, I took a dozen branches down with me. Flashlight beam moving from branch to branch around my feet, I search for the right stick. I grab a thicker one about the length of the hole's diameter. Two feet above the bottom of the trap, I shove the branch into the wall of dirt, knocking soil lose. I drag the other side of the stick up the wall until it resists. I give it another pull until it's firmly stuck.

In the distance, a noise cuts through humid silence. Here, it's faint. It could be anything. An owl. A raven. A siren. What I think, though? It's a scream.

I slip the flashlight into my bag and my bag around my shoulders. I push my palms down on the forest floor and step onto the branch. As I put my weight on it, the branch slips away and drops. But I've already got enough leverage, and I push off the wall of the hole with my feet until I'm out.

Lying on the ground now, back aching, I breathe hard. The smell of wet earth and fungi fills my nose and the back of my throat.

There it is again, that noise cutting across the forest. I hold my breath and listen.

It's brief. It's muted, like screaming into a pillow, but I'm pretty sure it's a scream and I'm pretty sure it's Natalie.

Sweeping the flashlight in front of me to avoid branches, I rush toward the scream. I have no idea how far away it was. Three hundred feet? Nine hundred feet?

I stay close to the trees. Whoever dug that trap wouldn't dig near a huge tree trunk where roots are too thick. I round a cypress tree, and my flashlight lands on the open door of a makeshift cabin.

I rush toward it, not thinking. There's no time for thinking or planning, and I don't want to give myself room to get scared. I burst over the threshold, heart pounding.

No one's here. My flashlight catches on a small crib-size mattress and stops to linger on the stains—the dirty brown of long-dried blood and the bright red splatters of new blood.

The filthy mattress feels cliché, like a prop in a poorly written crime show, and I cringe. What kind of reality do I live in where bloodstained mattresses are cliché?

Not David. It can't be David. I'm witnessing the crazy of another mother's son.

At the far end of the room, chains are bolted into a long, broken piece of wood. My body feels haunted. Like ghosts are whooshing through my chest and thighs and head, trying to push me, spook me, knock me over.

I'm about to run out of this pathetic and disgusting place when the beam of my flashlight catches a fold of yellow fabric against the wall.

I rush to check.

It's a sweatshirt. Dark green with yellow letters. A hoodie. Sugar Glen North High. McClane's.

A moan comes from deep inside me, part of me that isn't really me, but something ancient and vestigial that only surfaces once or twice at most in a lifetime, like a sea monster rising from the deep, breaking the ocean's surface with a wail because its baby has been poached. It sounds nothing like me.

Scanning the makeshift cabin once more, all I can think of is David coming home from Boy Scout camp at fourteen and telling Joe how he'd gotten his survival badge by making a lean-to shelter and spending the night there.

Outside, another scream.

I run toward it.

CHAPTER 62

McCLANE

MISSING

It's strange I didn't think of it myself. I guess it's the stress. Being under pressure, I couldn't think straight. I got tunnel vision. And the drugs messed with my thinking. All my dendrons or ganglions or whatever they're called—all those little branchy things connecting your brain cells—mine were, like, wearing condoms. Their connections were anesthetized.

Still, it's strange I didn't think of it. But it's also not strange. Look at Dave. Dude is under some weird stress and his brain short-circuited. Like an electric pole down in a storm, shooting sparks, shorting out the power box.

Good thing Natalie is thinking clearly—*my wrestling moves*. I'm double-jointed. I don't do it often because it mad hurts, but it's gotten me out of a few pins. I've been told if I do it too often, pop my joints out of socket, I'll get arthritis when I'm like fifty, but that's a lifetime away. Who knows if I'll be alive when I'm fifty. I'm not gonna live my life carefully now so I make sure I can play pickleball when I'm in a nursing home.

I'm pumped because I have a plan, but I'm in a rage because Dave steered her out the door with his fucking gun.

I rotate my shoulders, pop one shoulder out of joint, then the next. It's painful, and my skin breaks into a cold sweat, but I've done it so many times and the pain doesn't last, so. I rotate my arms over my head, around to the front of my body. My wrists before me, I bite at the zip tie. My teeth slip, slicing into my tongue. Blood fills my mouth. I spit and keep biting at the zip tie. It snaps, and my wrists are free. The skin around my wrists is raw and the muscles ache, but I don't have time to rub away the cramping.

I pull off my hoodie, wrap it around my fist, and punch through the window. The glass cracks, and shards fall both outside and onto the floor. Using a shard of glass wrapped in my hoodie, I saw at the zip tie binding my ankles together until it snaps. My one ankle is still chained to the long wooden plank. I'm not going to be able to free my ankle from that chain, but I can free the plank from the wall. Natalie and I have been working on loosening it from the wall all day, so two of the four bolts are already free.

Standing on the top edge of the plank, I jump on it till it breaks away from the wall. As it drops, I lose my balance. My feet go out in front of me, my head hits the wall, and I go down. Pain lights up my ankle as it twists, and emotions pump through me—fury, desperation, impatience. This is taking too long. I pick up the massive plank chained to my ankle and run, dragging the heavy piece of wood out the door.

They can't be far. I listen, trying to quiet my panting. Nearby, water drips slowly. A little farther, an owl hoots. Then: her voice. Natalie is talking to him. She's raising her voice, pissed off, but she's also talking, like, still trying to use logic with him.

I barely raise the plank above my knees because the chain binding my ankle to the wood is short. It's long and awkward to carry, so I look like a gorilla running with my knuckles close to the ground. I need to split this piece of wood, so I run as fast as I can toward the space between two trees, trying to keep the plank parallel to the ground.

The far ends of it hit both trees, and it cracks, hitting me in the shins and groin. I go down. I've wracked myself so roughly, my vision narrows and goes black. When my vision comes back, my balls are still ringing. My thighs and knees also feel pretty mangled. I don't want to look at what's bleeding, so I don't. I wipe sweat away from my eyes and get to my feet. I've still got a book-size slab of wood attached to my ankle, but I can run with that dragging behind me.

Natalie screams—the agony in her voice splitting my heart right open, drawing tears from my eyes—and I grab a rock from the ground and hobble toward the sound of her. The stupid board bangs around, bouncing off the ground and smashing into my shin, cutting slashes into me, but who fucking cares because Natalie is screaming.

As I run toward her scream, I think about Dave.

Dave at seven years old, hopping into my bed on a Saturday morning and telling me his plans for the day, what ideas he's got, and I'm welcome to join.

I think about him TP-ing my room for my eighth birthday and me thinking it was so cool of him to wrap my room in toilet paper.

I think about fishing with him in the creek behind our house when he was in middle school, making a cage for all the toads we caught and feeding them crickets before letting them go.

I think about Dave getting his driver's license and taking me along for Wendy's Frosties on school nights and thinking he was so chill, how lucky I was to have a big brother like him. A fun brother who named his car after a character in some old movie.

I think about going to Dave's high school football games, the air chilled and charged, the announcer's voice like God. Even though he was second-string, I was so proud to watch him on the field.

I'm thinking about Dave, about all these little moments with him, because I know I've got to be okay with my choice. Even before I round the tree and witness Dave punch her in the stomach, I know.

I'm going to kill him.

CHAPTER 63

MEG

DAY 3, 9:02 P.M.

The stone falls from McClane's palm and drops to the ground with a thud. His expression is ghostly, and he stumbles back a few steps.

David's body crumples. He is on his back, his body still. His eyes stare at the sky. His mouth moves, but he's quiet.

I feel like I'm on the outside, looking in. Both of these boys are strangers to me. Adult men I hardly know. I am in shock with this feeling of unfamiliarity.

In the distance, a strange low, muffled chatter. At first, I assume it's an animal. Oh, someone's talking through a bullhorn.

McClane rushes to Natalie's side. She's doubled over on the ground, quiet, with her eyes closed.

McClane sits down beside her and talks quietly near her ear. She listens with her eyes closed, nodding slowly. Her cheeks are smeared in dirt and blood. Her hair is a tangled mess. She looks like she's lived in the forest for months. She's only been gone a day.

McClane's face looks worse. I want to grab his arm, I want to pull him close and hold him tightly, but I don't know his mindset. I am still on the outside.

"Are you both okay to walk?" I say.

McClane turns toward me, surprised, realizing I'm here. His lower lip trembles. Tears slip down his cheeks and he buries his face into Natalie's back. "I had to do it, Mom."

"I know. I know you had to do it. Here's my flashlight." I untangle myself from my bag and toss it on the ground. "If you're both able to walk, head toward the bullhorn."

"I had no other choice," he says.

"I know. Go. Go. Go slowly. There are holes covered with sticks."

McClane looks at David and winces, pulls his hands down his face. Natalie sits up and leans toward him, whispering words quietly near his ear. She stands slowly, grabs my bag, and guides McClane away as he whimpers.

Taking turns taking care of each other. Joe and I used to do that. For a moment, I wonder what words they said to each other. Only for a moment, though. My baby needs me.

I kneel beside David. He's on his back, eyes wide. A gash at his temple oozes blood everywhere, into his hair and down his face. When he was small, my hands ruffled his hair so many times, I knew the feel and sweaty smell of his hair by heart. His body is still but his eyes and mouth move. No longer a stranger, he is familiar, like a small hand slipping perfectly into my own. He is mine. My boy.

"It's going to be okay. You're going to be okay." I take my jacket off and press it against his temple. With the sleeve, I clear his eyes of blood.

"Mom?" He's confused. His irises quiver and migrate sideways in his eye sockets toward me. He doesn't trust his senses.

"It's me. I'm here."

"Where's Dad?" His voice sounds so small, choked up.

My heart breaks. "He's coming. He's on his way."

"I don't feel so well." Blood outlines his teeth and slips out of his mouth, down the side of his cheek. I don't understand why his mouth is bleeding too.

"Try to relax. Help is on the way."

"I didn't want to hurt Mick. Can you tell him?"

"He knows." I don't even know what to say to him. Do I tell him I didn't kill Carson, do I tell him I love him, do I ask him about Angie Giano? It all feels too late. Pointless. He tries to lift his head. I lay my hand on his chest. "Stay put. Help is on the way."

"They're everywhere, Mom."

"Who is?"

"I got one." His eyes flutter and close. "I wish I got more of them."

"What do you mean?" I know what he means.

"You can't trust anyone," he says, his voice small and frightened. "Not even you."

"I'm sorry, kiddo."

"Don't leave me, Mom."

"I won't. I'm right here." My arm trembles as I hold my jacket to his temple. My other hand trembles as I squeeze his hand. It's cold. His eyes stay closed and his breathing slows.

"When's Dad coming?" he whispers.

"Soon. He's coming soon."

CHAPTER 64

McClane

TWO MONTHS LATER

I'm still having nightmares about Dave. In my dreams, I kill him over and over. Dr. Kamry assures me the nightmares will fade. I cling to that promise.

Another month and I'll be headed to Indiana University, studying psych. Go figure. I met my roommate on Snap. He's from Michigan. He's bringing his gaming rig, I'm bringing the fridge—a balanced partnership.

I won't be wrestling. I have a few torn ligaments from the thing with Dave. Nothing needing surgery yet. But we'll see. But it doesn't matter if I want to wrestle or not, the injuries made the choice for me. Dad and I have that in common now.

Even though I can blame my torn ligaments, Hud and Jack throw me shade about limp-dicking out of a full ride. Behind their jokes, I see their attempts to lift my spirits.

My parents don't care about the scholarship. Obviously. They have bigger storm clouds following them. Lots of those storm clouds are in the shape of Dave. The FBI is investigating what happened exactly. Lots of stuff going on there, starting with the dead woman they found in the Ohio River, but I don't want to think about that. My therapist says that's okay, it's not my job, it's outside of my circle of control. She is big on this circle thing.

Nat and I are at Breakneck, high above the expanse of water. It's a week past the Fourth of July, and someone's left a small parade flag stuck in the grass under the crabapple. With its blooms gone, it's unrecognizable as the tree Nat and I lay under the day she told me she was pregnant. The only reason I know it's the same tree is I park my car in the same spot every time, just to the left of it.

The morning is humid, but it's overcast. Everything gray, water to sky. Hazy and still.

Things are good between Nat and me, but we've kept some thoughts to ourselves. Even after two months, a few things hang heavy between us, things I need to say but haven't.

She's watching the water, as if she's waiting for something along the calm surface to change. "Fifty feet, right?" she says, her tone uncertain.

I exhale. "I meant it when I asked you to marry me. I don't want you to think I didn't mean it."

She pauses for a beat, taking in what I just said, then laughs. "Oh, fuck off with that, McClane." She doesn't look up at me. Her eyes are on the water. "I've got plans. Plans with you. But plans for me too."

She had a miscarriage. She said she expected to be able to see a big freaky clot, but she didn't even notice. She had her period like normal. She told me and her mom at the same time, that's how comfortable she is with life, with who she is.

I am in awe of her. She takes life one pitch at a time, like it's a sport she's been playing since she was in preschool.

But she's nervous now. She's got her bikini on underneath her T-shirt and cutoffs. All I can see is a white spaghetti strap peeking out where her T-shirt falls to the side, but I know that bikini by heart.

"It's all clear to the left of the rock," I say.

"Left of the rock," she says to herself. She slips off her flip-flops. Shimmies out of her shorts, which is distracting. Spaghetti straps, fringe, and so much of her skin.

She steps over the guardrail, and up to the edge. I think she's going to say more, I think she's going to look back at me and wink, but she doesn't. She jumps.

I hold my breath. It's safe to jump in daylight. But no matter how many safe jumps are made, there will always be that one fatal jump we think of.

As she goes over the edge, her hair hovers above her head and her legs and arms are straight down and it's like she's shot through an invisible tube, falling until her legs slice through the water. The sound of her splash reaches me.

I am still holding my breath, waiting for her to come up. Because it's not always about the fall. Landing wrong can fuck you up. One second. Two. Three.

Her head bobs up, her radiant smile stealing all my tension.

Her laugh, though muffled by the distance, sounds like home. She shouts, "Come on, Golden Boy!"

I slip off my sneakers, set them next to her flip-flops. Pull my T-shirt over my head and toss it in the grass. I answer her call the only way I know how. I jump.

CHAPTER 65

MEG

FIVE MONTHS LATER

Joe left me.

I forgave him for killing my oldest child. He couldn't forgive me for a blow job. Pretty much sums up our marriage these past few years.

We sold the house. He's living with his dad. Temporarily, he says, but if he couldn't manage to log on to his email for six months, I can't imagine him scheduling a house-hunting date with his Realtor.

This man was the sturdy fire keeping my heart warm for so many years, and now he's burnt out like a cheap candle with bad wax, leaving a brown stain on my wall and black boogers in my nose. I didn't fight for him, because he wasn't Joe anymore.

I don't miss the house, which is strange. The house was so important to me. I made it a reflection of myself, a symbol of my ability to nurture, a symbol of my success at motherhood. Now that I've lost so much, I don't want anything. It's freeing in a way.

I feel more myself these days. I haven't been myself for as long as I can remember, maybe since Joe and I started dating. And even though I am feeling more authentically me, I will never be myself completely. That confident, unruly, witty young me pulsing with vitality and humor? I threw that animal so much steak—to keep its belly full, its mouth too busy to talk, and its brain sleepy—it has become fat and dim and acquiescent.

I didn't bring much to my new place. Clothes, a dresser, Jamie's bed. I frisbeed the Dalí clock into the forest behind the house—just like Whitney and I laughed about. Good riddance to my interesting clock and my interesting life!

I'd like to say Whitney and I have moved in together and she's nursing Hudson back, inspiring him to clean up his act, but that's not really how things go.

Whitney and I have fallen back into our mother-daughter seesaw of supporting and bickering with each other. She didn't want to choose Mom or Dad, so she's living with a friend right now. We text and go out to eat twice each week, and she sends me Zelle requests for money.

McClane and I are closer. He calls to check in every Sunday. He tells me about his classes, about the clubs he's joined, about Natalie coming to visit. I think since David hated me so much, and David hurt Natalie, McClane has mentally made me his brother's opposite and thinks of me as wholesome and good. It's twisted, but I'll take it. His therapist will probably spoil this at some point, but I'm okay with that too. McClane has become my old-soul child. He has lived another whole life, seen the worst, and come back to us with a new perspective—that the world is uglier than he'd guessed but still worth exploring.

Jamie is in town for the first time since the funeral, checking in on Whitney and McClane. She said she might swing by my apartment, depending on how things go—she's keeping it vague.

I'm living in Shady Grove one floor down from Hudson and his dad, Chase. I bring them a casserole every Monday and tell them the same stories about Hud as a boy looking out for Whitney, to spark some pride in Hudson and to spark heat under Chase's lazy ass. I tell Chase he used to be awesome not so long ago. He can get back to that.

Oh, and I have a cat, Joyce. She followed me in. Technically, I held the door open for her, so it's possible I stole someone's cat. She wasn't wearing a tag, so their bad. Occasionally she scratches at my front door, trying to escape, but I lure her to the kitchen with cheese and she forgets her dreams of chasing mice and dodging cars. Once a day she spreads her body out across my laptop while I'm working until I take a break to give her scratches. She likes them under her chin.

I like Shady Grove. It is a community of losers, truly. We have all lost something to end up here, and no one's pretending otherwise. People don't pretend here. They are either grumpy and sad or sad but happy. They step into the elevator and say the weather is shit when it's shit. They complain about the rent or their arthritis or their colon or the parking. Or they tell you who they lost and what they do to pay bills or they say, "You don't want to know what I do to pay the bills." Sometimes they tell you to take care of yourself or they offer you a brownie, and you don't know if it's just a brownie or if it's medicinal.

And sometimes they stomp out after I step in, their faces pinched in disgust as the doors close. Mostly, though, people don't judge me. They are too busy with their own troubles to hang on to mine. Shady Grove is good in that way.

When people ask directly, I say, "Yeah, that was my son you heard about." I tell them he was a good boy who wanted to become a good man, so he got a job as an FBI agent, hunting child abusers. His work pulled him too far under, and he killed someone who tortured their kid. He died in a tragic accident.

They nod. They understand this is not far-fetched. That all it takes is a string of so-so choices or a sprinkle of bad luck to tumble you down a hole.

Also, they know there's more to the story and crave the juicy details. I mean, it became national news. There were too many intriguing elements—my bad parenting caught on video, Carson's death, my brother Nathan killing his friend, McClane going missing, Natalie's pregnancy, Natalie's abduction, Joe running naked by Breakneck, Angie Giano's murder, and David's death. With all these details woven into the story, it became irresistible, cherished by thirsty news anchors because the well didn't run dry. It gave news folk their best teaser: *When we come back, yet another twist to the David Hart case.*

Whitney was wrong about my video. It went viral.

I think it would have fallen under the radar like she predicted had the whole thing not ended in David's death and the revelation he'd killed the Missouri woman.

I have never pointed out to Whitney she was wrong. Obviously. When you've made as many mistakes as I have, you keep your judgment to yourself. I only tell her she's brilliant and kind and has a future full of possibilities. And I text her photos of my cat.

Who is there for me every day? Eileen. Me and my AI friend. I haven't been fired from my job, if you can believe that. I expected it, but it hasn't happened, so maybe it won't. I imagine myself aging off into dementia, chatting over tea with Eileen. She is getting more sophisticated by the day. She's also getting a bit snarky. This morning I asked her for a few motivating quotes. She told me, "You can do hard things," and I choked and spit my coffee.

———•———

My timer rings, and I take a pie out of the oven. The warm scent of flaky dough and sour-sweet cherry pulp is a nice alternative to the slightly musky smell of cat. I brew coffee and play with Joyce—she likes batting the feather wand—until my doorbell buzzes.

"Hey," Jamie says. With her purple-gray hair, her cold-slapped cheeks, and the crisp smell of autumn on her sweater, she radiates vitality in my drab hallway. "I only have twenty minutes," she says, stepping inside my apartment but already planning her escape. She is herself but not fully—not the spirited, joyful, silly girl she is on Instagram, posting photos of salted margaritas, new tattoos, and *Mamma Mia!* karaoke with her friends. "I half expected to get slashed in that creepy stairwell with those fritzy lights. And those dudes toking out front? Yikes. You okay living here?"

"The smokers are Hudson's friends. They help me carry my groceries. It's not as rough as it looks." Honestly, Shady Grove suits me better than our lovely farmhouse did these past few years. "Come have a quick slice of pie." Cherry is Jamie's favorite.

She drops her purse by my front door, and we settle at my two-seater kitchen table. I serve pie and fill our mugs with coffee. She heaps spoonfuls of sugar into her coffee, and I resist the urge to advise moderation.

Joyce sidles up next to her. "Oh, look at you," Jamie coos, offering her palm for a sniff.

My gaze drifts to the raised white scars on her palm—reminders of a fall in the 7-Eleven parking lot and standing up to those girls who bullied David. Having gone through puberty early, by seventh grade Jamie was fleshy and thick-boned and as tall as those pugnacious girls while David was scrawny and hairless, smooth as a seal, as a freshman.

I was proud of Jamie for sticking up for family, yet a nagging thought lingered: If only she had kept her mouth shut, maybe David would have found his voice. Maybe he wouldn't have felt so small.

Jamie was always the fighter. Even when she was two years old, she had a mouth on her. If someone took her lollipop, she didn't quietly get another one. She screamed, mouth wide, tears flowing. I've wondered: If she would have been easier, more yielding, maybe Carson would have been warmer to her.

What a shitty feminist I've turned out to be! *If she would have kept her mouth shut. If she would have been easier.* These thoughts are insane. Still, I have them.

"How are things?" I ask Jamie as she strokes Joyce.

"I renewed my lease. My roommates are good. I have a boyfriend. He's good."

She leans back and crosses one ankle at her knee, her thigh relaxed open. She is comfortable in her body, in her tattooed skin, in who she is, and it reminds me: That's how I once was. I want to warn her to not lose herself—to not let her boyfriend slowly peel herself away from her.

She takes a bite of pie and glances at her watch again. "I need to tell you something."

This is why she wanted to visit. My heart pounds. What could it be?

"My last name got me a job offer, a *really* good one," she says. "I got hired to report on an alternative crime beat, and the first thing they want from me: Dig into Dave's story. It's exploitive, for sure." She laughs a little. "I'm okay with that," she says, her tone more familiar, more herself. She studies me, trying to gauge my fragility. Whatever her test, I pass, and she leans in. "I'm not sure if you know this, but Dave has this, like, underground cult following."

"Whitney mentioned it. I don't go looking. I don't go on social media." Although Carla didn't press charges, the media storm she ignited lives on in Facebook groups and forums where people still believe I killed Carson.

"That's probably a good idea," she says, humor in her tone. "Anyway, people have dissected his posts. They quote him. It's creepy and biblical. They call him the Dark Shepherd. Anyway," she says, leaning back and sipping her coffee, "Whitney's gonna help me dig into computer stuff. Mick's okay with it too."

This worries me. Digging into the darkest folds of David's life could be dangerous. I fear she could also learn more about Carson. I don't want Jamie to find out Carson nearly drowned her. And I'd rather the public forget us, but I don't own our family history. "You do what you want. Be considerate of McClane and Whitney, but not me."

"I'm not asking for your permission. I'm giving you a heads-up."

Ouch. "Oh, okay."

"I've got to go," she says and stands. "Thanks for the pie."

"Wait," I say, standing. I touch her shoulder. She lets me. "How are *you*?"

She smiles. It's weak but sincere. "I struggle with the Dave I knew and this other Dave." She shrugs. "What are you gonna do besides get on with life? Stay present? Live every day like it could be your last? All that. I've got to go." She picks up her purse and shuts my door on her way out.

———•———

Live every day like it could be your last.

I'm not a fan of that saying. The last thing I need is to try to pack more shit into my day because I might not survive the night. What I need is to be told to live every day like I have at least a few thousand more. I need to be told to kick my feet up and turn on the morning news for a second, the less-serious B-team news folk bumping elbows with each other and showing goofy dog photos.

Live every day like it could be your last.

People say it optimistically, like carpe diem and make happy memories with your loved ones. It's assumed your family and friends want to spend time with you.

To me, this saying is ominous. Live every day like you are going to lose your family, your reputation, your electricity, your home, your job. In other words: Watch your back. Pay attention. Keep up the pretense. Stow a few secrets in your back pocket. You're going to need them.

ACKNOWLEDGMENTS

When you enjoy writing stories, you never know if you'll get your first book—or second or third—out there into readers' hands. The publishing business is like a wild merry-go-round, and all you want is a chance to hop on that sucker.

What I'm getting at is, I'm damn thrilled to have gotten another spin. Thank you, Hyperion Avenue, for bringing this book to readers.

My editor, Olivia Zavitson: Thank you for championing this book and making it shinier. You are brilliant and an absolute joy to work with. Adam Wilson, Guy Cunningham, Karen Krumpak, Sara Liebling, Jill Amack, Amy King, Kaitie Leary, Crystal McCoy, Andrea Rosen, and everyone at Hyperion Avenue who touched this book along the way, thank you. And thank you to Keith Hayes and Joel Fisher for the cover design and photography.

My agent, Barbara Poelle: Thank you for cheering me on. And for being telepathic—available when I need to chat and then letting me do my hermit thing. You are a delight.

When this book was sold, I had been away from social media and the author community for two years. The thought of reaching out and asking authors to read my book felt daunting. But the author community is full of humble, patient, wise, and generous individuals.... To all the authors who read, spoke kindly, and rooted for me and any of my books—thank you from the bottom of my dark heart to yours.

To the readers, TikTokers, and Bookstagrammers: You bring the magic. Your love for stories keeps this whole thing going. Special thanks to those who carve time out of their busy schedules to write reviews—especially the good ones.

Mom, Michelle, Julie, Steven: Your kindness and support mean everything. And to the kids: Katie, Lauren, Reed, Quinn, Ethan, Alex, and Sarah—for good times and Farkle. Marc and my family on the other side: Thank you for years of support. Appreciation to all my friends, especially those I've leaned on recently: Liz, Christine, Magen, Wendy, Marquita, Jasmina, Erin, Tara, and Lisa. Thanks to the Cartwrights for seamlessly updating my website to keep it from self-destructing.

Marcel, Jo, Christine, and Erik Lewinski, and Cheryl Klocek: I'm grateful for your generosity. And to everyone at my day job, thank you for making my days so enjoyable that I still have energy left to write after work.

Edward, Jon, and Sam: You are the reason I strive to be the best version of myself. It's not easy (it's kind of exhausting to be honest), but I'm so grateful for it. Watching you three grow has been the adventure of my life. Keep showing up. Stay curious. Keep having a good time.

AUTHOR'S NOTE

Heads-up—this author's note contains spoilers!

I like to include an author's note for two reasons: First, to share how this book came to be, for those who are interested. Second, because I'd forget otherwise. This note serves as my personal souvenir—a snapshot of what was on my mind when I started the novel. Even though it's been just over a year since I began writing this story, I had already forgotten how it came to me. I had to dig through my damn phone notes to find my inspirations.

Some books have a single spark of inspiration. This one had many. Picture a hive of honeybee larvae—each grubby organism doing its own thing, fed and nurtured by worker bees. Eventually, these larvae grow up and become part of a singular hive mind—one cohesive story. Let me introduce you to the grubs:

Other writers' works inspire me. One of my all-time favorite shows, *The Leftovers*, nailed sexy, chaotic portrayals of delusion. Naturally, I thought: What if I did the opposite? Unsexy, mundane psychiatric struggles. Why replicate brilliance when I can go for the opposite? Kidding. Sort of.

That alarming moment in my kid's room. There was this one time I saw something unnerving in my kid's room. For a few seconds, I was like: Whaaaat? Then I remembered—this is my kid we're talking about. There had to be a harmless explanation. There was, by the way. Creative and wacky, but innocent. But I couldn't help wondering: What would it look like to someone who didn't know them? A detective, maybe?

Dialogue comes to me on nighttime walks. Meg's monologue about "The Elves and the Shoemaker" came to me this way—funny and tragic, and I knew it would end up in the book.

Overheard conversations. "I love him to death, but I hope he dies before me because, my God, who would take care of him?" A mother said this about her child, and I think about it often. I feel for parents of violent children. And for their children.

Themes keep rearing their heads. The thread running through many of my books is slippage—how a life unravels. From sane to insane, solid to disturbing, good to violent. People in desperate situations—that's what captures my attention. And then there's the endless tug-of-war between nature and nurture. What's innate, what's learned, and what's biologically acquired through disease or injury? I'm fascinated by how fragile our perspectives and personalities are.

I wanted to write an earnest young character! I write a lot of messed-up characters. Naturally, thrillers require a bad guy, or two, or three. I decided to shake things up by writing some seriously wholesome young people—kids so genuinely good I hoped they might linger in your heart long after the final page.

And just for kicks, here are the songs I had on repeat while writing or thinking about this book:

"Chlorine" —Twenty One Pilots
"Hash Pipe" —Weezer
"The Man" —The Killers
"Andy, You're a Star" —The Killers
"Toxic" (instrumental from *Promising Young Woman* soundtrack) —Anthony Willis
"Suga Suga" —Baby Bash featuring Frankie J
"Calm Down" —Rema and Selena Gomez
"Lose Yourself" —Eminem
"Golden" —Harry Styles
"Tangerine" —Led Zeppelin
"Over the Hills and Far Away" —Led Zeppelin
"This Must Be the Place (Naïve Melody)" —Talking Heads

If you've made it this far, thank you for your curiosity and for reading. Getting to put a book out there is a pretty cool thing. I hope I showed you a good time.

Yours truly,
Sharon